* IN ̶̶̶̶̶̶
MIDDLE OF
✦ THE ✦ NIGHT ✦

Also available from Charlie Jane Anders and Titan Books

ALL THE BIRDS IN THE SKY

THE CITY
IN THE
MIDDLE OF
THE NIGHT

CHARLIE
JANE
ANDERS

TITAN BOOKS

The City in the Middle of the Night
Hardback edition ISBN: 9781785653193
E-book edition ISBN: 9781789091601
Paperback edition ISBN: 9781789093568
Signed paperback edition ISBN: 9781789095043

Published by Titan Books
A division of Titan Publishing Group Ltd
144 Southwark Street, London SE1 0UP
www.titanbooks.com

First Titan edition: February 2019
10 9 8 7 6 5 4 3 2 1

This is a work of fiction. Names, places and incidents are either products of the author's imagination or used fictitiously. Any resemblance to actual persons, living or dead (except for satirical purposes), is entirely coincidental.

Charlie Jane Anders asserts the moral right to be identified as the author of this work.

What did you think of this book? We love to hear from our readers.
Please email us at: readerfeedback@titanemail.com,
or write to us at the above address.

To receive advance information, news, competitions,
and exclusive offers online, please sign up for the Titan newsletter
on our website: www.titanbooks.com

A CIP catalogue record for this title is available from the British Library.

Printed and bound in Great Britain by CPI Group (UK) Ltd. Croydon CR0 4YY

TRANSLATOR'S NOTE

This manuscript has been translated from the original Xiosphanti and Argelan into Peak English, which as Jthkyklakno points out [ref. 2327.288] has become "the language which everyone reads, but nobody speaks," across several worlds and spacenodes. This exercise entailed a number of challenges, particularly with the "Mouth" sections, but given the amount of interest in these documents (and indeed, misinformation regarding their contents) a serious attempt at a clean translation appeared necessary. Despite all of the apparent fabulations and liberties taken in both of these narratives, they remain the closest thing we have to primary sources regarding the origins of this emergent new form of human sentience. Detractors such as Linghathy have argued for a mythocratic pseudoframe, choosing to view these hybrids as the products of a response to extreme environmental pressures, resulting in a kind of evolutionary assimilationism. These texts undoubtedly serve to complicate and possibly even subvert that framing. Note: Where the settlers on January chose to adopt archaic Earth terms for common items, along with local flora and fauna, I have attempted to render this into Peak English as seamlessly as possible. (Hence "radio," "lorry," "pager," "crocodile," "cat," "bison," etc.) Names and proper nouns have also been regularized into English spelling, where possible (e.g., "Sophie," "Bianca," "Reynold," etc.). For a glossary of Xiosphanti and Argelan terminology and common names, see Nuxhaven, ref. 11819.99. I welcome any feedback via the usual channels.

PART

ONE

SOPHIE

I

Bianca walks toward me, under too much sky. The white-hot twilight makes a halo out of loose strands of her fine black hair. She looks down and fidgets, as though she's trying to settle an argument with herself, but then she looks up and sees me and a smile starts in her eyes, then spreads to her mouth. This moment of recognition, the alchemy of being seen, feels so vivid that everything else is an afterimage. By the time she reaches the Boulevard, where I'm standing, Bianca is laughing at some joke that she's about to share with me.

As the two of us walk back toward campus, a brace of dark quince leaves, hung on doorways in some recent celebration, wafts past our feet. Their nine dried stems scuttle like tiny legs.

*

I lie awake in our dark dorm room, listening to Bianca breathe on the shelf across from mine. And then I hear her voice.

"Sophie?"

I'm so startled, hearing her speak after curfew, I tip over and land in a bundle on the floor.

Bianca giggles from her bunk as I massage my sore tailbone. I keep expecting some authority figure, like one of the Proctors, to burst in and glare at us for disturbing the quiet time. If you can't sleep when everyone else does, you're not even human.

"Sophie! It's okay," Bianca says. "I just wanted to ask you a question. I don't even remember what it was now." Then she stops laughing, because she understands this isn't funny to me. "You're *not going to get in trouble.* I promise. You know, we can't even learn anything here unless we think for ourselves occasionally, right? Some rule we learned as little kids doesn't have to keep us in a chokehold forever."

When Bianca first showed up as my roommate, I hid from her as much as I could. I crawled into the tiny space above the slatted hamper in the side washroom, next to the wide sluicing cisterns that people use as toilets here. Bianca was this whirl of hand gestures and laughter who filled every room with color. When she started trying to talk to me, I assumed she was only taking pity on this painfully shy girl from the dark side of town and I'd just have to ignore her until she gave up.

She didn't give up.

Now I look up at Bianca's shape as I pull myself out of my huddle on the floor. "But you follow the rules too," I say. "Like, you would never actually go outdoors right now. You probably could. You could sneak out of here, wander onto the streets, and the Curfew Patrols might not ever catch you. But you don't do that, because you do care about rules."

"Yeah, I'm not running down the street naked during the Span of Reflection, either," Bianca laughs. "But a little talking after curfew has to be okay, right?"

Bianca makes me feel as though she and I just stepped off the first shuttle from the Mothership, and this world is brand new for us to make into whatever we want.

Since I was little, I couldn't sleep at the right time, along with everyone else. I tried whispering to my brother Thom sometimes, if I thought he was awake. Or else I busied myself trying to do tiny good deeds for my sleeping family, fixing a broken eyepiece or putting my brother's slippers where his feet would find them most easily on waking. Except my father's hand would come out of the darkness and seize my arm, tight enough to cut off the blood to my hand, until I whined through my teeth. Later, after the shutters came down and the dull almost-light filled our home once more, my father would roar at me, his bright red face blocking out the entire world.

Everything is a different shape in the dark. Sharp edges are sharper, walls farther away, fragile items more prone to topple. I used to wake next to my family, all of us in a heap on the same bedpile, and imagine that maybe in the darkness, I could change shape too.

*

Bianca has found another book, way at the back of the school library, on one of those musty shelves that you have to excavate from a layer of broken settler tech and shreds of ancient clothing. This particular book is a spyhole into the past, the real past, when the Founding Settlers arrived on a planet where one side always faces the sun and had no clue how to cope. "That's what history is, really," Bianca says, "the process for turning idiots into visionaries."

The two of us stroll together into the heart of the city's temperate zone, past the blunt golden buttresses of the Palace, breathing the scents of the fancy market where she always tries to buy me better shoes.

Bianca reads all the time, and she tears through each book, as though she's scared her eyes will just fall out of her head before she finishes them all. But she never does the assigned reading for any of our classes. "I'm here to learn, not study." Her mouth pinches, in a way that only makes her narrow, angular face look more classically perfect.

Even after being her roommate for a while, this kind of talk makes me nervous. I'm still desperate to prove that I deserve to be here, though I've passed all the tests and gotten the scholarship. I sit and read every single assigned text three times, until the crystalline surface blurs in front of me. But everyone can tell I'm an interloper just by glancing—at my clothes, my hair, my face—if they even notice me.

"You're the only one of us who had to work so hard for it," Bianca tells me. "Nobody belongs here half as much as you." Then she goes back to telling me that the Founders were bumblers, right as we pass by the giant bronze statue of Jonas, posing in his environment suit, one arm raised in triumph. Jonas's shoulder pads catch the dawn rays, as though still aglow from the righteous furnace of decontamination.

II

E very so often, Bianca puts on a dress made of iridescent petals, or violet satin, and disappears, along with a few others from our dorm. There's always some party, or banquet, that she needs to go to, to nurture her status among the city's elite. She stands in the doorway, the silhouette of an upward-pointing knife, and smiles back at me. "I'll be back before you know." Until one time, when the shutters close and the curfew bells ring but I'm still alone in our room. I crouch in the gloom, unable to think about sleeping, and wonder if Bianca's okay.

After the shutters open again, Bianca comes into our dorm room and sits on her own bed-shelf. "The party went too late for me to make it back before curfew," she says. "I had to stay with one of the hosts."

"I'm so glad you're okay, I was so worried—" I start to say, but then I realize Bianca's slumped forward, hands clasped in front of her face. Her latest dress, made of silver filaments that ripple in waves of light, bunches around her hips.

"I'm just . . . all I ever do is play the part that's expected of me. I'm just a fake." She ratchets her shoulders. "Sometimes I'm afraid everybody can see through me, but maybe it's worse if they *can't*."

Seeing Bianca depressed makes me feel soft inside, like my bones are chalk. I sit down next to her, careful not to mess up her dress. Her curved neck looks so slender.

Neither of us talks. I'm not good at breaking silences.

"I don't even know why you would want to be friends with me," she says.

I get up and fetch the teapot from down the hall, and a few moments later I'm pouring hot tea into a mug, which I press into Bianca's hands. "Warm yourself up," I say in a soft voice. Bianca nods and takes a big swallow of the acrid brew, then lets out a long sigh, as though she realizes she's back where she belongs. We keep stealing the teapot for our own dorm room, because hardly anyone else uses it, but some busybody always sneaks into our room when we're out and reclaims the flowery globe for the common room, where it technically belongs. "Warm yourself up," I say a second time.

By the time the tea is gone, Bianca's bouncing up and down and cracking jokes again, and I've almost forgotten that I never answered her question about why I want to be her friend.

The two of us sit in the Zone House, in our usual spot in the gloomy nook under the stairs, which smells of fermented mushrooms. Upstairs, a ragtime band draws long, discordant notes out of a zither and a bugle, and people discuss the latest football match at that new pitch in the Northern Ranges. Bianca asks what made me want to be the first person in my family—my neighborhood, even—to go to the Gymnasium. Why didn't I just finish grammar school, settle down, and get an apprenticeship, like everyone else?

Her wide brown eyes gaze at me, as though there's more than one Sophie in front of her, and she's having fun trying to reconcile them.

I've always dreaded when people ask me personal questions, but when Bianca asks, I feel a flush of pleasure that goes from my skin all the way inside. She's not asking just to be polite, or using her question as a slender knife to cut me down.

"I always thought I would just go find a trade, like my classmates," I say at last. "But then they wanted me to marry. There was this boy I was friends with at grammar school, named Mark. He and I just stood around, watching everybody, not even speaking except for a word here and there. People saw us together, and they all decided Mark would be my husband. They made jokes, or winked at us, or sang this gross song. The thought of his hands just *owning* me made me sick to my stomach. After that, I ran away whenever I saw Mark, but I was told I had to go to matchmaking sessions, to find a different husband. They said, 'There's a time to marry and have children, just like there's a time to sleep, and a time to work.'"

Bianca pours more dark water into a tin goblet. "Yeah, they always say things like that. Or like, 'Heed the chimes, know your way.' This town! Everybody has to do everything at the exact same time as everybody else." She laughs.

"I *wasn't ready*." My voice is a sore growl. "I'd gotten my visitor less than two dozen times when they started with all this marriage talk."

"Your 'visitor,'" Bianca says. "You mean your period?"

I feel myself blush so hard my scalp itches.

"Yes. Okay. My period. But I found out that if I could get accepted to one of the top colleges, like the Gymnasium, I could get a deferral on the marriage requirement. So I became the best student ever. I memorized all the textbooks. I found this place to hide, with a tiny light, so I could just keep studying right up until curfew."

Bianca's staring at me now, a notch between her eyes and an uptick around her thin lips. I shrink into my chair, bracing for her to say something sarcastic. Instead, she shakes her head. "You took control over your life. You outsmarted the system. That's just amazing."

I take a swig from my goblet and search for the slightest sign of condescension or mockery. "You really think so?"

"Everyone else at the Gymnasium is like me," Bianca says, meaning a child of the temperate zone—or really, of comfort. Her parents died when she was very young, and she went to live at a high-powered crèche that groomed her for a leadership role. "We all came to the Gymnasium because we were expected to. So we could graduate and claim our places in government or industry, and help keep this bloody stasis machine whirring. But you? You are something special."

I don't think of myself as special. I think of myself as invisible.

Bianca orders some of the salty, crispy steamed cakes that you have to eat with a special hook, left side first. The first time I tried to eat one, I made a sprawling, wet mess on my table at the Gymnasium canteen, in front of a dozen other students, and then Bianca slid next to me on the bench and coached me in a hushed voice. I still can't look at one of these without reliving my humiliation.

As we eat, Bianca asks what it was like to grow up on the dark side of town, on that steep cobbled street that climbs into deeper shadow, with the acrid fumes from the tannery and the chill wind coming in from the night. Where you woke up as the shutters lowered to let in the same gray light as before, and you lost a heartbeat, remembering all over again that you'd be working or studying under that pall of gray. But I don't talk about any of that stuff. Instead, I offer her comforting stories about my tight-knit neighborhood: all our street parties, all the people who offered a hand when you were in need.

She looks at me in the weakly dappled half light, under the stairs. "I wish I could be more like you. I want to demolish everyone's expectations. I want to keep surprising them all, until they die of surprise." She's not laughing, but her eyes have the same brightness as when she makes a joke. There's more light in her eyes than in the whole wide sky that I grew up underneath.

III

The Progressive Students Union meets under basements and behind larders. Usually between five and fifteen of us, talking about systems of oppression. Bianca's long black hair hides her face as she leans forward to listen, but her hand brushes mine. A mop-headed boy named Matthew is talking about the ordinary people whose every waking moment is spent at the farmwheels, the factories, the sewage plant, or the power station, until they die.

Then Bianca stands up and her voice rings out, like we're all inside her heart and we can hear it beat. She wears streaks of purple and silver paint, to frame her eyes, and I never want to look away.

"If you control our sleep, then you own our dreams," she says. "And from there, it's easy to master our whole lives."

Everything in Xiosphant is designed to make us aware of the passage of time, from the calendars, to the rising and falling of the shutters, to the bells that ring all over town. Everyone always talks about Timefulness, which could be simple—like, making it home for dinner before they ring the final chime before shutters-up, and the end of another cycle. Or it could be profound: like, you come across a mirror and realize your face has changed shape, and all at once you look like a woman instead of a child.

But nothing in this city is ever supposed to change.

Time should make you angry, not complacent, Bianca says. Back on Earth, our ancestors could follow the progress of the sun from horizon to horizon. They saw change roll right over their heads. Enough of these journeys and even the weather would change, from colder to warmer to colder. This awareness made them fight with all their strength. They were always using violent metaphors, like "Seize the day," or "Strike while the iron is hot."

"Time isn't our prison," Bianca says, "but our liberator." We cheer and snap our fingers, until we all remember the reason we're meeting in a stuffy basement behind barrels of cake batter: we're committing deadly sedition down here.

After the meeting, Bianca gossips to me in our room about

Matthew, the guy who spoke before she did. "He took forever just to say that we should have solidarity with other activist groups. He's one of those people who likes to hear his own voice. Nice legs, though."

"Matthew's just nervous," I say. "I've seen how he fidgets right before he's going to try and speak. I think he's in awe of you. And you don't know how scary talking to people can be."

Bianca leans over and touches my wrist. "You'd be a great leader, if you just got out of your shell." She takes a stiff drink, and then says, "You always try to see the worth of everyone. Maybe you're right about Matthew. I'll try to put him at ease next time."

How long have Bianca and I been roommates? Sometimes it feels like forever, sometimes just an interlude. Long enough that I know her habits, what each look or gesture probably signifies, but recent enough that she still surprises me all the time. According to the calendar, it's 7 Marian after Red, which means the first term is half over. When I'm not talking to Bianca in person, I'm thinking of what I'll say to her the next time we're together and imagining what she'll say back.

Lately, when Bianca talks to me illegally after curfew, I crawl onto her shelf so I can hear her whisper. Her breath warms my cheek as she murmurs about school and art and what would it even mean to be free. Our skins, hers cloud-pale and mine the same shade as wild strawflowers, almost touch. I almost forget not to tremble.

Everybody says it's normal for girls my age to have intense

friendships with other girls, which might even feel like something else. Some childish echo of real adult love and courtship. But you'll know when it's time to abandon this foolishness, the same way you know when to eat and sleep. I close my eyes and imagine that when I open them again I will have outgrown all of my feelings. Sometimes I clasp my eyelids until I almost see sparks.

I still haven't gotten used to those times when Bianca has to go to some fancy ball or dinner near the Palace. She'll break out some shimmering dress, made of vinesilk, hanging at the back of her closet, which sways with her body. And she'll hug me and promise to think of me while she's doing her duty at the Citadel. Sometimes lately, I don't even see her for a couple of shutter-cycles, but she always comes back in a strange mood, with sagging shoulders.

One time, I don't see Bianca for a while. Then, I come back to our dorm room, and she's sitting on her bed next to Matthew, the Progressive Student organizer with the nice legs. They're holding hands, a couple buttons of her tunic are unbuttoned, her ankle-skirt is undone, and her lipstick smeared. His hand has a thatch of hair across the knuckles.

Bianca doesn't startle when I walk in on them, she just laughs and gestures for me to sit on my own bed. "Matthew's leaving soon anyway. We've been talking about solidarity, and how to make it more, uh, solid." She laughs, and so does Matthew. I try not to stare, but there's no place to put my eyes.

After Matthew leaves, Bianca flops backward onto her bunk and says, "You were right about him. He's a sweet guy. And he cares about making a difference. I think he could be fun." I feel like my tongue has dissolved in my mouth, and I'm swallowing the remains. I slump onto my own bunk.

Bianca notices my face. "He's not that bad. I promise! And it's been too long since I had someone. It's not good to be single too long. I feel like you helped set the two of us up, so maybe we can help you find a boyfriend next."

I shake my head. "No boyfriend."

"Right." She raises her hands. "You told me about Mark. That sounded ghastly. But I'm sure you'll get over it, once you meet the right guy. You'll see."

Bianca's eyes are the most awake I've ever seen them, her cheeks suffused with color. She's so transported that she's wriggling on her bunk and humming to herself. I wonder if that's how I looked when I finally let Bianca take an interest in me. I've been so stupid.

Every time I think I know what's wrong with me, I find something else.

The five leaders of the Progressive Students Union sit in the cellar of the Zone House, emptying a jug of gin-and-milk and swapping personal stories. The jug and cups wobble on a low table with unlevel legs. This isn't an official meeting, so we're not hiding deeper underground, and people only mutter about politics in oblique half references. You can still tell from all the olive-green pipe-worker jackets and rough-spun scarves that we're a group of freethinkers. Upstairs, the ragtime band thumps out a slow, dirgelike rendition of "The Man Who Climbed into the Day."

Bianca is holding hands with Matthew, right in front of the group, and the two of them exchange little glances. I'm convinced everyone can sense my jealousy, hanging like a cloud in this moldy basement. She throws me a quick smile that packs a million snarky in-jokes into its contours.

I look away and see one shaft of light, coming through a tiny window over our heads and striking the wall opposite. They don't cover that window, even when all the shutters close, so this faint sunbeam never lets up, and over time it's stripped away the paint and torn off the plaster, just in that one spot. Even the exposed bricks have deep ugly fissures that meet in the middle like the impact site from an ancient meteor. I wonder how long before the entire wall comes down.

Maybe if I can speak in front of the group for once, Bianca will pay attention to me again. She'll realize Matthew has nothing interesting to say, and she was right about him the first time.

I open my mouth to make some joke that I know won't be funny, and I ignore the hot prickle that I always get under my skin when I try to talk to strangers, or to more than one person at a time. This shouldn't be so hard, I tell myself. You can tell one joke.

Just as I say the first syllable, the police cascade down the rickety stairs in a blur of dark padded suits, corrugated sleeves, and shining faceplates. They're carrying guns—high-powered fast-repeaters, which I've never seen up close before—and they stand over our little group.

Their leader, a short man with a sergeant's insignia and no helmet on his square head, comes in last and addresses our tiny gang, using the polite verb forms but with a rough edge to them. "Sorry to disturb you. We've had some information that one of you student radicals stole some food dollars from the Gymnasium. Those notes are marked. Whoever took them ought to speak up now."

He keeps talking, but I can barely hear what he's saying.

A memory comes to me: on our way here, I saw Bianca slip inside the Bursary, on the ground floor of our dorm building, and emerge a moment later stuffing something in her pocket. She made some joke about being able to buy a round of drinks for the leaders of the revolution.

"You people. You 'revolutionaries,'" the sergeant is saying in a growl. "You always act as though the rules don't apply to you, same as everyone else."

I look at Bianca, next to me, and she's frozen, hands gripping the sides of her chair. Her face closes in on itself, nostrils flared and mouth pinched. If they find the food dollars in her pocket, this could be the end of her bright future. She could do so much for this city, for all the struggling people. This could crush out the light in her eyes forever.

And me? I'm invisible.

I slip my hand into Bianca's pocket and close my fingers around three cool strips. I pull back and slide them into my own jeans, just as the cops start searching everyone.

"We're not any kind of 'group,'" Bianca is hectoring the cops. "We're just a few friends having a drink. You are invading our privacy with this unwarranted—" She chokes in mid-sentence as they start patting her down, her whole body rigid as she stands, swaying, over her chair.

When they don't find the stolen cash, Bianca goes limp. She almost topples into her chair, and then she recovers. Her eyes dart around the room. Husky rasping sounds come out of her mouth.

Then the police come to me, and I have just enough time to brace my hips before one of them finds the pocket where I stashed the money. "What did I say?" He laughs. In the cop's gleaming visor, I see a distorted reflection of a girl with a wide-eyed expression.

Bianca looks at me, and her face changes shape, her mouth slackening, as she realizes what I've done. She tries to speak, and nothing comes. Tears cluster around the inner rims of her eyes as they turn red. Matthew reaches for her and tries to offer comfort, and she shakes him off.

She tries to step forward, to put her body between the police and me, but she hesitates a moment too long, and two of them are already grabbing me. I'm aware of nothing now but my own loud breathing and the tightness of their grip on my arms.

When I can hear the world around me again, Bianca has gotten her composure back and is talking to the sergeant in her best talking-to-stupid-authority-figures voice. "Fine. You found the money. Congratulations. I'm sure none of us have any idea how it got there, including Sophie. But this is an internal Gymnasium matter, in any case. You can take us to the Provost, and we'll just sort this—"

"Not this time," the sergeant says. "Time you 'student radicals' learned a lesson. You want to just sit down here and natter about how you're going to ruin everything we've built, to take the bread out of my mouth. Out of everyone's mouths, with your anarchist nonsense. You don't get to do whatever you want just because you're clever."

The cops grab me by the armpits, two of them, and drag me to the rickety staircase that Bianca and I normally sit under. My legs scrape the floor as I try to plant my feet.

"It's just a few stupid food dollars!" Bianca is screaming now, her voice already hoarse. The other Progressive Students are still frozen in their seats. "Bring her back! This is wrong. She's done nothing, she's a good person, maybe the only good person, and I . . . Stop! *Please!"* Bianca's face turns crimson, shiny with tears, and she's grabbing the sergeant's sleeve in her fists until he throws her away.

The men with opaque faceplates pull me up the stairs, still gripping my armpits so hard I get friction burns. All my kicking and squirming just leaves me bruised.

"You can't take her!" Bianca's shriek comes from her whole body. My last glimpse of her is a crying, shaking, furious blur of black hair and clenched fists. "She doesn't belong with you, she belongs with me. She's done nothing. *Bring her back!"*

Then I'm yanked up the rest of the stairs and into the street.

The cops keep pulling me by my arms instead of letting me just walk between them, so my feet scuffle to gain purchase on the slate street. They make a lot of noise on purpose, so that even though I try not to cry out, a crowd still gathers. Workers, teachers, some of my fellow students from the Gymnasium. Daniel, who's in my Chemistry class, throws a dirty food wrapper at me and misses.

Bent over backward by the hands on my armpits, I can only see the sky, which is the same milky color and consistency as always. Like a wide dome made of mother-of-pearl, always pressing down. The cops' helmets keep swimming into view, and each time, I see a half image of my own teeth, biting air. I hear the hoots as we reach the Boulevard, and get my head up enough to see the streaky lines of the mob reflected in the giant plate-glass windows of the shopping center.

My ears fill with noise, but I can still hear my own breath: tiny wheezing sounds.

We reach a small police lorry and they throw me in the back, with a cage around me. They drive slowly, like a parade, and I watch as we pass the side of the Palace and the Founders' Square. The high-garretted houses and sleek sandstone buildings loom over us as the sky puts on its shroud, layer by layer.

People in the main market look up from peering at vegetables, and stare as we drive past. More hooting, and now some shouting. This whole scene feels like something happening to someone else a long way off, as if my amygdala has transformed into a special distorting lens.

I keep bracing for us to swerve onto a side street, so they can deliver me to the police station and bombard me with questions about subversive groups. I picture the look on my father's and brother's faces when they find out. I haven't spoken to either of them in so long.

But then we drive past the station, and the jail, and the cops just laugh at my confused face. There's one more magistrate office, just up ahead, but then I realize we're not slowing down for that, either. The sergeant, in the front passenger seat, sees me staring out the window, and chuckles. "Eh. Not wasting anyone's time with you."

Then we pass the farmwheels, which fill my entire view: towering stone structures, each the size of the Palace, they push up out of the ground. A thousand spokes revolve in slow motion, rotating crops from shadow to indirect sunlight and back. Every few moments one of their tracts blots out half the sky.

After that, the Grand Arches, and their recessed carvings of crocodiles embracing tigers, with the Golden Sphere nestled between them. I used to love those carvings.

Everywhere we go, people point at the ungrateful child who challenged the system that provides for all of us. I might as well have tried to pull the farmwheels down with my bare hands. I still feel as though I'm somewhere else, watching this scene from high above.

The Boulevard splits into five kinked streets that form one wedge of a maze, and we take the middle path, plunging into the dark side of town. Everything takes on the same gray cast that I remember from childhood, and the crosshatched view through my caged window fills with factory towers and apartment blocks. Pipe-workers and builders wander past, wearing coveralls, and most of them just shake their heads and look away. One or two spit at the car, but I don't know if they're spitting at me or the police.

I know where we're going now, and all of the terror that I've kept at a distance rushes in. I start breathing harder, and making more noise, and beating my arms and legs against the wire cage inside the lorry. The fear drenches my insides, suffocating me, and I can't bear it, I need to break free, I keep kicking the mesh. The sergeant laughs and looks at his timepiece, as if he has a wager for how long I would take to start freaking out.

I can't bear this crashing inside me.

I need to escape, I can't escape.

The cage was built for much stronger legs than mine, and I can't catch enough breath to scream, even if I wanted to. I can already see the outer wall of Xiosphant, along with the slope of the Old Mother, the mountain that protects the city against the night. Out here, the sky is the color of damp soil. Down at the far end of the Warrens, the slate-roofed houses, factories, and warehouses seem to huddle against the cold.

Maybe they'll relent at the last moment. Put the lasting fear into me. They could shove me out of this lorry right on the edge of town and let me go with a warning.

But when we reach the big reinforced stone wall, one of the helmeted officers fumbles for a big key and unlocks a thick metal gate, which opens with a weary hiss. They pull me out of the backseat cage by my wrist, and I overbalance, falling onto one knee. The sergeant shoves me through the doorway between dusk and full night, then gestures for the two nearest officers to accompany me. Two large men each take an elbow and steer me the rest of the way through the door, into the coldest air I've ever felt.

The Old Mother rises over us, a great dark tooth silhouetted against the black sky.

I'm still wearing my casual flirty café-wear. Jeans made of a thin hemp-and-wool blend, a loose chemise coming down past my waist, and a little skirt pinned around my ankles. And light woven sandals. The cold rips into me, coming off the mountainside. The police wear thick padded suits, heavy gloves, boots, and protective headgear.

But still, the two officers shove me and gesture with their guns, until I climb the sheer surface the best I can, with my frozen hands and feet. I can't see where I'm going, and every meter or so I stumble and fall onto my palms. I almost lose my purchase on the stone and tumble backward a few times. They kick my leg until I keep going.

A thought forces its way past my firebreak of panic: *Bianca will never even know what happened to me.*

I claw at the rock, kick it with my bare toes, find handholds and footholds, relying on sheer wretched desperation.

A slow keening comes from the night, as though the crocodiles are baying in anticipation of fresh meat. Maybe they can already smell me coming somehow.

By the time I climb about halfway, I want to quit. What's the point of even reaching the top? Nobody ever comes home from the night, except for the occasional survivor of a hunting party. But when I stop and sit on a tiny ledge, trying to aim a defiant look behind me, the cops raise their guns.

I take a deep breath and turn back toward the rock face, because I'd rather keep scratching at the mountainside, even lose all the skin on my fingers and the heels of my hands, than just give up and accept the death they've chosen for me.

The only warm hope in all this frozen nothing is that Bianca is okay. She'll have the life she deserves, and maybe she'll end up in a position to change this city. She'll forget about me, after a while, but maybe some tiny pocket of her heart will preserve my memory, and it'll inspire her to do something for others. I can die out here, knowing that she's going to be amazing. I try to tell myself that's enough, that it's as good as a whole life by her side.

*

The wind stings my face, washes out my sight, and forces me to shed more tears than I can spare.

But some mechanical part takes over and I keep groping for handholds and pulling myself up, meter by meter. I lose all awareness, almost like sleepwalking, and my hands and feet are already numb.

I'm startled when I pull myself up one more time and reach the summit. I find a tiny plateau, where I can stop and drag some frosty air into my lungs. A dozen meters away, a sliver of direct sunlight hits a raised crag, hot enough to sear your skin off with a single touch. Even that one bright spot is too painful to look at.

Behind me, the city is splayed out, already asleep behind thick shutters. And beyond that, the Young Father slices the bright horizon—the smaller, smoother mountain that shields us from daylight.

I stand there on this wide ledge, panting, and try to regain some feeling by putting my hands under my bruised armpits, when the cops grunt at me. They're eager to get back to the city, to drink their own pitcher of gin-and-milk, next to a fireplace. They nudge me with their guns, and I turn back toward the other side of the mountain.

Ahead, I see . . . nothing. The night stretches endlessly, a place where light and warmth never come. Out there, glaciers carve through the tundra and storms tear through everything. Storms and megafauna kill anyone who ventures past this mountain, if the cold and disorientation don't take them first.

The police officers step forward in unison and shove me with one gloved hand each, until I fall face-over-legs into a cold so intense I feel as if my heart will stop.

The night side of the Old Mother bludgeons me, landing blows on my torso and legs, as I careen. I try to find a handhold, get my feet under me, but I overbalance again and again, until I stumble into a sheer drop, a smooth wall coated with ice that burns the remaining skin off my hands as I grope at it. I can't see how far I've fallen, or what's below me, or how to avoid getting dashed to pieces on the rocks.

I try to push myself away from the rock face with both elbows, twisting and groping at nothing but icy wind, and then I just fall through space.

I land on a layer of snow, hard enough to drive all the breath out of me, and gag on the frozen air that replaces it. My whole back and sides flare with agony, and for a moment I think I've broken something. But I force myself to rise onto one knee, spasming, and the worst of the pain seeps away.

I can't even see the mountain that I just fell down. My fingers and toes go numb, and so does my face, and my lungs are bursting, and my stomach turns. The wind gets angrier, and its scream steals all other sound. All I can feel is a dark vortex inside me as I rise to my feet. I've only been in the night for a few eyeblinks, but it's already killing me.

Everybody says that if you stare into this unseeable waste for too long, you'll be struck with delirium. If you even survive.

But I make myself face it. I stand, hugging myself, and walk into the churn of ice on the high winds, trying to grope my way forward without any sense of direction.

My body collides with something. I feel dense fur, over an even thicker carapace. A single warm tentacle brushes my face, and I realize I'm standing a few centimeters away from a full-sized crocodile.

Her giant front pincer is close enough to crush my head in one lazy motion. I hear a low sound under the wind's endless chorus, and I'm sure this crocodile is opening her wide, round mouth full of sharp teeth to devour me, bones and all.

SOPHIE

{*After*}

I

Back in grammar school, they taught us all about crocodiles, and what to do if you ever meet one.

Don't try to run, because you're on their territory, and they can ensnare you in one of those long tentacles before your first stride. Plus they can clear vast distances with their powerful hind legs, each one the size of an adult human. And their strong forelegs can climb any surface and dig through almost any barrier.

You might be able to hide, because we don't know how they sense their prey, since they can't rely on vision or hearing in this pitch-dark wind. They may use scent, or maybe they can detect motion somehow. Nobody's ever hidden from one, but you might be the first.

The only viable strategy is to attack. Crocodiles do have a

few weaknesses that a human can exploit. They have soft spots on the underbelly, where the carapace doesn't extend all the way around. I know where all their major organs are, because I watched Frank the butcher carve one up for some fancy banquet after a few hunters had gotten lucky, returning from the night in one piece and with fresh game.

But their main weakness, the easiest one to reach, is the exact center of the pincer that's right in front of me, sticking out of the creature's head. The impenetrable shell contains two knife-sharp claws, but at their midpoint is a forest of a hundred wriggling tongues, each one about the size of your little finger. If you manage to strike at the pincer's heart, and hit those slimy appendages, then you might kill it in one stroke.

That pincer is so close I can feel one of its edges scrape my throat. It could slice my head off before I could react. I try to summon all my courage, brace my feet on the slippery ground to deliver one great blow to the warm spot at the pincer's fulcrum. I can do this, I'm strong enough. I raise both fists.

Then I stop.

Because I feel warm breath coming from below the pincer, where the creature's mouth is. And that part of me that always stands back and pulls everything apart, instead of just blurting out words, is asking: Why is a crocodile's mouth so far away from all these tongues, anyway? She can't possibly use them to taste anything or make any sounds. Why are they right at the center of this armored scissor, vulnerable yet shielded?

I lower my fists. Instead, I push my unprotected face forward, almost losing my balance in the dark. The pincer is all around my head and neck now, but it doesn't close and kill me.

Instead, this crocodile lets me press forward and push my frostburnt nose into the moist heat of her slimy warm grubs. They brush my face, and my head floods with urgent smells and disorienting sounds, a beautiful ugliness, too much to handle, like I'm out-of-my-head drunk with no up or down, nothing but a whirl of sensory overload.

I almost keel over, but somehow I stay upright until—

—I'm somewhere else. I'm way out in the middle of the night now, surrounded by huge sheets of ice on all sides. A mountain of ice and snow sidles past, along the horizon. We're thousands of kilometers farther out than any human has gone in twenty-five generations, since we lost all our scoutships and all-terrain vehicles.

Somehow I can see in the dark now, except that I realize I'm not seeing at all. I'm using alien senses, and my mind is turning them into sight and sound.

I tear through the landscape so fast the wind can't keep up. A sudden storm could rip me apart, the tundra could swallow me, but I don't even care. My back legs push against the ground and the ice surrenders, while my smaller front legs rip into the slick surface, propelling me even faster and keeping my balance. I'm not running—this is something much better. I've never felt so much power in my body, and so many sensations flood into the ends of my two great tentacles as they taste the wind around me.

I want to laugh, and then I turn and see that four other crocodiles are running alongside me, grasping some spiky devices in their tentacles and guiding a sled full of some kind of precious metal. I feel a surge of pride, safety, happiness that they're with me, and we're going home.

Then we reach it: a huge structure in the shape of a rose with all its petals spread, a circle surrounded by elaborate crisscrossing arch shapes. Only the very top pokes above the surface, and the rest extends far below the ice, but still its beauty almost stops my heart. A glimmering city, many times larger than Xiosphant, that no human eyes have ever seen.

I must have blacked out, because I wake up and find the crocodile has swept me up in her tentacles and is using her front legs to brace me, while also climbing the sheer rock face that I fell down. I'm still frozen to the bone, but she has wrapped some kind of thick blanket around me that feels like something between moss and fungus. The fabric feels warm and dry, wound around my face with just enough slack to let me breathe. One tentacle covers my nose, and her cilia brush against my skin. I still can't see anything, but I feel our rise in my inner ear, and even with the crocodile's body shielding me I feel the bitter wind flow around me.

She deposits me at the same spot where the two officers pushed me over the edge. I'm on the ground before I even realize she's laid me down, and I wriggle out of her covering only to be blinded by the faint light for a moment. The cops are long gone.

My rescuer is even bigger than the other crocodile I saw being butchered as a child—with a thick carapace and weathered skin on her legs and tentacles. There are two large indentations, one on either side of her head, which look like big sad eyes, but aren't. Her round shell hunches as she shields herself from the sudden exposure to partial sunlight, which no crocodile can ever endure. Her pincer opens and closes, as if saying goodbye.

Before I can take a proper look, or try to communicate again, or do anything really, the crocodile has turned around, already disappearing back down the mountain.

From up here, Xiosphant looks like a great oval, with a bite taken out of the right side. The farmwheels keep rotating, but all the buildings have sheer faces, so the whole city is asleep.

The part of town nearest me, the Warrens, is a heavy, colorless off-black with slate rooftops and tall white-brick rectangles, but the city picks up a glow as I look farther inward, toward the farmwheels and the main shopping district. The pall lifts slowly, until my gaze hits the center of town, where the great spire of the Council House and the golden domes of the Palace gleam under a silvery light. From there, the light blazes fiercer and fiercer, until you reach the day side of town, which hurts my eyes even from here. And beyond that, the rays of the sun just poke out from behind the Young Father, though I don't look that far, for fear of hurting my eyes. Off to my right, outside the wall in the Northern Ranges, cattle jostle each other, surrounded by high fences. The outcroppings at the base of the Young Father have mining tunnels going into them, and a few craggy shells of old treasure meteors have come to rest farther north.

Life returns to my body with an itchy soreness. My hands

and feet feel as vast as this mountain range, and the blood stings as it flows into them. Even once I can move, I want to stay on this plateau forever, just watching the city go through its never-ending cycle of waking and sleeping. Striving and dying. I can look down from my rocky perch and think: *Fools.*

A high-pressure cloud system scuds across our strip of twilight, too high and too dense to make out any individual clouds, and staring up at it will give you a headache every time.

The thought of going back home, after what just happened, shakes me, every capillary and every inch of skin. The first time I try to stand and make my descent, I imagine the police spotting me as soon as I get back inside the city, shouting from behind their helmets, and suddenly I can't move or breathe, as if they already have me. They'll catch me again, they'll know I survived, maybe this time they'll force me into the day instead.

But after a chain of breaths, I start talking sense into myself. *Nobody knows you're alive,* I tell myself. *They didn't know you were alive before, and now they're sure you're not.* That last thought makes me laugh out loud for some reason, and I pick myself up and force my frost-stung body to climb down to the outer wall of Xiosphant.

I walk around the wall for a lifetime before I find a weak spot that they only half repaired after the last rockfall. I pull loose stones away until there's a crack big enough for me to force myself through.

*

II

The streets of Xiosphant always feel narrow: so crammed with people, carts, and a few lorries that you can't get anywhere. But now, the empty streets yawn like chasms, and the whitestone slabs and cinderblock walls amplify every footstep. Boots play a brisk rhythm off in the distance, a Curfew Patrol coming my way, and I realize that I still have plenty of fear left in me. I breathe faster. They'll find me, a feral creature wearing nothing but a mossy blanket and torn scraps of clothing, covered with cuts and dirt.

I need to get off the street before—

A klaxon rings in the distance and echoes across town. That's the warning bell right before the shutters open, a courtesy in case people want to make themselves presentable before they're bathed in light. When I used to hear that bell at home, the time between that sound and the return of the sun felt never-ending, torturous. But now, I realize I have perhaps a couple hundred heartbeats until every window is thrown open and people rush onto the streets.

I can't go home to my family, not after what we said to each other the last time I saw them. I'll never make it back to the Gymnasium before the shutters rise, and even if I reached Bianca, she'd have to try to hide me.

I duck into an alley, hide behind garbage, sneak past slatted windows. I realize I'm going in circles, the same five dirty streets over and over. My breath gets more and more ragged. Everywhere I look, factory buildings, warehouses, and tenements turn their backs to me, and then I remember a place where my mom used to go when she was alive. She took me there a few times when I was out of school, and it's not far. She always said it was her safe place. That was a long time ago, but maybe anyplace that's truly safe can't ever disappear.

I follow the route my mother showed me, past a linen warehouse and a chemical plant, along a series of alleys that seem even darker than the other streets around here, and then into a lane that you have to be looking right at, or you'll miss it.

At the end of that lane, the paving stones of which are a little finer than the worn cobbles of the surrounding streets, there's a wide, ornate door made of some kind of heavy wood, but painted bright gold with crimson notes and two rows of decorative iron nails. When I reach the door, I almost fall in a dirty heap onto the mat. But I find the hidden buzzer, behind one of the elaborately carved curls of the surrounding wood.

I press, and nothing happens.

The second time I stab at the buzzer, I hear a shrill noise, then a grinding sound of cranks and pulleys, coming from all around me. The shutters are opening. I look back the way I came and see the windows of the building at the end of the lane losing their metal shields, revealing dirty panes with faces behind them.

I ring the buzzer one last time and pound the thick door with my fist, while doorways open and people flock onto the street. I'm trapped here, at the end of this blind alley.

The door swings open, and an elderly man looks down at me. He wears a looser silk tunic, to disguise his paunch, and an old-fashioned cap embroidered with golden thread, to cover his encroaching baldness. But Hernan still has the same kind eyes and wide smile, with a hint of an old pain behind them.

He squints down, and doesn't recognize me. Then he blinks. "Sophie? Oh dear. What happened to you? You'd better get inside, before people think we've started having mud-wrestling in here."

Hernan doesn't ask any more questions, just hustles me indoors, past an ornate waiting room that I remember from my mother's visits, full of dark-stained wood, bright carpets, and slow pendulums. A moment later, we're in a part of the building that I've never seen: the living quarters and service areas. Plain brick walls, cold stone floor. At the end of this hallway, a door opens to reveal a washroom with a big tub.

I try to thank Hernan with what's left of my voice, and he just smiles. "Tell me all about it when you're yourself again." He stoops and fills the tub to the lip with water so hot I breathe steam. Then Hernan leaves, shutting the door behind him, and I drop my blanket.

As soon as the hot water touches my skin, I break apart. Feeling comes back into my fingers and toes, and my skin glows even as I scrape layers of dirt and blood off it. I hyperventilate until I choke, and as the hot water stings all my scrapes and cuts, I let out a long, high-pitched wail. I will never be clean again, never be warm inside. I scrub until I bleed in more places, and I keep scrubbing.

The water turns murky from all the filth that was on my body, and my sinews and veins come back to life, and I finally let myself feel everything that just happened. *They took me away. They tore me away from you. You cried and shouted. They paraded me in the street. People threw things. My classmate threw something. They laughed at my fear, like they were hungry for it. They forced me up the mountain, they pushed me into darkness.*

As these things go from being "moments that I need to survive right now" to "things that will always have happened to me," I start to shiver. I feel so chilled that the scalding water might as well be solid ice. Once I start, I can't make myself stop. The shivers build and build, until water goes all over the floor tiles. I hug myself, and I shed tears that I can't blame on windburn, and they taste much too pungent, like the tears of a dead person. I hear myself from a tremendous distance, wailing and chattering my teeth.

Just as my own wailing gets too loud for me to bear, and I can't endure this body, and I feel like I'm going to leave a hundred pieces of myself in this tub, another thought comes, that almost drives out all the others: *I was a crocodile, running across the tundra with all of my friends.*

PART

TWO

mouth

The Sea of Murder vanished behind them, and then they had nothing but the road. Deathly shroud on one horizon, white furnace on the other. Sky so wide it pulverized you to look up. No other features but the cracks and marbling in the stone underfoot. The rhythm of their footfalls, *chump chump chump,* became a piece of music that never stopped, accompanied by the sled's churning wheels. A couple times, a bison charged in from the night and tried to seize a person in its powerful maw, with more teeth than you could count, and razor-sharp threads crisscrossing between them. Once, a storm fell from a great height and set upon them, knives of rocky ice clutched in a million fists. They had to build their shelter though they could barely stand, and hug each other as they shielded the sled with their trembling bodies. At last, though, when they seemed to have walked a dozen lifetimes, they saw a glow on the horizon: the lights of Xiosphant. The lights grew prouder and then vanished, because the city was having its curfew. When the lights reappeared, they looked much closer.

Everyone cheered at the thought of unloading their cargo,

unlacing muck-stiffened boots, finding a lukewarm bath, eating hot food. Except for Mouth, who felt a rising dread at the thought of being trapped inside a city again.

The other members of the Resourceful Couriers were city people who traveled for a living. Mouth was a born traveler, who tolerated cities for brief periods.

In a city, you could only walk in circles. Trouble knew where to find you. People lived with more things than they could carry, and they pretended that built structures were geographical features. Mouth couldn't travel alone, and the Resourceful Couriers were the closest you could find to a gang of nomads in this age, but the long drags between trips were torture. Especially in Xiosphant, where the residents were obsessed with making sure you slept at the right time, and they didn't even know how to make decent coffee.

Maybe Mouth would get lucky and the whole city would fall into a chasm before they reached it.

The city wall loomed in the distance: granite blocks, topped with tungsten spikes, which they'd raised after one of their stupid wars, generations ago. And soon the noises rang from inside that wall, and Mouth couldn't tell factories and mining gear from shouts and musical instruments. Cities teemed with synesthesia. So many sounds and smells, a din of imagery, until your senses just gave up.

Omar gave the signal when they were almost under the wall, at the designated spot. Nothing happened. The Resourceful Couriers tried to get the sled as close to the cover of the wall as they could as its axles protested, and they all huddled there in the pale half light. The damn wall vibrated.

They had started out with eight people, including three new recruits, but Jackie had taken one look at the Sea of Murder and run back to the relative safety of Argelo. Then Franz had acted like a fool on the boat, and had toppled and drowned. Even Mouth wanted to raise a glass to poor Franz, and to all their absent friends and family.

Everyone around Mouth started to panic they would be stranded at the foot of an ugly gray-brown wall forever. Omar did the signal again, and then again a moment later.

A passage opened a dozen meters away, a dark tunnel going under the base of the wall, propped up with rotten vines. Justin, their contact, told them to hurry inside because it was late. As if they hadn't been waiting out here for an age and a half.

Justin had three people with him, and they all got hands on the sled, which kept getting caught on the tunnel's grooves. Something about the way Justin's helpers positioned themselves, once everyone was grunting and the sled motor started overheating, made Mouth suspicious. So she hung back. Halfway into the tunnel, Justin whipped out a gun, an ancient slow-repeater, and said he was taking the cargo. All of the Resourceful Couriers had their hands out—except for Mouth, who emerged from behind and raised Justin's head into the support beam so hard it half collapsed the tunnel. After that, just a big knife fight in the dark.

You don't get to be a Resourceful Courier without having blades stashed in every contour of your body.

The Resourceful Couriers eased the sled into a junkyard right before the tunnel collapsed behind them, on top of Justin and his crew. This was shit. They needed to find a new contact—because dried apricots, fancy fabrics, and swamp vodka don't sell themselves, and who could understand the stupid money here. Plus when time came to leave town, they would need a new tunnel. All in all, a shit end to a shit journey. Nothing for it but to get ass-faced.

One thing Xiosphant did have plenty of was bars. Something about all that repression. They found a dive called the Low Road and traded a case of the swamp vodka for food, drink, and permission to crash in the back room after curfew. Soon everyone had gotten good and wasted.

Mouth had developed a persona that camouflaged the social awkwardness and the trapped-inside-walls feeling: loud, boastful, full of jokes. Sometimes even Mouth was fooled, after enough booze.

But Xiosphanti was a clumsy language to joke in—all those consonants, glottal stops, verb tenses, fancy pronouns. Mouth mangled every other sentence, even though people seemed entertained by the story about the bar brawl (adjacent to a hot oil cauldron) against a man twice Mouth's size. At the same time, in the quiet part of Mouth's brain, the memory kept replaying: Justin's head giving way against the support beam, as Mouth's muscles levered upward. Had Justin gotten a shot off? Sometimes Mouth thought yes, sometimes no. The only constant was the feeling of a man's head losing solidity, the body tensing and then slackening, and a scent between urine and motor oil. The usual post-murder hangover nauseated Mouth, but meanwhile she was also full of furious loathing at the sort of person who would try to rob hardworking smugglers who had hauled garbage halfway around the world, crossing the goddamn Sea of Murder even. If Justin had appeared at the Low Road, somehow alive and unscathed, Mouth might have torn him apart. She couldn't decide if the murder had left her queasy with guilt or just unsatisfied.

Both, maybe.

"Dude is dangling headfirst over the boiling hot oil, by his throat." Mouth's story had reached its crowd-pleasing climax all on its own. "And he looks up at me and says, 'Shit, is that peanut oil? I'm allergic.'" Everybody howled with laughter and a couple people bought Mouth more gin-and-milk, along with some of the swamp vodka that the Resourceful Couriers had bartered in the first place.

The Low Road emptied out as the chimes signaled the Span of Reflection, the last bell before curfew. Mouth sat next to Alyssa, staring at the street full of suckers trying to outrun a clock. Alyssa was Mouth's road buddy, meaning they spent every moment together, slept together, watched each other's backs, and each knew what the other was thinking. By rights, they ought to be sick of each other.

"Are you excited to be back in Xiosphant?" Alyssa laughed at Mouth's grimace. "I bet you're overjoyed to be speaking a language that's so full of qualifiers you can hardly get to the point," she said in flawless Xiosphanti, the polite form. Her sentence specified what time it was, the tense implied (present conditional), and the genders and social statuses of both herself and Mouth. None of it sat right with Mouth, who never liked to be categorized.

Mouth snorted. "I don't care. I won't stay here long enough to let it bother me."

"You're an optimist," Alyssa said in Argelan. "Remember how you caved in our tunnel with a man's skull? And we lost our main contact? Might be a while before we get another gig. And to be honest . . ."

She didn't finish that sentence. She almost didn't have to. Here, under a roof for the first time in forever, she had all sorts of shadows and creases on her face that hadn't been there before. Alyssa had curly dark hair, a strong jawline, and big firm hands that had clutched Mouth comfortingly whenever they had shared a sleeping nook. Alyssa had always seemed inexhaustibly young and capable of surprise—except now, she looked older.

"You want to quit." Mouth shouldn't have cared. The lineup of the Resourceful Couriers had always changed, since forever, except for Mouth and Omar. You couldn't get attached.

"Not so much that I want to quit, more that I don't know if I can go on."

Mouth laughed. "If you were going to quit, you'd have been better off staying in Argelo. Your hometown. At least they know how to have fun there."

"Argelo was a little too much fun last time. Actually, I like Xiosphant. It's quiet. They make nice cakes, thanks to all the flour from those farmwheels."

"I really hope you change your mind." Mouth drained her jar of swamp vodka. After hauling cases of the stuff across nine kinds of hell, it didn't taste nearly good enough. "I would hate to lose you. I don't want to have to share a sleep nook with Reynold."

Reynold, sitting a couple meters away, overheard and

rolled his eyes. He was a big ugly dude with tattooed arms, a broken nose, and weirdly tiny hands. Nobody ever wanted to share a sleep nook with him, because he snored and farted at the same time.

"That's not why this is upsetting you," Alyssa said.

Mouth didn't feel upset, but Alyssa was usually right about these things. "Why, then?"

"You're scared that if I'm too old to keep doing this, then maybe you are too."

"It's different for me," Mouth said. "I'm going to keep doing this until I die."

"Why? Because you were raised by nomads?" Alyssa laughed. "You do get that nomads aren't smugglers, right? Smuggling is for young people with decent reflexes. Do you think you'll be able to break a man's head with one hand after a few more of these trips?"

"Nomads have to break heads too sometimes."

Mouth wanted out of this conversation.

"Are you ready to be the only old person in a crew of young smugglers?" Alyssa asked.

"I'm ready to drink until I pass out. Beyond that, I hadn't made any plans."

"Drink faster. Time's running out."

And sure enough, just as Alyssa spoke, there was that grinding, squalling sound that Mouth remembered from previous visits to Xiosphant: the shutters cranking up all over town, blocking out the half light. The Low Road went from pleasantly dim to can't-see-your-own-feet.

Mouth hated darkness. The idea that you would want to

sleep under conditions where anything could ambush you, that just closing your eyes wasn't risk enough, seemed barbaric. Atavistic. All the other Resourceful Couriers fumbled for a corner of the back room to sleep, alone, with their road buddy, or just in some random pile. But Mouth sat, staring. She'd never really been in the dark until she'd first visited Xiosphant as a child and the shutters had closed on her. Discovering a new phobia was like the opposite of falling in love.

The road didn't age you. Settling down somewhere, gaining attachments and expectations, assimilating—those things aged you. This was a childish way of looking at things, but Mouth couldn't help it.

The nomads who raised Mouth had included elderly people as well as children, but they'd worked out all sorts of customs to make sure vulnerable members of the community were taken care of. And of course, the Citizens hadn't been trying to carry fragile, semiperishable goods from one city to another at a decent speed.

Mouth barely slept, even in spite of exhaustion and tipsiness. When the shutters rolled down at long last, and the blue-gray light poured into the room, Mouth felt ugly. The bar owner, a cheery old man with short gray curls named Ray, brought around plates of hot pastries that made Mouth feel less like smashing another head or ten.

Alyssa was right: they really did know cakes in Xiosphant. But their coffee still tasted like shit.

Now the streets were filling up instead of emptying, the Resourceful Couriers all went out to explore. The streets of Xiosphant were narrower than in Argelo, but straighter and laid out in a semi-grid—and better paved, because they'd had more access to fancy technology from the Mothership when they'd laid out this town. One building they walked past had a big stone awning that had to have been fabbed, with little creatures flying around it. Then there was a narrow townhouse, with gold leaf all around the fancy piping that had crumbled to bits but still had some grandeur.

The Couriers made a big effort to clean up and look like they belonged here, because even being a foreigner in Xiosphant was basically against the law. Mouth wore a big ribbony cap that covered up her mohawk and scars, and one of those ponchos that the local women were wearing, but she drew the line at putting a lacy fringe around her ankles. Everyone else blended in, more or less. But in this town, you could tell the pipe-workers, the factory grunts, the shop kids, and the bureaucrats apart just by looking at their clothing and the stains on their hands. Everyone seemed to sneak glances at Mouth whenever she risked walking on one of the busier streets full of food vendors and schoolchildren. A few little kids pointed at Mouth's mismatched poncho and trousers, and the lack of an ankle-skirt, and made noises.

Everything that happened now, Mouth turned into another opportunity to feel old, after everything Alyssa had said.

They had left Kendrick guarding their stuff, back in the junkyard, and it was all still there when they got back. But time was not a friend here. The police had a million eyes, and everyone in Xiosphant was too curious about your business. With Justin gone, they needed to find someone else to move the merchandise and help them get a new cargo to bring back to Argelo.

"I've been thinking," Kendrick said, his high forehead crinkling in a way that made his many piercings jangle. "We won't find another fence, not in a hurry. The black market in Xiosphant is pretty tiny, and disorganized, compared to Argelo. But I know a guy named George who might be able to help. He's the bank for this big roofing company, which means he handles every kind of currency, not just infrastructure chits. And he does a certain amount of bartering to make sure the roofers have access to dental care and toys for their kids. I heard last time we were in town that he also does some moonlighting."

"Let's go see George the Bank." Omar whooped.

They hid the rest of the swamp vodka in the back room of the Low Road, then spent ages disguising the sled with their other goods as a delivery vehicle for one of Xiosphant's leather warehouses, using mostly stuff they found in this junkyard. Those chimes were rattling again: time running out. "We'll just have to stick to the back alleys," Kendrick said. "I know a route." Kendrick was the guy who knew the way to the spiciest food or the weirdest liquor, wherever you traveled.

"I still don't get how someone can be a bank," muttered Yulya. She'd never even been outside Argelo until she talked Omar into letting her tag along, and everyone had expected her to freak out and run home, like Jackie. Instead, she'd taken to the wild road, carrying her share without complaint. She even kept her spirits up on the Sea of Murder. Yulya said she'd always wanted to be a traveling performer, a profession that hadn't existed since . . . well, since Mouth was little.

"It's the screwy economy here in Xiosphant," Kendrick told her. "They have like ten different kinds of money, for different things. Food dollars, med-creds, infrastructure chits, energy rations, and so on. So the roofing company gets paid in infrastructure chits, but George the Bank also has to make sure the employees receive all other kinds of money, by making side-deals with medical providers, food companies, and the power plant. And so on."

"That's . . . literally insane," said Yulya, still speaking Argelan, in a low voice.

"It's their way of avoiding scarcity and hoarding." Mouth shrugged.

"It's how they keep everybody in line," said Alyssa. "Everybody's so busy trying to get enough of all the different kinds of money, nobody has time to stop and think."

Just then, red-and-blue smoke filled the sky, which signified the midpoint between shutters-down and shutters-up.

The roofing company was all the way over on the bright side of town. Still indirect sunlight, still just creeping over a big-ass mountain, but there sure was a lot of it. Mouth could see all the little hairs on the back of her hand, and everything had colors. The air smelled different this close to the day: sulfurous, tangy, kind of salty. Sweat collected inside Mouth's collar.

"I guess being stuck in this part of town would make you think about the importance of a good solid roof." Alyssa snorted.

They came to a huge slab of limestone, so tall you couldn't tell if it even had a good roof, with a sign over the corrugated shutter that read roof masters. A few guys in coveralls were carrying boxes into the building, and Omar asked them where the Couriers could find George. Half of them ended up staying with the sled while Mouth, Omar, Alyssa, and Kendrick went through a maze of warehouse shelves and pasteboard walls, at the center of which a young man squatted on a big rubber ball, inside a wire cage.

"You really just came all the way from Argelo?" George blinked at them. He had an autofocusing lens in one eye and a scarf tied around both arms, in the same style that Mouth had seen on some of the financial professionals swarming through the streets. But he wore his dark hair in six fancy braids. On the wall behind him hung one of those overcomplicated calendars that looked like a million lines crisscrossing inside a big circle. "I never even met anyone who's been to Argelo. We used to have open trade with them, you know. I know some elderly people who still remember this one kind of cat butter that used to be imported from Argelo, and—"

"Mason's Salty Cat Butter," said Omar. "We've got five kilograms of the stuff, in special preservation packs."

"Well," George said. "That might be worth rather a lot of food dollars, or whatever you're interested in. I also know some folks over at the mines who can get you bauxite, tin, copper, and a few other things. The mines are not what they once were, but they still produce some surprises." He used the polite form of Xiosphanti, for addressing strangers, and identified himself as a manager and the Couriers as visiting laborers.

Mouth tuned out the negotiations and poked around the room. This space was as big as the front room of the Low Road, but seemed much smaller because filing cabinets ringed the whole back area. The good kind, made out of refractory crystal with a fine aluminum rotary index. George had collected information about not just his own trades but also tons of other stuff that people had swapped, bought, or sold here in Xiosphant. This one dentist near the cold front had amassed quite the collection of old uniform insignia from the Mothership. (Still sailing overhead, in her lonely, slow-decaying orbit.) George had lists of rare and collectible items sold at various auctions around the city, too.

For a place that prided itself on having exactly the right kind of money for everyone's needs, Xiosphant sure had a lot of deals under the table. For a moment, Mouth imagined settling down here along with Alyssa and some of the others. You could get rich and soft here. Or you could get dead—just ask Justin.

Mouth kept spinning the wheel, letting different engravings on the crystal pop up on the viewer, out of boredom, as George asked all the usual questions about Argelo and its famous parties. Like, did people really just never stop dancing, ever? Would they let someone just walk around half naked, on the street? Was it even true that they let men go with men there? They let anyone do anything in Argelo, was the answer to every one of his questions.

And then an item on one of George's auction lists caught Mouth's eye. Mouth nearly choked, vision gone white, like the road after a hailstorm. She must have misread—but no. There it was. She even found a picture when she pulled up the entry. And the name, written in fancy cursive Xiosphanti script. "The Invention."

The Invention.

"Where?" Mouth coughed. Heart thrashing like a wild snake. "Where did this item end up? 'The Invention.' I have a friend who, uh. I have a friend who would kill to get their hands on this."

George groaned. Mouth had interrupted just as he and Omar were getting to the fun part of their conversation about the crazy shit that went down in Argelo, the City that Never Sleeps. "Which list is that?"

Mouth scrolled back up to the top of the list and scanned for the title. "The McAllister Acquisition." There was an amount, in luxury coins, plus some time-related details which would only make sense to a Xiosphanti.

George tutted for a moment, then said, "Oh. Right. Yeah, that was a special auction. Some rare items. As near as I can recall, it all ended up in the Palace." Sure enough, the bottom of the manifest had a notation that included the prince's personal seal.

The Invention was here. In Xiosphant. In that stupid cotton-candy Palace. Everything Mouth had lost, everything that the Resourceful Couriers had failed to replace. Just sitting there, and Mouth only had to go in there and grab it. Mouth lost a breath, thinking about holding the Invention, opening it up, looking inside.

She felt like passing out from happiness.

SOPHIE

The new boy is named Jeremy, and he doesn't know how to do anything. I have to lace his sandals for him five times, and his polished leather tunic keeps threatening to fall off one shoulder. He can't hold the tray steady, or light the candle with a supple enough wrist. He doesn't breathe right. He keeps asking me questions, in a precise accent that reminds me of Bianca. I just shrug and keep redoing his laces and buckles and flower arrangements, hoping this time he'll get it.

"Please," he says. "If you won't even talk to me, how can I ever understand anything? Hernan said you would help." Jeremy is pale, with wavy reddish brown hair and narrow eyes with dark brown pupils, and he shuffles around in the antechamber between our tiny shared bedroom and the staging area for all the client sessions, with its racks of ornate samovars, fine plates, and tiny serving implements.

It's true, Hernan did ask for my help: putting his hand on my shoulder and crinkling his gray eyes underneath his pale wispy eyebrows. "Sophie, I know this is hard for you. But just try to remember when you were new at this, and you felt like you were going to break everything, all the time. Other people, including Kate and Walter, went out of their way to help you. So now, it's your turn. Please help us with Jeremy."

As if I could forget those times when I was still so raw, one layer beneath the skin, that I felt an endless ice storm raging in my blood and my bones. The time, right after I came to the Illyrian Parlour, when I was sure the police would arrive at any moment to finish what they started. I've lived here long enough that I can venture out into the street, even walk past a police lorry, without trembling or trying to hide my face. Nobody would recognize me now, even if they somehow knew me from before, since I've grown a few centimeters, while also forcing myself to learn a whole new posture and way of holding my body. I walk even slower than I breathe, and each new breath comes and goes, as gradual as the blooming and wilting of a flower.

Yet I still can't venture into the temperate zone, or anywhere near the Gymnasium, without hearing the drone of police engines and the shouts of the mob, echoing in my memories. Some part of me is convinced that if I walk too close to campus, men in uniforms will instantly cuff me and throw me into a police lorry.

So I try to help Jeremy as much as I can. I owe a lot to Hernan, and to all his staff, past and present. But I never liked talking to people before, and now I hate it twice as much. Part of me is still waiting to finish telling the joke I started blurting out in the basement of the Zone House. As though time halted in the midst of that one syllable, and has never found a way to resume, no matter what the calendar says.

Speaking of the calendar, it's already 4 Wander before Blue, which means Bianca must already be at least halfway finished with the whole program at the Gymnasium, maybe closer to two-thirds finished. She'll have forgotten me by now. She'll have an incredible life, help so many people, make so many friends. I make friends even slower than I walk, but everyone who meets Bianca wants to love her. I'm trying not to think about it too much.

"Please," Jeremy says again, in his voice that reminds me so much of hers. "I need to learn. I don't have anywhere else to go but here."

I give him what I hope is a kind look, and whisper: "Just watch me work."

People arrive at the ornate front door of the Illyrian Parlour out of breath. They've rushed here from work, and they only have a short interval before they have to run back. The gears on all the timepieces keep chewing through moment after moment, and they can't stand to walk under this cruel sky any longer. They buzz and knock a few times before the golden door opens, and we can see them out on our stoop, fidgeting and even chattering to themselves. Shoulders hunched, necks clenched enough to show tendons.

When I finally open the door, I just wave them inside, and hold out a red-and-gold-woven bag to store their timepieces. Then I show them into the waiting room, where a pendulum appears motionless at first. On the other wall, to their left, words of comfort unscroll across a cream-colored sign, so slowly you could doze off and wake to see one new word. The hand-loomed Argelan carpet absorbs all sounds once they've removed their shoes. On one of the chairs, a marmot named Cyrus sleeps, with rippling golden fur and blue velvety pseudopods that can extrude or disappear as needed. Most people have never seen a marmot before, let alone a full-grown one that weighs as much as a human toddler. Some of them dare to lean forward and touch Cyrus, and his contented rumble first startles and then relaxes them.

We don't start preparing the soothing blend of coffee and the geometrically complex interlocking pastries until they arrive, and that process takes three of us a while. Most of the time, the customers' breathing slows down little by little, and they stop jerking their heads in every direction. A few of them just get up and leave.

After the waiting room, they come into the main salon and stare at the embroidered floor cushions, low tables, wall hangings, and shelves full of books so old their crystals are fogged. They stand there, still breathing too fast and hunching forward, and try to assert themselves. And the only person facing them in that cool, persimmon-scented room is me.

I always smile and gesture for them to sit on the cushions with one palm, and then pour a little clove-scented coffee into their cup, in a thin stream. They start talking, to fill the silence, and I let them. When at last they make a silence, I whisper something, such as a line from one of Hernan's favorite books, and they have to concentrate to hear. Eventually someone comes in, Kate or Meg, and plays soft tones on a zither.

Behind me, a pinwheel slows down at an imperceptible rate, and the music, too, slows little by little—all the tricks, aimed at putting their Timefulness to sleep, just for a while. I count my breaths, and breathe slower each time, the way I practiced. I sit languidly, ankle-skirt tucked under my feet.

And meanwhile, I study each one of them. Hernan has been training me to read people, to pay attention to all the little cues and hints about what's really going on with them. So, in turn, I can soothe them with tiny actions. I've discovered a whole side to myself that I'd only glimpsed before, and I've found it's easier than I expected to take control over a scene with another person, as long as I have a well-defined role and we start from a place of quiet. And I like helping these people, who keep the farmwheels spinning or the waste flowing through the reclamation plant, to believe that they can survive another turn of the shutters.

Around the time they've settled enough to hear me, I do something that feels like a huge exertion. I make conversation.

The Illyrian Parlour is designed to look like a coffeehouse back in Zagreb, the greatest city back on Earth at the start of the Brilliant Age. But at some point, Hernan realized that what people in Xiosphant really needed was a place to lose track of time.

The latest client has burn scars on his face that occlude one eye and create a slight inlet of baldness on one side of his head. Due to an industrial accident, perhaps, or brief exposure to direct sunlight (I think of my mother and flinch, but not visibly, so as not to upset him). "They call me Mustache Bob," he says, "on account of my mustache." This is a joke he's told many times—or not quite a joke, more a deflection. His mustache is certainly impressive: dark, bushy, and tapered on the sides of his full lips.

My first instinct is to think that he just wants to be someplace where nobody will ask him about his injury, where someone can just look at him without drama. But I study him more closely: the downward eye movements, the way he clutches his multitool from work, the twinge of anxiety when I quote from a poem about the Golden Thread of obligation and care. He's feeling guilty about something that he can't talk about. Whatever it is, he's afraid people will find out and destroy him—something I can identify with better than almost anyone.

So we do what Hernan calls the Indirection Dance. I don't ask him any questions, and we just carry on a superficial chat about art, music, philosophy, all of the things nobody ever talks about in Xiosphant. Back in Zagreb, at its height, fashionable people traveled all the way from the other city-states—even as far away as Khartoum, New Shanghai, and Ulaanbaatar—via slow railways that snaked far below the toxic surface. Just so they could sit in rooms like this, and talk about nothing.

Bob won't even let out a hint about his secret transgression, but meanwhile he gets excited talking about this cartoon he saw as a child, which they streamed at the Grand Cinema before shutters-up. He makes pictures with his hands while he tries to describe the story. Then, on a hunch, I mention other forms of art, specifically sculpture, and he shuts down.

Just before our session ends, I find out Bob's sin: he needs to keep his hands busy when he's monitoring all the big machines at work. So he's taken to carving tiny figurines out of spare chunks of banyan wood, and he wants to give them away to people. But gifts make Xiosphanti people uncomfortable, suspicious, maybe even angry. If someone just gives you something, they're saying that you need help, or they're trying to insinuate themselves into your life. Like everyone always says, "Freely given, twice cursed." Except maybe Bianca, I guess.

There's no time left to find the right way to reassure Bob gently that he's done no wrong, even though we pretend, in here, to have all the time in the world. So I just say in my soft voice, "If you come back, I'd like one of your carvings. I'll keep it next to my bunk." For a moment, he pulls away, because he doesn't want my charity. But then he sees that the look on my face hasn't changed, and he nods, smiling a little, then runs because he's late for work.

When I get back to the staging area, Jeremy babbles a stream of praise for my craft, but he's more scared than ever that he can't handle this job. I shush him, and he waits a long time for me to speak. "Maybe the next client we can deal with together." He's way too grateful, almost crying, and I remember the part about him having nowhere else to go.

I can't help studying Hernan the way he's taught me to study other people. He sits in an armchair that looks more comfortable than it is, with big white wings and carvings of waves and boats on the arms. Cyrus the marmot is snuggled in his lap, growling with pleasure as Hernan scruffs his ears with his right hand.

Hernan is taking a huge risk—because Cyrus has rolled onto

his back, exposing the gland on his belly that'll squirt a half liter of acid if anything startles him. The acid won't kill Hernan, but it would sting horribly, and could cause permanent damage. Still, Hernan looks contented, wearing his usual gold-threaded tunic and linen pants, just with no shoes. Except that Hernan's left thumb is caught in a vise of his own fingers, like a fear he's keeping at bay.

I'm perched on a big pile of cushions, ready to topple at any moment, in Hernan's personal study, which is tiny and crammed with beauty. The dark walls are covered with little statues made with precious stones that must have come from a treasure meteor, red-and-gold watercolor paintings of the Young Father that someone risked blindness to create, strings of vivid blue feathers from some creature I've never seen.

I've worked here for ages, but I still don't understand Hernan at all. Everything about him, and about the Illyrian Parlour, spits in the face of Xiosphanti values. Not just the way we try to loosen the reins of Timefulness around people's necks, but also this elaborate tribute to Zagreb, one of the seven city-states that pooled their resources to build the Mothership and come to this planet.

There was a man in my apartment building, when I was little, who casually mentioned in public that he thought he had ancestors in the Calgary compartment on the Mothership, and people whispered that he was trying to set himself apart from everybody else. I heard my parents whisper sharp-edged little phrases about him, right before shutters-up. Soon after, he lost his job and had to move out, and I don't know what happened to him after that.

"We're all Xiosphanti now," people always say, as if those seven cities dissolved into one people the moment we stepped onto this planet. Even Bianca would never talk about her roots when she and I whispered together after curfew.

Hernan proudly mentions his family came from Zagreb, which is an even more shocking confession, given what the history books say. He doesn't flinch, or cavil, or act embarrassed by his own rudeness. He just comes out and says it, often right before he lectures me and the other servers about the beautiful way that everything was done in Old Zagreb at its peak.

He doesn't talk so much about what came later.

But still, Hernan is afraid of something, or perhaps just waiting for tragedy to arrive. This place can't last, we all know that—but he knows it more than we do.

"Do you know why your mother used to come here?" Hernan asks me, without looking up from Cyrus.

"Yes," I say, without thinking about it.

"You do? Oh good. Please do tell me. I always wondered."

"Oh, uh, well," I say. "She was always so frazzled. My mom, you know, she was a bank for one of the farmwheels. And it was her job to fix everybody else's messes, all the time. And then she would come home, and my father . . ." I stop, and pull the conversation back from what was about to be a bad place. "So she came here, to be at peace. That's what I thought, anyway."

"Your mother was a very talented artist who never had a chance to share her art with anyone," Hernan says, "which you'll find is true of many of our clients here. But she also believed in assimilation and being a good Xiosphanti, and she spent her life keeping all these wheels turning. I think on some level she disapproved of the Parlour, with all our decadence, but we were the only ones who could give her what she needed. Whatever that was. As I said, I still don't know."

"What kind of art?" I say, in a whisper that's not my usual whisper. I don't want to ruin whatever is happening here, this moment that Cyrus and I have catalyzed.

Hernan just gestures at one of the paintings cluttering the wall: a little girl, standing in front of a pile of barley fresh from the farmwheel. The girl is a smudge of light brown, set off by green-and-white highlights on her chemise and ankle-skirt, and the stalks of barley are a rusty blond.

My mother painted my picture, and I never saw her do it.

I stare for a long time, until the image resolves into brushstrokes, but I can't turn it into a scene whatever I do. It's just a girl, and some barley, and no context. The harder I try to imagine the whole moment and place my mother in it, the more powerful the sense of absence becomes, until absence is the meaning of the picture. I hear stuttering breaths from my own mouth, like an echo of Cyrus's purr; I suckle my own lower lip.

When I get my voice back, I say: "She couldn't have disapproved of this place too much. She brought me here with her."

"True," Hernan says, just cradling Cyrus now. "Or maybe she just thought you would need this place eventually, even more than she did."

mouth

Alyssa and Mouth met for drinks at the Low Road, right after Mouth had come back from yet another one of those political meetings where everyone kept quoting from ancient thinkers like Mayhew and Grantham. ("Sleep when you're sleepy, play when you want," and "People are most imprisoned by the walls they help to build.")

"What are you even playing at?" Alyssa demanded, once she caught the stench of another dank factory basement on Mouth's clothes. "Why are you getting sucked into politics anyway? You always told me politics is for settlers."

"Politics is a bloody waste of time," Mouth snorted. "This isn't about politics."

Alyssa knew Mouth too well, that was the problem. She was the one who held tight during all of Mouth's bad dreams, nursed Mouth through her bouts of lightsickness, and cried on Mouth's shoulder when the road started to eat at her soul. Mouth had shown Alyssa how to catch those little weasels under the crust of the road, which you could live off if you had to, and Alyssa had trained Mouth to shoot a gun. Alyssa even taught Mouth some of the songs from her bat mitzvah, and the stories from the Torah, some of which were about nomads. By now, Alyssa knew all of Mouth's tells.

"This is about what I said before, that you and I might be getting too old to be smugglers." Alyssa sipped and made a face. "Now you're trying to prove something by hanging out with Granthamites who are barely old enough to wank. You don't have to prove anything to anybody, love. You're not even that much older than me. And anyway, I didn't mean 'old' in terms of physical decay. I meant that I'm burning out. I have dreams about the road, and they all end with my bones in a hole. Even if we had a tunnel and a supplier, we might still be stuck here."

Mouth sighed and guzzled gin-and-milk. This goddamn local drink tasted like cat butter that had gone bad. To be fair, even fresh cat butter tasted as if it had gone bad. Who exactly was going to trade bauxite for cat butter? Mouth understood enough of that "calendar" to know George had been stringing them along for thirty turns of the shutters.

"I'm working on something."

"Uh-huh." Alyssa stared at Mouth. "So you're scamming these kids? Or what?"

Mouth looked around, like government spies could be hiding behind the ugly placard outside, which commemorated the victims of the great cattle stampede long ago, during the Seventh Age of Luck.

"I need to get inside the Palace." Mouth gave up on trying to keep a secret from Alyssa. "There's something in there that I need. They probably don't even know they have it. It's worthless to almost anybody, but it's priceless to me. Remember how I vanished after our meeting with George the Bank? I was scoping out the entrances and exits, and there's no way I can get inside the Palace on my own. The guards have guards."

"So, you need a thief. Someone who knows all about breaking into places like that." Alyssa had always loved stories of palace thieves, the whole time Mouth had known her. Something about the glamour, the disguises, or the inevitable seduction of some handsome count just did it for her. Mouth had seen Alyssa kill three people with a single knife, but she still melted when she listened to one of her old audios of long-dead actors playing out some sexy burglary. Alyssa's hometown had no palace, no prince, no councilors. All the Argelan kids grew up with dramas and stories about the fine houses here in Xiosphant, until it became a fairytale of gold leaf, mahogany, and velvet, with trumpets and swooning any time anyone entered a room. You only fantasize about princes when you've never seen one.

"No thieves," Mouth just grunted. "They don't have a lot of thievery in the fancy part of town, after what they did to the last one they caught. Anyway, I don't have time to recruit a debonair master of disguise, just to steal one item out of a giant vault."

"What exactly is it?"

Mouth hesitated. "It's . . . all that's left of my culture. The people who raised me."

"The nomads?" Alyssa perked up, because she'd always wanted to know more about Mouth's childhood.

Mouth was going to need a lot more gin-and-milk if they were going to talk about this. She had long since turned her upbringing into a handful of cute anecdotes about "the nomads who raised me," which she'd crafted with great care, to avoid straying into painful territory. But Alyssa was giving her that look, the one she had whenever Mouth had lightsickness and was trying to cover. And maybe Mouth owed Alyssa more than just a rehearsed story.

Just in time, Ray came over and refilled their cups.

"We called ourselves the Citizens," Mouth said, slowly. "We had a whole other relationship with the road than the Resourceful Couriers have. Like, the road was where we lived, not just where we passed through on our way to someplace else. It sounds stupid when I say it like that. We believed that if we kept walking out there, we could learn to keep company with the day and the night. We always stopped in these small towns along the way, and we became something different each time. One town, we'd be traveling performers, like a theater troupe or some musicians. The next town, we'd be carpenters. Or pest controllers. We were experts at becoming whatever the local people wanted us to be, so we always earned our keep. Until the end, anyway."

Now Alyssa had the same expression as when she listened to her old-timey actors having a stolen romance—like Mouth's loss was the loveliest part of a heartbreaking story. Mouth tried not to hold it against her.

"One time," Mouth said, "we walked farther than ever before, probably farther than anybody ever had. We came to the other side of the world, and we found a canyon. Wide enough to fit five Xiosphants inside. No way to cross, you couldn't build a bridge wide enough even if you had all the heavy metals in the world. We just stood there and gawped at the other side, through all the mist, and tried to see all the way down to the bottom. And then we turned around and went back the way we came."

"So how do we steal this thing that's in the Palace?" Alyssa said.

"You don't do anything," Mouth said. "You enjoy your vacation and live off the spoils from our last job, assuming George doesn't screw us, which I'm putting at fifty-fifty right now."

"You really think I'm going to let you do this on your own?" Alyssa slapped the table with one fresh-manicured hand. "What kind of bitch do you think I am?"

"The kind of bitch who knows this is none of her business."

"Shut your filthy hole. You're my sleepmate. We always have each other's backs. That doesn't stop just because we're off the road."

Mouth looked at Alyssa. Eyes all bright and wide. Nostrils flared a little, head thrown back to expose a delicate neck and collarbone. "I'm asking you, just this once. Stay out of this. I can already tell it's going to get ugly."

Alyssa kept arguing, but eventually she gave up and went to check on the rest of the Couriers, who were still shacked up in the back of a furniture store while George worked out the kinks in their deal.

Mouth always met her informant in the same place, at a small table made of unvarnished banyan wood, in the spicy-yeasty cellar of an oatmeal restaurant. And always at the same time:

three chimes after the red-and-blue smoke. Mouth usually arrived first and then sat alone, as motionless and slumped over as one of those black banyan trees that lined the dry gullies in the Northern Ranges.

The girl arrived late, as usual, limned with a grief that dulled her gaze and put heavy lines on a face that seemed like it was made for laughter. "Hey," she muttered as she sat opposite Mouth. "Thanks for waiting."

Bianca had high cheekbones, ears shaped like dewdrops, and the sleek confidence of the Xiosphanti ruling class—you could tell some of her ancestors had ridden in the New Shanghai compartment, though you could never say so in this town.

"I've been having one of those times when I see her face everywhere, and I just want to scream," Bianca said.

"I've lost a lot of people, and I'm very familiar with the thing where the past becomes an optical illusion." Mouth chewed every other word before she spoke it.

"How do you deal with it? How do you keep from just screaming and breaking things every time you see someone that you know is dead?"

Mouth didn't have a good answer for that. The whole reason she was meeting with Bianca was to appease the dead, but that was none of Bianca's concern.

Those fools had stuck the Invention in a vault inside the Palace, just two kilometers away from here, and maybe this, at last, was the reason why Mouth had elbowed her way past death so many times. So Mouth tried to come up with something to say to Bianca.

"I don't know. Dreams intrude into reality all the time, and you can't waste your energy getting mad at them."

The banyan trees this table was made of had been grown from Earth seeds, spliced with DNA from local flora, and the result had been oily flesh, hard-pebbled skin, and misdirected growth.

"I'm not pissed off at dreams." Bianca laughed and shook her head. She had to stop talking because a waiter showed up, and she was ordering swamp vodka for both of them. Mouth realized that Bianca's Xiosphanti had gotten less formal, with fewer clumsy attempts to pin a social status on Mouth, than the first time they'd talked.

Mouth had made three short visits to the Founders' Square, near the Palace, to try to scope out entrances and exits, and had found no obvious holes in the security. But she'd noticed something else: a gang of twitchy young people who were clearly doing the same thing she was. She'd eavesdropped enough to figure out this was the Uprising, and they were planning something serious. Some kind of political action inside the Palace, and they knew about some secret passage that led all the way in. Plus they had some way of getting past the guards outside. Since then, Mouth had attended as many political gatherings as she could.

But none of the leaders of the Uprising trusted Mouth. Except for Bianca, who ate up Mouth's stories of visiting other places where they did everything different—including Argelo, the City that Never Sleeps.

The swamp vodka arrived.

"Your friend gave her life for the Uprising, right? So you're honoring her memory the best you can." Mouth forced herself to drink, even though the fumes made her sick to her stomach.

Bianca shook her head. "Sophie wasn't part of the Uprising. Neither was I, back then. We were just kids, playing at being revolutionaries. We never would have overthrown a coffee table. But then Sophie . . . she took the blame for a few food dollars that I borrowed." She choked down some swamp vodka and hissed in her throat. "The ludicrous part is, if they had found that money in my pocket instead of hers, they probably would have let me off with a warning. They took one look at her and decided she ought to die."

"They were trying to send a message," Mouth said.

"They were being operated by the machinery of the state. They weren't trying to do anything, really."

A single electric torch lit the cellar behind Bianca's head, casting shadows that gave her two black eyes and a long mouth.

"Most people die for stupid reasons. The most anyone can hope for is to make some noise before that happens." Mouth forced herself to gulp more swamp vodka, to encourage Bianca to keep drinking.

"I never even got to tell Sophie how much she meant to me," Bianca said. "I didn't even realize myself, until she was gone. Nobody else ever saw the side of her that I got to see, when we were alone together. She had these amazing insights. I couldn't wait to see what she would become. The whole world would have learned to admire her. If only—"

Bianca spat out a little blood from chewing her own tongue, but she still didn't let the tears out, like she hadn't earned them.

Mouth didn't get why Bianca had to join these rebels when she was probably destined for a leadership position inside Xiosphant's government anyhow, if she just kept her head down, and then she could change things from the inside. But Bianca kept saying she didn't want to be co-opted, to become part of the problem, and she couldn't play it safe after what they did to her friend.

"Well, whatever it is you and your friends are going to do sounds tricky," Mouth whispered. "And maybe you could use my expertise at sneaking sensitive items in and out of secure locations." Mouth tried to keep her voice casual, like she was offering to help Bianca's friends out of pure altruism, but she could tell she was running out of time. They were going to make their move soon, and she needed to be there when they did.

Facing the end of the Resourceful Couriers felt like losing your family a second time. Like Mouth would need to recount every one of the tears she'd shed after the Citizens all died. Somehow Mouth had convinced herself that if she could just grab the Invention, and get back one small piece of the Citizens, then she'd be okay with whatever happened after that.

Mouth tried to think of the right thing to say to get past Bianca's guard. "You won't find anyone else in this town with as much experience moving high-value items."

"Why would you even want to help us?" Bianca stared at Mouth and frowned. "I thought you were just passing through town. So why get involved with local politics?"

Mouth considered telling Bianca the truth. But instead, she just scratched both her ears with her knuckles, and said, "I don't even know when I'm going to be able to leave. Our tunnel, uh, got caved in. And I can't stand to see the way this town exploits people. Everybody here just works and sleeps, works and sleeps, until they drop dead. I'm just not the sort of person who can see injustice without wanting to tear it down with my own hands." Mouth paused, to make sure she hadn't oversold it.

When Mouth looked up, Bianca was studying her, like she wanted to believe that Mouth was for real, and could help. Bianca was getting ready to throw her own life away because of her pointlessly dead friend, and she was just smart enough to be terrified.

SOPHIE

I look over my shoulder all the time when I venture outside. Every soot-stained garret hanging over me, every food cart on the sidewalk, becomes a mob or a police squad, and I go stiff and breathless every time I think I'm about to get caught. Even though nobody's looking for me, I see threats everywhere. It's more like the memory of my execution is carved into every weathered sandstone wall and every loose brick of these streets, and I can't go out without feeling as though the police still have me, and I'm still about to be thrown to my death.

But as I dart my head around, I see only the normal life of the city. Children play shadowseek in the big fenced-in workyard, hiding behind industrial lathing tools and carving machines. The workyard used to be an actual playground, before my time, but they decided the space was needed for more important things. Kids insist on playing there anyway. The pipe-workers are having their shift change because it's Ninth Chime, and they all meet on this one block of sidewalk, in their muddy coveralls, where the pipe-workers going off shift say the old ritual phrases of consolation to the ones who have to work into curfew. This one old man is hand-churning cake batter, in the exact same storefront where he's done it since my parents were little. I step on flyers for the Grand Cinema and discarded copies of a cheap magazine full of romance stories, both printed on recycled banyan wood.

As I walk in the direction of night, I imagine what I would say to Bianca if she were here, but I no longer have any idea what she would say back.

Some of the buildings in this neighborhood have survived since the beginning of Xiosphant: you can tell by the perfect blocks of whitestone, quarried by the Mothership or an airborne excavator, plus all the classical detailing. The next oldest buildings, including the Illyrian Parlour, come from right around the time of the Great Insomnia, when half the population of Xiosphant left to found another city across the sea, or a slew of smaller towns. You can tell their age by the smoky quality of the bricks, which were fired in this one type of furnace we don't know how to make anymore. Next, there's a mishmash of building styles, including rougher bricks but also hand-lathed stone, hauled from beyond the Northern Ranges, with some crude attempts to copy the older style of decorations. We also had that brief period, between wars, when prospectors kept finding new treasure meteors, and trade with Argelo brought lots of beautiful handcrafted decorations. And then there's everything from the past eight generations, when we just built as much as possible, as cheap as possible, big blocks of cement like the one I grew up in. You can see the whole history of the city, looking at the buildings in any one neighborhood.

I reach the crack in the wall that I've squeezed through so many times now, and remove the skirt around the cuffs of my pants. I hesitate, looking up at the side of the Old Mother and remembering the guns and the taunts, the kicks to the back of my leg. The bruises are long faded, but I still feel them under my skin.

And then I start climbing, because I'm looking forward to seeing my friend.

I know every crack and promontory on the Old Mother by touch alone, and I'm pretty sure I could scale this rock blindfolded. This climb, which nearly killed me when I did it at gunpoint, has become relaxation, a vessel to empty my mind. I let my body recite the litany of grip and hookstep, while I breathe out all my preoccupations. Even when I lose my footing or miss a ledge with my hands, I know how to recover, and I know to rest if I have a cramp. Except if I look behind me and see the steep drop and the sharp rocks at the bottom, or if I stare ahead and dwell too much on the memory of the first time I did this, then I panic. My breathing gets out of control and my fingers weaken, and those things only increase the fear, and there are guns in my face, and I'm going to fall.

That's when I have to stop, breathe deep, and remind myself: *You're climbing by choice this time. You're in control. This is the proof that you're stronger than the monsters who forced you up this slope before.*

When I get to the top, Rose is waiting for me. Her tentacles are cocked in big loops, like she's been tracking my progress, and she lowers her head and opens her pincer in what I know is a gesture of welcome. Her forelegs are bent so she can crouch close enough for me to embrace her. The milky inlets on the sides of her head, above her pincer, close in slightly, giving her a wistful look. That round crocodile mouth— which always looked ravenous and vicious in all the pictures they showed at school—seems to grin, but also pants a little in the warm air. Her woolly fur shimmers with a touch of iridescence. Rose shrinks away from the light up here, but lets me approach.

"I'm so glad to see you, you have no idea," I say, still out of breath. "I didn't mean to keep you waiting so long. I guess I've become an expert at keeping people waiting, but that shouldn't include you."

Rose doesn't seem to understand a word I'm saying, which is one reason I'm so comfortable talking to her. But she shows signs of picking up on my emotional states, which is more than enough. I decided to call her Rose, after the rose shape of the city she showed me the first time we met.

I open the satchel I've been keeping on my back during this whole long climb, and pull out some stuff for her. "It's not much this time. I wish I could repay you properly. Or at least be a better friend." I hand over some blackberries, which come from the smallest of the farmwheels and are almost impossible to get, except that one of my clients knows people. And then a few scraps of Xiosphanti tech.

"This tests water quality." I hold up one gray-and-red box, shaped like a rectangle, with a big loop coming out of one end. "You hold the curved part in the water, and watch for the color on this side. We have a lot of problems with contamination, and I thought maybe you do too."

Rose thanks me, and with one tentacle she holds up her own present for me. It's a ball of dark green spikes with bright blue tips, connected to a long yellow-white stalk. The spikes are each as long as my ring finger, and they quiver in the wind. The frosty stem burns the skin off my fingers. I take a piece of cloth from my pocket, so I can hold it.

I stare for ages before I realize: it's a flower. Some kind of hardy plant that grows out there in the night and exists without sunlight, maybe even without liquid water. It can't use photosynthesis, so how does it live? The spikes catch the twilight and seem to glisten, the greens and blues seeming more vivid and delicate the longer I stare. There's no way this flower will survive the trip back to Xiosphant, so I just commit it to memory while Rose rests next to me.

"I'm actually feeling kind of happy," I say to Rose without taking my eye off the rippling blue-green petals. "I don't know if I ought to be. I can't stand to wonder what Bianca's doing right now. But meanwhile, I have a new family, and we're helping people. I'm doing work that I enjoy, and I can see the results. My life feels wrong, but good. Maybe that's the best I can do."

Rose just tilts her head toward me, like she wants to understand. The flower is already wilting. The cloth I'm pinching around the stem is soggy. The spikes droop, but as they do, they reveal an underseam of brilliant orange.

"I wish I could have talked to my mother about her paintings," I say. "I never even knew she painted."

Rose is holding her pincer open, ready for me to go inside

again. I try not to drop the flower as I lean toward her. I've found that it's easier to do this from a kneeling position, when Rose is hunkered down, than standing up. I'm still thinking about Bianca, and my mother, and the impermanence of the flower in my hand, when my face and neck make contact with the slimy tendrils, and—

—I'm out in the ice. This is the part where usually Rose shows me some aspect of the crocodiles' society, like how they built that huge city by mining deep caverns and tempering metal in the heat of a volcano, and by growing other structures organically. Sometimes she shows me some engineering feat that would make the professors at the Gymnasium sick with envy, but then it's tinged with a sadness, a worry, that I don't understand.

This time, though, I don't see other crocodiles, deep furnaces, or soaring girders. I see a young human, dying in the snow.

(This is the second time I've seen how I look to someone else lately, and this time I almost don't recognize myself. To Rose's senses, I'm a pile of hot meat, giving off fear chemicals and making vibrations in the chill air. A jittering, stumbling human, smaller than most, with upper limbs closed in on themselves. The most unusual thing about me, to Rose, is that there's only one of me.)

I hesitate, because the smart thing in this situation would be to leave this creature to die. But something makes me stop and examine closer. We have plenty of experience with human fight-or-flight behavior, including the usual stances and the chemicals that humans give off. And this one tastes different on the wind: like some mixture of defiance and tenderness.

So instead, I approach the shivering, mewling human and embrace her. For a moment, she seems about to lash out and try to attack my tendrils, and maybe I'll be a dead fool. But no, she moves into my embrace, and I give her one short memory, with a simple message: *We have our own city. We can work together—*

—I think that's it, Rose has shown me everything she's going to, but the memory shifts, and—

—I'm standing with a group of other crocodiles, and we're watching one of our friends bleeding from a spear that juts out from under her carapace. She's surrounded by humans who carry explosives and weapons that could tear through us. My stomachs grind and every heart in my body beats against its cavity with the need to help my friend, but the other crocodiles cross their tentacles in my path. It's too late for her. I break down, venting a noxious cloud of misery and grief, as the humans lash my friend with cords. They drag her, still flailing, up the mountain toward the punishing glare—

—Rose lets me go. I'm already on my knees, but I sink further, and double over, sick to my stomach. My face is moist from the secretions on Rose's tendrils, which create an afterimage when I breathe deeply. I'm hyperventilating, which makes Rose's memories flicker in and out of my head.

"Why don't you just hate us?" I stammer. "Why don't you want to kill us?"

Rose just pulls away slowly, and pulls herself up on her hind legs.

"I know you could. I've seen enough of your geoengineering by now. You could bring rocks and ice down on our city, and we'd never even know what happened." I take a deep breath and rise up on one knee, swaying. "I'm . . . I'm sorry. I'm sorry about your friend."

I've never eaten crocodile meat. Few people have, it's a huge delicacy. But I've seen the hunting parties leaving town before, young people full of loud songs and swagger, and I watched Frank take one apart with knives and spikes. Something rotten settles in my guts and I have to hug my knees. "That was evil. And I wish there was something more I could do."

The ice flower is a dark smudge on the ground.

Rose can sense my distress, like before, and maybe she understands I'm expressing remorse. She comes back again, and opens her pincer one more time. I rise up and bring my face in, and I get a single impression of a block of glossy orange metal. *Copper.* I feel its cool weight on my hand. She pulls away again.

"Okay," I say, still unsteady on my feet, still heartsick. "I'll get you some copper."

Rose turns and clambers over the edge, back toward the night, her front legs picking at the rocks so she doesn't overbalance. A moment later, she's gone, and I turn back to stare at the complacent city, washed in its usual gradient. The farmwheels and tar rooftops shine like new.

I think about how in the world I can score some copper, and then it hits me: I'll need to go back to the temperate zone, the home of all my fear and regret. For a moment, I'm sure I'll die—that if I go anywhere near the Gymnasium, people will see me, they'll shout, the cops will arrive, and this time—

Then I breathe and remind myself, *You're in control. You're stronger than those monsters.* I pick myself up and hurry back to town before they ring the last curfew bell, running down the slope so fast I nearly kick myself as I skid and spill onto the ground.

mouth

Mouth and Bianca took a walk on the edge of the slaughter-house district, where livestock raised outside Xiosphant came in to be butchered, on lorries or in long trains of wide-eyed cows and fidgeting goats. These buildings clustered near the city wall, on the side facing the Northern Ranges, and they made a crisp profile of clay-brick gables and steeples against the wall's edge. Mouth had only eaten meat occasionally in Xiosphant, but she did appreciate the leather.

Since they were out in the open, walking along a wide slate-paved road with the indentations of countless lorry wheels, they spoke in whispers, and only discussed politics obliquely. Still, Mouth welcomed a meeting someplace besides the oatmeal restaurant.

"When they took Sophie, I lost all my dumb illusions about how the world works," Bianca said. "I had all these lofty theories about culture, and internalized mechanisms of control, but I hadn't ever faced up to how much the world runs on crude, mindless violence until it was right in front of me."

"Violence doesn't settle everything," Mouth grunted.

"Sometimes violence just postpones a conversation that's bound to happen sooner or later. But that can be useful in itself, to some people."

Bianca had barely slapped anyone in her life, and Mouth was the first person she'd ever met who'd killed people as part of her job. At times, Bianca seemed to crave reassurance: that she could do this, that fighting and maybe killing would come naturally, that it would pay off. Other times, she almost seemed to wish Mouth would say, *You're not cut out for this, leave this to the professionals.* To justify Bianca's qualms, or make a space for her anxiety about whether her grief over Sophie would give her enough strength.

Sometimes at the oatmeal place, Bianca would quiz Mouth about her skills. How many people had she killed? Could she fight in close quarters? What weapons did she have particular experience with? Those questions always came with an appraising stare, like Mouth was a piece of merchandise that might be overpriced.

Now, in the wide driveway near the rows of abattoirs, Mouth tried to remember what the Citizens had said about self-defense when they'd trained every child to hold a weapon. Bianca seemed lost in thought.

At last Mouth said, "Part of how they make you obey is by making obedience seem peaceful, while resistance is violent. But really, either choice is about violence, one way or another."

"That almost sounds like a quote from Mayhew." Bianca laughed, then covered her mouth because they were out in the open, where any number of government spies could be lurking behind these walls, along with the muffled drone of cutting machines.

The longer Mouth stayed in Xiosphant, the further off-center everything drove her. They had foods that you could only eat right after the shutters opened, and other foods you ate right before they closed. People would raise a glass *before* the blue-and-red smoke filled the sky, because they expected it. When Bianca talked about the workers' rebellion that happened during her great-grandparents' time, she couldn't help saying it took place during the Third Age of Plenty.

And right now, Mouth was hustling to George's roofing plant, because the klaxons said the city was getting ready to pull up all the shutters. You could smell the starchy aroma of everyone's pre-sleep meal, and the soapy fumes of last-chance laundry. The sky remained pale, and calm, thanks to those mountains cutting off the worst of the weather systems, but people rushed as if they were about to get hailed on. A look of good-natured anxiety on everyone's face. You could almost hear them mutter, "Oh dear, this is very bad, well, it's okay, but it's very bad, must get indoors, if only I had a little more time, oh dear."

Everyone in Xiosphant was weirdly polite, just as long as you pretended all their made-up stuff was real.

George was in a good mood, because he'd been able to unload some of the textiles they'd brought from Argelo, and had done some wizardry to get them a "basket of currencies" in return.

"Is that like money?" Reynold snorted.

Mouth had to help the other Couriers to carry the crates of silk and muslin across town. They couldn't use the sled because it drew too much attention, and they had to move these crates before the shutters closed. George came along, since he knew all the teeny alleyways that cut between the big boulevards and the crisscrossing avenues. The main obstacle in these shortcuts: heaps of garbage that smelled like the poisonous swamps out past Argelo, where they made vodka out of the sap of this one carnivorous plant. (Swamp vodka tasted better if you didn't know where it came from.)

Six of them carried crates on their shoulders, nearly tripping over rubbish every few steps, and Mouth heard Alyssa cursing as she stepped in puddles. Their route took them closer and closer to the night.

The final bell sounded, meaning they were too damn late.

"Here it is." George pointed at a stone staircase, at the end of a narrow alley.

By the time they hoisted the crates up the uneven stairs into the garment factory, the shutters were going up all over town, with a sound like Xiosphant was grinding its teeth.

"We'll have to stay here until the shutters drop again," Omar said before they even had a chance to look around the garment factory. Looms, rows and rows of sewing machines with rusty pedals, vats of dyes and ammonia. The place smelled even worse than the alleys, or the sub-basements where Mouth had snuck into political meetings. No place to lie down, and only those benches to sit on. The factory manager apologized in a few grunts as he handed over the "basket of currencies" in a bag made of cheap canvas, then locked himself in his office with the single cot.

"I can tell I'm not going to be able to sleep here," Mouth said.

"Better get some shut-eye if you can. It's also illegal to sleep when the shutters are open," Alyssa said, settling onto one of those benches in front of a sewing machine.

"That's not true." Yulya gaped, speaking in broken Xiosphanti. "Is it true?"

"Actually," said George, "the penalties are almost as bad for sleeping during shutters-down as for being out and about during shutters-up. You're supposed to be contributing to society when everyone's awake, so we're all united. They've put people to death for being repeat offenders: sleeping at the wrong time more than once."

"Sleep when you're sleepy, play when you want," Mouth said, without even thinking.

George leapt to his feet and looked around, like they were all about to be arrested. "Where did you hear that?"

Everyone stared at Mouth. Alyssa raised one eyebrow. Omar's eyes narrowed. The Resourceful Couriers had an informal rule against getting involved in local politics, for obvious reasons, and Mouth had sort of forgotten.

"I dunno." Mouth tilted her head. "I was drinking somewhere and there were these students. I thought it was a funny thing to say."

"It's a dangerous ideology," George said, "aimed at cutting my throat. Cutting all our throats. Wrecking our whole society. People don't realize how much we're all just hanging on by our fingernails. This planet really doesn't want us here."

"I don't know." Alyssa decided to rescue Mouth from an awkward moment. "Maybe people in this town could stand to loosen up just a tad, you know? I've been in synagogues in Argelo that were more laid-back."

"I know you people have been to other places, where they deal with this hostile environment differently," George said. "But we have almost a million people in Xiosphant, and everyone has food and shelter, pretty much." He turned back to Mouth. "That phrase you quoted was part of a whole manifesto about living in harmony with nature, which on this planet is antithetical to human life."

Mouth was starting to understand what that guy had meant when he said people were the most trapped by the walls they helped to build. But she just nodded at George and pretended to fall asleep.

Once the shutters came down again, Mouth would pretend to be awake.

SOPHIE

The memorial to the Second Argelan War looks even uglier up close: the seams in the lumpy black underside, the ochre streaks where it's rusting away.

The sculptor tried to create the impression of waves and froth below the little section of boat, but they were working with an ungainly metal that couldn't hold any fine details. I always heard that parts of this sculpture were made of melted-down artillery, but either way the result came out crude, like something your somnambulist hands might shape in the throes of a bad dream. Above the slice of deck, a faceless man in a heavy uniform stands holding a weapon on one shoulder, ready to fire some projectile.

I hunch behind the statue until I hear her voice, then I peer between the soldier's legs. Bianca walks across the Gymnasium's plaza with a satchel across her almost-translucent chemise, and her laugh sounds as dazzling as ever. She smiles and waves to the other students who trot past her on their way to class, and then she stops and talks to Cally, an earnest red-haired girl, about homework. I can almost guess which class they're heading to, and what jibes Bianca is making about the professor.

The crumbling edges of the statue scrape my arms and repel my attempts to lean against them. The soldier scans for enemy boats in the distance. I sink below his leaden feet and look at a tiny rip in my ankle-skirt.

I tell myself this is what I wanted for Bianca. I wanted her to let me go, to get on with her life and be happy. I knew she was bound to forget me. If anything, I should be relieved. But I feel as if I'm made of the same dead weight as this top-heavy soldier, who seems more and more doomed to pitch over. I see nothing but rust and metal fatigue, but Bianca's voice still comes, from far off.

Copper nuggets weigh down my jacket pockets. I took all the infrastructure chits I'd ever earned at the Illyrian Parlour and went around town to all the markets and scrapyards, buying a little at a time. I couldn't buy too much in one place, or someone would ask questions.

I'm about to sneak back to the nearest alley, a dozen meters away. But I turn back for one last look. Something to preserve in my mind for later. This time, I see a different Bianca.

She stands alone in the plaza, and her posture has transformed, now that she thinks nobody sees her. She stoops forward, her mouth wraps into a scowl, and her eyes have dark lines. Her right hand makes a half fist. All of the other students have gone, because class is starting, but Bianca stares at the paving stones. At last she forces herself to go to class, walking short measures that make her loose skirt ripple.

My heart wakes at the thought of running over to Bianca. I

want to pull her into a hug and cradle her head with one hand, tell her that I'm here. I'm alive. I came back for her. I stare at the tight lines around Bianca's mouth as she walks to class, and I feel so much longing and compassion and joy and sadness and rage I can't help stepping around the statue, right in broad view.

But as soon as I'm out in the open, the memory-panic hits. I imagine the cops seeing me, in the middle of campus, and surrounding me. Their black faceplates blotting everything, their hands on my arms and legs. I won't escape this time. All my former classmates will swarm outside to watch.

I feel my body go taut, and my lungs empty. I'm never going to escape that moment, no matter what I do. I almost white out from oxygen starvation. My armpits feel fresh-bruised, but the rest of my body has no sensation. I manage to stagger back behind the cover of the statue, praying nobody saw me, and then I sink into its shadow. By the time I get blood back in my head, Bianca has gone inside one of the classroom buildings.

I'm left alone, catching my breath, next to the whitestone plaque commemorating our heroic dead.

I can't stop cursing myself as I work my way back toward the darker end of town. Bianca was *right there,* she needed me, and I did what? I stayed hidden, because when I saw the Gymnasium and the students and everything, my execution turned brand new, as if it had just happened. They took me away from her, and they're still taking me from her. It's not my fault. I know it's not my fault. The whole purpose of arresting me and hauling me away, with so much fanfare, was to put fear into people.

So why be surprised that the fear is in me?

Those gloved hands haven't loosened their hold on me, even after all this time.

I have to stop and check myself, because I'm carrying valuable metal and I don't want to be noticed in this neighborhood. I try to clear my mind and pretend I'm playing a game of shadowseek.

Every child in my neighborhood learns to play shadowseek at a young age, even middle-class kids like myself. To win, you have to know where the shadows are, and move from one to another without a break. The shadows never change shape or position, so a clever child can memorize them in advance. And if you're really good, you can stay in the shadows by pure instinct.

But my mind is stuck in the moment when Bianca let her grief show and I almost went to her. I hardly even see my surroundings, because in my mind I'm still stepping out from behind a decaying metal slab, about to console her with an indelible tenderness. All the potential that was in that moment, I let it fill me up so that maybe next time I can . . .

That thought consumes me—so I don't even notice the mob until it's rushing toward me.

They snort and pant, ash-colored jackets swirling as their arms and legs pull at the air. A few hundred of them stampede in my direction, and there's no way to escape. I'm convinced that I'm about to be swept away. I'll kick, I'll struggle, but their momentum will be too much for me. They'll carry me to justice. No escape this time.

But the mob reaches me and keeps moving. They're heading somewhere, and I just got in their way. I stop fighting, and move in the same direction as everyone else, and soon the crowd shelters me, buries me inside its raucousness. We arrive in Founders' Square, facing the Council Building and the Spire.

I stand, pressed in on all sides by people, and stare down at the paving stones, which have a pattern that looks like star charts when the light hits them. My parents used to bring me here to listen to the vice regent or even the prince, and instead of looking up at all the gaudy costumes, or the grandeur of the Palace and the Spire and everything around me, I just ran my fingers over this pavement, marveling at the flecks of mica and agate.

Trumpets sound, and the vice regent comes out on the plinth: a tall man with a slack chin and mean eyes, wearing a long gold tunic held together with a bright red sash. We hear his voice around the square, thanks to speakers but also the amazing acoustics that our ancestors engineered.

The vice regent talks about all the achievements of Xiosphant since our great-grandparents' time, when the Fourth Age of Beauty began. We were falling into decadence, our society was collapsing, all our resources were dwindling. But then we severed contact with Argelo, we stopped tolerating disruptive elements, and we renewed our Xiosphanti values, thanks to the Circadian Restoration. Now we're truer to our ideals than ever. And yet, we've made sacrifices—like all the people who just journeyed past the Northern Ranges to find more arable soil for the farmwheels, steering lorries across thousands of kilometers, with only their timepieces to tell them when to sleep.

The vice regent puts on his most comforting voice. "Thanks to these brave souls, and our hardworking farmers,

I'm delighted to announce an increase of two percent in the supply of food dollars. Alas, at the same time we are still facing . . . certain resource constraints. And thus, the supply of both water tokens and med-creds is being reduced by ten percent each. I'm sure we'll all make the best of this challenging situation, because we're Xiosphanti, and we—"

Everyone roars. I don't hear the end of that sentence, because the mob is rushing forward again, this time charging straight at the vice regent's plinth, in front of the Council Building. A woman standing next to me has a moldy radish that she must have brought just for this moment, and she flings it at one of the riot cops in front of us. People chant slogans, but I only hear vowels. The vice regent tries to restore order, but the officers have clubs and shields raised.

I have no choice but to run toward a line of police, who wear the same murky faceplates as the figures in my worst memory. They're raising weapons and clubs, and I feel myself blank out as the people in front of me crash into the wall of the Council Building. We speed up as we hit. I have to close my eyes for a moment. They're going to clutch me, I'm trapped. When I look again, the people closest to the front are crushed between the mob and the police shields, and I hear them scream. The police bring their clubs down.

The calm part of my mind takes over, the same part that figured out how to communicate with Rose the first time. I pull back and look at this whole situation as if from far above. I stop staring at the mob and the armored cops, and search instead for a way to survive. I don't let myself look at the helmets and guns, or think about how close they are.

The woman next to me snarls and hoists another vegetable. Then the whip-crack sound of a gun, and she's gone. Just . . . vanished. I don't even think to look down at first, and then I see her. A red mess has replaced most of her head, but the people around me trample her body.

I'm still not letting myself feel any of this. The crowd has broken. People shove each other in all directions. Someone pushes me and I nearly fall in the path of more trampling feet. But I recover, and then I spot the golden statue of Jonas, and I dodge the flailing limbs and angry faces to reach it. I pull myself up into the hollow underside of Jonas's shimmering All-Environment Survival Suit and hide. I hear shouts, falling bodies, and more gunshots.

The noises peter out, but I don't leave my hiding place. A few times, I'm about to make a move, when I hear the police making another sweep or, later on, the aggrieved cleanup crew trying to mop all the blood and dirt off the spangled paving stones. But at last they all decide to knock off and get some gin-and-milk, so I risk slipping away.

I reach the Parlour with just one bell left to shutters-up, and turn the brass doorknob three times left and four times right, as I was taught. Five people with severe windburn and ill-fitting Xiosphanti clothes are sitting in the entry lounge, with Cyrus sneering at this invasion of his cozy space, exposing his lower incisors. One of these strangers has a spiky haircut that covers only the middle of her scarred head, and another has metal sticking out of his face. I almost turn and leave again, because these people don't look like clients. The images of the police shields and helmets, the gunshot and the headless woman are still seeping into my mind, and I can already tell they're going to replay in my dreams.

But Hernan appears and waves one arm. "Sophie, come on in. These lovely people are the Resourceful Couriers, and they're visiting from Argelo. They won't be staying long. I've done business with them in the past, and this time they've brought some great delicacies, including genuine cat butter."

I can't help gawping. I've never even met any foreigners before. The Resourceful Couriers nod at me, and one tall man with a large black mustache and neat beard does a little bow. They're all staring at me, and the need to get away from all these people is almost overwhelming. But I'm curious, too.

"I was worried about you," Hernan says to me. "I thought you might have gotten caught up in the . . . unpleasantness at the Founders' Square." He measures his syllables, as if to remind me that, inside the Parlour, we do not rush.

"Some unpleasantness, yes." The leader of the Resourceful Couriers, the man with the dark whiskers, laughs. "People here are not accustomed to seeing economic disputes settled with guns, but every economy runs on bullets, one way or another." Omar's accent sounds like nothing I'd ever heard, and his syntax keeps slipping from polite to familiar.

"In my experience," says Hernan, "absolutely everyone can pretend to be a pacifist, just so long as there's enough money to go all the way around."

I want to keep listening, but without anyone paying too much attention to me. So I fetch a pot of lukewarm coffee and load up a tray with tiny cups.

The youngest Resourceful Courier is a woman named Yulya, close to my age, with long dark hair and skin that looks less windscarred than everyone else's. Yulya believes her ancestors traveled in the Zagreb compartment, just like Hernan's, and she stares at every little item and decoration. "I can't believe you managed to build all of this. In Xiosphant, of all places," she says, with worse grammar than Omar. "I wish my father could see this place."

"I always heard that Zagreb didn't put in its fair share when they were pooling resources to build the Mothership," says the large man with the metal piercing his face. I think his name is Kendrick.

"That's what they say, when they talk about it at all," Hernan says.

I've heard Hernan's version of the story a few times now. By the time the great city-states of Earth were building the Mothership to escape a ruined planet, Zagreb was in steep decline from its worldwide supremacy back at the start of the Brilliant Age. But you still couldn't call yourself cosmopolitan if you hadn't spent time there, so all the other cities made concessions to allow Zagreb to have a compartment on the ship. In return, the Zagreb contingent made sure to bring everything from musical instruments to cooking spices to beautiful handcrafted furniture to great works of literature— everything you'd need to re-create true civilization.

But after the radiation leaks, the explosive decompression, the Hydroponic Garden Massacre, and all the tiny wars, the Zagreb stock ended up ruined. They arrived with nothing. All anybody remembered about Zagreb was that they didn't contribute as much as all the other city-states, but we let them come along out of charity.

Hernan grew up believing he came from a long line of beggars. He and all his extended family lived on the bright edge of town, where the shutters conducted heat and you felt like you were cooking alive in the dark, and he hated every one of his relatives. Until Hernan somehow discovered a long-forgotten book about the salons of Old Zagreb. That's why he opened the Illyrian Parlour, although he had to pretend that it was just a beautiful coffeehouse, and downplay any Zagreb connection, or else they'd never have let him accept food dollars instead of just luxury coins.

Some of the other Resourceful Couriers pipe up with their own theories and stories about things that happened to their distant ancestors on the Mothership, during the journey, or after planetfall. This conversation has strayed into territory that would get all of us arrested, at a time when the city has already set about eating itself, and then I realize the smugglers are amused by my discomfort, to varying degrees. Which makes me more uncomfortable.

Thank goodness everyone realizes the shutters are about to close, and the conversation ends. The Resourceful Couriers leave the Parlour in a hurry, looking flustered, almost like proper Xiosphanti.

Four of us sleep in a tiny room, even smaller than I used to share with Bianca, with two rows of bunks. I'm sleeping above

Jeremy, who thrashes when he dreams about whatever drove him away from his comfortable old existence. All Jeremy has told me about his past is that he was doing an extended course in geophysics, hoping to help solve the great riddle of our world: how the climate can be so stable, with fire and ice so close together, and whether it'll stay that way. But there was some scandal, an improper romance, and he had to flee.

Opposite us are Kate and Walter, who've been here the longest and always start shoving, running, and pillow-fighting the moment we're done playing at languid slowness.

Everyone else seems to be asleep, but I just lie there and hug myself. I remember the defiance on that woman's face at the Square, right before she didn't have a face anymore. All of my old fears feel even more rational than before, and the gloved fingers grip my armpits more tightly. My last thought before sleep is of Bianca's ghost smile, slowly dispelling.

When the shutters open, I wake groggy, and remember dreaming of helmets on a mountainside. Meanwhile, Walter, Kate, and Jeremy are whispering that our next clients will be the worst, now that everyone knows someone who got trampled or shot at. A feeling of dread seeps through all of the hand-gilded murals and reproductions of classic wooden furniture.

Hernan takes me aside as soon as I've dressed and tied my wavy hair back with a neat ribbon. "Sophie, I know you had a terrible experience. Do you feel up to working this shift? We can always give you some time off."

Over in the far corner, Jeremy's eyes widen, because if I take a surprise vacation, Jeremy will be left dealing with all these people on his own, and he's still not ready.

I shrug. "I'll be okay."

Hernan stares, because he knows I'm lying.

"I'm close enough to okay," I say. "I know how to get out of a situation if I start feeling less okay."

"That will have to do, I suppose." Hernan smiles, and then offers me a hug. I hesitate a moment, then lean into his stocky chest, close enough to see a loose silver thread on his brocaded jacket. "I wish I knew why you were sneaking off all the time, with my old padded jacket and those new boots that you spent all your clothing vouchers on. You never quite explained how you survived being forced up that mountain, and now I wonder . . . I just hope that whatever you're doing, you keep yourself safe."

I feel like saying, *Nobody is ever safe,* but instead I smile and say, "Of course."

Long after I have forgotten what everything in the Illyrian Parlour looks like, the scents will stay with me. The musk that hangs in the air after I've slept in our tiny bunkroom with Jeremy, Walter, and Kate, the flowery, pungent scent of coffee brewing in the tiny cracked-tile kitchen behind the beautiful client room, the aroma of sandalwood and fresh-cut lavender, the comfort of soap. These scents have come to feel like home, and if I even notice a hint of sandalwood or dark coffee anywhere else, I feel a recognition that my mind only catches up with after a moment.

I find myself trying to memorize every detail, so I'll remember this place whatever happens, and also because

Hernan created a place where the world feels bigger, and yet also more intimate, than anywhere else in this city. I wish I could figure out how he pulled that off. My mother used to smile at me and say these funny things, which I now recognize as quotes from the books Hernan has made me memorize. *A fen has more dignity than a mountain, because the fen settles according to its own weather.* Or: *Listen to yourself, hear your own footsteps, your breaths, your heartbeats, oh, how many rhythms you make as you come and go! you are an orchestra.* I remember my mother saying that to me: "You are an orchestra." And laughing, until I laughed too without getting the joke.

Jeremy and I work together, while Kate and Walter play music or hustle behind the scenes, and Jeremy's grateful enough that I'm working that he covers for me when I have to shut my eyes and ride out a small memory-panic. Some part of my mind has combined the guns that forced me up a mountain with the ones that took a woman's head apart, as if those were one incident. And meanwhile, the people who sit across from us flail around, grope for stillness, and make too much noise and commotion, in spite of all our work. Jacek, a pipe-worker who always seems ashamed of his fetid odor in this clean, fragrant space, keeps looking in all directions, biting all his fingers one by one, muttering, "They didn't need to shoot anyone, they didn't," and twitching. Our next client, a tall athletic woman from the power plant, seems better, breathing slow and shallow, hands on knees, until I realize she's in shock.

Nobody is okay. Nothing we do helps. I breathe slower and

louder, confuse them with morsels of old stories, sprinkle petals in their coffee. Client after client. The shutters close, and open again, and it's the same thing again. Even after two more shutter-cycles.

It's okay, I want to say, *I know how you feel. Like slow-dancing with a rockfall.*

After another endless shift, I let myself slump, so exhausted my arms fall like rags. I turn to Jeremy and ask, "Have you ever had something happen to you that scared you so much you felt like you were going to keep reliving it forever?"

Jeremy pauses for a moment, his round face creasing. "Hernan always says that a perfect moment of beauty can last forever. But maybe some moments are so ugly that they never end, either. All you can do is be patient with yourself."

mouth

Mouth spent way too much time obsessing about how to get inside Bianca's head when the two of them weren't sitting together in the oatmeal place, eating overseasoned mush and drinking bad liquor. Bianca's main weakness seemed to be the dead girl, Sophie. Mention that name, and she just devolved into a weepy mess, but this always led to a conversation about loss and revenge rather than any actionable information about their Palace job.

"Every time the shutters roll down and the light comes into my room I lay there, and I just look up at the milky sky. I curse, and I stare at the shelf where Sophie used to sleep." Bianca closed her eyes and inhaled through her nose. "Hope doesn't get me out of bed. Duty definitely does not get me out of bed. The only thing that does is making the bastards who took her from me pay."

By this point, Bianca had talked about the dead girl half a dozen different times—but Sophie never once sounded like a real person. According to Bianca, Sophie had possessed no flaws, not even the slightest jealousy or negativity. "She always wanted to see the good in everyone." Bianca held the bowl of oatmeal to her face and breathed in the sour vapor. "She managed to see through all the hypocrisy, using kindness instead of anger."

"There's no way to replace someone who had so much life. But I guess you can still make her death worth something." Mouth could smell all the spices and the rankness of boiled tomatoes in the kitchen upstairs. The scent brought back a powerful recall of this one herb that the Citizens used to pick out in the far plains way past the other side of Argelo, which Yolanda insisted was great for your digestion, but which tasted like salty dirt.

"You're the only person I can talk to about her," Bianca said. "Everybody at the Gymnasium just decided to pretend Sophie never even existed as soon as she was gone. And Derek and the other organizers of the Uprising don't want to hear about my selfish motivations for joining the fight. Everybody's supposed to be in this for the pure light of justice, and liberation from the endless cycle of toil."

"There's no right reason for wanting to make a difference." Mouth kept seeing that picture of the Invention from the catalog in her head. She imagined picking it up and letting light into all its contours, and feeling as though maybe her life had a purpose after all.

"Don't get me wrong, I believe in the Uprising. I think Xiosphant was a great place once, before the wars and the isolationism and the Circadian Restoration, but now it's grown into something elitist and corrupt." Bianca looked up at the pockmarked clay ceiling. "The only goal this city has is to maintain. We're just supposed to keep the city the same for another four or five generations, and after that, everything breaks beyond our ability to repair."

Mouth wanted to say, *You shouldn't get yourself killed in a pointless gesture.* But she thought about the Invention, and instead she said, "I bet Sophie would be proud of what you're doing."

"I hope so." Bianca smiled, and the backlit shadows turned it into a scowl. "I just can't keep feeling like this. Ever since they took her, I've hated every breath. And I want to take all of this pain and give it to someone else. Let them see how they like it."

Mouth sensed she was running out of time to find out how these revolutionaries were going to get inside the Palace. If she could just sneak inside under their cover, she'd only need a few hundred heartbeats to get upstairs, crack the vault, and grab the Invention.

Mouth almost said, *You know, you'll just end up killing the working stiffs if you attack the Palace. The guards, the cleaning staff, the drudges. You'll never even touch the people in power.* Instead, she poured Bianca more swamp vodka and said, "You need to stay angry, and remember why you're fighting. Hold on to that fire, because you owe it to your friend. Trust me, you can't leave these debts unpaid, or it'll ruin you over time."

As Mouth spoke, she was thinking of the fire that had consumed the Citizens' remains, and the debt that she had carried ever since. Bianca was nodding, heavily, and Mouth made herself smile.

SOPHIE

The last few times I visited Rose at the summit of the Old Mother, I've been empty-handed, because it took me some time to figure out how to get copper. This time, I'm weighed down. To add to the chunks I bought in the temperate zone, I stripped some old wiring that I scrounged in an alley near the Illyrian Parlour, and found a few more bits in a scrapyard, plus one of our clients made me a present of a pendant that has some copper in it. The extra load adds to the strain on my already-stiff arms with every steep rise. I keep taking breaks, and thinking about Bianca's heartsick expression.

When I reach the plateau, I sit and wait, staring outward, and I try to make sense of all this mess. No human being has ever shared their thoughts with me the way Rose has. I know more about what it feels like to watch hunters drag my friend into the searing twilight than I'll ever know about most human experiences, and every time I think about that image I feel something lower than shame. Even with all the other anxieties that overturn my thoughts, the image of a crocodile being dragged away for an obscene feast, bound and bleeding, keeps coming back.

I hear a crunch, and a massive shape rises out of the dark. I nearly lose my balance on the slice of rock where I'm perching, even though I've been waiting for Rose. The wind ruffles her fur, and her front legs crinkle as she plants her wide, clawed feet. She shields herself from the meager daylight with her tentacles, and crouches near me, greeting me in the crocodile fashion. Her round mouth seems to smile.

"Hi," I say, over the sorrowful wind. "It's good to see you. I hope you've been safe out there. I hope all your friends are holding up. Things in Xiosphant have been . . . intense. Everyone is so freaked out they almost can't think straight."

I'm ashamed of my tiny amount of copper, which Rose clutches in one tentacle before tucking it under her woolly carapace. We used to have tons of the stuff, because the Mothership had steered a lot of ore-rich asteroids down to us. People used copper to decorate everything, but all the treasure meteors are exhausted and our mines are empty. Scientists believe that a lot of the most valuable metals on this planet are concentrated on the day side, where we can't mine or even investigate.

So to make up for this sad bundle, I reach into my satchel and pull out the timepiece my father gave me when I was a child, to help me pay attention. I had this tiny clock in my jeans pocket when they banished me to this place, and the fine metalwork survived somehow. You can still make out the care that somebody put into every angel, every flower, and the way the fine gears turn.

"This is important to my people," I say. "This is how we

know what to do, or what everyone else is doing right now. If you could read this, and you knew enough about me, you could use this to know where I am, all the time." I try to show Rose how to wind it, and which dial points to day or night, the different times and settings. She seems to pay attention, or at least to understand I'm making a fuss about this object. When I place the timepiece into her tentacle, she tries to give it back. I press it into her grasp and let go.

"A present. For you."

Rose accepts the clock, placing it next to the copper. Then she beckons with her open pincer, and I only hesitate for a moment. I push my face and neck into the fulcrum, where slick warm fingers brush my face—

—We live in a great city, far from here, under the crust of the night. Cliffs of ice, deep fissures, towering structures of stone and metal, and wheels turning far beneath us, fueled by underground rivers, and furnaces hotter than the touch of the sun. At the heart of our city, tiny creatures who look like us hang in a mesh of warm, dark threads, helpless and spindly. They cry out, their tentacles and pincers still too tiny to communicate properly, but we can feel their distress, and our blood runs thin. They stay inside that web because their slender bodies haven't finished developing, and when an adult places some bright roots among the threads holding them, the babies absorb this nourishment right away. The roots shrivel as the web swells with nourishment. But these infants still cry out. Their pincers open and close, and the message is clear: *I'm cold. It hurts. I'm scared.* No matter what we do, these children aren't growing the way they're supposed to. Their soft unshelled bodies hang, weaker and weaker, as they struggle to take in any nutrition.

We don't understand the cause of the sickness for a long time. But then we discover: a poison rain, falling on the ice sheets far above, gives off scents that make us almost lose consciousness if we even approach. Some caustic liquid that was trapped long ago, somewhere in the hottest part of the day, has been released into a cloud, because the sky has gone out of balance. Even the slightest touch burns the cilia off your tentacles, and it turns the air too noxious too breathe. This poison seeps down into the soil, until it reaches the protective threads around our children, tainting them. We feel sorrow, trapped in our deepest cores like a memory too painful to share, when we travel back down into the depths of the city and see their toothless mouths open and close, their unshaped tentacles reaching out for nothing. This sickness taints a whole generation of our children, and there will be nobody to give our most cherished memories to before we die—

—When Rose releases me, I reel, and topple in the direction of the night before I recover. My face is wet, even apart from the residue from her tendrils. I fall on my back, looking up at the dark clouds.

I babble something. "Those babies. I'm sorry. I wish . . . I don't know what I can do. How can I help? What is there? I'm so sorry. I would do anything—"

Rose just lowers her head again, like she's encouraging me to climb up on her back and ride. We stand there, on the line between one world and the other. I hear thunder a long way off, on the other side of endless ice fields, but never see any lightning. I wonder how long that toxic rainfall has been blighting the crocodiles' nurseries, and what caused it. There was a sliver of an idea buried in Rose's shared memory: the atmosphere was in balance for a long time, the day and night in perfect arrangement, but now the sky itself has gone wrong.

I'm too cold to stay up here any longer, even with Hernan's warm padded jacket, and I hear the chimes sound the Span of Reflection. I touch the end of one tentacle, gently, then pick my way back down the mountainside.

I don't know what I'm supposed to do about toxic rain falling on a city thousands of kilometers away, across an endless field of ice and storms. I can't banish that image, but I also can't make my mind encompass it.

So I find myself drifting back to my other obsession.

I need to make sure Bianca's okay, after I've seen so many other people flying out of their skins. I'm not even sure how many times the shutters have gone up since the riot, but at last I dredge up the courage to go check on her again.

When I walk near the Gymnasium, I feel myself freeze up again. But this time I'm expecting it, and so I take Jeremy's advice: I'm patient with myself. I stay in a safe alcove, protected by shadows, until the worst passes. Then I find another hiding place and watch Bianca, chatting with the other students, striding away from campus. I see her stroll past Matthew and a couple other old members of the Progressive Students, and they barely acknowledge each other. Good. The police are probably still watching that whole group, including her, and right now they're ready to shoot anyone who makes them the slightest bit nervous.

I almost try again to talk to Bianca, but there are always too many people around. Instead, I just walk a safe distance behind her as she strides downtown. Bianca doesn't look at the Plaza, the Market, or the row of clothing stores along the Grand Boulevard. She just keeps her head down, and doesn't even change her posture when she passes through the cold front. Colored smoke fills the sky, and the bakery switches from wake-up pastries to after-work treats. Watching Bianca from a safe distance, I feel so homesick, in the middle of my chest and the prow of my back.

Bianca wanders into the grayest part of town, close to the Warrens, and knocks on a plain metal door in an abandoned paint factory. I find a tiny window, on the other side of the building, that has a view into the dingy room where she emerges and starts hefting an ancient rifle in both hands. Around her, people study plans and maps of the Founders' Square.

Seeing Bianca next to this pile of guns, I feel the cold go through me. She's going to do something stupid. Spots fill my eyes, almost like an attack of lightsickness, as I think about the helmets, the guns, the casual murder. The thick gloves seizing Bianca this time, or hoisting her dead body.

I have to close my eyes and picture myself out in the ice floes, kilometers from the nearest drop of illumination, clawing the tundra in total darkness.

When I make myself look into the basement again, I notice someone who seems out of place, even among rebels and misfits. They turn their head, and I recognize one of the foreigners who came to the Parlour. The Resourceful Couriers, they called themselves. This is the tall, angry one, with the strip of hair cutting across the hash of pale scars on her head. She's hoisting a large gun in both arms, like a baton in some obscure game.

mouth

The air felt sickly, like the chemicals from the old paint factory had seeped through the groaning cement ceiling and the meter-thick insulation down to this maintenance pod. They'd taken all of Mouth's weapons, except the two that were hidden in places nobody ever searched. Bianca escorted her past a couple of smudge-faced pipe-workers and three artfully scruffy Coliseum students, until they reached a small pale man with a wispy beard.

"Derek, this is Mouth. She's the foreigner I was telling you about."

"Bianca says good things about you." Derek gestured at a well-annotated map of the Palace, the Spire, Founders' Square, and the surrounding areas. "We're ready to move soon. When they shot unarmed protestors, they showed their real faces and exposed the contradictions at the heart of this broken system. If we strike now, the people will be on our side."

Derek worked at a shoe-tacking place, and his callused fingers were always moving things around and making marks on paper. Everyone in Xiosphant seemed to have fidgety hands.

Besides Derek, the other key people included a physics student named Jeff (tall, with big hands and a great mane of black braids), a rangy, red-faced pipe-worker named Vicki (who made sculptures from detritus she found in the abandoned mine tunnels), and a big crusher named Brock, whose shaved pink scalp had lost too many fights with ringworm. Plus three skinny white-haired men who worked together in the same linen factory, whom everybody called the Gumdrops, on account of the bright-colored stains on their faces and hands.

"I've seen you at a few of our meetings, sitting way at the back." Derek squinted. "You always stood out, even with your head covered up."

"I wanted to see if I could help." Mouth smiled. "Somebody needs to do something about this town." Then she quoted from Grantham: "'The worst way to deal with failing technology is to transform human beings into machines.'"

"So, you've been paying attention." Derek grinned, revealing crooked teeth that he hadn't had enough med-creds to fix. And he seemed to reach a snap decision. "Here's what we could use your help with. We have seven incendiary devices we put together, and they're located in a safe place nearby. Somebody needs to transport them to the Founders' Square after the next shutters-up, arriving before the Span of Industry."

"That's when the blue-and-red cloud appears, right?" Mouth said.

"Right. If you can help us get them to the far end of the street market off the Founders' Square, you'll be met by our team there. The explosives will create a lot of noise and smoke, but they won't hurt anyone. The perfect distraction for me to lead a small team inside the Palace service tunnels by removing this solar power transformer box, which provides access to the maintenance crawlway. We'll take the High Magistrate hostage when his guards move him from the Receiving Room to a secure location once they hear the blast."

"Okay," Mouth said. She only half listened to Derek, because she was trying to memorize the maps and plans in front of her. Now that she knew how they planned to get in, she could just go right now, make a run at that vault—but she'd probably have a better chance during the chaos after those incendiaries went off.

Whoever designed the Palace had gone for a circular design, in homage to Jonas's original principles of Circadianism, but the rooms were still rectangular, which created some weird bottlenecks. A handful of access hallways bisected those "spokes," but most of the rooms only opened onto the central hub. The service corridors ran around the outside of the circle, with stairs leading down to the basement level, where the kitchens and maintenance areas were, or up to the second floor, where that vault lay at the end of a side corridor. Mouth imagined herself holding the Invention. Reattaching a long-lost part of herself. She had been half awake for too long.

"This Palace is made of chokepoints," Mouth said aloud. "You get into a firefight with Palace guards, they'll get you from both sides."

"We'll worry about that," Derek said. "You just help Bianca get the explosives into position." Then he turned to Bianca. "You're responsible for this smuggler, since you brought her in. Keep her with you the whole time."

"Will do," Bianca said, with a sober expression.

"Okay," Derek said. "Both of you show up here right after the next shutters-up. This place will be our rally point." He walked away to talk to the Gumdrops, who were inspecting some rifles.

"I can't believe it's going to happen," Bianca whispered as she led Mouth back to the entrance. "Just one more shutter-cycle, and we're doing this. What if we succeed? What if we really capture the High Magistrate, and force them to negotiate? I can't even imagine what it would look like for Xiosphant to treat everyone like an actual human being."

Brittle ice coated every nerve lacing through Mouth's body, but her blood was hot. She looked at Bianca and saw the same confusion of symptoms. "You're doing the right thing," Mouth said. She repeated this, like a blessing. "You're doing the right thing. You're doing the right thing."

"I'm so glad I met you." Bianca put her hand on Mouth's forearm, right when she was in the middle of strapping all her weapons back into place.

"I'm glad we met too." Mouth smiled. "You're going to set this old town on fire. After this, everyone will remember Sophie's name." Then Mouth heard those fucking bells, once again, and realized she was late to meet up with the Resourceful Couriers.

On her way back into the glare, Mouth stuck to the trashy alleys, and tried to convince herself that she had some kind of shot. Derek's plan had enough weak spots to ensure that every single member of the Uprising died, including poor Bianca—but all Mouth needed to do was give Bianca the slip after they delivered the bombs, and make her way to that loose solar power transformer in time to follow Derek's crew inside. Then it was just twenty meters from the maintenance hatch to the service staircase leading to the second floor, with the vault, while the Palace guards were distracted. Mouth tried to form a clear mental image of how this would go down, and then she realized someone was following her.

Even with this ridiculous hat and poncho, Mouth had enough visibility to catch the motion in her blind spot, and whoever it was ducked behind a garbage pile or a doorway whenever she turned. Mouth retraced her own steps, until she came to the spy's hiding place, a narrow gap between two factory buildings.

Mouth's tail was the quiet girl from the Illyrian Parlour, the one who'd brought spiced coffee while they'd unloaded some of their cat butter. Dark, pretty, big hazel eyes, small twitchy nose—she looked solidly Xiosphanti middle class. Full mouth, which never smiled or opened. She recoiled, but showed no fear, even though Mouth outweighed her by a lot.

Mouth smiled. "Did I forget to pay for my coffee?"

The girl just stared, not flinching or backing away. Mouth let go of her collar.

"Why were you following me?" Mouth said. "Who do you work for? What's your game?"

No response. Mouth hadn't heard her speak at the coffee place, either. Maybe she was mute? That would be a handy trait in a spy. Mouth tried a few more questions, but got nothing.

The two of them were stuck together in the pale shadow of the leatherwares plant. Dank, reddish smog pooling around them. Mouth didn't want to hurt this girl, not without a much better reason. No point trying to capture her, because then you'd be stuck with her.

This whole situation felt weird, like Mouth had been stalking the girl instead of the other way round. At last Mouth gave up.

"Don't follow me anymore. Or I'll tear you apart with my bare hands."

She turned and walked away, without looking to see if the girl had obeyed.

When Mouth got to George's roofing plant, Alyssa was waiting out front. "Don't go inside," she said. "Just walk away right now, before anyone sees you."

Mouth turned and walked in the opposite direction, and Alyssa walked alongside her.

"They've all gotten wind of some of your political activities," she whispered. "Omar is pissed. He's pretty close to putting together a deal to carry some Xiosphanti leather to Argelo. But they're going to hit you with an ultimatum: you quit with the politics, or the Couriers leave you behind when we go."

Alyssa's hand was on the back of Mouth's neck, which was the first clue that Mouth was bent double and heaving, with a stream of vomit pooling on the slate pavement below. Mouth had gotten into a crash position without even realizing—she just kept breathing harder, tasting more puke.

"I can't," Mouth said. "I can't. Please, I can't."

"Oh fuck," Alyssa said. "I've never . . . I thought nothing ever got to you. What the hell. This is a whole new side of you, and I don't . . ."

"I'm sorry." Mouth was face-to-knees panicking. "I'm sorry. I'll get it together. I will, in a moment. I just, this is all too . . . I mean, they have the last surviving piece of my childhood, my heritage, in that stupid Palace. It's the only thing that can save what's left of me. I can't just walk away from it. But I can't be trapped here, either. This town. I just hate it. I hate it so much. I think this town thrives on hate."

"Well." This was the problem-solving, reasonable tone, which usually meant Alyssa was about to cut through some logistical issue on the road. "The thing you're trying to get, the Invention, isn't going anywhere. Right? I mean, they've had it for a while. They'll still have it for ages more. We can grab it the next time we come back to this dump."

"Can't risk it." Mouth straightened up. "Anything could happen. I could die. They could burn that ugly mausoleum down in one of their stupid political actions. They could decide to clean house and throw away a bunch of stuff. I have a duty. I can't explain this right. I owe everything to the Citizens, the nomads who raised me. And this is all I can do. I just have to string those revolutionaries along a little longer."

"Well," Alyssa said. "If you want to leave town with us, you better move fast."

"Please, just stall them," Mouth said. "Tell them I got too drunk to walk. They'll believe that."

"As long as you never hear Omar's ultimatum, you might

not get in trouble for disobeying it." Alyssa smiled. "That's why I grabbed you before you could go in there."

Everything still tasted awful. Alyssa looked down and gave Mouth a radiant smile, in spite of how gross she must look hunched over, with bile on her chin.

"I don't deserve a friend like you," Mouth said.

She laughed. "Nah. It's more like, I'd be a shitty friend if I gave you what you deserved." Alyssa punched Mouth's arm. "And you've gone all the way to the edge of the night for me, more times than I can count." Mouth couldn't actually think of a single time, but let it go.

"Well, thank you," Mouth said. "I . . . I really care about you a lot, and I can't imagine what I would do if I had to break in a new sleepmate."

"Ugh. I'm the only one who can put up with your kicking. Anyway, get out of here. I need to get back before they start to wonder why I'm taking so long in the bathroom."

Alyssa hugged Mouth, who clutched her tight for a moment. She was gone a moment later, and Mouth was left almost choking on puke and carbon dioxide again.

"Please," Mouth whispered again, to the sunburnt air. "Please, please, don't fuck me over this time. I know that a good traveler is supposed to leave everything in their dust. I know that impermanence and loss are just the distance markers on the road. I know that. Just please, this one time. I can't get fucked this time, or I don't know what will happen. Please."

Then Mouth stood up straight and pulled herself into fighting shape. She was running out of time—and depending on other people was worse than tasting your own digestive fluids.

SOPHIE

I grapple with the last handholds before the ridge of the Old Mother, like a clumsy old bear. Once on top, I stumble and teeter toward the other side, then I sit and stare at the textureless dark, trying to imagine the city out there, all the great machines, the webs full of sick children. I think about that smuggler—Mouth—telling her friend, *I just have to string these revolutionaries along a little more.* This was after she told me not to follow her, but I just followed her anyway. In my mind, the cops are already on their way to arrest Bianca, and I don't know what to do.

Nothing moves in front of me. No shapes grow, or change their position. I'm wasting my time looking for help here, when Bianca needs me. I slap my legs to get blood back into them, and try to stand.

Rose raises her head up over the cliff, tentacles and front legs straining. She finally gets her whole body up in front of me, and I see the soft, tawny hide around her front legs. I hand her the pitiful amount of copper and tin I've scrounged this time, and she studies it with the cilia on the end of one tentacle, then puts it away on her back.

"I'm sorry, I need your help again. I don't know what to do. My friend is in trouble. I know your people have amazing technology. You showed it to me. But do you have any weapons? Weapons? Something to protect a person from getting hurt."

Rose bows her head, big indentations on top narrowing, like she's frowning or sad. She raises a tentacle to touch me, and I let her brush against my face and feel my pulse through my neck. She wants to understand, and not just because I brought her copper.

I push my face toward her tendrils. "I'm scared. Please understand that I'm scared. I'm still scared from the way I almost died, back when you saved me, and now I'm scared that something will happen to Bianca. She's everything to me. Can you feel my fear? Can you at least understand the feeling, even if you get nothing else?"

Rose seems to nod, or maybe it's just my imagination. She reaches into her own wool-covered carapace, searches, and pulls something out, holding it in a knot of her tentacles. The size and shape of a starfruit, the object has five spines, going off in different directions. I almost try to bite into it, but I look closer and realize it's made of some metallic alloy, with flecks of a crystal or mineral, like quartz. This is like nothing I've ever seen, but I can tell that somebody designed these diamond shapes and the complex way they intersect.

Still, this device is just as confusing to me as my clock was to Rose, and I hold it up to the twilight, squinting.

Rose lets me fumble for a moment, then finds another, identical metal-and-crystal starfruit. She twists one of the diamond-shaped segments around, so it's at a strange angle to the others, and the one in my hand vibrates, giving off a faint rumbling sound.

"Wow. What did you—" I grapple with my own device for a few moments before I manage to turn one of the slices, and a similar growl comes out of Rose's device. So it's like an old-style phone, or the telex machines in Xiosphant. And maybe you can use one of these to find the other? Rose helps me to rearrange the diamond slices until the device forms a circle. I snap it around my right wrist: a spiky bangle.

I stare at this device, snug against the base of my thumb. These creatures must have invented it over a long time, as they found materials under the ice, dug up metal and rocks and studied what they did and how they worked, and put them together. It's not like almost all our technology in Xiosphant, which people invented millions of kilometers away on Earth, dozens of generations ago, and we're just trying to keep it all working.

Rose comes closer, slow and careful, and puts her claw around my face and neck again. I always have to make a conscious effort not to pull away as these tongues affix themselves to my skin, but it gets easier each time—

—A crocodile built a flying machine and soared over the flaming glaciers, shielded against the sun, but still cowering a little under its rays. Crocodiles stood on great soaring platforms, making a study of the atmosphere. The sky on fire, gouts of flame roaring into the ice. A team of crocodiles journeyed to the very end of the world, going inside a mountain with smoke pouring out of it. The sky turning and reversing, turning and reversing, clouds doing a strange dance. None of this stuff makes any sense to me, until I form those images into a story: *the sky was on fire, when the world was young, and we risked everything to find a solution.*

Then I sense the weight of the bracelet that just closed around my own wrist, only it hangs on the tentacle of an elder crocodile who travels across a shale landscape dotted with frost in a carriage that is half rock, half flesh. She may not make it back home before she dies, she feels weary in her clicking joints, and a sense of fallowness leaches into her core when she thinks of being away from her extended family. But the bracelet grunts in answer to her lonesomeness, and it connects her to all the explorers and scientists—the menders—who had flown above an icefield painted with flames—

—Rose pulls away, and I touch the bracelet, which now seems an emblem as well as a device.

"Thank you." I put my arms around her, as gentle as I can. "I wish I could tell you . . . I don't really have a family anymore, but I'm going to feel like you're with me, wherever I go, as long as I wear this. No matter how far into the light I travel. And I need to stop calling your people crocodiles, because that's just a dumb name that humans decided to call you."

I look at Rose, and at last I don't see her body only in terms of sheer power. I was taught to see her as a great destroyer, and in my fear I had wanted to keep seeing her that way—so I could identify with her, and feel powerful by association. Her front legs move like great pistons, but they're also supple, made for exploring tricky spots. Her tentacles swirl and grip like serpents, but their cilia are exquisite, sensitive, delicate.

I remember a word that came to me, during the last thing she shared: "menders."

"My ancestors should have tried to call you what you called yourselves," I say aloud. Rose cants her pincer a little, as though she's listening in her own way. "You think of yourselves as menders, as builders, as explorers. There's no one word for all those things in Xiosphanti, but the old language, Noölang, had one: *Gelet*. It's like architect, and traveler, and five other things, all in one. So . . . I'm going to start calling your people the Gelet."

Then I remember about Bianca, and turn to rush back to the city. "Thank you," I say again. "I hope I do something to deserve this." Rose is already halfway off the plateau, her massive frame clambering back down into the dark.

When I pull myself through the hole in the fence and get back inside the city, I hear the clatter of all the people trying to finish their business before shutters-up. Parents hustle their children, or try to do one last odd job to score infrastructure chits, med-creds, or water tokens. The repair crews apply their last bits of sealant to the cracked walkways. I haven't carried a timepiece since I gave mine away to Rose, but I can tell you what the clock says just by the scents of cooking, cleaning, or brewing of hot drinks. The laundry steam, the long line at the bakery, fathers carrying their children home from school. You can't fight Circadianism, because it's soaked into our pores.

Jeremy finds me sitting on the steps leading to the Parlour's lacquer door, staring at my new bracelet. My face must diagram all the suffering in my heart, the way I'm seeing Bianca's death more vividly than my own feet under their tiny skirt, just as the crocodile visions—the Gelet visions—always seem realer than real. Being ashamed of fear doesn't make me less afraid.

"I've tried to cut off my old life," I whisper. "But I have a friend from school, and she's trusting someone that she shouldn't. She's going to throw her life away. I'm scared to face her, and everyone at school will lose their minds if they see me."

Jeremy sits next to me and breathes, deliberate and even, as if I'm a client and he wants to steal away my awareness that time is flowing. He doesn't have that easy look on his face, though.

"You can't hide from the people you care about. A love that hides is already halfway to becoming regret." I have a feeling he's quoting one of the books we were supposed to memorize, but I don't care.

I say nothing back—just take the biggest breath I can of the ozone-scented air, touch Jeremy's shoulder with one hand, and walk toward the light.

Everybody said if my mother had lived a bit longer she could have prepared me: for my body changing, for marriage, for life as an adult. She'd been waiting for the right time to explain to me what was expected, everyone said. But sometimes I wonder if my mother would have sat me down and told me to grab as much freedom as I could, as hard as I could, instead of getting stuck in a marriage to a man who called her the Brick, because of the way she slept in a rigid fetal position. Maybe my mom was working on a way to break free of my dad. I'll never know.

My mother was with a group of managers, inspecting their farmwheel, and the crops burst into flames at the top of the superstructure. Someone had come up with a scheme to raise the farmwheel slightly, expose the food to more light, increase yields. This plan worked for a while, but they didn't count on one thing: erosion. A few boulders fell off the Young Father, or the peak just grew shorter, and the crops caught a full sunbeam. My mother was one of the people closest to the disaster, and while everybody else screamed and laid blame, she climbed up and stopped the fire from spreading. But the rays of the sun roasted her skin and boiled her eyes, and even if she hadn't fallen, she would have been dead anyway. Everyone called her a hero, but I always wondered if she had seen a way out of her dead-end life and had taken it, without even stopping to think about me.

The final warning sounds, and I hear the shutters close, but I keep playing shadowseek in these empty streets. I can't loosen the chokehold inside me. The sky looks like a flat pan of dirty water, which brightens as I make my way. The closer I get to daylight, the higher my risk of arrest for curfew violation. I hear a few patrols, but I always manage to slip out of view before they get close.

The Gymnasium looks the same as ever. The War Monument swallows the same light in which all the whitestone buildings bask. But emptied of students, teachers, and staff, these places look abandoned, as if after some catastrophe. I let the old familiar anxiety claim a few heartbeats, then I touch my new bracelet and remember I'm not alone. And I make my hypervigilance work for me, scanning in all directions. I've already seen the worst, and I'm still here.

I unpin my skirt and climb the wall of my old dorm—anybody could see me, awash in pallid light—and swing from sill to sill without making a noise, until I reach my old window. I lean on the shutters with all the strength I've developed climbing a mountain so many times, and they go down, with a rusty groan.

Looking into the dorm room where I used to sit and talk after curfew is the most powerful experience of Timefulness I've ever known, reminding me that time is real, the past is the past, and part of me really did die when they executed me. I always thought moments of Timefulness should be either practical or wistful—but here's an acrid chunk of poison lodged in my throat.

Bianca rests on her little shelf, same as always. I almost expect to see myself sleeping there, on the opposite shelf, but it's empty. Bianca looks so happy and peaceful I almost want to let her sleep. Then I see some shape hidden under the blankets beside her. Something rigid, bulky. A crutch? No, an ancient rifle. She's cuddling a gun in her bed, as though the fight could begin any moment. Bianca keeps opening one eye, watching for something.

She notices too much light coming in the window and opens both eyes. She reaches for her gun, while I get the window open and stumble inside. By the time she has her gun out of the snarl of blankets, I'm on top of her, with a hand on her mouth.

She looks up and her eyes widen, and I feel her teeth sink into the fat of my thumb. She has too many tears for me to see her reaction. Her nostrils flare, and the bulky stock of her gun juts between us. I freeze, the old tremors rising. I have a million things to say, but I can't speak. I slowly lift my hand away.

"Sophie." Bianca's breath feels hot enough to scald the skin off my hand. "You're— You're— Am I going delirious at last? Is this delirium? Am I just dreaming? Say something. Fuck you, say something *now*."

"I'm alive," I whisper. "It's me. I'm alive. I'm here." Everything in this room smells of laundry detergent and stale cakes and tea and comfort.

"How? How can you . . ." Bianca bites her tongue, the way she always used to when she worked through a logic problem, twice as fast as anybody else. "Oh shit. They locked you up. Didn't they? You've been in some dark cell this whole time. I thought they killed you, forced you outside, but all along you've been in some dark hole, and I didn't even look for you. Did you only just escape? What happened?" She wheezes a little. "I'm so sorry. I didn't know. I should have searched for you."

I shake my head. "It's not . . . they didn't lock me up. They tried—they tried to execute me, but I didn't . . . I got away."

I'm still sitting on top of Bianca, half straddling her. I feel her heart convulse, as the realization spreads across her face: I was alive and free this whole time, and I chose to let her think I was dead.

"It's not like that." I'm still juddering, unsteadying myself. "I just couldn't come back to you. I didn't want to put you in harm's way, and I . . ." I don't have the words to explain how the fear immobilized me whenever I tried to reveal myself to her.

Bianca looks forlorn through the sheen of tears, as if she just lost me in a whole new way. Or even worse, as if she's just realized that I was never really hers, and this realization is costing her some part of herself. Her expression resolves into something as blunt and unbending as the rifle in her bed.

"Fucking . . . I would have broken everything, I would have killed anybody, to have you back here with me. I would have torn it all down. I can't even tell you. And you were just alive the whole time, and you, what? You didn't bother to let me know."

"I'm sorry," I stammer-whisper.

My mouth is a desert, but the rest of me is chilled. I know for sure that even if we survive this, she'll never smile at me the way she used to.

Bianca sits up, though I'm still pinioning her lower half, and she raises her arms as if she wants to embrace me, but she can't.

"I would have torn it all down," she says again. "I still might."

I'm clutching her bedcovers with one hand. "I came to warn you. You can't trust that smuggler. Mouth. She's just using you. I heard her telling her friend."

Another moment of Timefulness—because everything has changed, the world is all askew, and it will never turn back.

"I should have known. That bitch. I should have seen the signs, but I wanted this too much." Bianca pushes me off her and jumps out of bed, already dressed, including boots and a belt crammed with supplies. "She knows the whole plan. We have to warn everyone." Bianca heads for the open window, gun slung over one shoulder, with its long handle and fluted barrel.

"Wait," I say, but she's already swinging herself out the window and pulling herself down, the same way I climbed up.

Bianca is already halfway across the residential quarter of campus by the time I catch up with her. "I seriously have been living in a dark tunnel since they took you away," Bianca hisses. "I can't even tell you. Where the hell have you been hiding?"

Bianca walks too fast for me to catch up, talks too loud for curfew. She doesn't wait for an answer, if I even had one.

"How long have you been hanging around, and just not letting me out of all this grief? How long?" She spits on the ground. "And then you decide to show up, right when I'm finally ready to avenge you. Why couldn't you have just come back to me?"

I don't know what to say, and she's moving away too fast, and the sky is much too bright here, and we're out in the open where anyone could see us. I have to shut my eyes for a moment without slowing my march, to keep the memory at bay. I feel certain this is our final moment, and I have one last chance to rebuild our friendship, if I can just say the right thing. The sunswept pavement burns my eyes, without any other people to cast shadows.

I grab Bianca by the arm and she turns to face me, so I can see the pain still only starting to unfold inside her.

"I thought of you every moment," I say, as she pulls me forward. "But I couldn't come back to where—"

We round the corner, and a Curfew Patrol is standing in front of us. Two men and a woman, carrying much newer rifles than Bianca's, with opaque helmets and vests just like the police who paraded me through the streets. My lungs, my heart, turn to stone.

Bianca seizes me and pulls me back around the corner, and then the two of us are sprinting, as the leader of the patrol shouts a warning. I spot one of the city's narrow crosswise alleyways, on the right, and drag Bianca inside just as the first gunshots slice through the air. We keep running—ducking under a low canopy, jumping over rotten boxes, veering into a long tiny space between two rows of buildings—as the alarms sound and more boots land on the streets around us.

mouth

Mouth had gone out in Xiosphant during curfew a few times before, so she was prepared for the wide-open eeriness of empty streets as she crept out of the Low Road. But this time, the city teemed with people wearing black suits with corrugated sleeves and carrying guns and batons. As if the whole town had decided to play dress-up instead of sleeping.

Mouth headed for the dark side of town, first by following the same alley the Couriers had used to move the sled uptown, and then by climbing a hemp-shrouded scaffolding that ran lengthwise along the front of a grand old building with apartments above shops. Five meters off the ground, Mouth crept along the jostling side boards as Curfew Patrols, cops, and even soldiers marched under her feet. Mouth had taken far too long to travel just a few blocks, and she had another kilometer and a half to cross before the rendezvous point, that old paint factory.

Hand-carved granite figures on a ledge acted out the stages of life, from birth to apprenticeship to marriage to mastery to death, and their giant bulbous faces leered at Mouth as she crept along the scaffolding. In the background of each panel, complicated designs showed how each stage of life corresponded to part of the cycle of sleep and work, from shutters-down to shutters-up. Mouth remembered Bianca saying that she used to think the root of all Xiosphanti oppression was planted in culture and ideology, until they'd taken her friend away—and then Bianca had decided that violence was the real answer.

Stuck between these educational gargoyles above, and the police below, Mouth couldn't find a clean way to separate ideology from force.

One of Derek's people must have gotten caught, or turned informant. So these thugs were going to tear the whole town apart, twice, to catch anyone who might have ever had a subversive dream. Mouth hoped the Resourceful Couriers had found a good place to lie low. From overhead, the people and their weapons made a shape like hinges, and Mouth tried to tell herself a story about how she could still turn this to her advantage.

She needed to find Bianca, in whom she'd invested so much time, and then secure her help getting inside the Palace. Bianca might even lean on Mouth harder than ever, with everything falling apart.

But when Mouth reached the paint factory, choking on the formaldehyde mist, there was no sign of Bianca. The one person who you'd expect to show up no matter what, to berate everyone else for being even a little tardy, and she wasn't here. Instead, Derek stood in the middle of the maintenance pod, with nine people around him, including Vicki, Jeff, and the

Gumdrops, and he was giving them a rousing speech. "We can't give up now. This is still our moment. They're still not expecting a strike against the Palace."

If Mouth could just snag those bombs and get them to the Palace herself, she could still use them to get inside. She could slip past those patrols and get to the vault while the authorities were focused on the Uprising's last stand in this paint factory. But Mouth scanned the room, and poked into the crawlspace and storage lockers behind her, and found nothing. Derek probably hadn't been dumb enough to store the explosives inside the same building where he held his strategy meetings.

Derek spotted Mouth searching a gantry, a half level up from the maintenance pod, and shouted, "Mouth, get down here. We need to figure out a new strategy."

She nodded, then turned and climbed back out of the building without saying a word. Mouth was wasting time here without Bianca to vouch for her, and these people were already dead. She heard Derek shouting for her to come back as she turned sideways to squeeze into one of those tight throughways between buildings, trying to put as much distance as she could between herself and the Uprising.

"Shit." Vicki's voice still carried. "She just left us. Without even saying anything."

The building opposite the Uprising HQ had a door with a busted lock, and Mouth climbed the stairs and stole down a filthy unlit corridor to an unshuttered window that looked down on the street, where people in riot gear clustered like a cloud of horseflies. They had the paint factory surrounded and were parking two armored lorries in the street.

Even from this distance, Mouth could hear Derek's hectoring voice from inside the paint factory, though she couldn't make out any words. Then an exchange of gunfire. What if Mouth just ran toward the Palace right now and slipped inside while everyone in a uniform was distracted? The Xiosphanti authorities would grow exponentially dumber as the crisis grew out of control. She could still do this.

No way Mouth could leave without the Invention. She could see herself pulling it off a shelf inside that vault, hoisting it, tucking it under one arm. The Invention would make sense of everything, justify all the walls of shit.

Just as Mouth was getting up the nerve to run headlong into the temperate zone, she heard a noise that was so loud it had no other characteristics besides loudness. She lost her balance and crashed halfway out the window. Then Mouth saw a coil of smoke rising up from a few blocks away: Derek's bombs had gone off early.

As the police stormed the disused paint factory where the Uprising had holed up, the sound of gunfire became more continuous and drowned any further shouts. Someone turned and saw Mouth looking down at them. A bullet caromed off the wall nearby, and Mouth turned and ran back the way she'd come.

A tower of smoke still undulated, a deeper ash gray against the night sky. Mouth heard Derek's voice one last time, some shout of defiance that ended midsyllable with another chorus of gunshots that descanted on the ones closer at hand.

This was not going to work out.

Mouth heard voices from the stairway. Cops, coming up to search this building. Mouth shrank against the wall, staying low, until they reached her, and then she stabbed one in the leg with her longest knife and elbowed the other in the neck. They both went down, and Mouth helped herself to the nightstick that the one with the leg injury was carrying. She left both cops unconscious but alive, and then a third officer came up the stairs. Mouth swung the nightstick, and the officer ducked, leaving herself open to the knife in Mouth's other hand. Mouth stabbed the cop's thigh and arm in quick succession, trying to avoid any arteries, and then drove the woman's head into the wall.

The musty smell of blood unsettled Mouth's stomach, already queasy from paint fumes, and she missed a stair. This staircase was arranged in a spiral, around a central pillar, because everything had to be circular in this stupid town. Mouth slid down the stairs on one leg, around the next curve, and spotted the two cops coming up the stairs before they saw her. She left them in a heap, leaning against the inside of the stairwell.

By the time Mouth reached the street, she had other people's blood all over her. Her whole body ached from the exertion, but also from the draining away of her righteous purpose. She kept trying to tamp down the awareness that she'd blown it, the Palace job had ended before it even started, those smug bastards still had custody of Mouth's heritage. She should just let the police take her, because where could she go now? She took a breath as she pushed through the building's front door and forced herself to keep walking.

When the rattling came from beneath her and around her, Mouth mistook it for another weapon. Then she stuck her head out and saw the metal sheaths coming off all the nearby windows. She muttered a quick thanks to the Elementals, and then lost herself in the swarm of people in coveralls and neat suits who had erupted into the streets, on their way to work.

Nothing stopped the Xiosphanti rank and file from keeping the gears revolving, not even a citywide emergency. Mouth couldn't help thinking of those sculptures on the side of the building, with their bulging red eyes and slanted grins. She pulled out that stupid Xiosphanti hat, squished it down onto her head, and stayed low inside a group of farmwheel bureaucrats as they pushed past the police cordons.

The Low Road sat empty, except for a few cups and plates, and the dust caught in the light from the big front window. No sign of the Resourceful Couriers. Mouth went about searching for clues, but just then Alyssa came up from the cellar, with her backpack and Mouth's. "There you are," she said. "The other Couriers left already. Things got too hot around here."

"You should have gone with them," Mouth grunted and took her backpack from Alyssa.

"If I had, we might have left town without you. And I couldn't just leave you. I promised." She looked closer. "Oh shit, you're covered with blood."

"Not mine."

Mouth let her backpack fall long enough to fold her arms around Alyssa, who leaned against her bloody torso. She felt warm, and her cheek was soft against Mouth's shoulder. But her body was tense.

"I should have let Omar stop you. I was sure you must be dead. Shit, I thought *we* were dead, a few times. They've been dragging people in the streets for even looking unusual, let alone foreign."

"This town knows how to throw a party," Mouth said.

Alyssa didn't laugh. When Mouth pulled away, Alyssa had a wan expression, like when she'd said she was ready to retire from smuggling.

"So, did you get it? Your artifact from the Palace vault?"

"No. Didn't even get close." Just saying this aloud gave Mouth a barbed knot inside her chest. "They probably have a hundred items that they plundered from other cultures sitting inside that vault, and nobody even bothers to look at any of it."

"I'm sorry." Then Alyssa looked over her shoulder. "We'd better join the others."

Xiosphant felt like a whole different city. Everywhere Mouth looked, police lorries blocked every major intersection, and people blurted instructions into megaphones until all their voices merged into a shrill din. The air tasted different: cordite, static electricity, and the tang of pepper spray instead of the usual starchy turpentine fug.

The sky had already flashed blue and red, and a few chimes had rung by the time they managed to reach the Illyrian Parlour, where the other Resourceful Couriers were fidgeting.

The marmot, Cyrus, had curled up on a plump cushion in the corner and was squinting at all of these intruders, flexing his snout.

"There she is." Omar was on his feet, coming toward them. "Time for an explanation. First you start spouting political slogans, and then this whole town loses what little mind it ever had. We damn near got skinned alive out there. What have you been playing at? I'm still tempted to leave you behind."

Mouth hadn't managed to think of a good lie. "Uh . . . I didn't get involved in politics. I swear. It wasn't that. It's just . . . You know how I was raised by nomads?"

"You only mention that fact every time I see you," Omar said.

"Well, they're all dead. Nothing left of them. Nothing to show that we were ever here, except for me, and you might have noticed I'm not looking too durable. But I got wind that there was . . . an artifact locked inside the Palace vault. The last surviving trace of the Citizens. I wanted to try and snag it. And it went kind of bad."

Omar was already rolling his big brown eyes, like he didn't have time for this idiocy. Which was a good sign. "Just promise me this was a one-time foul."

"I promise," Mouth said. "I had to try. I failed. If I live long enough, I'll put this behind me."

Omar shrugged, and was about to say something else, like driving home the message that Mouth was on probation now, or this could never happen again. But just then, the proprietor emerged from some inner room with cups of spiced coffee, leaves floating on top. Hernan was wearing a plain dark suit instead of the silk brocade he had last time.

"So, I trust we have a deal." Hernan handed the coffees around, with a little smile. "I show you another route out of town, a disused mining track big enough for you and your vehicle. And you bring along one of my employees, who's drawn some undue attention from the local law enforcement. Plus her friend."

"Sure," Omar said. "If they can pull their weight. Then yes."

Hernan gestured, and two girls stepped forward out of the back room. One was Bianca, who glared at Mouth, as if Mouth could somehow be to blame for everything falling apart. Eyes like broken weapons, shoulders sagging under the weight of her big rucksack. Mouth tried to say something, but she wouldn't reply.

The other girl Hernan ushered forward was the mute, the one who'd followed Mouth around. She looked at Mouth as if she was seeing pure evil for the first time ever.

Mouth looked at Alyssa, who just shrugged, as if reminding her that she was lucky to be here at all.

Hernan was talking about the two girls, both of whom looked about the same age as Yulya, and he mentioned the name Sophie. Mouth looked at the mute girl again and realized: this was Bianca's dead friend, except not so dead. Bianca had said this girl was some kind of saint, with both a pure heart and a brilliant mind. But that perfect dead girl was standing here, watching Mouth with the worst expression anyone had ever aimed at her.

A too-familiar death rattle signaled that the shutters were closing, and Omar said, "Now's our chance. Let's just get going before this town gets any nuttier. Just show us the way out of this shitpile, and let's get our sled and go."

Everyone drained their coffees and loaded their packs up with all the provisions Hernan had to spare. Mouth was trying not to stare at Bianca and the not-dead Sophie, and they in turn seemed to be sharing a complicated silence.

If Mouth was lucky, maybe both these girls would catch

something nasty from one of those giant insects in the deadlands, or get swept overboard in the Sea of Murder. You didn't want to wish anyone dead, of course, but Mouth couldn't handle the thought of traveling all the way to Argelo, empty-handed, under both of these accusing stares.

Mouth slid a massive pack on her back and prepared to brave the empty streets, which were still full of checkpoints and hyperactive triggers. Omar came up and grabbed Mouth's shoulder in one long-fingered hand. "So I believe you when you say you didn't get involved in politics and you were just pulling some ridiculous hustle. But I just need to know. What exactly was this thing you were trying to steal from the Palace?"

Bianca was standing right behind them, listening in. So was Sophie, the undead saint.

Mouth swallowed. She and Omar went a long way back, plus she owed him a lot right now, so she couldn't look him in the face and give him a glib line. Not to mention, this particular disappointment was too fresh for her to have turned into a cute story yet.

"We called it the Invention. It, uh, it was a big crystal volume? It contained all of our songs and lyric writings. And verses."

"A poetry book." Omar laughed much too loud as the Couriers crept out into the tiny side street. "You tried to break into the Palace to steal a fucking poetry book?"

Mouth was tensing up, but got a grip just in time. The fists she had made turned back into hands, and Mouth found a smile someplace. "Yeah. It was the only copy, though."

"Now I know you're a maniac. A poetry book. You'll have to do a recital for us once we're out in the deadlands." Omar was still chuckling as he strode in the direction of the junkyard where they'd hidden the sled full of merchandise once more, hunched over from his backpack. Lorry engines squeaked in the distance, and smoke billowed from no particular direction. Mouth turned and saw the hatred in Bianca's eyes, until the rest of the Resourceful Couriers bumped against them, in a hurry to escape this city at last.

As they rushed across one of the main thoroughfares, Mouth spotted scraps of cheap paper that had been trampled into the cobbles: a poster declaring that the leaders of the Uprising would be executed in Founders' Square after two more turns of the shutters. She tried to avoid stepping on the drawing of Derek's bony face, out of respect.

At last they came to the junkyard. The wide-open street looked gloomy, here on the edge of night. All of the metal slats on the windows seemed to reject them, and the air seemed colder than usual. Every step Mouth took in defiance of her own rust-spiked heart. The Citizens had been good people, just trying to go through the world making themselves useful, and striving to preserve their culture as best they could. The world had stepped on their memory like it was dirt, and Mouth had blown her one chance to salvage something.

Alyssa came alongside Mouth and whispered, "Keep your shit together." Mouth nodded, and she tried to empty her mind, the way she had so many times before.

PART

THREE

SOPHIE

I can't see Hernan's face, but he has a kink in his neck that keeps his shoulders uneven, and sadness creeps into his voice, even as he gives directions in a jolly tone. Before taking each step, he stares down at the cracks and sawteeth of this mining tunnel. These ancient mines have a hundred dead ends, and countless deep crevasses, and Hernan knows the safe route because a longtime client of the Parlour had inherited a map. Some of the wall struts seem to be starting to buckle.

I touch Hernan's arm and whisper, "Thanks for helping Bianca and me get out of town."

"Just keep yourself safe," he whispers back. "I think I might disappear for a while myself, once I make sure Jeremy, Walter, and Kate are taken care of. This city barely tolerates people like us when things are calm, but during a crisis . . ."

"I can't bear to think of the Illyrian Parlour disappearing." I almost hit my shin on a tiny spur of rock, but stumble aside at the last moment.

"I always knew that place couldn't last forever." Hernan sighs. "We'll preserve what we can, and reopen when we can."

The end of the tunnel seems so brilliant at first I have to shade my eyes until they adjust.

"This is where I turn back," Hernan says. "Don't forget everything I taught you."

I lean against Hernan's slate-gray suit jacket and clutch him as tight as I can. His scent comforts me for probably the last time, the same lavender and sandalwood as the Parlour itself. I try to slow down the flow of time, the way Hernan showed me, to keep this moment from ending, because I can't even bring myself to walk away from the man who gave me a new family and nurtured my mother in spite of herself. The man who showed me how patience could work as much transformation as a million geothermal vents.

"Thank you," I say again, "for everything."

"It was the very least I could do," he murmurs. "I wish your mother could see the brave young woman you've grown into. She'd be as proud of you as I am. Goodbye, Sophie."

Hernan fades into the darkness of the ancient tunnel, while the rest of us climb down to the dry riverbed that marks the outer boundary of the deadlands.

The Old Mother and the Young Father extend past the city walls, but they dwindle into mere foothills ahead of us. Beyond the mountains' end, there's only a reddish-gray rocky terrain that stretches past the horizon, with naked darkness swallowing one side and scorching daylight exposing the other.

As soon as we're past the walls, the Resourceful Couriers start singing. None of them sings the same song, or in tune, but the raucous clash of shanties seems to cheer them up as we trudge and steer their wobbling sled down to somewhat more level ground.

Bianca hasn't spoken since we left the Illyrian Parlour, but now I hear her voice, even over the six different choruses.

"I have unfinished business in that city." Bianca doesn't look back at the sheer stone wall. "I'm going to make sure the sacrifice of Derek and the others counts for something. Even if it takes the rest of my life. I'm going to burn that fucking Palace to the ground." She grips her backpack in one hand, like a cudgel.

I try covering my eyes and looking down at the regolith, but the sky still hurts. Bigger than dreams, sweeping from cinder gray to acrid white, with no buildings or mountains in the way. Even if I wrench my neck, I could never see the whole thing. The "road" ahead looks lifeless, drained by Xiosphant's endless water demands, but every now and then I see the head of some burrowing creature emerge. The reddish-gray dirt, marbled with ochre and crimson, becomes either rich embroidery or a bloody shroud, depending on which way I turn my head.

I can still look back and see the city that banished me twice; no matter how long we trudge, the golden Spire still glares at our retreat over a hill covered with tufts of scrubgrass quivering in the cold wind from the night.

When I fantasized about walking beside Bianca again, I always imagined this happening after Xiosphant had thrown away all the old rules in some unimaginable revolution, or when we had grown old and found each other again. But now she and I are together, here and now, and we're traveling to the City That Never Sleeps, where we can be whoever we want. I can't even trust this much good fortune.

Except that Bianca won't even look at me.

Maybe I've been dead to her too long, and she can't accept me back into life. All this unsaid garbage is heaped up between Bianca and me, as tall as the Old Mother. And she just keeps staring, red-eyed, at Mouth, the scar-headed smuggler who tricked her. Bianca hasn't spoken since she said she had unfinished business in Xiosphant, and she hasn't looked back once. She marches with emphatic strides and gritted teeth, as if she's heading toward something rather than away from it.

I can't hear the city's chimes anymore. I don't know what time it is, and I feel as if I've been out here for half my life. Only the slight changes in the landscape prove time is still passing. I feel like falling on the ground, pummeling my own knees, or refusing to walk any farther along these endless plains.

Some part of me keeps expecting things between Bianca and me to go back to the way they used to be. She's supposed to be the one who jolts me out of my silence. She ought to be reminding me that we're young and we can just laugh at everyone's stupid limits.

No matter how much she ignores me, I can't stop leaning into her line of sight and trying to get her attention, like a neglected child.

Ahead of us, a sudden wind sweeps from night to day, shaping loose soil and rocks into a shimmering fist.

My new bracelet makes my forearm itch, and I keep thinking I feel it vibrate. When I touch it with my eyes closed, I almost feel as though I'm traveling through the night instead of the dusk, on four powerful legs. I wonder if Rose, or one of the others, is out there beyond the side of the road, watching our progress. This bracelet feels like a reminder that I have other friends besides the ones I just left in Xiosphant and Bianca. But also, there's a claim on me. I owe a debt that I haven't repaid yet.

Sulfuric dust gets in my eyes, nose, and mouth. With no mountain in the way, the night looks like it's right there, next to me, calling to me. And over to my right, the unquenchable blaze seems ready to burn me to cinders, like my mother.

In front of us, the sled jerks and halts, even though Kendrick, the giant with the face piercings, insists he upgraded the motor back in Xiosphant. Alongside piles of leather, ore, dried fruit, and cakes, the sled also has a quilted denim pouch on top, just big enough for two bodies to squeeze inside. That's the sleep nook, and we'll all take turns inside, sleeping two by two. The front of the sled seats two: Omar and Mouth. Four of us walk alongside the sled, two in front and two in back, carrying packs and rifles. Bianca's had a bit of rifle training, but I don't even know how to hold mine properly. The youngest smuggler, Yulya, keeps promising to give me some lessons, and maybe also teach me some Argelan—she already tried to explain about something that sounded like "Anchor-Banter," which she says is a major concept in Argelan culture.

Mouth keeps nudging Omar and pointing out a million

dangers on the road, from sinkholes to storms to deadly wildlife charging out of the night. The two of them have a whole shorthand that doesn't sound like language. I keep watching out for the horseflies that will descend without warning and eat a person whole, or maybe infect you with a flesh-eating disease. Yulya keeps saying you can go from safe to dead in an eyeblink out here.

As soon as we're away from Xiosphant, Omar adjusts his clothes, lets down his mane of dark hair, and wraps a big scarf with an elaborate pattern around his neck. Some time later, I hear him say to Reynold, "You know, Khartoum built all the computers on the Mothership, and then they got shafted." Then Omar looks over his shoulder at Bianca and me, because of course you're not supposed to talk about such things in Xiosphant, and he can sense our discomfort. "Better get used to it." He laughs. "Everywhere else, you better believe we talk about this stuff."

To hear Omar tell it, New Shanghai built the Mothership's life support, food supply, and gardens before leaving Earth, while Calgary built the water reclamation and sewers. And then once the Mothership had launched, those two compartments ended up in a position to demand whatever they wanted—and all this time later, their descendants still rule Xiosphant. That's not the version we were taught in school, and it makes me wonder what else we were taught that nobody else believes.

Not knowing the time makes me feel young and ancient at once. I don't know if the shutters are up or down at home, whether people are eating sweet pastries or savory pies, if the children are playing in the scrapyard. I could get used to seeing a dark horizon and a line of bright red occupying the same sky more easily than this unawareness. I don't even know how weary I am. The knapsack straps gnaw on my shoulders, and I keep zoning out as I walk.

All those people who paid Hernan to lose track of the passage of time could have just come out here, to the deadlands.

A few times, the trail slopes downward, and the night rises up, making a hillock or cliff against the darkness. Maybe I glimpse a shape standing on the cliffside, a big shadow on the edge of night, flexing tentacles and a great pincer, or maybe I'm dreaming on my feet. Even if I could survive walking into the night, the smugglers would think I'd gone delirious if I even tried.

I brought a toothbrush, but there's no spray and I just have to use some weird soap they gave me. And I'll never get used to squatting behind a rock to go to the toilet, and then running to catch up with the sled.

Every time I catch sight of Bianca—her still eyes downcast, shoulders caving under her own giant pack—I forget to breathe. She's the only thing worth looking at, even with the coruscating light coming off the mineral deposits on the rock formations. But she watches her own footfalls, without seeing much of anything.

But then I hear the tattooed man called Reynold mutter in Xiosphanti: "Waste of food. Why do we even bother to keep these two girls alive when there's no way they'll make it to Argelo in one piece? If you ask me, we should just—"

I charge forward, overtaking the sled, with my face searing

hot and my fist already wound up. My knuckles connect with Reynold's jaw, and I hear a sound like a door slamming. The big ugly man falls and rolls out of the way of the sled's wheels right before he gets run over. He looks up and has a good view of the fury in my eyes.

"Sorry," Reynold blurts. He stumbles to his feet and jogs to catch up to the sled, where Omar laughs in his throat.

"So, that's going to leave a nice bruise," says Alyssa, who's also walking up front. "I like this one. She doesn't need to talk, she expresses herself just fine."

A massive storm comes over the horizon ahead of us, but dissipates before we reach it.

I see shapes on the edge of the night, but nothing comes to try its luck—and I never even glimpse a Gelet, though my bracelet still keeps throbbing, especially whenever I veer toward the light.

My entire body throbs from the repetitive motion of stepping on the hard ground, over and over, steadying my load with each footfall. I brought my best pair of mountain-climbing boots, but they're already wearing out. The sky feels like it's crushing me under its gray weight.

Maybe I'm dead already, just condemned to keep walking forever, with the angry ghost of Bianca by my side.

Long after I'm sure that I'm going to fall and they're just going to leave me in the dust, Omar announces it's time to change sleep shifts. Kendrick and Yulya slide down out of the sleep nook in a smooth practiced motion. But when Bianca and I try to climb inside with the sled rolling, we misjudge our leap, falling in the dirt while everyone laughs and cheers. We make it on the third try.

I'm lying face-to-face with Bianca, in the blindfolded warmth of a quilted tube just big enough for us, resting on all the precious leather. I breathe in a hint of the floral soap Bianca always used, laced with our sweat and the tang of rawhide. My knees rest against her thighs.

"I'm sorry about your friends," I whisper in Bianca's ear. "I know you think you could have saved them somehow, but you would have just died with them. And if anything had happened to you, I couldn't even . . ."

"Let's just sleep," Bianca mutters. "I don't want to talk about it."

I'm sure I won't be able to sleep, but then I black out. For once, my sleeping mind doesn't replay scenes of cops pulling me by the armpits, or hunters hauling a wounded Gelet away. Instead, I remember a time that never was, when Bianca and I lived in a hollow space carved into the center of a tall rock face, which was perfectly round on the inside, like a globe. The two of us furnished the space with a hundred kinds of fragrant grass, and brewed hot drinks that took a whole lifetime to steep.

When I wake up, someone's screaming.

"Omar! Fuck. It got Omar! Fucking, it fucking ate Omar. Kill it! It's getting away!"

Bianca and I have as much trouble getting out of the sleep nook as we had climbing in, and we tumble onto the hard ground just in time to see the lower half of Omar's body vanish into the night, in the jaws of a bison. Muscles ripple underneath ochre fur-covered plates, and a forked tail thrashes so hard it carves the air around us. The sled careens, in danger of tipping over, without anyone left to steer. Mouth lunges across Omar's seat and wrestles with the steering levers.

Kendrick takes a shot at the bison, but misses. Omar's face has a look of dismay, but not pain, as if the razor-sharp threads in the bison's mouth severed his lower half too fast for him to feel anything.

The sled stops moving. Everyone just stares at Omar's head and torso, then at each other. Mouth still leans over from the passenger seat, her hands shaking. She mutters something under her breath, and I realize that it's a prayer in the original language, Noölang: something about the Elementals, and footsteps in dirt. Next to the driver's seat, Alyssa's hands splay, rigid as claws.

mouth

Mouth's final memory of Omar would always be laughter.

She had been lucky to sit in the passenger seat, on watch, where she could enjoy a long conversation with three participants: Mouth, Omar, and the landscape. They had been reminiscing about a time the sled broke down in the marshes, and Omar had chuckled, remembering how upset they'd all been. And they'd pointed out things to each other, like the furrows in the stabgrass near the day that could be from some creature, or an air-pressure drop that could mean a storm. Plus all the native Earth plants that'd spread since their last trip—like the soybeans, engineered to flourish in local soil, which had mutated into something inedible. Mouth had been thinking that Omar, out of all the Resourceful Couriers, could have been at home among the Citizens. This warm feeling had pushed away some of Mouth's remaining sickness from the failed Palace heist, like she still had friends and still belonged here.

And then the bison had cut Omar clean in half.

Now Mouth stumbled out of the passenger seat and fell on

the clay ground, trying to get away from Omar's unseeing gaze. She went numb, her vision unfocused, her ears hissing. No sense left but smell.

"Fuck no," Kendrick was saying. "He was like a brother, he . . . This isn't right."

"He kept me from losing my shit out here, so many times," Alyssa said.

"Omar . . . Omar was the heart of this group," Yulya said. "He never once made me feel like the newest. Even after Jackie and Franz."

"We need to keep moving," Kendrick said. "If Omar was alive, he'd say we can't stop here, where we're easy targets for more bison attacks."

Alyssa sighed. "We'll give him a burial at sea. Mouth, you've driven this sled before, right?"

Mouth gave a toss of the head in the Argelan style, meaning yes. "But I don't want to be in charge."

Kendrick snorted. "Given that you almost got thrown out for breaking our most important rule, that seems wise."

Mouth helped Alyssa and Kendrick to lift Omar's torso, gently, out of the front seat, and wrapped him in some of the cloths secured at the top of their cargo. Every time Mouth glimpsed Omar's face, she went hypothermic.

There was no time to clean Omar's guts off the driver's seat before Mouth sat and got them moving again. Alyssa slid into the passenger seat, cursing in Argelan. The day and the night loomed on either side, like old enemies that could wait forever for their chance to finish you off.

They stayed silent apart from the crunch of their boots and

the chugging of the sled, until Reynold spat on the ground. "We're so screwed without Omar. He was the only one who knew how to make this journey in one piece. Can we even find the boat without him? Does anybody else know how to reach our contact in Argelo?"

"We'll figure it out," Alyssa said in a lifeless monotone.

"He's got a point," Kendrick said. "What's the point of hauling all this junk now? The one guy who kept the Resourceful Couriers going is dead."

"Oh yeah, we're done," Yulya groaned. "We're so done."

"We're still moving because we're too dumb to realize we're already dead," Reynold said.

They all kept encouraging each other to panic, until everyone was shouting and crying at once.

"Whoa!" Bianca yelled from behind the sled. She rushed forward and tried to shoot her rifle into the air, but she'd left the safety on. "Whoa whoa whoa! Everybody shut up."

They all went quiet, and turned to look at Bianca.

"I thought you dicks were supposed to be the greatest smugglers," Bianca said. "You keep bragging about how you walked through the jaws of death so many times you became their personal dentists. I know it sucks, you lost your number-one guy, but he seemed pretty anal retentive. He must have left contingency plans, right? I bet this asshole knows what you're supposed to do."

Bianca was pointing at Mouth, who still felt frozen. Mouth shrugged. "Maybe I know some stuff."

"See? This lying shitstain may have used me, and betrayed everyone, and gotten my friends killed over a damn poetry book, but she still has her uses."

Mouth couldn't look at Bianca, and not just because she had to watch the road.

"I didn't get anybody killed. The cops were already on high alert when I went out to meet you. Someone else must have turned informant, or gotten themselves caught after curfew."

"Not the right time to sort this out," Alyssa said. "But Bianca's right. We don't just quit because we lost our leader. We're smarter than that. We've survived so much already."

"The Resourceful Couriers always complete the job," Reynold said.

"So? Let's complete the job," Bianca said.

Everybody got back into position, flanking the sled, and put on an imitation of their usual swagger. They marched in silence, casting more watchful gazes into the night.

Mouth kept having bouts of lightsickness: stabbing pain behind her face that gave birth to white haloes, whenever she spent too long outdoors, with all this sun and shadow. She tried to concentrate on driving straight, but everything hurt. And then she realized Alyssa was looking at her instead of scanning for more bison, or axle-snapping craters, or those burrowing mud-crabs.

"What is it?" Mouth asked when the first glimmers of marsh appeared. Thank the Elementals, her head was clearing somewhat. "Why are you looking at me like that?"

"Just thinking," Alyssa said. "I didn't realize Bianca was one of those revolutionaries that you were using to get at your poetry book. And now all her friends are dead. And yet she saved all of us from self-destructing just now."

"I feel bad for her too," Mouth said. "I wish I could have helped. But loyalty isn't some sugary confection that you hand out to everyone. And Bianca's the one who chose to get dragged into politics."

The marshes lapped at their wheels, and the people walking sloshed with every step. Here come the horseflies.

"Wasn't your thing political too? Getting this book that belonged to your dead tribe?"

"That was cultural survival." Mouth swerved to avoid a sinkhole. "It's different. Politics changes all the time, and it doesn't matter who's in charge now versus a generation ago or a generation from now. But culture ought to last forever, if we protect it like we're supposed to."

"I guess I just value actual breathing people, who are alive now, more than the writings of people who are already dead."

"You were the one who wanted to help me steal the Invention—anyway, it's over. I failed. I'll never get another shot. And I couldn't have saved Bianca's friends. They were doomed before I met them."

"Maybe the part that worries me is where you care about ghosts more than the people who are right in front of you," said Alyssa, who sat close enough for the scent of sweat and hair oil to reach Mouth. "You know, with Omar gone, we depend on each other to survive more than ever."

"I'm here," Mouth grunted. "I'm not carrying any ghosts. And now that we're out of that city, I feel more alive than in ages. Walls and other people's rules fuck me up."

Mouth needed half her concentration to drive the sled, and the other half to avoid falling into despair. She kept thinking that if she only had the Invention, she could have said the right words over Omar's corpse, a proper goodbye to one of the few decent people she'd ever known. The Invention would've helped her to cope, to understand what she had lost when she was a child, and all the loss since then. But instead, the loss of the Citizens felt like an old wound gone septic.

But Mouth tried to put on a good face for Alyssa, who'd risked her neck waiting for her at the Low Road after the others had gone. They'd been sleepmates for five and a half round trips now, and there was something about your sleep patterns syncing with another person's that felt like intimacy. Mouth wasn't sure how to say any of this out loud.

"Do you remember any of it?" Alyssa said a while later. By now, the marshes were a stained-glass mirror spread before them.

"Any of what?" Mouth was grappling with the control for the mudguards.

"Any of that poetry. The poems you were so desperate to get your hands on."

"I guess. More just the rhythm than any actual words. Snatches."

Mouth tried to reconstruct one of the verses in her head, and her heart beat so fast she thought she might die. She had a sudden memory of Yolanda leading all of them in one of the songs of gratitude, and had to gasp out loud. That ball of barbed wire was back inside her chest.

"Could you recite some of the poetry now? For me?"

Mouth looked around. None of the other Couriers could hear. Sophie and Bianca were all the way behind the sled, having some fancy student drama.

The marshes swallowed their wheels. The mudguards barely helped. Everyone on foot sank up to their knees. The air smelled like rotten fish and sewage, the marshwater glinted with daylight, and the horseflies swarmed, ready to carry off a piece of you in their mandibles.

"Yeah. Right here. Why not." This felt like a test, of whether Mouth trusted Alyssa, or whether these poems had been worth so much scheming.

Mouth could only stall for so long.

The Citizens' poetry was written in the old language, Noölang. The one Mouth remembered best was about an old peach tree growing by some fluke, out in the wild meadows between the towns of Untaz and Wurtaz. Every time the travelers passed, they had fresh peaches, big and purple as life, with juicy strands inside them. Until a small town sprang up around the tree. The townspeople tried to plant an orchard and harvest the fruit according to their own schedules, and make peach bread to sell to other towns.

The next time the travelers passed, the soil was dead, there was no fruit, and the town was gone.

Mouth thought of Yolanda, the Priors, everybody, and felt like throwing up.

"Come on," Alyssa said. "Speak up. I want to hear. Please."

Mouth recited, louder and with more oratory, like when they used to do one of their "theater troupe" things, long ago:

Sing the tart juice, taste the sweet peach bread
But never say you own the tree
The hot wind flows from the day
Tempered by a hedge, across the cooling waters
A crag guards the peach tree from ice storms
Cradled by chaos
Sing the tart juice, taste the sweet peach bread
Give praise to the meeting of day and night
Through hedge and rocks, and the generosity of fruit
You cannot organize luck, or make the perfect wind
Or bridge night and day with your foolishness
You will never again taste such beauty
Cradled by chaos

Alyssa was nodding. "That was beautiful. You have a lovely voice when you're not threatening to kill everyone in sight."

"I should kill people sooner and skip the threats, then. My voice would be fresher."

Alyssa laughed at that.

"The Citizens." Mouth hesitated. "They were supposed to give me a name. I was . . . I was at the age. We had a whole rite of passage. You got your real name around the time your body changed, along with the story of who you were. 'Mouth' is just a temporary name, for a person who hasn't earned one yet."

"I always wondered why you were called that." Alyssa shook her head, swatting away horseflies. "So what happened? They all died before they could name you?"

"No." Mouth wove the steering wheel back and forth. "They kept delaying, until I was almost too old. They said, over and over, that I wasn't ready. Some test, I don't know what, I never passed. And then, yeah, eventually they all died."

Mouth had never talked to anyone about any of this. And talking about it now made her feel much worse—guilty for talking to an outsider, but also heartsick. Nothing Mouth could say might do justice to the reality of the Citizens, or just how completely Mouth had failed them, both then and now. She was out here, on the road, with one horizon blazing and the other drowning everything in its emptiness, and she felt as though the Elementals were watching her. Counting her failures.

A horsefly took a chunk out of Mouth's hand. They came in swarms, tearing your skin, until you bled all over. Little bastards. Nearby, Reynold waved a bat around, making a splattering noise whenever it connected with two or three at a swing.

"Ugh." Mouth drove faster through the last of the swamp, so horseflies exploded against the sled's front window, coating it with their glutinous bodies.

They reached the rocky strip, covered with pebbles, that separated the marshlands from the Sea of Murder. Mouth climbed out of the sled and searched for the hidden skiff. There ought to be a bunch of landmarks, like this one inlet and a thumb-shaped rock, but brand-new thistles (another invasive species) waved their candy-colored heads everywhere and camouflaged the shoreline. You could memorize landscapes all you wanted, but everything was like that peach tree: here one time, gone the next.

Bianca stared out at the Sea of Murder. "It's just so gorgeous," she said. "I've seen pictures but . . . this is breathtaking."

Mouth followed her eyeline, and had to gasp after all. You

spent all your time on the Sea of Murder trying not to end up one of the corpses who drift down to the bottom to be eaten by the giant squids that lurked inside the hulks of old warships. But the water smelled crisp and salty, especially nice after the swamp gas. Moonlight spangled the waves—and that was the other thing. You could see the moon. Stars, too. Something about convection, or the air currents, peeled away the clouds that kept an off-white haze overhead everywhere else. The sky turned a dark creamy blue, and you could make out a handful of craters in the shape of a footprint on the moon. Bianca was probably seeing stars with her own eyes for the first time.

"One guy I knew," said Mouth, "swore he saw the Mothership fly overhead when we were out on the ocean."

"That's incredible," Bianca said. "He could actually see it? I always thought if I saw it, I would make a wish or something. Did he make a wish?"

"I don't know," Mouth said. "He was dead a moment later. Because he was looking up at the sky in the middle of the Sea of Murder, instead of paying attention."

Bianca laughed, which made Mouth like her again.

Mouth searched for ages before she found their boat, and then they had to clean a swan's nest out of the intakes while Mouth steered the sled gingerly onto the deck. But at last they chuffed across the Sea of Murder. Alyssa steered them along treacherous currents, between two deadly extremes.

Mouth helped Yulya, Kendrick, and Reynold to hoist Omar's remains and heave them overboard, making a pitifully tiny splash in the cold water. "We'll drink to his memory in Argelo," said Kendrick, who was sort of in charge now. "For now, we all stay watchful."

They were closer to the night than the day, so they could just make out the ice shelf where the sea froze. But if you squinted at the horizon to your right, you could see where the water hit daylight and boiled, creating a wall of steam so high you couldn't see the top.

SOPHIE

can't stop throwing up. This boat is just a crumbling wooden platform built on top of a rusted metal frame, with an ancient polymer sac on its underside, which battery-operated pumps inflate, making a stuttering gasp that sounds more and more feeble. We secured the sled on the deck via a dozen attachment points, and there's a silty blue platform for the "crew" to stand on, including a panel with the knobs that Alyssa uses to operate the rudder. The deck tilts in one direction and then the other, until I'm sure a giant squid has us in its grip. Seawater sprays up and burns all the places where the horseflies tore me open, and I can't keep my damn stomach inside. I lean over the unfirm guardrail and spray into the water, with only Yulya's grip keeping me from tumbling over the side.

I'm going to die, long before we can cross this ocean. I've never been so sick in my life, and the laughter of the Resourceful Couriers doesn't make things any better.

"Ice! Watch out! Ice!" Reynold shouts. Total darkness, almost dead ahead, swallows up the water and the sky. Frozen chunks drift past, bobbing with a rhythm that makes me sick once more.

"I'm trying! I'm trying!" Alyssa wrenches at the controls. "Watching Omar steer this boat is one thing, but steering it myself is—ugh—something else. Grab ahold."

Just as Alyssa says that, we lurch so hard I fall on top of Yulya, and Bianca slides across the deck so fast she almost falls overboard before I grab her. A scraping sound, loud enough to feel in your teeth, fills the boat as we rub against a blade of ice. Some of the hull plating snags on the ice for a moment, then we're free. I touch my bracelet and think of Rose.

"Keep it steady," someone shouts.

"What do you think I'm trying to do?" Alyssa growls.

No more ice, and the sky lightens enough to see ahead. The other horizon glows once again, sending flashes along the water that hurt my eyes. Jets of bright vapor rise up from where the ocean is always boiling.

Bianca and I both try to scan the horizon for danger, but everything looks equally terrifying. My stomach has subsided and I have a moment of awe at the impetuousness of this ocean, which tosses waves in our path and tries to shake us off. I can't help thinking of the Sea of Murder as a beautiful giant beast that needs nobody and obeys nothing.

Bianca still isn't talking to me, and I'm trying not to look at her. But she must have seen the starvation in my eyes, because she comes and stands beside me against the rail as the sea goes calm for once.

"I don't know how you expect me to deal with you being alive," she mutters. The pale mist turns her spectral. "After I threw away everything to avenge your death. You've been living at some gracious coffeehouse, and meanwhile I've just been falling apart, piece by piece."

The deck plummets without warning, and we both cling to the railing.

I breathe spray and blink salt out of my eyes, and Bianca is blurrier than ever. My longing feels so intense it's more like raw panic. This could be our last moment alive, and I feel nauseous, and I don't know what to say.

"I'm sorry, I'm so sorry. I wanted to spare you, I didn't want to hurt you." I have to talk much too loud just to be heard over this wind. "I thought, I don't know, I thought you deserved to be free, and live your life, and you would have so many other people who cared about you, and you would just forget about me eventually."

The ocean erupts with gray foam. I think I glimpse dark shapes far beneath the surface, but they're gone before I can be sure.

The wind surges, but over the boat's terrible creaking I hear Bianca's voice. "How could you think I would just move on and find new friends, after what they did to you? How could you even think that? When they took you, they tore a hole in my—"

A wave strikes almost hard enough to flip the boat over and sprays both of us with freezing water. Drenched and gripping the railing with raised knuckles, Bianca still stares at me, tears mixing with the seawater on her face. Every inch of me is soaked, and I'm sure the next wave will snatch me into the depths.

The wind subsides again, by some mercy. For a moment, I have a clear view of the shadowed icebergs on one side, the geysers on the other, and the moon and stars above.

"You're the most alive person I ever met," I say, eyes burning, chest closing up. "I was sure you would find a way to keep going. I knew you were going to amaze everybody, with or without me."

Everything else on the ship holds steady for a moment, but Bianca still clutches the rail and sways with the echoes of turbulence. "Maybe if you'd trusted me, I wouldn't have been so stupid. But I trusted the wrong person." She glances at Mouth, who's too far away to hear us. "And now a lot of good people are dead, and my heart is just this rotten pile. Why couldn't you have just come back to me sooner? Why couldn't you come back to me—"

She breaks into sobs and lets go of the railing to hug herself as her shoulders rise and fall. The Resourceful Couriers are busy watching the ocean, so nobody sees me put my arm around Bianca. She stares at me, like she still can't look at me without reliving my execution and everything that followed.

Then Bianca puts her face on my neck and sobs so hard it feels like she'll shake herself to pieces. My grip is strong enough to hold her up, and to encompass her crying jag.

"Storm!" Kendrick shouts. "Storm coming!"

I hear the typhoon, without seeing. The roaring starts low and hoarse, then gets louder and shriller. The shrieking feels as though it's inside my own head.

The Resourceful Couriers rush to cover the sled and the precious cargo as much as possible with their last tarpaulins.

Everyone secures themselves to the deck with ropes and chains, and Bianca and I imitate them. I try to wrap my bracelet with some loose twine, though I don't know if it's prone to water damage. Alyssa stays put, trying to keep the ship on course.

Bianca has tied a thick rope around her waist, but the rope snaps and she careens down the wet planks, toward the rail. Her mouth is open, but I can't hear her.

Part of me gets lost in the memory of tumbling down the Old Mother, but then the part that stays hyperfocused in a crisis takes over. I grab her just in time, and hold on to her with all my strength. I still have a chain slung around my belt, lashed to one of the deck's attachment points.

"I am not letting you fall," I say, though Bianca probably can't hear. Her face is pale, her eyes wide and nostrils flared. "I am never letting go, ever again," I say louder, in her ear, over the screaming wind.

The boat shakes almost onto one side, and she almost slips away, but I tighten my hold.

"I'm here," I say. "You're safe. I've got you. I'm going to keep holding on for as long as I have arms. You're safe in my love."

I keep saying these things as the winds wrench the ship one way, and then the other. A million jets of water knock us flat on the deck and try to wash us off the ship altogether.

"I will never again let you out of my sight," I say as the front of the skiff draws upward, like a foot kicking a ball. "I'll guard you while you sleep." The hull makes a cracking sound and the motors sputter. "I've got you. You're safe in my love."

The storm falls away, and we can hear and see again. The

sea and sky shimmer—blues and greens and reds that leave afterimages even when I close my eyes—because we've drifted too close to the day. The wall of steam soars ahead of us: taller than mountains, wider than cities. I can't look at the white churn without squinting, and my face feels burnt. Alyssa isn't sure she can steer, with all this damage to the undercarriage, but she fights with the controls until we turn away from the cauldron. The engine sputters. I'm startled to be alive. I was sure that "love" would be the final word I ever spoke.

I don't know if Bianca heard anything I said, and I'm scared to look at her face. I hear her disentangle herself from the railing while I keep my eyes on the simmering ocean and the dark clouds congregating over the waves in the distance. Bianca moves closer, and then her hand reaches out and touches mine. I turn to face her.

The pure white light of day, filtered through steam, bathes Bianca's face. Her eyes are all pupil, opaque with tears, and her hair looks electric. She smiles at me, still weeping softly, and takes several gusts of warm sea air in through her mouth. Her hand remains on top of mine as we veer back into the middle of the ocean and the air turns damp and chilly once more.

mouth

The pirates sounded their horn just as the skiff got back on course, tearing through the air like a bison's attack cry. Fucking pirates. They approached in three tiny fishing boats, with barbed hooks made of rusted iron attached to the gunk-smeared prows. Seven or eight scrawny people to a boat, some of them holding rifles or harpoon guns. Their floating jackknives could outmaneuver the skiff even without storm damage, and they moved in a pincer formation that they must have practiced.

"We're gonna be surrounded," Reynold said. "Are you guys seeing this?"

"We see it," Kendrick grunted.

"Those attachments on the front are sharp enough to rip a giant chunk out of our hull," Alyssa said. "If they get us with one of those, we've got a long swim ahead."

Mouth raised her own rifle and tried taking a shot at the main ship, the one in the center, but her aim was for shit with these unruly waves. She couldn't stop remembering how Alyssa had accused her of caring more about ghosts than the people around her. There had to be some way Mouth could prove that she had everyone's back, just like always.

These pirates were just stupid fishing people who'd overfished their shore, so they'd turned to other ways of surviving. The Couriers' skiff must have been the first vessel to cross their path in ages, and Mouth pictured them rushing to bolt these corroded abominations onto their sturdiest trawlers.

"So what do we do? Maybe if we surrender they'll just take a cut of our cargo and let us go," Reynold said.

Alyssa shook her head. "They'll take everything. Ships don't come along often enough to make it worth just collecting a tariff." She looked at the three boats, bobbing in and out of view, and seemed to reach a decision. "Everybody hold your junk, and if you need to scream, do it in your own head."

Alyssa gave a little smile, like someone hatching a prank, and wrenched the controls so the skiff swerved toward the ice. The ship listed so far it seemed about to flip over, and the railing seemed about to buckle under Mouth's weight. Then they flattened out again and sailed into near darkness, with just a tiny glow to orient them.

A dense mist rose from the freezing water and turned everyone into an outline, like a reflection in a plate-glass window. You couldn't see the ice crags in the skiff's feeble lights until they were dead ahead. Alyssa kept jerking the rudder to and fro, and the boat quaked.

The sound of a thousand men grinding their teeth came from beneath. "We're going to need a new hull," said Yulya.

"The hull will make it," Kendrick said. "Remember how carefully Omar maintained that undercarriage? We can handle this."

"If we can just keep it level, we can slip past them," Alyssa muttered.

The claws of ice kept scraping against the skiff's hull, and someone on deck was moaning. These two sounds, together, became much more unnerving than either on its own. Mouth caught sight of Sophie clutching at something on her wrist, like a talisman.

A shape loomed in front of the skiff, and Mouth shouted before she even recognized one of the tricked-out fishing vessels. Besides the lance bolted onto the front, the other major modification they'd made to the ship was a skull, painted in phosphorescent green, on its hull, with unevenly shaped eye sockets. Seven people stood on the other ship's deck, two of them holding range weapons, and they looked just as startled to have found their prey here.

Alyssa veered to try to avoid the pirate ship as the man standing closest to the prow raised a rifle. Mouth already had her own rifle out and hit the man before he could get off a shot. He toppled into the ice water. One of the surviving pirates on the boat fired another rifle, but missed.

The pirate boat still raced right toward the Resourceful Couriers, with its metal thorn aimed at the weakest part of the skiff's hull.

"We're super screwed this time," Yulya said.

"This was such a bad idea," Reynold hissed.

The cockeyed skull came close enough that you could count

its teeth. Then it stopped and flipped sideways, like the skull's owner had decided to take a rest. They must have hit one of those icebergs dead on. The skull's smile looked whimsical, philosophical, accepting an unjust fate with a chuckle.

"We got them," Alyssa whispered. "I can't believe it."

"Shit. We're in the water! We're sinking. It's too cold to swim. I can't feel my—somebody help. Please, somebody. Please help."

Everybody looked at Kendrick, who shrugged.

"Even if I wanted to help those bastards," said Alyssa, "I don't think we can."

The screams of drowning pirates fell away, leaving nothing but the crunch of ice against the hull, and Kendrick's low curses as the skiff became less and less seaworthy.

"I can't believe this is going to work," said Reynold. "Just a little farther, and we can come around behind them and make for the Argelan shore. No fuss."

Mouth didn't see the second pirate boat until it was too late, and her warning shout came right before she felt something break irreparably under her feet.

Shouts and cheers came from the other ship, and its crew rushed forward, guns and long knives already raised.

Mouth kept thinking about her conversation with Alyssa, in the middle of fighting hand-to-hand with eight half-starved pirates. *You care more about ghosts than the people around you.* Maybe Mouth did feel bad for leading Bianca on, or the way her scheme had gotten the other Couriers stuck in the middle of a citywide freakout. Or maybe that guilt was just a poultice over the much deeper wound of failing to rescue the Invention, and knowing the Citizens would be forgotten when Mouth died (soon, most likely).

The pirates had abandoned their rusty guns because they had the Resourceful Couriers surrounded and that spelled a nontrivial chance of friendly fire. Mouth managed to get off three shots at actual targets, and even injured one young woman with flowing auburn hair and a strong brow who cursed and knocked the gun out of Mouth's hands with her unhurt arm. Mouth headbutted the gorgeous pirate and felt her nose crack, then elbowed her in the neck. The freezing sea air clogged in your throat like woodsmoke, turning every breath into a misery.

"My name is Jenny, and I'm in charge here. This is our ocean, and you fuckers are trespassing," shouted a tall woman with a huge mane of black hair and some mix of Zagreb and Ulaanbaatar features. "We're taking your cargo either way, but we'll spare anyone who surrenders right now. This is a one-time offer." Nobody even responded.

Mouth usually did most of her best thinking in the midst of battle, when everything was simple for once. But this time, her thoughts were a mess, and this foggy deathtrap wasn't making anything better.

The fight sprawled from the Resourceful Couriers' skiff to the pirate ship that had rammed them. Freezing water pooled around their feet, sloshing as Mouth kicked a stocky man with more beard than face and the kind of bad skin that comes from serious vitamin deficiencies. Mouth's foot connected with the man's stomach and sent him sprawling on the wet deck, and then Mouth trampled him on the way to punch a large hair-knotted man with both fists.

"You're all dead," Captain Jenny kept shouting, even as her voice grew hoarse from screaming into the sea wind. "You're going to feed the squids. You fucking smug city people, I'm going to kill you all." She had a big corkscrew-shaped blade with a handguard, and Kendrick howled as she stabbed him in the leg.

Everything stank of rotten fish and human entrails.

Mouth had seen too much death and not enough life, and maybe that was as bad as not letting in both the night and the day. Her knee connected with the face of the knot-headed pirate, who was already bent double, and he went overboard into the icy surf. Those young radicals, Derek and the rest, had been doomed from the start. But Mouth found herself getting stuck on the part where she'd encouraged Bianca to leap into the abyss in spite of all her doubts. Or maybe Mouth only felt remorse because her efforts hadn't done a thing to preserve the Citizens' memory.

Kendrick was losing a lot of blood from his leg wound, and Mouth was standing over him, holding Jenny by the throat. The pirate's corkscrew sword was coated with blood.

What was the point of feeling guilty, when people just kept hurting each other all the time?

Mouth tightened her forearm against Jenny's neck. "Time to close down the show. We're all going to drown here."

"My people live on this ocean. We eat and sleep and fuck these winds and these currents." Jenny laughed. "I never expected to die any other way."

She managed to pivot and bite Mouth's ear, so hard you could both smell and taste the blood. Mouth managed to get a foot on her instep and wreck her balance. Jenny fell mid-swing of the corkscrew blade and toppled over the side of the boat into the cold water.

But Mouth had leaned too far, with too many limbs off-balance, and so went overboard too.

Mouth grabbed at the slippery edge of the boat, suspended over blades of ice that moved faster than her eye could track. Her fingers clutched the rotten wood, and only managed to collect wet splinters. Terror chilled Mouth's insides, and the tastes of bile and sea foam blurred together. All the regret churning around her head had left her too raw. She couldn't help screaming.

She almost got a purchase on the lip of the Couriers' skiff, but the metal crumbled. She clutched instead at the barb jutting off the pirate boat, her feet kicking just above the sharp ice teeth. When the last of the Citizens died, their lore would die too, like all those songs they had forced her to memorize. Mouth probably should have tried to write some of it down, but couldn't manage that old-fashioned script. Everything the Citizens ever taught, everything they ever learned in all the generations, wiped out forever.

Nobody could hear her, and tears pooled in her scars.

A hand reached down, then stopped. Bianca leaned over. "I should just let you get cut to fucking pieces by the ice," she said. "I should just watch you die."

"Please, please help me up. Please, I'm begging you. I don't want to die."

Mouth would have expected, without question, to meet this situation with dignity. The Resourceful Couriers always faced death with a "well, fuck" attitude, like they'd expected to die, and now was as good a time as any. Mouth had almost died before, with a heart of stone. But this time, fear owned her—or more like, fear was building a house inside her, one with too many windows. Mouth wanted to try to get her dignity back, but she couldn't stop whinnying.

"I can't believe I trusted you. All your talk about loss and fighting back," Bianca spat. "I thought you were for real. You were just laughing at me for actually daring to believe in something."

Mouth's fingers froze and lost their strength, and she kicked against the side of the boat in vain. Bianca's raw hatred looked like an amplification of the face she'd worn in the shadows of the oatmeal restaurant all those times Mouth had been working on her. Mouth heard herself back in Xiosphant, telling Bianca to stay angry, and her vertigo and chills grew worse, as though she were falling an infinite distance to a bed of frozen knives.

"I wasn't laughing," Mouth babbled. Her fingers slipped. "I never laughed at you. I'm sorry. You're right, it's my fault. Everything's my fault. I'm a shitty person. I don't deserve to live, but I can't die like this. Please."

"You're horrifying," Bianca said. "I can't even stand to touch you." But she reached down and grabbed Mouth's wrist with both hands. She leaned so far she was in danger of falling herself.

Sophie appeared alongside her friend, and then her strong hands had Mouth's other arm. Mouth spilled onto the deck of the damaged pirate boat, coughing up a ruckus. The deck was flooding, four or five centimeters deep already.

Mouth pulled herself together, still looking at Bianca. "I would have done anything for my people, the same as you would for yours. I don't know why you thought I was going to risk my life for your cause. You can't control anyone unless you know what they want."

Bianca recoiled. Then her face closed up, and she took on the same dead-eyed expression that Mouth had seen on the faces of so many practiced killers. "Thanks for the advice. I'll try and remember that."

Back on the Resourceful Courier's skiff, four or five meters away, Alyssa faced off with the last pirate. "Hey, can I get some help over here?" But the pirate had surrendered by the time Mouth, Sophie, and Bianca arrived.

"There's no point." The pirate, a pale Zagreb-looking dude with a long beard and no eyebrows, was throwing all of his weapons into the thick water on deck. "No point fighting any more. My name is Gerry. I surrender. We're all dead anyway. I hope your stupid cargo was worth it."

So the survivors of all this were Mouth, Alyssa, Bianca, Sophie, Yulya, Gerry, and the badly injured Reynold and Kendrick. You couldn't even tell how Reynold was injured, he was just red all over, leaning on the sled with no strength. "I used to have a lot more blood. Funny the things you take for granted."

"You idiots chose to fight," Gerry said. "We were fighting for our whole community. You don't even know what it's like to grow up hearing the shallow splash of fishing boats coming home empty, and seeing the exhaustion on people's faces, the sheer inability to keep trying to pull life out of these waters."

"You can just shut up," Yulya spat at Gerry. "You fuckers attacked us."

The skiff and Red Jenny's boat were well on their way to sinking. "We need to get as much of the cargo onto that boat as possible." Alyssa gestured at the remaining pirate boat, which looked ancient but still seaworthy.

But Sophie, the mute girl with the big dark braids, pointed while grabbing Alyssa's arm.

At first, Mouth didn't see what Sophie was pointing at, but then it made sense: she was pointing at nothing.

"That's full night." Alyssa cursed. "We're too late."

How are you supposed to prepare for death, anyway? The Citizens had done a whole hospice thing, where you were supposed to make peace, and leave the world the same way you left your campsite: clean and empty, except for whatever knowledge might be helpful to those who came after you.

The others were discussing whether they should all get in the pirate boat and hope it held up better than the skiff. But no boat could survive hitting the ice shelf.

"Wait," Mouth said. "The sled. The sled has those big tires that we took off an old all-terrain rover."

"Help me untie it," Alyssa said. They worked quickly, Mouth, Alyssa, and Sophie, cutting the ropes that secured the sled to the skiff. And then they helped Reynold and Kendrick into the driver's seat. Everyone else climbed on top of the cargo, crawling under the tarps.

The impact of the skiff's metal underside against the thick ice floor almost knocked Mouth off the sled. "Hang tight!" shouted Alyssa. The sled rolled off the doomed skiff and hit the ice with so much force Mouth's jaw and spine contracted. Then they slid forward.

"I can't see where we're going," said Kendrick.

"Can we stop?" Alyssa said. "Try and stop."

"I'm trying!"

They kept sliding on the ice, and their headlights provided no guidance. Mouth kept wanting to crawl out from under the tarp and help, but couldn't. At last the sled hit a snowbank, with another bone-splitting impact.

SOPHIE

I wrap myself around Bianca, trying to shield her from the freezing wind, and I try not to think about the look on her face when she almost let Mouth die. The night feels even colder here than near the Old Mother, thanks to the frigid sea air. Every breath feels like swallowing an open flame. My eyelashes turn solid, like needles, and my lips freeze. Mouth and Alyssa wave electric torches, but everyone else fades into the mist.

Someone tugs my wrist, hard enough to jolt me. I don't even realize at first that the bracelet has woken up and is trying to pull me deeper into the night. I nearly stumble away from Bianca and the others before I get my footing.

Rose gave me this bracelet so I wouldn't be alone, no matter where I went, and there has to be some way I can call for help. The bracelet exerts more pressure, trying to coax me into deeper darkness, and I keep trying to figure out the interface.

Alyssa has the tarp from the top of the sled, and she wraps it around all of us, even Gerry the pirate. We all huddle together, sharing as much warmth as we can.

My bracelet stops yanking at my wrist, and instead makes a low warbling that carries over the squalling wind. As if my message has been received.

"What the hell is that sound?" Alyssa says.

I whisper to Bianca, "I managed to contact a friend of mine. They're sending help. We're going to be okay. But when they show up, everyone needs to stay calm."

"What are you talking about?" Bianca says aloud, each syllable chopped up by shivers. "What friend? How could you have friends out here?" But I just shush her, because I can't draw enough breath to explain, even if I knew how.

So Bianca just repeats my message to the others, and adds, "You idiots shouldn't do anything stupid. Just keep it together."

Everybody is too cold to talk, except for Mouth, who murmurs something that I can't make out at first. Then I realize Mouth is speaking Noölang, which we studied at the Gymnasium—something like, "Keep my face a secret until you are ready to make a safe place for me, oh Elementals, keep me unknown even to myself unless I can know my friends by the sound of their feet on the road. Keep me cold naked unless I warm myself with compassion. Keep the road straight. Keep me safe between day and night in your eyes."

"I knew you guys were maniacs, but shut up already," Gerry the pirate stammers.

"You shut up," Alyssa hisses at him. "You don't get to have opinions."

My bracelet gives a louder, more insistent spasm, and I look up to see soaring mounds gathered around us on all sides: a whole group of Gelet, though I'm the only one who can identify them by faint torchlight. Bianca yelps with surprise, and the others all stiffen. But then the Gelet lean forward and wrap each of us with the same mossy blankets that warmed me after I was banished into the night.

I nudge Bianca, until she says, "These are, uh, Sophie's friends. They're here to help us."

Everybody tries to spit out questions, but I just ignore them. The Gelet nudge us forward, and we push the sled along the ice with us. Next to me, Mouth falls face-first on the ice, picks herself up, and keeps going.

I can't make out enough details, with these feeble torches, to tell if any of these Gelet is Rose. Even if I could see better, I still probably couldn't tell. I sense their tenderness, their concern, as they usher me forward through uncountable meters of snow. I can count on a few fingers the number of humans who have cared for me as much as these night-dwellers seem to. I'm conscious, even through my frost-drunk haze, that my debt to the Gelet has doubled.

Just as I'm feeling as though we've been walking our whole lives and any memories from before must be false, I see a glimmer on the horizon. Everything wakes up and gains substance. We come into the twilight on the far shore of the Sea of Murder, close enough to see the swaying of the waves and the distant notch of the last pirate boat.

"Well, I guess we made it after all." Mouth sounds deliberately casual, like this was a lark.

"Sea of Murder, always a rare pleasure," Kendrick grunts,

his leg still bleeding despite his crude attempt at a bandage.

The Gelet are already retreating back into the night, tentacles swirling and pincers flexing, but not before Bianca gets a good look at them and squeezes my arm in shock.

Now that our faces are visible once more, I turn and smile at Bianca. I still don't know if she heard anything I said during that storm at sea, and the longer this goes on the more I wish I could unspeak those words. Before Bianca looks away, I glimpse the same stony expression as when she almost let Mouth fall onto the blades of ice.

PART
FOUR

SOPHIE

Argelo sneaks up on us: I don't even realize we're in the city until I can't find my way out again. A few mud-and-brick shanties hug the rocks, and the muddy trail from the shore turns to slate, and then the next time I look up the buildings are cement and brick, taller and wider than before. The slate path becomes tar and then cement, and the buildings clump into city blocks. Argelo has no skin, and its bones jut almost at random, and none of this feels like a real city to me, after Xiosphant.

Argelo doesn't have a convenient mountain range to protect it from the day and night, or a beautifully landscaped valley, or a street grid, let alone one that was partly carved from space. The people who founded this city were fleeing Xiosphant with whatever they could grab, Alyssa explains, though they did manage to dig the Pit, and a few other underground structures. The weather is a lot rougher here, and sometimes you get rainstorms or even ice storms. Gerry the pirate says they had a new kind of rainfall, a while back, made of some substance that burned your skin away.

I'm bent nearly double, holding up a big box of leather, plus my backpack, and I'm also supporting one corner of the improvised stretcher that contains Reynold. We're all loaded down with whatever cargo we could salvage. Alyssa keeps saying that if Reynold dies, so will Gerry—until Reynold manages to lift his head. "Stop saying stupid shit, Aly. If I die, it won't be Gerry's fault, at least not personally." Meanwhile, Yulya and Mouth are holding up Kendrick. Bianca stumbles and lurches next to me under her own load.

After the huge empty landscape on the road, everything feels too close. All these walls, all these people, pushing in on me.

My bracelet hasn't stopped twitching since the Gelet left us on the shore. Like they're reaching out from the darkness, their claim on me strengthened by this new debt. Even across all this light and piles of stone, they're with me.

I look up and realize Bianca is staring at me. "I can't believe you learned how to control the crocodiles and you didn't tell me." Her jaw tightens and releases. "All this time. You could have made them work for the Uprising. They could have rained frozen rocks on the Palace, and we could have won almost without a fight."

I can't believe what I'm hearing. "I don't control them. How could I?"

"I just saw you do it. Just now. You were telling them what to do and they did it. Fine, okay. You tamed them. Domesticated them. Is that better?" Her eyes stay fixed on me.

"They're not pets. They're my friends. They're sentient creatures, just like us. They have a civilization of their own, with a huge city and everything. I call them the Gelet, because it's the closest thing to how they think of themselves."

Bianca snorts. "They're *animals*. You remember the Biology lectures at the Gymnasium. You were still there when we did that unit. Crocodiles don't have a complex nervous system."

"That we recognize. That is similar to ours. The Gelet have something different." I can't believe that Bianca, who always taught me to question everything we were taught, is throwing textbooks in my face.

"Something different. Okay. Fine. But you have some kind of influence over them. Right? They do what you want. I knew you were amazing, but this . . . What else can you get them to do?"

I turn away from her, as far as I'm able, while we're both holding up the same dying man. "You don't know what you're talking about, and you should stop talking about it."

Everything smells like spicy food gone bad. After the knifepoints of sunlight reflected on the ocean, and then the blackout of the night, my eyes are still adjusting back to regular twilight. So my first impressions of Argelo are just scents and sounds. Music blares around us, and people shout in Argelan, a language that sounds like a throat disease. I've never had this experience of being surrounded by people speaking a language I don't know, and I'm convinced everyone is yelling at me, or about me. The smoke comforts me with a coal-and-spice flavor one moment, then nauseates me with rancid fumes the next. So many fires, burning so many things, and meanwhile I haven't heard a single bell since we got here. When I get used to the light, I see too many faces jammed close to mine, and I have to close my eyes again and convince myself that I'm not about to be carried away by a mob. At least there are almost no police here in Argelo—except a special force for certain crimes that threaten the whole city, Alyssa said.

I open my eyes again, and there's another burst of disorientation. The streets weave and double back on themselves, widen and narrow, become tunnels or bridges, without warning. Lorries and handcarts clog the road ahead of us, and people selling food or clothes at the side of the road yell for our attention. I keep looking around for a timepiece, or burst of colored smoke, or some other cue to let me know whether people have just woken or are about to sleep, but I see a million details, all of which tell me nothing.

And everywhere I look, I see strange clothing. No ankle-skirts or chemises like back home, no coveralls or linens. People wear colorful one-piece suits or multilayered dresses made of some kind of shiny fabric, or else thick denim jackets and trousers. Or they wear outfits that celebrate whichever compartment on the Mothership they trace their ancestry to. Girls walk past, wearing glittering facsimiles of the carbon-fiber-polymer crowns for which Ulaanbaatar was famous, along with rugged woven jackets and long cotton skirts. A few people who look somewhat like me wear loose shifts and light high-waisted trousers that look like the CoolSuits people wore in old Nagpur. I see some Zagreb-style jackets and cravats that Hernan would appreciate, too. I've only seen tiny pictures of these clothing styles in history books. Alyssa sees me staring and says that most of the people who came to Argelo after the Great Insomnia were the ones who felt oppressed because of whichever compartment their families had arrived in, a few generations earlier, so there aren't as many people from New Shanghai or Calgary.

Bianca shoots me another look. I ignore her.

Every joint in my body hurts and my breathing sounds like a busted motor, and even thinking about what Bianca said about the Gelet makes me want to scream. I still feel unsteady, seasick in retrospect, when I think about everything I said to her on the boat, but now that memory is cloaked with anger. But maybe I'm partly upset because Bianca's right, on some level. She's only seen me ask the Gelet for help with my own problems, because that's all I've ever done. They've saved my life twice, and what did I do for them? Bring them a few nuggets of copper. Shed a few tears for their sick children and their butchered friends.

Alyssa keeps pointing out things around us and laughing. "There's the tiny courtyard where we used to smoke and make plans for how we were going to own this city, the other Chancers and me." She bounces, even though she's carrying a large oak box and supporting one corner of a stretcher. "This here is where that old guy used to just turn up, selling the tastiest fish bread. Down that alley is where that saloon used to brew its own wine. God, this is a real city."

"I thought you were sick of this place," Mouth grunts.

Alyssa starts to answer—but a man comes out of the alley she just pointed at. He aims an oil-crusted harpoon gun at us, and says something in Argelan. Mouth is standing nearest to him, and she gets one hand on the harpoon gun and the other on his throat before I even have time to react. The man pulls the trigger without a good shot, and ends up impaled on his own weapon.

Afterward, Mouth is in an even uglier mood than usual, as if killing one more person makes any difference.

Soon everybody but Bianca and me is speaking Argelan, so we'll make less obvious targets. I understand a word here and there, because some of the vocabulary is almost the same, and Yulya taught me a few phrases, including that confusing "Anchor-Banter" thing.

We're passing through some neighborhood called Little Merida. The aromas of spiced meats and some kind of lime-scented fish broth come out of every doorway, and I hear strange rhythms echoing off the walls. According to Yulya, this neighborhood was where the Great Argelan Prosperity Company had its central office before they tore all that stuff down. By now, I'm sure none of us knows where we're going. The longer I listen to the gargling racket of this language, the more I wish I could plug my ears. I'm getting lightsickness, which makes my head throb and fills my vision with streaks.

I'm about to just throw my box of leather on the street, refuse to carry it any farther, when we turn down another alley and venture inside a small tavern, or bar, where everyone hunches over small tureens that smell like hot rat stew, but also like liquor. We lay Reynold on a big oak table, and I'm able to unload the box and my rucksack onto the floor, and blood flows back into my shoulders and hands, so I feel light-headed with relief. Nearby, Yulya and Alyssa help Kendrick into a chair. When I look back at the table where we left Reynold, a man is already cleaning his wounds and has some fancy wound sealant ready. Gerry has already made himself scarce.

Over in the corner of this tavern, or whatever it is, a quartet of musicians pounds out a discordant rhythm on mandolins, drums, and a brass piano, while also playing some board game that involves beautifully carved pewter fish. I think the drummer is winning.

Alyssa, Yulya, and Mouth greet a man who looks familiar, and then I realize: he looks a lot like Omar, our dead leader. Same long curls over a cotton shawl, same whiskers and sideburns. I hear this man say the name "Omar" in the middle of a question, and then Alyssa and Mouth both shake their heads and mutter apologies. The man, whose name turns out to be Ahmad, weeps into one sleeve and brushes off all attempts to console him.

We all just sit for a while, Ahmad staring into the distance and occasionally trembling.

Somebody hands me a bowl of the pungent alcohol-spiked broth, and I force myself to gulp down a few mouthfuls because I can't remember the last time I ate. It almost doesn't stay down. My whole body is sore, but I don't know if I'm supposed to be sleepy right now.

At last Ahmad comes over to Bianca and me. "You came a long way," he says in perfect Xiosphanti. "Welcome to Argelo."

"Omar was a really good person," Bianca tells him. "He saved us from an awful situation back in Xiosphant, and kept us safe on the road when we were too stupid to live." She smiles at me, and I half smile back. I'm starting to forgive her for the things she said about the Gelet.

"Thanks," Ahmad says. I notice he's not eating the stew. "I used to travel with my little brother, and keep an eye on him. Now I wish I hadn't stopped."

Bianca nods and takes a swig of the stew. "He kept his sense of humor in conditions that would make most people scream. I didn't even realize how much he meant to all of us until he was gone."

They talk about Omar a while longer, while the musicians pack up. I feel so exhausted and numb inside I can't hold my head up, and I feel drunk on three spoonfuls of stew. But Ahmad's grief reminds me just how recently Omar died, and how little time we've had to mourn.

At last Ahmad says, "Alyssa is hoping you can stay with my wife and me. We don't have a lot of space, but there's a small extra room. The goods you managed to bring from Xiosphant will cover your costs for a while."

"Thank you," Bianca says. "I always dreamed about coming to Argelo and experiencing real freedom, but now that we're here . . . I don't even know. How do we even live here?"

Ahmad brushes this away. "We'll worry about that when you're rested. Come on, I'll show you our luxury penthouse."

We shoulder our backpacks again, say goodbye to the Resourceful Couriers, and follow Ahmad's swaying gait down a series of zigzag alleys coated with vomit. At one point, he says: "I remember the first time I came home to Argelo after traveling with Omar. Took me a while to get used to the noise and the chaos again." Like he's trying to relate to our disorientation, but also his grief is still so new that everything reminds him of Omar. We emerge into the sunny side of town, at a plain cement block.

Upstairs, the apartment is just a single long room, with a dining table, a tiny kitchen area and washroom, clean white walls, and tapestries showing beautiful patterns of geometric shapes. Ahmad and his wife sleep in the back, with their son nearby, but Ahmad shows us to a tiny storage space with two bedrolls, for Bianca and me. It's a little bigger than the sleep nook, at least. Bianca's already falling onto one of the bedrolls, without bothering to wash or even undress, and I join her, my boots still on.

For a moment, I feel wide-eyed with fear, bordering on delirium, because I still don't know whether the shutters are up or down at home. Plus, too much light is coming into this space. Now that I'm back inside walls and surrounded by people again, some part of my brain expects some order to my sleeping and my waking.

I'm pulling my body into a snake shape, turned away from Bianca, when she murmurs: "I heard what you said in the storm, on the boat." Now I'm wide awake, and I have a sprinter's heart.

"I need you to know that I'll never let anyone take you away from me again. I would burn everything to fine ash, both cities, the world, to keep you with me. You belong here, you're fucking mine. Whatever comes next, we're going to demolish it together."

I catch my breath, and then I lose it again. I lie next to her with my heart speeding, until exhaustion drags me under. The whole time I'm asleep, I'm hearing her words in my head, and when I wake I'm not sure that I didn't just dream them.

mouth

The light in Argelo didn't look like the light in Xiosphant, or anywhere else. Xiosphant had those two perfect mountains to block and reflect the sunshine, creating a pale glow across the whole town that tapered as you approached the night. Out on the road, the light was naked, and you learned not to turn your head too far in either direction, but there was a different quality to the shadow—full of texture and energy—thanks to those storms that came right up to you and sometimes tore you apart. In Argelo, though, everything felt more muted because most of the city was recessed into the ground, and so you sometimes felt as though the dark was coming up out of the Pit and spreading over everything. There was a poet once who said something like, *Xiosphant is the city of dawn, but Argelo is the dusk city.*

Mouth and Alyssa spent most of their share of the Couriers' haul, plus some savings, on a tiny apartment overlooking the bright end of the Knife, Argelo's biggest nightclub district. With a balcony, so they could watch all of the party kids throwing up on each other. They filled the apartment with artisanal rattan furniture, and decorated with dried flowers and hilariously ugly paintings of children riding around on cats, using the cats' neck spikes to steer. (In real life, if a child tried that, their parents would have one less mouth to feed.)

Mouth couldn't lean too far over the balcony or she'd have an instant recall of hanging over sharp ice, pleading for her life. She was starting to remember how painstakingly she had built a cairn inside herself, a stable structure that kept her upright and fighting, protected her from any emotional assaults, spared her from being afraid of dying. But these things always crumble when you need them most.

Alyssa spoke up from the big rattan chair. "So. You remember that conversation we had in Xiosphant? About retiring from smuggling? Time we made it official."

Alyssa got up and poured out some of this fancy wine, made from blackberries that grew on bushes out in the bright hills past the steppes, which only fruited once in a while, when the hot wind came off the day just right. She handed Mouth a glass, and she looked into its scrim. The smell was better than the taste: like air from a cloistered orchard, where nothing bad could happen.

"Even if I wasn't broken after that last trip," Alyssa said, "there's the fact that the Couriers are basically you and me. Kendrick doesn't want to travel ever again, if he even recovers. Yulya said one round trip was enough for her. We don't even know if Reynold will ever wake up. We'd need to recruit a whole new crew, and neither of us is an Omar. And my guess? Nobody travels anymore. It's just gotten too dangerous."

Mouth felt like the wine had gone down the wrong pipe.

But she put on a smile. "So. What are you going to do?"

"I'll tell you what I'm not going to do." Alyssa laughed. "I'm not going to waste my remaining money on partying and gambling and buying fancy bottles of booze—even though this wine tastes lovely—the way that Argelo always wants you to do. This town is designed to separate losers from their money, and all the prices keep going up. So I'm going to live cheaply after this. Maybe invest in something. Start a business, you know, open a shop."

"You're going to be a shopkeeper." Mouth couldn't help laughing. "You? Standing in the middle of a salesroom, trying to get people to buy shirts? I can imagine you robbing a store, but not owning one."

"Wow, thanks." Alyssa cast her eyes at the ceiling for a moment. "Really appreciate the vote of confidence. So glad you think I'm doomed to failure."

"That's not what I meant. I just . . . You might as well shave your head and become one of those bald music teachers."

Alyssa sat for a moment, and her face turned dark. "Seeing Ahmad made me think. He seemed happy, apart from the thing where his brother died because he wouldn't quit smuggling." She paused to choke down some wine. "And you know what? Ahmad used to look much older than you or me. We were kids, next to him. Not anymore. If anything, he looks younger than we do."

Mouth bit both her lips, but still wanted to say something she would regret, some remark that might break the only worthy thing she had left. She took a breath. "Maybe you just need to take some time off. That situation with the pirates was . . . intense. We just need to take some time and regroup, and then we can put another crew together. I don't think I can do it without you."

"You probably couldn't do it even with me," Alyssa said. "Anyway, you just want help getting back to Xiosphant, so you can have another shot at stealing that poetry book."

Mouth flinched. "I don't think I get another shot at that. After what happened, the security will be way tighter. That whole town is going to be a prison."

Even since they came to Argelo, Mouth and Alyssa had kept sleeping next to each other, in this tiny cubbyhole. The apartment had a nice sleeping area, but they still used the nook, for the same reason they slept in a knot: they were used to it. Eventually, though, you could get used to something different, if you weren't careful.

"Listen," Mouth said, reaching out one hand to the big rattan chair where Alyssa sat cross-legged. "You're the closest thing to a friend that I have, who's still alive."

"How close, though?" Alyssa looked at the street below their balcony, where some drunks were beating each other senseless. "How close to actual friendship are we?"

"I'm good at reckoning distances, by looking at the shades of light on the ground and the length of the shadows," Mouth said. "I'm not so good at figuring out near or far from abstract ideas."

"To me, friend is an either/or: you're a friend, or you're not. You're always saying that you're a real traveler, you were born on the road, not like the rest of the Couriers. You always made sure we all knew you were better than the rest of us, and I always let it slide. But now? Now you have to decide if you have room to care about anyone besides your dead nomads."

Mouth felt like getting up and storming out, maybe smashing the rattan couch on the way. But then this might be her last ever conversation with Alyssa. The two of them would become strangers, and Mouth would be even more lost.

"I thought you understood. About the pain of losing your whole extended family. When we first knew each other, you used to talk to me about the Jews, and how they were nomads, and your ancestors were almost wiped out more than once. You were the one person who was supposed to understand." She still wanted to break things, but also to cover her stupid weak face.

"That's just it." Alyssa's tone softened, and she reached out for Mouth's hands. "You're not the only one who's lost everything. Or even the only one who belongs to a culture that was all but destroyed. There are still some descendants of the people who survived the Hydroponic Garden Massacre walking around. I get it, you lost your whole world when you were a child, and I can't even imagine the awfulness. But that doesn't give you a lifetime pass. You know?"

The Citizens had many ideas about death, but mostly, if you died on the road, then the rest of the group would carry you with them. Metaphorically, not physically. Even the group was doomed to extinction; only the road was eternal, and the only real death would be if you lost the road.

But none of this was Alyssa's fault, and in fact she'd saved Mouth's ass too many times. So Mouth dug up a kind voice from somewhere, clasped her hands, and said, "I get it. I can recognize reality, I swear I can. I just have a hard time with change, which is probably weird for someone who grew up on the move. But I get it. I won't pressure you to keep smuggling. Okay?"

"Okay." Alyssa poured some more wine. "And maybe you're right, and we're not cut out to be shopkeepers. Maybe there's something else we can do to make money, since we're going to be here for the rest of our lives."

Mouth tried to suppress a shudder.

Mouth kept asking Alyssa where they were going, and she just laughed. At last she said, "Our new job." She started singing one of the Couriers' old songs, about the dog and the ostrich and the man who lived underground. This just ratcheted the tension in Mouth's gut, which had aspirations of becoming a full-blown ulcer. Alyssa veered uptown, so close to the day that Mouth felt the first stirring of lightsickness.

Just as Alyssa got to the part of the song where the dog tugged at one neck of the ostrich and the man pulled the other, she stopped and banged on the stone door of a wooden building that was so blanched it had cracks. They were in a tight alley where four streets collided and you'd need to be a wizard to find the continuation of the street you'd come in on.

"Here we are," she said. Mouth followed her inside a high-ceilinged one-story warehouse stacked with crates that Mouth knew at a glance would contain guns.

"This is going to be way better than opening a shop," Alyssa said.

Mouth made sure to wear a neutral expression.

"You must be Mouth," said a tall man with swept-back hair, tiny eyes, and a pointed beard. Behind him, a short woman wore her raven hair in two thick braids. They both looked like they identified with the Merida section of the Mothership.

"My name is Carlos," the man said, "and this is Maria." Handshakes all around. "Alyssa tells me you're a good person to have in a bad situation."

Mouth gave a head tilt, which could mean "yes" or "depends," or "I don't know you, and don't feel like volunteering any information."

"We're about to be in a world of bad," Maria said, looking at Alyssa. "The Nine Families haven't been managing their shit, and it's time for some smaller, leaner operations to move up."

"It's all up for grabs," Carlos said. "The sea is fished out, meteor quarries coming up empty, textile factories at half capacity. Toxic rainstorms have been trashing our crops, and the aquifers are getting polluted or drained. Shortages mean one thing: opportunity."

Mouth could think of one other thing that shortages could mean, but just gave a tiny bob of the head. Alyssa, meanwhile, was saying, "Yeah, yeah."

"So we're going to hit the Perfectionists while they're weak," Maria said. "We understand you two have some experience at getting things where they need to go."

"We were part of the Resourceful Couriers, as I mentioned." Alyssa punched Mouth's arm.

"That's excellent. Really excellent. We don't need you to take anything to Xiosphant, or Moorestown, let alone Untaz or

Wurtaz," Carlos said. "God knows, just getting from one end of town to the other can be vicious."

Mouth finally spoke: "How big are the items we'll be transporting?"

"Not super big," Maria said. "Don't worry, you're not carrying these." She gestured at the crates of guns. That had, in fact, been Mouth's worry.

The rest of the conversation was just logistics: signal, pickup, delivery, and, most important, payment. Nobody in Argelo could ever agree on what time it was, so Carlos and Maria's crew, the Superbosses, used tiny wireless devices that could receive up to a dozen preprogrammed signals. Complex electronics were getting harder and harder to come by as everything ran out, but someone had figured out a way to manufacture a ton of these gadgets.

After the meeting, Mouth waited until they'd walked several streets away, then said: "You fucking kidding me? *That's* our new job?"

"It's a good opportunity."

"After everything we've been through, we're going to be working for gun-running bottom-feeder gangsters."

"You owe me," Alyssa said. "I stuck my neck out for you so far I could barely see my own body." They got lost while arguing. Here at the edge of morning, all the ugly streets looked the same, and they all swallowed their own tails. Even the shadows were no help.

"Listen," Mouth said as they retraced their steps. "This isn't like smuggling out there, on the road. It's not open spaces, where storms and local fauna are your biggest worry, except on the water. Here, it's enclosed, it's all firefights in tight spaces. This city is one big killzone."

"That's what everyone loves about you," Alyssa said. "Your sunny personality."

"Don't call me that. The sun has killed too many friends of mine."

They ended up at a bar at the top of Archer's Hill. From up here, the Knife seemed always to be in midswing, about to stab the Pit's black heart. You could still see where they'd torn up a ton of the old alleys to make a grand thoroughfare back during one of the People's Congress eras, and then more recently the Nine Families had torn down an entire neighborhood to build a few of their mansions, leaving a nest of streets that led nowhere.

"You know that I will do this if you ask me to," Mouth said after the third overpriced swamp vodka. "Even if I didn't owe you, you're family. But it's a bad idea."

"We have to do something," Alyssa said. "You're starting to scare me. You get weird when you have too much time on your hands, and you're not built for honest work." She paused and drank enough to destroy the lining of her throat. In between coughs, she blinked tipsily at Mouth. "You really think of me as family?"

Mouth leaned across the table, almost knocking over the half-empty bottle, and caught Alyssa in a hug so encompassing, it was like one of those streets that folded in on itself. As she relaxed into the hug, Mouth whispered, "You're my only family."

*

Mouth refused to sleep while they were watching for the Superbosses' signal, and then when at last the tiny black gadget spat out a single glyph, Alyssa all of a sudden needed to make a pit stop on their way to the pickup.

And now Mouth wished she'd slept when she had the chance, because she kept hallucinating out of the corner of one eye. Someone was selling roast pheasant on the street corner, with smoke permeating the scaly flesh and the webs between all of its legs. Alyssa bought one for each of them, and the hot juices felt like a corpse reviver.

The "pit stop" took them far from the pickup location, which was that same building on the edge of daylight. Mouth got more and more confused, following Alyssa into the guts of Argelo, and then farther into a row of muslin and silk warehouses. Alyssa knocked on a blank stone wall and said, "It's me," and the whole wall swung aside.

Inside the stone building, a bunch of men and women perched on expensive mahogany furniture, holding new-looking single-shot rifles with slide-loading action. Mouth recognized the flying-horse insignia of the Perfectionists, one of the nine ruling "families" here in Argelo.

"I got the signal," Alyssa said to the man nearest the door, a wall of muscle with long dark hair, a neat beard and mustache, and a tailored black one-piece. "We're supposed to move the stuff into position."

"The pickup location you told us?" the guy said.

Alyssa nodded.

"Great," said another large man with no beard, sitting closer to the bar area on a five-legged stool. Nobody bothered to introduce themselves to Mouth. "Do it just like we talked about. When you get their route, follow it as long as you can, and then make a detour on the dogfish lane. End up at the maiden's fountain, and we'll collect your cargo. Meantime, we'll deal with the social climbers."

Alyssa nodded again, then turned to go.

This time, Mouth didn't even wait until they had gotten a block away. "You've seriously lost your shit."

"Too late to discuss now. You going to back my play or what?"

Mouth didn't answer.

"This is Argelo," Alyssa said. "This is how you move up here. I grew up in this town, you didn't."

Alyssa had started out in the boiling-hot Snake District, with her mother and uncles, and became the leader of her own gang of kids. Petty theft and arson for hire, mostly, but a few other hustles. Alyssa had thought they would stick together forever, but all the other members of the Chancers had decided to graduate to the big leagues. By then, Alyssa's family had all died of skin cancer, and that was when she'd decided to try smuggling.

"Look at it this way," Alyssa added. "You'll be doing your part to keep the fabric of society intact. And those are good people to have a relationship with."

"As you know, social cohesion and making friends are my two primary concerns," Mouth said.

At the cracked wooden building, Carlos handed them a banyan-wood crate that was smaller than the gun crates, but still a good square meter, and almost too heavy for the two of them to carry alone. "We don't need to know what's in here, I guess," Mouth said. "But we do need to know if anything will happen if we drop it or bring it too close to an open flame."

"Let's just say the contents are delicate," Carlos said. "I would handle with extreme care." He handed Alyssa a map, which had as many words as lines, then wished them luck.

"See you soon," Alyssa said. Then they were off.

"Please tell me we at least have a way to make this box less conspicuous," Mouth said. It was already making inroads into her shoulder. "I don't much care, but we did tell them we were professionals."

"Way ahead of you." Alyssa steered the box down a steep slope and an outdoor staircase to a tiny cul-de-sac below street level. There, Alyssa pulled some potted plants aside and revealed blue delivery smocks and sticky labels from the grocery store nearby. Mouth followed her lead and helped her put stickers all over the box. A moment later, they were two grocers carrying a box of potatoes and carrots.

"Okay, I have to admit, you did good."

"Damn right," Alyssa said.

Now all they had to do was make this heavy, "delicate" box look like root vegetables. Mouth tried to square it against her chest, but Alyssa still had to hoist her end over her shoulder to keep it level, and they were both gasping after a few of these up-and-down streets.

"Makes me hungry for some fried carrots," Mouth said.

"Shut up," Alyssa grunted.

Gunshots seemed to come from every direction, thanks to the bunk acoustics. Mouth was pretty sure they were getting closer to the fighting. She flinched, but even before Alyssa said

215

anything, they both knew they just had to keep walking.

"Hang on," Alyssa said. "I gotta check the map."

"Really?"

They laid the cube down, straining not to drop it, and Alyssa pulled out the map that Carlos had given her. "Oh, man. I think we already took a wrong turn."

A naked man fell out of a window in front of them, blood already spurting from a wound in his shoulder before he even hit the pavement. "Fuck," he said, and died.

Mouth did not want to know what would happen if a bullet hit the crate. She was reliving the memory of hanging over the ice, babbling supplication. She tried to stay businesslike, rough-hewn. "I guess we ought to move."

Alyssa nodded, and they got the crate in motion again.

"Potatoes," Mouth said. "Get your fresh potatoes."

"Shut up."

The way forward was blocked by the large bearded man they'd met at the Perfectionist building. "You made it," he said, and Mouth realized that ugly blob behind him must be the maiden's fountain. "Nai is going to hear about your service, and you're going to be—"

A hole had opened in the man's forehead. He pitched forward, onto the pavement.

Standing behind him, gun raised, was Maria, wearing a floral dress that was probably nice before it got coated with the blood of four or five different people, going by the spray patterns. "Fucking smugglers," she said.

"You don't want to shoot us while we're holding up this crate," Alyssa said.

"We all do things we don't want to do," Maria said, and shot Alyssa.

People in Argelo had no real way of reckoning the passage of time, but they had plenty of ways to talk about regret. A million phrases to describe what might have happened, what you should have done. Several major sentence constructions in Argelan had to do with information that had been knowable in the past: knowledge that a person had taken to her grave, observations that could have been collected, texts that were no longer readable. The Argelans had developed dwelling on lost opportunities into an art form, but they couldn't say with any precision when any of those doors had closed.

Alyssa hadn't woken up, and the longer that continued, the worse her prognosis. The bullet had missed everything major, but she'd lost blood and suffered head trauma from her fall. Mouth kept replaying the scene, trying to figure out what could have gone different. As Maria had shot Alyssa, Mouth had thrown the crate, which turned out to contain batteries. Now the Perfectionists had gotten Alyssa a bed in a back room at one of their health facilities, with tubes gnawing at her.

Now that Mouth had helped clean up what was left of the Superbosses, the number-two guy in the Perfectionists, Sasha, held out a token with the four-winged horse.

"Keep this where people can see it," Sasha said. "Nobody will ever hassle you. You'll get the best stuff. If you ever have kids, they can go to one of our schools. Finest schools in the city."

Sasha was that clean-shaven bruiser who'd been sitting in the back when Alyssa had stopped by to tell the Perfectionists she'd gotten the signal. Up close, he had a receding hairline that you could still see, even with his head shaved, and lines on his face that charted how quickly his smile could turn vicious.

Mouth took the token and tried to look overjoyed, because she could already tell that Sasha had been surrounded by sycophants for too long.

Here's what Mouth learned about Sasha from eavesdropping: he collected paving stones from different towns here on January, plus a few that supposedly came from Earth. He loved to play that type of music where you also play a game at the same time, and everybody let him win. He only ate humanely raised meat, and he made a big deal out of the fact that he'd never killed anyone with his own hands.

"You look like you had some ancestors in the Ulaanbaatar compartment," Sasha said.

"People tell me that," Mouth said. "Never even knew who my biological parents were."

"Well, it's a good thing. Most of us in the Perfectionists can trace our roots back to old Ulaanbaatar. The greatest civilization that ever was, back on Earth. They built this one tower that held twice as many people as Argelo, with its own built-in farms. I've seen pictures. Ulaanbaatar was where they made the outer hull of the Mothership."

Mouth rotated her hands. "I always thought it was a sad story. They were lifelong travelers. Horse-herders. They lived in tents, found whatever they needed. Then they put down roots and became city people."

"You could see what they had built from space." Sasha was not used to being contradicted. "They built to last, something people in this town could learn from."

"Of course," Mouth said. Alyssa was the one who knew how to handle people like this. "They were amazing. You're right."

Mouth wouldn't leave Alyssa's bedside, except for bathroom breaks. No matter how much Mouth tried to keep Alyssa clean, or beg others for help, she kept marinating in her own piss and sweat. Alyssa's eyes, which usually laughed or scowled or glared or rolled in reaction to the stupidity around her, stayed closed and motionless. Mouth couldn't stand to see Alyssa like this, but also would not look away.

Mouth wept into her own free sleeve. Gave a silent prayer to the Elementals.

She had started having little bursts of dreamsleep where crocodiles were standing next to Alyssa's bed, or the walls crumpled, when Alyssa opened her eyes. "What the fuck" were Alyssa's first words out of her coma. "Did you just dump me in a ditch? Am I in a ditch now? What ditch am I in?"

"You're not in a ditch." Mouth sobbed with relief. "You're in a bed. You're safe. You're here, with me. I fixed it. You're being taken care of." Then Mouth screamed for the doctors so loud Alyssa tried to raise an atrophied hand to cover one ear.

Some time later, a doctor showed up, shone a light in Alyssa's eye, and examined her. Concussion, she said. No lasting damage. Should make a full recovery, but take it slow at first. Lots of fluids, painkillers, and gentle physical therapy.

"Thank you." Mouth's eyes were so wet the light refracted into those cheap rainbows you see on soap bubbles.

"How long have you been sitting here watching me?" Alyssa asked, and Mouth had no answer. "You should get some sleep. You look like shit."

"You look shittier," Mouth said. "You look like if shit took a shit."

"You look like if shit made a shitty monument to the god of shit."

"You look like if shit built a whole shit city, but then it went to shit."

They went on like this for a while, and then Mouth fell asleep in mid-sentence. This time Alyssa watched Mouth sleep, or at least her gaze was the first thing Mouth saw on waking.

SOPHIE

My bracelet keeps giving tiny nudges in the direction of the night, which feels just like a person grabbing my wrist and pulling me toward them. I want to jump out of my banyan-wood chair in the front room of Ahmad's apartment and run headlong toward the dark so I can talk to one of the Gelet that rescued us from the Sea of Murder. We didn't even get a chance to speak after they saved us, and I can only guess at what they were thinking. These were the first Gelet I'd ever met other than Rose, but I know nothing about them. And I keep thinking that this might be a turning point, when I actually asked for the Gelet to help, and now I belong to them even more than I did before.

Bianca can't stop talking about everything we're going to do now that we're in the City That Never Sleeps. "I want to go to the Knife," she keeps saying. "I want to find all the best parties, and meet absolutely everybody. We have one chance to make a huge splash." Bianca sounds giddy—all of Argelo is a present she's dying to unbox—but then I catch her staring into the corner, her hands coiled into fists.

Whenever I see Bianca falling into this silent rage, her face compressed and her hand clutching at some invisible weapon, I try to distract her by talking about all the fun we're going to have. "We can dress up in colorful clothes, like the ladies here. We can explore together, just the two of us, as a team," I say. She smiles and nods, and her posture slackens.

But first we need to speak the language. I've been studying Argelan for ages, but I still can't make any of the sounds, and I hate the bludgeoning syntax: the order in which you say the words makes them subject or object, past or present, and so on. No tenses, qualifiers, or distinctions. And then, in the empty space where they've removed all the useful parts of speech, Argelan substitutes a million different terms for relationships: lovers, parent/child, teacher/student, friends, some combination of those. Many of these relationship terms don't translate to Xiosphanti—not to mention the strange thing that Yulya tried to teach me about on the road, the phrase that sounds like "Anchor-Banter." You could be father/daughter, creditor/debtor, murderer/victim, but "Anchor-Banter" will replace or transcend any of those. Whatever that means.

Even the body language is different here: people toss their heads off to one side, meaning "yes," and sort of roll their heads for "no," and I can't tell these gestures apart.

Ahmad wants us to memorize the crests of the Nine Families of Argelo so we can avoid messing with anyone who bears one of them. "You tangle with anyone wearing one of these emblems," Ahmad says, pointing, "you're basically dead." Are the Nine Families the government? Bianca asks, and Ahmad just laughs.

Time passes, and we sleep sometimes, both of us breathing like swimmers. Sometimes I get up and wander to the washroom across the hall, then realize the rest of the household is sleeping, and I feel a surge of guilt, like I'm awake at the wrong time. Or I catch sight of a window without any shutters, and feel a jolt of worry, as if there are Curfew Patrols on the street, and they'll see the uncovered panes and rush inside to grab us.

At some point, Ahmad starts organizing a proper funeral for Omar, and he invites Bianca and me. But I can tell he's being polite, and it's more of a family gathering, so we stay home.

Ahmad's wife, Katrina, is a short round woman with spiky brown hair and pale skin who laughs constantly, and seems happy to have more people in the house even though she speaks almost no Xiosphanti. She gives us bowls of some kind of spicy fish and root vegetables, plus mugs of bitter tea. Their son Ali, who looks a bit younger than I was when I went to the Gymnasium, comes and goes without talking to us.

Bianca keeps asking questions: How do you know when to go to work here? How does Ahmad know when to pray, or go to a mosque? How do women keep track of their cycles? Ahmad's answer to all the questions is the same: You make your own arrangements.

We get outdoors whenever we can, with Ahmad or Katrina, but I still don't understand enough to distinguish between regular crowd behavior and a mob coming to tear me to shreds. People come too close and speak too fast, and I stiffen, and start seeing every angle at once, looking for a way out. Everything feels wrong, and I go from hungry to nauseous without any warning, and these streets all look the same and lead in circles.

I start helping Ahmad in the kitchen, learning how to slice carrots against the grain, and peel the thick shells off swamp crabs. I've almost gotten used to a diet with more dairy, fish, root vegetables, soybeans, and seaweed. Argelo has no farmwheels, but they have orchards and swamps, plus types of cloth that we don't have in Xiosphant: muslin, silk, denim, and some polymers.

By now, Bianca and I are both wearing secondhand Argelan work clothes: loose pants, long-sleeved denim smocks, thick canvas belts. I pull my sleeve down to cover my spiky bracelet. I'm learning how to walk like an Argelan girl, swinging my arms and shuffling my feet, but my body carries all these memories from the Old Mother and the Sea of Murder, and they catch me off-balance. I wonder what it would be like to try to dress like my ancestors. Like, if I wore a Calgary jersey, like my father's people, or a sari, CoolSuit, or embroidered silk jacket with long tapered sleeves, like my mother's. I've been thinking about my mother more often lately, trying to imagine what she would think of all these strange sights and sounds, all this clutter.

Sometimes I see Bianca by my side and feel so grateful my heart almost breaks, as though I still can't trust this much luck. But another part of me can't stop worrying at the distance between us. I wonder if Argelan has a word for when you get what you've always wanted, but it's still not right.

Soon I'm dreaming in Argelan (mostly about the same thing as always: glass-faced men forcing me to climb a freezing mountain). Bianca and I start speaking to each other in

Argelan, which turns our conversations stilted but weirdly direct, because we just spit out nouns and verbs, like "I eat food." When I try to slip back into Xiosphanti, to try to draw Bianca into talking about what happened back in Xiosphant, and the things she said to me when we first went to sleep here, she just keeps responding in Argelan. "Let's keep practicing. I want to make the most of our time here."

Whenever we go outside, I feel the bracelet pull harder in the direction of the night. I'm wasting time here, when I ought to be following this summons. But if I wander too far on these streets, I'll never even find my way back to Ahmad's apartment.

I'm sitting in the front of Ahmad's restaurant, reading the same page in one of Ali's old schoolbooks for the ninth time, and I look up to see Mouth towering over me. "Hi, Sophie," she says in an easy drawl. "Want to take a walk? I'll buy you some lemonade. The good stuff. I just want to talk about, you know, *our friends in the night.*"

I stare into the wide planes of her face. "You can't tell anybody about what I did, or the fact that I can understand them. It's complicated." Almost the first words I've ever spoken to her.

"I won't tell anyone, I swear. I just want to talk to you about it. Please." I shrug and stand up. I need to talk to someone about the Gelet, and I can't talk to Bianca without hearing more of her nonsense. Plus I could use a break from studying this ridiculous language.

Mouth decides to take me to one of the fancy drink stands

in the Pit, which is a giant subterranean complex that the Mothership dug for Argelo before we lost contact with it. On the way down there, she tells me that Alyssa got herself shot, but she's fine. "She only needs one more gunshot wound, and then she gets a free stuffed marmot." While Mouth cracks jokes about Alyssa's injury, her neck creases and her lip trembles.

"You should come visit Alyssa, though. She'd love to see you." Mouth gives me one of those Argelan addresses with too many numbers and not enough words as she guides me down the riotous street.

Soon I'm sitting in a wicker basket chair, looking down into the Pit, with its perfect circles of railings going all the way down. People perch on the rails, selling junk or panhandling, while workers and shopkeepers shove past them. Mouth says if you watch long enough, you'll see one of those rail-sitters fall into the gloomy depths.

"This lemonade costs twice as much as the last time I was in town." Mouth sets down a pitcher of green liquid, full of brackish weeds. I still can't get used to the idea that there's only one type of money here—how do people know what to spend it on?

I take a sip of the lemonade, and the bitterness makes me choke at first, until I get the sweet aftertaste.

"We ought to be friends," Mouth says in Xiosphanti. "I can help you learn Argelan. It's a deceptively simple language. If you just go by the meaning of the words, you'll miss half of what's being said."

"A good language for liars, then," I mutter.

Mouth snorts. "Every language is good for lying. Even body

language. If we didn't lie, we couldn't communicate. Here in Argelo, they're fond of the concept of 'miser generosity,' which is like you're being generous by being stingy. They write songs about it. If you only give a little bit—of the truth, of your time, of money—then you're being sincere. Give too much, and you're probably just careless, and it means nothing."

I feel all of my defenses rise, making me want to close myself off, but something about Mouth's defense of lies goads me into talking. "Bianca opened herself up to you, the same way she did to me when I was a scared young student. And you used her, and you treated her like a disposable piece in your stupid game, and now I'm afraid she'll never open up that way again. So no, we can't be friends."

Mouth's impassive "bruiser" persona drops away for a moment and she looks stricken, the same as when she tried to joke about Alyssa's injury.

"I don't know what to say. I used to have a handle on ethics," she says. "Maybe if I had access to the Invention and could read all the teachings, I would be a good person again. When I was in the Citizens, every situation had a guiding principle, but now I have to figure out everything by myself. If I had rescued the Invention, it would be like getting to talk to them one more time."

"That book wouldn't have helped you," I say. "If you read those poems by yourself, they'd just be more of your words. More 'stingy generosity.' You can't replace people with words, especially if you're a liar."

In the Pit, an elderly woman has her hat out, asking for loose change or extra food, and everyone ignores her.

Mouth changes the subject. "I can't believe you went into the night and learned to speak with the crocodiles. We spent a lot of time talking about them in the Citizens, and some people thought the night was the land of the dead and they were there to guide us. Or maybe they were just wise spirits. But in any case, the Citizens would have considered you some kind of mystic. Or maybe even a saint."

I feel a weight, like Mouth is trying to settle some crown onto my head that will slowly break my neck. The word "saint" feels even worse than when Bianca said the Gelet were my pets.

Mouth sees me shrinking into my basket chair and says, "I'm just saying, I owe you my life, but even more, I'm in awe of you. And maybe there's a way for you to use your gift to help more people. I know here in Argelo there are scavengers who go into the night looking for the wreckage of environment suits and land cruisers our ancestors left out there. They could really use someone to help them reach an understanding with the crocodiles."

At this point, I'm done with this conversation, because the idea of making a profit off my relationship with the Gelet is the worst insult yet. I get up and walk back toward Ahmad's place without even looking to see if Mouth is following. I only get lost three or four times.

Everywhere we go, people stare at Bianca, because of her New Shanghai features that look like nobody else's in this town, and because she can't help being loud and excited, with an obvious foreign accent. At first she glared at people, with a barb in the wrong language on the tip of her tongue. But now she's decided that if she's going to be a spectacle either way, she might as well have fun with it. She's wearing a sheer silver dress that leaves her shoulders and most of her legs exposed, a wrap made of loose filaments, and silver sandals. Plus blue-and-silver streaks around her eyes. I'm wearing a golden dress made out of some fabric I've never seen before that clings to my body in coruscating ripples.

"Everybody is going to stare at me," I grouse under my breath.

"Good." Bianca claps her hands. "They should. You look glorious."

Goose bumps raise up on my bare arm. Bianca smiles at me, and I remember what she said in the storeroom when we first slept here: *We're going to demolish this together.* I smile at her, too, and she takes my hand, right out on the street, like she's letting everybody know we're together. I almost don't care anymore that we haven't talked.

She's wearing some fragrant oil, and every time I breathe it in, I feel dizzy, half wild with joy, out of control. We're holding hands! In the street! She's chattering to me about the place she wants to take me, in the nightclub district. The Knife. We're going to dance together, just the two of us, at some club that has walls made of speakers and air made of glitter. I can't help feeling like this is some buoyant fantasia, like I fell asleep watching an opera, and now I'm dreaming in song.

Bianca's hand and the Gelet bracelet are guiding me in different directions, at right angles to each other. I silently promise to find my way to the night as soon as I can.

"Everybody who's anybody will be there, and it's our chance to start getting an introduction to the right people," Bianca says in Argelan.

"I don't care about the right people," I breathe. "I'm just so happy to be here with you." I keep remembering how she said she would burn the world for me, and I'm so ready to set at least a few small fires—together. I keep noticing more things, like the way some of these older buildings look influenced by Xiosphanti architecture, but with cruder decorations and other kinds of rock painted to look like whitestone. I whisper and point, and she nods.

I can tell we're getting closer to the Knife, because bright lights shine from every building, and I hear the thumps and whistles of a dozen kinds of loud music in the distance. Argelan dance music is like Xiosphanti ragtime, only much faster and with more drums.

"Maybe we can find some students to hang out with," I say in her ear. "People our age, who are studying the same things that we were studying. Having the same conversations we were having. I bet there are some groups like the Progressive Students here."

She shrugs. "I'm not interested in spending time with a bunch of naive students. We're going to need powerful friends to survive in this city and achieve all our goals. You heard Ahmad, that's how it works here."

I still feel the bracelet pulling me in the opposite direction, but it only bothers me if I pay attention to it.

"We're finally here, in the place we always talked about back home, the city where anything can happen," Bianca says.

"We're young, and we're free, and our city tried to kill us. Let's make some noise!"

I would burn the world for you, I hear in my head.

"Yeah. Let's make some noise." I clasp her hand tighter.

We round a steep corner on this potholed street, and then we're standing at the hilt of the Knife. I've never seen so many colors in one place: every nightclub and bar has a sign that glows pink, or red, or a color between blue and green that I don't even know the name of. The sharp edge of the Knife curves away from us, along a street paved with reflective stones that look like candies. Each building has a different style and texture, from burnished steel beams to whitestone columns to a huge transparent cube, and out front, a sea of young people sways and drifts from place to place, holding drinks or gnarled pipes. Most of the people in the crowd are only a little older than Bianca and me, and they wear sheer clothing that exposes parts of their bodies. The sky looks just as gray as ever, but everyone's face is bathed in a hundred shades of orange and green. I can't help gasping at this radiance, this decadence, this liberation.

I stop resisting and let Bianca pull me into the throng. Every time the scent of perfumed sweat and the view of squirming exposed flesh start to overwhelm me, I look at Bianca. Her whole face is bright and open as she points out each new thing, and everything shines with more beauty because she's showing it to me.

mouth

outh didn't know how long they'd been in Argelo. Long enough for the money to start running out, and for all the prices to rise again. She was already sick of overhearing pretentious Argelan conversations about living in harmony with nature, and whether the unchanging canopy overhead granted liberation from all constraints, or merely required a greater exertion of individual will to keep sleeping, working, playing, and eating in their right proportions and intervals. And so on. People could talk forever here.

At least back in Xiosphant, Mouth had known what people saw when they looked past her camouflage: a foreigner. Here in Argelo, somebody might see an enforcer for one of the Nine Families, or a mercenary, or an escapee from the undercity. Everyone squinted at Mouth and wanted to know which compartment her ancestors had occupied on the Mothership (the nearest guess was usually Ulaanbaatar) or, worse, to speculate about her scars. People kept propositioning Mouth, for business or sex, and she just scowled until they went away. You could do whatever you felt like in Argelo, but so could everybody else.

*

Mouth visited every bakeshop in the city, looking for those little cactus-pork crisps that Alyssa ate. Something about almost losing Alyssa reminded Mouth of all the other deaths she'd seen, which led to thinking about the Citizens, which in turn led to remembering that she would never know how to mourn, because all the rituals were stuck in a book in a vault in a damned Palace. But at least there was one person left alive for Mouth to treat to fried food.

The cactus-pork crisps were still hot, still carrying the tart scent of the tiny bakeshop near the bottom of the Pit, when Mouth got them back to the apartment. Alyssa barely needed her cane to get around anymore, and her energy seemed to be back. Mouth was about to say that Alyssa needed rest, then realized that they weren't alone. A short, elderly man sat in one of the big rattan chairs, holding a chipped cup full of coffee in one veiny, pale hand and a huge stack of books and notepads in the other.

"There you are," Alyssa said. "I've got a surprise for you. I hunted and hunted, it took forever, but this was so worth it."

Mouth just stared at the old man, who had a thin mustache, tiny glasses, and a threadbare muslin suit. "I brought you a surprise too." She held up the greasy bag.

"Oh yum. We'll all share them." Alyssa bustled to the kitchen, fetching plates and brushing off Mouth's attempts to handle kitchen stuff. "Mouth, this is Professor Martindale. He teaches at the Betterment University, up on the morning side of town. He's a professor of religious studies."

"I've enjoyed talking to Alyssa," Martindale said, taking a plate with a cactus-pork crisp on it with a smile. "I haven't met a Jewish person in quite a while. There's only one temple left in Argelo, as far as I know. No offense."

"None taken," Alyssa said. "But never mind about me. Professor Martindale, tell her."

"So . . . Alyssa tells me you were a member of an itinerant group called the Citizens," Martindale said. "I've been studying them my whole career, both before and after they vanished. I used to interview their leader—her name was Yolanda, correct?—and several other members. I have a section of my archive devoted to them."

The floor was unsteady, like this building could have been set adrift on the Sea of Murder. "What did you say?"

"I've been studying the—"

"Alyssa," said Mouth. "Can we talk in the kitchen?"

"Uh," Alyssa said. "Sure. We'll be right back."

They crammed into the tiny kitchen, which was only separated from the rest of the apartment by a flimsy partition. "What's up?" Alyssa said, pouring herself more coffee.

"I don't want to talk to this guy."

"What do you—"

"I don't want to hear some outsider tell me about the Citizens, or what some 'expert' figured out. They were my family. My community. I'm not interested in what some fancy professor has to say."

"But he talked to them. He interviewed that Yolanda woman over and over. He can tell you—"

"I don't want to know!" Mouth was shaking, light-headed.

Seeing flame trails. She tasted salt again. "I don't want to hear somebody's stupid, overeducated . . . I don't want my people to be his specimens that he dissects. He probably wants me to share more of the secrets. It's none of his business. It's none of your business."

"I see how it is." Alyssa choked down her dark water and then poured some more. "You were willing to sacrifice all of us to get your hands on that stupid book, because you needed answers and closure. But here's the guy who can give you answers and fucking closure, you stupid bitch. He's sitting right there, in our living room, because I turned this whole city upside down to find him."

"I'm sorry." Every word Mouth spoke was colored by weeping. "I'm sorry. I know I'm selfish. I try not to be. I brought you the crisps."

"Never mind the fucking crisps. Let people do for you. Let me do for you. I found that professor guy to help you. Those nomads died before you even finished puberty, right? You never got to know them as an adult. I know you're scared that you'll taint your memories of them, but I can tell you it doesn't work like that. You'll only add to your understanding. That's all."

"Okay." Mouth hugged Alyssa with a ferocious strength. "Okay."

Maybe you don't get to choose how you make peace, or what kind of peace you make. You count yourself lucky if peace doesn't run away from you.

"Let me do for you," Alyssa said again. Mouth nodded.

Then Alyssa was back out in the front of the apartment. "Sorry about that interruption," she was telling the professor.

"Mouth wanted to remind me that we have better plates than these, and we always save them for company, and then the one time we have company over we forget to use them." Hearing this, Mouth reached to the top shelf in the kitchen and pulled down all three of the good plates.

Mouth sat in the rattan armchair and listened to the professor talking about how the nomads were among the few examples of a type-three intentional community in recorded history, even on Earth. "What's particularly interesting about the Citizens is the teaching that everybody gets to have their own personal mythology, as though you don't have full Citizenship unless they construct a cosmology that explains how the Elementals brought you to the road." This was the thing that Mouth had never earned, according to Yolanda and the other Priors.

"I never knew the details of how it worked," Mouth said to fill the silence.

"When I used to speak to Yolanda, she always said the Priors would walk from morning to evening and back to morning, to consult with both the day and night Elementals, and then they would know what someone's personal myth ought to be," said the professor.

Mouth just grunted at that.

Then Martindale pulled out a thought box. "Ever seen one of these before?"

Mouth nearly fell out of her chair. Nobody was supposed to have one of those, and this college teacher was handling it like a regular wooden cube. The wood had been harvested from one particular grove, beyond the last frontier town, way farther than anyone else ever journeyed, and then the Priors had stained it with a lacquer that they made out of the resin from a different copse, on almost the opposite side of the world, and then carefully blackened it over an open fire. Mouth had only held a thought box one single time, when they'd said, *You're still not ready for a name.*

"Where did you get that?" Mouth slid back onto her seat, trying not to act shaken.

"At this little market stall, down seven levels from the shoe repair man, in the Pit," said the professor, with a faint smile. "You can probably still buy one for yourself. The Citizens used to come through town and sell these, and they built them to last."

Mouth stared at the box, which was scored with all the markings that Mouth was told never to explain to an outsider, along with other signs that even Mouth had never understood. People were buying these in the Pit, like they were ashtrays or cactus-pork crisps. The Citizens had encouraged this. "Did—" Mouth swallowed. "Did they sell these as religious artifacts? Or just as random boxes to put your stuff into?"

"Both. You should talk to Jerome. He runs the woodcrafts stall, and he did business with the Citizens all the time, whenever they passed through. I'm sure he'd love to meet you. The Citizens were pretty pragmatic about it—they knew some people would love to own an authentic religious item from a 'primitive' community, but other people just wanted a nice box to store jewelry in."

"We used these to contain our negative, harmful thoughts. It was a whole cleansing ritual." Mouth would have given anything to have access to a thought box back when the others had all died and there was no place to put all of the guilt.

"Well, I would love to hear more about what it was like to be raised among the Citizens." Martindale put the box back into his old satchel. "I already gathered some background from Yolanda and the others when they were in town before. And of course, since the Citizens vanished, I've been able to get more context from talking to Barney."

"Barney?"

"Apologies." He looked over at Alyssa, who was shaking her head with a skittish look, like maybe this was all too much, too soon, after all. Mouth tried to smile. "You probably knew him as Barnabas," the professor went on. "He was a member of the Citizens for most of his life. He left the group during their final visit to Argelo, and his place is just a kilometer and a half from here. I assumed you were already in touch with him."

Mouth had forgotten all about Barnabas, who had cooked for the group and used to sing and laugh at the same time during feast breaks, but now a few s cattered memories came back. Nobody had talked about Barnabas after he'd gone missing, that last time in Argelo, and Mouth had just assumed Barnabas was dead.

"Thanks for coming over, Professor," Alyssa was saying, by way of letting Martindale know that maybe this was enough for now, and they didn't want to make anyone's head explode. "We'll be in touch. I am sure Mouth will be excited to talk some more about the Citizens, and their unique culture."

"Great, great." Martindale got up and tugged on Mouth's hand and then Alyssa's, and then he was gone.

Mouth stayed glued in the big rattan chair, staring at the chair opposite, where the professor had sat handling the thought box and talking about the ancient mysteries like they were a funny story. Day and night might as well have changed places.

"He doesn't have a copy of that book you were trying to steal," Alyssa said. "I already asked him."

She saw the look on Mouth's face and sat down in the chair where Martindale had sat, offering her hands.

"Look," Alyssa said. "I know that was weird, and I shouldn't have sprung that on you as a surprise, I guess. But you need to find out more about your nomads, or they'll always be the people who judged you when you were a little kid and then died before you could stand eye-to-eye with them as an adult. I can't even imagine."

"You're right." These were the two hardest words Mouth had ever spoken.

"I am?" Alyssa was so relieved she laughed and then started to cry. "I thought you were going to kill me for a moment."

"No, you are right about this. And thank you." Mouth was in horrible pain, all the way down to the cellular level where all that guilt had lived for so long. But maybe this pain would turn out to be the healing kind. Clutching Alyssa with both arms, Mouth let out a deep, ugly, gasping breath of what might eventually be relief.

SOPHIE

"I found this place," Bianca says, "where they make this drink. You will never want to drink gin-and-milk again." As if making me hate gin-and-milk is some accomplishment.

I still stick to the same main streets most of the time, because otherwise I'll get lost and Argelo will just swallow me whole. I can't get used to a place where so many people shove each other, and I can never tell who's just woken up and who's about to go to bed. I don't even know if I'm supposed to be tired, and that makes me more tired. Random people want to talk to me about Nagpur, a place I know almost nothing about.

But Bianca already knows all the best places in every neighborhood. "This is the café where they do these donuts. Abraham here is a genius at grinding the stalks and getting them just the right muddy consistency." She drags me by the arm into a wooden cavern, which reminds me of the Illyrian Parlour except they just drink coffee by the light of tiny candles. She gives me a bite of a donut, and it's incredible: sweet and crumbly, pure happiness. Abraham, a big guy with a bald head and stretched-out ears, pauses in the middle of grating some dark sticks into a bowl to wave at her.

I stare at all the people crammed onto all the seats, stools, and ledges in this thick air. Two girls squeeze onto a single oak chair, holding hands and whispering. At the table next to ours, a group of students wearing loose, torn clothing argue about the nature of consciousness, in a flurry of Argelan that I about half understand. Are we conscious because we perceive the outside world, or because we are aware of our own thoughts? One young man, with a high forehead and bony shoulders, says that by definition consciousness is the ability to act on our environment with intent, because otherwise sleep would be a form of consciousness. What about crocodiles? someone asks. They have some kind of insectoid hive behavior, but does that make them conscious, or just a complex manifestation of instinct? I tune out this conversation, because they're idiots. And meanwhile, the two girls are kissing, right in front of the whole café. I can't stop looking at these girls, with a Xiosphanti voice inside my head blaring *Unnatural*—and then I'm ashamed to be caught staring, and I look away with my face hot. Bianca's already standing up, ready to leave.

"Here's what I learned about Argelo." Bianca stops to wave at everyone who passes on the street, and they all wave back. "People spend all their time and energy trying to live in the perfect spot, with just enough light to let you see some color. And then, once you've got your home in the light, you spend all your remaining money in bars and cafés, where it's pitch dark." Bianca dresses like a fashionable Argelan lady, with ribbons, silk, and lace, but people still gawp at her, especially now that she's put a bold red streak into her lopsided black hair and started wearing luminescent makeup.

At last Bianca takes me to the place with that wondrous drink. It's one of the hottest bars in the Knife, called Punch Face. (The name in Argelan sounds a lot like the word for "shutter malfunction" in Xiosphanti.) The darkness inside Punch Face is so thick and smoky I almost step on a famous torch singer named Marilynne.

But Bianca sees better than me, and also she knows the whole scene by heart. She talks in my ear, just in Argelan, except for a few words in Xiosphanti. "That man you almost kicked, that's Gabriel. He's been making a fortune speculating on sour cherries, because they are in huge demand right now thanks to being a key ingredient in this amazing drink that you are about to try for the very first time." The drink is called an Amanuensis, and my first sip is tart, but with a fizzy sweet afterburn. "See? Forget you ever even tasted gin-and-milk. You could rob Gabriel right now, and nobody would care. Except don't rob him in here, because I don't want to get thrown out of my favorite club."

Punch Face looks no bigger than the Zone House back home, as far as I can tell, without ever seeing the walls. The center of the room is taken up with a black fire, which devours light instead of giving it off—this is something they rescued from one of the old space shuttles, and it has a complicated explanation that I cannot hear over the noise. A group of musicians hunch on one side of the space, slapping a pair of drums and grinding out a rhythmic melody on guitars and a piano, with a singer hissing, "You can trust me, I want to bite you." People dance in loose clothes that billow like the waves of the Sea of Murder. The air has a sugary tang, as if everyone is sweating out their sweet drinks.

The music speeds up. We all crush into the center of the room, arms under legs. Our torsos slide sideways across each other, and I'm going to implode with happiness. I don't know this dance we're doing, but I don't need to. I follow the music and the other people, and our bodies speak to each other with heat and pressure. All my nerve endings go wide awake. We put everything we have up in the air, then fall on top of each other. I hear Bianca laugh, feel her grabbing my waist with both hands to lift me into the air. And then there's a man nearby, with no shirt and sweat running along the ridges of his muscles. He laughs too, as his body whips between us. All my usual anxiety is gone. Everything feels brilliant. Bianca and I are alive and we're together, here on the other side of the world, in this dark warm room full of beautiful dancers. I want to fall into this moment forever.

Bianca keeps trying to pull me toward another food stall, or a trendy bar. "Come on," she pleads, "there's so much you haven't seen yet." But I follow my bracelet in the direction of the night, because I've put this off for much too long.

"You should come with me," I say to her. "You can learn to understand the Gelet the way I do, then you'll know they're not animals. They can show you their city, and all of the incredible things they witnessed before our ancestors even arrived."

Bianca considers this. "If I talk to them now, would they come when I called, the way they did for you? Would they help me out if I needed to cross through the night?"

I stop and look at her, and a cart runs into me, loaded up with fabrics on this narrow winding street, with a large man pedaling.

"I don't know," I say. "I spent a long time earning their trust and getting things for them. Maybe they would expect the same from you."

"That seems like a huge commitment. And you're basically saying I would have to be their servant." Bianca purses her lips. "No offense, but this whole thing feels creepy. Do you even know what these creatures are doing to you? Like, are they controlling your mind?"

I turn and start walking again, down darker and darker streets. I don't know how to respond to any of this.

"Plus you can't just walk into the night from here," Bianca says behind me. "You heard what Ahmad said. There's no wall, no mountain, between us and the edge. A lot of people live right up against the evening, and it's the worst part of town. I bet the crocodiles won't even come anywhere near that place." I give her a look, and she says, "I mean the Gelet. Right."

I pause, because this already feels like night. Rough clay-brick buildings still cluster around me, but I almost can't see my own hand, a few centimeters from my face, even with a small electric torch. I feel frost-sick, even wearing three layers. Farther ahead, I can almost make out more buildings, and people moving, but they could be my imagination. If you starve your eye enough, it will invent things.

"If anything happens to you, I'll lose my mind."

"I'll be careful."

"Good luck with that," Bianca says. "There's some effect I read about, where every hundred meters you go deeper into the night, the temperature drops exponentially. Plus you won't even know which direction the day is. Seriously, come back with me now. I'll buy you donuts. Please."

I turn to look at Bianca, who's a few gray lines. "Don't worry. I know what I'm doing." At least this time, I have my torch, and the warmest padded jacket and pants I could find in Katrina's closet.

"I'm turning back. You should too. I'm sure the crocodiles—Gelet—don't want you to just get yourself killed." The horizon only has a dim ember left. Bianca disappears back into the city.

I almost collide with a house before I see it. The structure shakes at my touch, and if I'd run into it with my whole body I'd have left just a pile of boards. Someone has lashed some pieces of an old temporary shelter to rotting poles, under a roof of packed mud and slate, and I could stick my hand through with no effort. I can't imagine what they do when there's an ice storm.

"Did you find it?" someone inside the tiny house asks. "Please tell me you found it. I can't hold on much longer. I only need a little bit." I almost turn away, but instead I grope until I find the door, and it opens inward.

Inside the shack, a figure huddles under a pile of survival cloths and old torn strips of insulation. A tiny lamp perches on a few crates next to this "bed." The tenant keeps asking if I have it, in a voice like an old man. But I get closer and realize I'm looking at a girl, a little younger than me, with no hair and shrunken features. She raises a hand with no fingers.

"Do you have it? Did you bring it?" She squints upward, realizes I'm nobody she knows, and gasps.

I reach in my bag for all the food I have—the remains of a fish pie from this place Bianca took me to—and I put it next to her bed. Then I turn and run out of there, and don't look back.

Back in Argelo, the streets spin me around again. Music blasts from all sides, and under my feet. I smell kettles of whiskey-scented stew. Laughter rings out from a half-open doorway, just upstairs on my right. But I can't stop thinking about the girl in the bed of old survival gear. I feel sick—like nausea, but duller and deeper. Even closer to the temperate zone, I have to step over beggars every couple of meters, something I never saw in Xiosphant.

A sickening phrase comes back to me: "miser generosity."

By the time I get back to Ahmad's, my horror has hardened into pure fury. What kind of city is this? They have enough resources to spare for light shows and sour cherry drinks, but not enough to rescue the people living in a shantytown at the edge of evening. Every self-satisfied chuckling face I pass, I want to scream into.

But Bianca is in high spirits. "Oh, thank goodness you're back safely," she says in Argelan. "I've been worrying myself to pieces. Did you manage to meet with your friends?"

"No," I say. "You were right, it was awful. I just saw the ugliest side of this city, and now I can't unsee it."

"Well, cheer up, because you're about to see a whole other side." She holds up a golden card, embossed with our names and a bunch of Argelan directions that I can't understand. "My persistence has paid off! I was dancing at Punch Face, and I met one of the top lieutenants in the Unifiers. You remember them, right?"

I toss my head, because of course I do. Ahmad made us memorize the Unifiers' insignia, along with the other eight ruling families here in Argelo.

"They're hosting a giant formal ball, with two of the other families, and I just scored the two of us an invite. Absolutely everybody who matters in this town is going to be there." She claps her hands together. "We'll have to get ball gowns made, and borrow some jewelry, and dance until we can't even see straight, and then dance some more, and it's going to be epic."

I still see the fingerless girl in my mind as I shake my head. "I can't. I just can't. You should just go without me."

"Sophie." Bianca takes my shoulders and looks into my face, and she looks like the fearless rebel who stole all my waking thoughts back at the Gymnasium again. "I want to share this with you. I want to dress you up in the most stunning piece of clothing you have ever worn, and then show off your beauty to all of the fancy people here in Argelo. This is going to be the greatest experience of our lives. I promise you, I know what I'm doing, and this is all for a good cause. But for now, just trust me, and come with me to the ball."

I'm so startled that she called me beautiful I find myself smiling and nodding. "Okay," I say. "Let's go to the ball together."

mouth

The tiny diner had three tables and seven chairs, with a wide counter along the back, at the bottom of a small hill where two streets made of stone slabs converged. The name barney's was etched across the front window in chipped gold letters, and there was a faded menu. Mouth stood outside and studied the proprietor's round, beard-shadowed face, and didn't recognize him. But Mouth mostly remembered Barnabas as a loud voice, and the scent of stews cooking.

Barney had owned this restaurant for as long as anyone could remember, not far from the college where Martindale taught, on the light side of town. Martindale hadn't even realized there was a surviving ex-Citizen selling cheap food to students and some faculty right down the hill from his office until recently.

Mouth wanted to keep standing outside and staring at the old man in the dirty apron, but Martindale was already pulling the glass door open. Barney saw the professor enter and gave a welcoming shout from behind the counter, then came over and put fresh plates and cheap silverware on the innermost table, with a grin that exposed his front teeth.

Barney filled every moment with patter. "Good to see you, Professor. I got some of that meatloaf you like, and I think we've got a few bottles of that grape juice, too. It's always great to see you. We've been lucky enough to get a lot of students coming in here lately. I always treat them right. Students always have the most interesting conversations, you know, Professor. Reminds me of when I used to live on the road, and we'd have all sorts of deep introspective talk when we were miles from anywhere, with nothing but sky in all directions. A man starts to feel his true size against the vastness of the universe. You know? What are your friends having?"

"Actually, I've got something of a surprise for you, Barney." The professor was enjoying himself way too much.

"Oh?" Barney was putting meatloaf onto a tray, and the meatloaf looked, or maybe smelled, familiar in a way that Barney's face hadn't.

Martindale gestured at Mouth, who fidgeted and backed toward the door. "This here is another surviving member of the Citizens. Barney, meet Mouth."

"Oh. Oh!" Barney rushed over and looked up into Mouth's face, searching for something. Barney's eyes widened. "Mouth. Of course. Little Mouth, I remember you. Such a tiny pain in the ass. You nearly lit my cooking tent on fire one time. I always wondered what name they ended up giving you."

"They didn't," Mouth said. "Never got around to it."

"Oh. That's too bad. Well, I'm sure they would be proud if they could . . ." Barney stopped and looked down, into the glistening slab of meatloaf. "I mean, if they could be here. If they were still around. To see you grown so big, and so self-sufficient. Not that they really valued self-sufficiency, I guess. They were always about interdependence. It drove me nuts. You couldn't wipe your ass without . . ." Barney trailed off again.

There was a long silence. Alyssa grabbed Mouth's arm, as if one or the other of them needed reassurance in this moment.

"I never found out what happened," Barney said. "All I knew is, we would come through town pretty regular when I was a member. And then I quit the group, and they never came back. I asked around, nobody saw them again."

"It was ugly," Mouth said. "You were lucky."

Barney had half sat down, but raised himself up again. He staggered over to the front door of the deli, suddenly moving like a much older, frailer man, and flipped the placard to indicate the place was closed. Then he went behind the counter and dug out a bottle of swamp vodka so dirty, it could have come straight from the swamp.

"So you were there?" Barney whispered. "You actually saw?"

Professor Martindale chose this moment to try to reassert his control over the reunion that he had facilitated. "Well, this is all very fascinating, and I think it's important that everything about this first meeting between two former members of the Citizens be documented for posterity. I'm interested to see the two of you compare notes, as it were." He pulled out a large stenotype machine, the kind that let you write quickly with one hand.

Barney and Mouth looked at each other, and then at the professor, and stayed silent.

The professor tried a couple of times to start the

discussion going again, by making an assertion like, "Well, of course, the Citizens are known to have placed a heavy emphasis on direct revelation, via spiritual experiences which would come, for example, as a result of visiting certain dormant volcanoes or other natural formations." And everyone would nod, and the silence would continue.

At last Alyssa poured herself some swamp vodka and destroyed the lining of her throat in a single gulp. "What I want to know is"—she panted a little—"what the hell were they even thinking? I mean, sorry, Mouth, but I've been on the road more than most people, and the only thing that ever made the road tolerable was knowing we would get off it for a long spell once we reached civilization again. What kind of people decide to just go out and lug all their stuff from town to town forever?"

Mouth kicked Alyssa under the table so hard she yelped.

But Barney just laughed and poured more swamp vodka. "That's a good question. I used to wonder about that all the time. Just like Mouth, I was born into the Citizens, and I lived with them for most of my life. I heard lots of stories of how the Citizens came to be, but they were all contradictory and full of weird holes. But here's what I think."

Mouth had switched from kicking Alyssa to trying to kick Barney before he said something he shouldn't, but Barney was a nimble old shit and kept moving just out of reach of Mouth's boot.

"The operative word in what you said was 'civilization.'" Barney swigged vodka, and poured more for Professor Martindale, who hesitated and then took a swig. "A lot of what people call civilization is just neglect. Most people on this planet live in the two major cities, because that's where we have the infrastructure, right? We have the farms and the factories, the power plants and sewers. Although the Argelan sewage system is breaking down, because none of the Nine Families is responsible for it. And the shortages are getting worse and worse, and prices keep going up and up. But anyway, with that many people on top of each other, you don't know who the people around you are. You might interact with a hundred people in a row without knowing much about any of them. Versus a smaller community, where you're surrounded by people you've known your whole life."

"When I used to talk to Yolanda and Daniel, the leaders of the Citizens, they said that walking outdoors for long periods of time was almost like a form of meditation." Martindale drank a little vodka, to be polite, and gagged. Barney encouraged the professor to wash it down with more vodka. "If you categorize religious activities on a three-dimensional map, with prayer as one fixed origin and meditation as another, you could helpfully classify the Citizens' travels as a hybrid devotional-transcendental activity."

"Yeah." Barney poured more vodka for everybody, making sure Martindale got plenty. "I mean, so you used to travel from one city to the other with your smuggler crew, right?" Alyssa tossed her head. "So you were out on the road for one trip at a time. Probably felt like it lasted forever, until you were back in a city, and then the road was just a dream you'd had. But when you're living out there, everything is different. You were born on the road, you lost your baby teeth on the road, you grew old on the road. And just moving forward, with the world stretching as far as you can see, your mind starts to empty out. You get in tune with the subtle changes in the wind, the way the landscape changes as you travel, the way that day and night can seem near or far, depending on the terrain. People did feel like they heard the landscape talking to them. Like they were closer to something real."

"I hate to break it to you." Alyssa pounded her vodka and took some more. "But the changes in the wind are not subtle out on the road. It can get ugly in no time."

"Weather's gotten more violent." Mouth spoke for the first time in ages. "Since I was with the Citizens, the storms have gotten worse, and more frequent. Used to be easier to travel, even without pirates."

Barney shrugged. "We get storms here, too. Toxic rain, even. We just hunker down underground."

"They're worse out there, closer to the ocean and the deadlands."

Professor Martindale was swaying, like a losing brawler.

"Oh, looks like you had a bit too much, man. Better lie down a moment," said Barney, already supporting the professor out of his chair and helping him over to a little cot behind the counter, near the cookstove. Soon he was out cold.

"Some people just can't handle the good stuff." Alyssa noticed the professor's vodka cup was still half full, and took possession.

"He's a decent fellow." Barney gestured at the sleeping professor. "Sometimes makes you feel like a bug under glass. But I get the feeling he and Yolanda appreciated each other. They both loved to hear themselves talk about theoretical questions of how many teeth make a bite. Whatever. Still. There are some things you don't talk about with outsiders."

Barney looked at Alyssa as he said that, and Alyssa made a big show of getting up to leave, but Mouth said, "She's family. She can stay."

"Okay." Barney brought a fried ham out of some cubby behind the counter, and carved a few slabs. "So, they really never gave you a name? That's cold."

"What made you leave? Why would you just abandon us like that?" Mouth did not mean to sound angry or wounded, since after all it was the past now, and Barney couldn't have made any difference if he'd stayed.

"What happened to them?" Barney demanded in return.

"You first," Mouth said.

"I left because I got arthritis, and they insisted I could get over it if I just listened harder to the road. I left because we were trying to sell our sacred shit to trendy people here in Argelo, for them to use as conversation pieces in their fancy homes, but meanwhile as Yolanda got older she got more sure that she was right about everything, and she wouldn't listen to anyone. But also, I . . . I felt like I got it."

"You . . . got it?" Mouth said.

"I had reached the goal. I had the clear head, the voices of the Elementals in the back of my mind, the whole concept of being able to look into the night without losing your will, that thing they taught of having evening and morning inside you, so you could reconcile the extremes within yourself. I had it. I was sure. It felt right. It still feels that way."

Mouth had been ready for Barney to say he had left because he lost faith, or realized it was all a sham, or anything defiling and dirty. But this was impossible to hear. Mouth felt drunker than the professor for a moment.

"But if you really had the clearness, the reconciliation, all of that," said Mouth. "That's even more reason for you to stay. So you could help teach the rest of us. I mean, shit. If there had been an actual sage, a real day-and-night integrator, living among us, I might have turned out different. Maybe I would have become somebody."

"You are somebody," Barney said. "Look at you. You turned out fine."

"I am nobody," Mouth said. "That's the lesson they left me with. No name, no myth, no identity. I never got any of it. And now it's too late."

"Listen." Barney seemed to pity Mouth, which was the worst insult. "I couldn't teach anybody. What I learned—if it was even real, it felt real to me, but who knows—what I learned could not be taught, I was pretty sure. And Yolanda didn't want me around anyway after I told her. The point of religion, for Yolanda, was to keep trying to reach someplace, and the last thing you want is for someone to actually feel like they've reached it. I couldn't stay. But I'm sorry for how they treated you."

Mouth had sometimes fantasized about hearing an apology from Yolanda, Cynthia, or one of the other Priors, for the no-name, no-self thing. But this was as close as she'd ever get, and it felt like hot dust.

"Whatever," Mouth said. "I was a child. Now I'm an adult. I've made plenty of my own mistakes since the other Citizens died out. I mostly wished I had a name and status so there could be someone to mourn them all. If I'd even known how."

"You still haven't told me what happened." Barney touched Mouth's hand and poured more booze for everyone. Alyssa was looking at Mouth too, because she had never heard the story either. Nobody had.

Mouth swallowed some spit, drank some vodka, hesitated, and decided to tell a cleaned-up version. "We stopped in the plains, near Pennance Hollow. I went to this lagoon to get some water for our new cook, who wasn't as good as you had been." Barney smiled at this. "I was carrying the water back to the encampment, in that big tub that had all the weird faces on it. And then I heard loud voices coming from the camp."

Even remembering that much drained all the life out of Mouth. Like sleep deprivation, or muscle fatigue, but much harder.

Alyssa rested her face on Mouth's chest for a moment, then sat up and poured more swamp vodka.

"At first I thought they were singing, like I had somehow missed a ritual, or a celebration. Then it sounded more like an argument. The idea that they were screaming, that I was hearing their death cries, didn't even figure. Then I got to the top of the ridge and it was like an ocean had appeared in our campsite."

"An ocean?" Barney said, so loud that Professor Martindale stirred.

Mouth didn't want to talk about this anymore. Now Alyssa was the one kicking Mouth under the table. Certain words burned. Chest wall encroaching on what it contained, eyes pushed out of focus.

"An ocean, just, bluer," Mouth said after a long time. Every word its own stammer. "I didn't even see the wings at first. So many wings. It was . . . it was a swarm of blue roaches. They rippled and waved, and then I was running toward them down the slope with the tub in my hands. They broke before I got there. They became a cloud, and then they spread out in the sky. They left nothing but bones. Bones and metal."

"They ate through everything?" Barney's voice was barely audible. "The crystal books? The ceremonial garments? The tents? The carts? All of it?"

Mouth just nodded.

Now Barney was weeping too, and so was Alyssa. They were probably all drunk. Mouth made an inarticulate wheezing sound, like an apology for sharing this horrible story, or maybe for having survived. They hunched over with the bottle in the middle, and their three foreheads met, and maybe their spines would never straighten again. Mouth felt lonelier and more unconsoled than before, when that story had been a one-person secret. Alyssa's hand clutched at the back of Mouth's neck and head. She was whispering something like *I'm sorry it's okay,* and Mouth just breathed into her hair.

The three of them stayed huddled like that for a long time, until a noise shook them so much they nearly cracked their heads together. Professor Martindale was waking up, groaning, with an almighty headache.

SOPHIE

I can't even move in this ball gown. If I lift my arms more than halfway, I feel the seams strain. Even though red taffeta, tulle, lace, and ribbons have nothing in common with the gloved hands of Xiosphanti police, I still have a suffocating threat reaction to these restraints. But I close my eyes, and give myself patience, like Jeremy taught me. And then I breathe, and smile, because Bianca's looking at me, beaming, and clapping her hands. "People will lose their minds when they see you."

Bianca can't stop giggling and twirling in her dress, making her skirt billow. Bianca wears another kind of fragrant oil, with hints of cinnamon and marigold, and her face glows, thanks to the bright lines around her eyes and the faint contours accentuating her perfect face bones.

My starfruit bracelet looks out of place with all the sparkle strung from my neck and arms, but I draped a flowery wristlet over it. I feel the gentle pressure on my wrist all the time, even when I sleep—reminding me that I owe the Gelet much more than just my life. I need to try again soon to find a way past that shantytown, into the night.

"So how do we even know when this party is starting?" I ask Bianca, who's studying the golden invitation she scored at Punch Face.

"There's this one angel fountain on the edge of the fancy residential area," Bianca says. "The party starts the next time it starts flowing, and you can predict when that'll happen if you know about the water levels in the city's reserve pumps. It's like a game, sort of."

Bianca leads me past the Pit, and we get on a train inside a pneumatic tube, which rushes us to the southernmost part of town, facing away from Xiosphant. Soon we're in a vast granite courtyard, ringed with a spiked iron fence, facing a ten-garreted mansion made of bricks so white they sting my eyes. We introduce ourselves to a man in a dark purple suit, who checks some list for our names.

I can't stop staring at the layers of crimson satin across Bianca's shoulders, and the delicacy of her every tiny movement. Back when we were roommates, at the Gymnasium, she would start to move like flowing water, and her voice would grow more cultured and precise, right before she went out to one of her galas or banquets. I always sat on my bed-shelf, watched the petals on her dress refract the light as she swayed, and fantasized about going as her escort, only so I could admire this other version of Bianca in her proper setting, among all the lights, perfumed candles, and soaring waltzes. Now, here we are.

But that thought just makes me wish that we could go back to our dorm after this party, to cradle our teacups and talk about books we've read, brand-new ideas we've discovered, things that nobody but us realizes are wrong.

The man in purple leads us to a giant space, full of marble floors that reflect the overhead light in bold streaks, walls made of some dark wood I don't know the name for, and billowing drapes of velvet. All the men are wearing collages of different-colored fabric strips that create an effect like a million shards of tinted glass, while the women wear costumes that make the red gown I'm wearing look plain: feathers, glowing threads, tight corsets, shimmering strands of beads. Someone hands me a drink, and it has the same effect on my taste buds as all these colors on my eyes. I realize the room is divided into three groups, and each group wears the same insignia, as jewelry or a badge, to mark which family they belong to.

I stand, frozen, as everyone studies us. I'd much rather be on the edge of the night, receiving the Gelet visions and learning about all the spaces beyond the narrow road, than be stuck trying to impress these people.

But the next thing I know, Bianca has a small crowd around her, and she's telling them how she got here, in a melodramatic style, like something from a storybook. Everyone here in Argelo grew up reading glossy romances about palace intrigue in Xiosphant, Ahmad told us, and she plays to this sentiment. "They killed all of my friends and hunted me in the street," Bianca says. "I fled from my home with only what I could carry, and we faced every kind of death on the Sea of Murder." Nobody can look away from her eyes. Her crimson gown exposes a teardrop of skin on the small of her back, above where the pleats grow out of her waist like petals, and every time she moves, the entire room forgets to breathe.

To distract myself from my nerves, I study a giant silver-relief frieze along one wall that depicts one of the great stories of "Anchor-Banter," which seems to involve people riding on top of old-fashioned crawling machines and fighting with sticks that light up. And then in the middle of all the scenes of machine-jousting and voyages across the steppes, two silvery people intertwine, half naked, like lovers or maybe like wrestlers. I can't tell if they're men or women, or one of each.

Men and women in purple costumes walk past, offering piles of food and more goblets of expensive liquor, and I can't help taking some. The most beautiful man I have ever seen strides up to me just as my mouth is full of food, and I chew as fast as I can while he asks my name and says that Xiosphant must be a desolate waste, with its two brightest lights gone.

I'm still chewing, and the man keeps asking questions. This food is delicious but takes an entire lifetime to reduce to something I can swallow. And after I swallow the food, I still can only stare at this gorgeous person, with his wide face, limpid brown eyes, and square jaw.

"Forgive my rudeness. My name is Dash." He gestures around. "This is my house."

Bianca notices that I'm stuck, and comes to my side. "I'm Bianca. Thank you for your hospitality. This is the coolest party I've ever been to."

"Well, you are the best thing that could possibly have happened to my party." Dash kisses her hand, like a prince in one of those Argelan storybooks.

"You'll have to forgive Sophie," Bianca says, with a stage wave. "She's been through a lot. It's a terrible story. She was wrongly accused of a crime and torn away from the rest of us by the Xiosphanti police, who paraded her through the street and humiliated her in front of the whole town. And then they drove her to the mountainside and tried to force her to climb the steep slope, into the night. She nearly died! She was cast out of society and had to hide from everybody. It was really something."

I stare at Bianca, and though the food is gone, I still have trouble swallowing.

Afterward, when we step off the train near the Pit, Bianca can't stop laughing and flouncing in her dress. "That was the biggest rush of my entire life. I forgot how good it feels to sweep into a giant room full of immaculate people, and just dominate all of their attention. This is what I was made for. I haven't been this happy since . . ."

Bianca stops, because she notices an expression on my face that she's never seen before, not even when she said the Gelet were my pets. The entire wall of superheated vapor on the Sea of Murder, with all of its dazzling spray and choking steam, is bursting inside me.

"What's wrong? Are you angry at me? What did I—"

"*Don't ever do that again*," I spit. She starts to ask, and I cut her off. "Don't turn my personal . . . my real-life suffering into a cute story to entertain those people."

Bianca starts to explain, to justify herself, and I give her a look that makes her stop talking.

"Just. Don't," I spit. "Never again. I don't even understand why you care so much what some stupid rich people think about us. You can tell them whatever you want about your part, but you don't get to turn my execution into party banter." My own breathing sounds like a giant rusted machine. "What I went through after they took me away, it still hurts. I have to work so hard. You have no idea. Even I sometimes forget just how hard I keep working, to stay at peace with it."

"Okay. I'm sorry." Bianca pauses. She swings her puffy arms, almost hitting the gray-brick wall. "But you know, it . . . happened to me, too. I watched them take you away, and I blamed myself. Because I mean, it was all my fault. I stole three stupid food dollars. I've imagined myself putting that money back before anyone noticed it was gone, a million times."

I never thought of how guilty Bianca must have felt. I only made it through everything in one piece by telling myself a story of how I had saved Bianca, and she would be fine. But of course she must have felt like garbage.

"I get that," I say aloud. "I know it wasn't easy for you, either. But . . . it's not the same thing. You don't know. There's no way you could know. You weren't there. You can't understand what I went through after they took me."

"But there were some good parts to what happened to you too, like you got to work for Hernan. And I was the one who had to live with—" Bianca must be able to see the scream building inside me, because she catches herself. "You're right. Okay. I can't even imagine what you went through, and I still don't understand this connection that you have to those creatures." She puts her arms around me, covering my face with her billowing shoulders. "I keep thinking how brave you must be, to have survived everything, and then still save all of us on the ice."

I look into a neon puddle. "I don't know if I survived or not. I feel like part of me never came back from the Old Mother. Like I'm here, but I'm also still there, too."

"Like the memory won't let you go. Like the past becomes an optical illusion." Bianca takes a deep breath, not letting go of my neck. "I think all you can do is not blame yourself for how you feel, and be aware of things that bring the memory back. Take care of yourself. Okay? And I promise, I won't talk about your real-life trauma in front of other people. That topic is off-limits from now on."

She lets me go, and I take a long look at her, in her crimson satin, turned strange colors by the reflected sign from a nightclub close by. I nod, slowly, and clasp her hand with mine, as if to say that we are bound together by more than just the past.

When we get back to Ahmad and Katrina's place, I'm swaying on my feet, but Bianca is still on a high. She can't own the biggest party in town, and then just sleep. I keep trying to imagine if the shutters are up or down back home. I almost wish I hadn't given Rose my father's timepiece. The confusion, the lack of shape to my sleep, is almost as bad as the sleeplessness, and I feel like I have lightsickness, even indoors.

"We can sleep later!" Bianca pulls my arm toward the door. "This is Argelo, remember? We'll sleep when we damn well feel like it."

Ali is dozing in the corner. Ahmad and Katrina trudge to their own bed and draw a curtain, but Bianca keeps jumping up and down. "Let's go out to the Knife. We've had our coming-out party, and now we need to be seen in all the best crowds. Come on. Let's go dancing!"

I just stare, because she must be joking.

"I get it," she says at last. "You can't shake off the Xiosphanti mind-set. You're still internalizing all the nonsense they taught you at home, and there's a wheel inside your head that won't ever stop turning. But don't try to hold me down."

At last Bianca agrees to climb into the storage area, and we peel out of our complicated outfits. We lay there, with Bianca squished against my chest just like in the Couriers' sleep nook. I dream of riot cops and ice, same as always, but Bianca wakes me, thrashing and yelling, "I have to warn them, they need to know," over and over. This is what she said to me in Xiosphant, right before the end.

When I wake again, she's already gone, and I'm still weary. But I feel the weight of the bracelet on my wrist more than ever, and my arm keeps landing in the direction of evening. I'm sick of being trapped in my own skin, and I crave that experience of going outside myself, when I let go of my memories and sink into someone else's. I can almost feel the softness of the tendrils, and smell the faint residue they leave behind. Those rare occasions when I remember a happy dream, it's always about venturing inside the midnight city. So I get up and put on the warmest clothes I can find.

When I slip past the last ramshackle buildings before full night, I still see nothing but faint snowdrifts, and the frost still tries to drain the life out of me. The extra layers of clothing feel useless, and I can't see which way is daylight. This is the farthest I've ever been into the night on my own, and I'm already too cold to move.

As I walk, I'm remembering the party, and how I finally got to be a part of something that Bianca always did on her own back in Xiosphant. And she burned me, but then afterward she opened up to me at last. I hope this is the beginning of the two of us sharing everything.

Just when I'm about to turn and go in the opposite direction of the bracelet's pull, I spy an indistinct glimmer in my torchlight. A Gelet tilts her body until I see her pincer flex, right in front of me. I try to speak, even though the air chills my mouth. "I came out here as soon as I could. It's been complicated. I'm sorry I didn't bring anything for you this time. Next time, I promise."

I hear something move, somewhere behind me, but then it stops.

The big claw closes around my mouth and nose, like usual, and—

—I'm in the Gelet city: the giant vaults and galleries, struts of ice and iron and stone, machinery deep beneath our continental shelf. I see clearer than ever that the Gelet city is alive, with a heart of fire from inside our mountains, and a mind made up of the shared memories of every Gelet who's ever lived there.

But this time, I'm not one of the Gelet, crawling inside their own city. I'm there as a human. As myself. I see Gelet leading me down the walkways, and everyone comes out to greet me. This isn't a memory, it's a vision of something that they hope will happen. Like when Rose asked me for copper, except more detailed, as if they've thought about this a lot. The Gelet are celebrating my arrival, as though I'm a friend who's been away a long time, and I'm rejoicing too, at being someplace safe—

"You want—" I stammer as this Gelet pulls away. That vision of myself in the midnight city lingers, as real as my own senses. "You want . . . me to come live with you. You're inviting me. But I mean, I wish, so much, but . . . Bianca. She's my friend. You met her, or a few of you did, and she needs me—"

The frozen air shatters. The Gelet falls backward, and my searchlight reveals a dark line sticking out of her side. I hear men shouting in Argelan, like they have glass in their throats.

I reach out and touch a harpoon, from one of those harpoon guns, and then the Gelet shakes, and the harpoon flies off her. I feel hot ink spatter my hand. Not ink. Blood. "No, no. Please. No, please no. I'm so sorry."

The voices get closer, men and women, shouting. I hear them call to me.

"Run!" I hiss. She flees into the darkness. A jolt of light from some huge lamp blinds me.

The humans beckon me, and I understand most of their chatter. They saw this Gelet holding my throat in her claw, and they thought she was strangling me. As I get closer, three men and one woman step onto the brittle frost, their faces ghostly in their floodlight. The biggest of them holds a harpoon gun that also shines a beam of light from its stock. He aims at the Gelet, who's too injured to leap to safety.

I throw myself at the man with the harpoon, shouting, "Do

not kill" in Argelan. (A moment later, I realize I got the word order wrong, so I was shouting, "Would not have killed.") I knock the man on his back, and his second harpoon shot goes wild. As he falls, he lashes out and knocks the woman to the ground while the other two men shout. The big man and I roll on the frozen ground, until I bite his hand and smash my forehead into his.

I pull myself free and run back to the city, hoping with every panting lurch forward that I didn't just get a friend killed.

mouth

Budkhi was a small town, about four hundred kilometers south of Argelo, the opposite direction from Xiosphant. A giant bog produced this one kind of moss there that tasted kind of decent if you grilled it, plus the bog-fish were good to eat if you removed their poison sacs first. A lot of people died when they first settled there, but that was true of every place.

The Citizens had passed through Budkhi every once in a while, but most of their visits had ended with them being chased out with axes and slings. What did the people in this swamp-gas village need from a group of odd strangers? The Citizens tried trading, bringing supplies from Argelo or one of the bigger towns to exchange for food and woven swamp-grass, but the Budkhians had a taboo on using anything they hadn't made themselves. So maybe the Citizens could be a theater troupe instead? Or just offer additional labor, for anything that needed some extra hands? Or they could be teachers? Doctors? Priests? Each time the Citizens arrived, they tried to present themselves as something new and different, and then the Budkhians only doubted them more. Yolanda kept saying,

"Every community has a need that it cannot meet in itself. The more they say they do not need us, the harder we must try to become what they need most."

But the truth was, the Citizens needed the Budkhians much more than the other way around, because this was the only town within a hundred kilometers in either direction, and the food sources in and around that bog were not easy for visiting strangers to harvest. The last time the Citizens tried to visit, the townspeople saw them coming and lit bonfires on the road, with a large shirtless man spinning a lit torch in each hand, as a warning to come no closer.

Still, Budkhi was always the last stop on the way to a big volcano, which was one of the Citizens' sacred places. So the Citizens skirted around town as best they could, coming perilously close to darkness, and pulled some just-about-edible frog eggs out of the bog on their way out.

Mouth was starting to realize it was odd for a religious order to be so willing to play any role you wanted, in any given situation. Mouth hadn't spent that much time around other faiths—Alyssa had talked about her Jewish upbringing, and there were a few mosques, two churches, and assorted other houses of worship here in Argelo. But as far as Mouth knew, most people who devoted their lives to a creed wanted everyone to know about it. You only put on different identities for different people if you didn't care about spreading the good reputation of your teachings.

So Mouth had been trying to break the old habits, and to be the same person with everyone. This was more difficult than you might think, because it turned out, everybody wanted you to be someone else, depending on their needs. A soldier, a friend, an enemy, a reminder of the past. Treating other people with honor was harder than Mouth had ever expected.

Speaking of, Barney was a whole other person when he was waiting on a table of students—clowning, doing little dance moves, snapping his dirty rag. Mouth watched Barney work, wondering if this really could be a living sage, until Barney noticed and came over. "Mouth, good to see you." Barney smiled so hard his eyebrows changed shape, but his posture also straightened, and he looked older. "Didn't know you were coming. What you in the mood for? I have a nut roast that's pretty similar to the stuff I used to cook on the road."

Mouth got some straw tea from the table against the far wall, choking just a little on the rank aftertaste. She ate the nut loaf—which did bring back powerful sense memories—and drank two more cups of the bitter tea. The starchy aroma made all the old memories of the Citizens feel more present, and Mouth had caught Barney in a good mood.

He watched her eat with a half-open smile, peppering her with odd reminiscences. "Remember that old blanket Yolanda always wrapped around herself, that was so frayed it looked like scrubgrass? And ugh, those canvas shoes that Cynthia made for everyone, with the spongy soles that started so comfortable and always melted after the first hundred kilometers. Remember those?" Mouth kept nodding while she ate.

She'd started visiting the diner regularly, whenever she wasn't running errands for the Perfectionists, or helping with

Alyssa's rehab. Sometimes so many students were sitting on every available surface and on top of each other you couldn't get in. Other times, the diner was closed, with a sign saying that the place would reopen when the university raised its study flag. Argelo was full of things like that: your favorite candy store would open whenever the crosstown train was running, and the crosstown train ran whenever the hydraulic systems were primed, and the hydraulics depended on the water levels in the reservoir, which fluctuated in a more or less predictable fashion. If you knew all these things by heart, you'd be able to get to the candy shop at the right time to buy those peppermints you liked.

But even when Mouth could get into the diner, Barney was often too busy to talk. And if Mouth managed to arrive when the diner was both open and empty, Barney would be intent on cleaning dishes rather than answering Mouth's questions. "You already know everything," Barney had said over and over. "Seriously, you got it. You made a life for yourself, didn't you? You know what you know, and there's no need to know any more. The Citizens are long gone. Although sometimes I wake up and it feels like I'm in the middle of the camp, and everyone is packing up around me, and it takes me a couple eyeblinks to remember where I am."

Once in a while, Mouth would catch Barney in a thoughtful mood, and he would muse about everything they had all been through, and all the things the Citizens had tried to do. "We kept to ourselves, you know, but we did try to help people integrate their lives, whenever we could. We would come into these smaller towns as a group of carpenters or plumbers, but after we'd done the work, sometimes people would ask us questions. And we'd try to share some thoughts about how to pay attention, and stop getting distracted by trivial crap. Hang on, I need to check the oven. Where was I? Oh. So we talked, and listened as well. People in those frontier towns see the craziest things."

"Before Alyssa found you, I thought I had blown my last chance to understand any of it," Mouth told Barney when the nut roast was gone. "I found a copy of the Invention in a vault in Xiosphant. The only copy, I guess. I just wanted to say the right verses for the dead. A lot of people died, pointlessly, and I didn't even get the book."

"Mostly I remember that book being a lot of doggerel," Barney said. "Their way of keeping everybody from complaining during those long hikes. I mean, don't get me wrong. If I read it again, maybe it'd speak to me. I do remember there were a few moving passages here and there."

You might as well have kicked Mouth in both sides of the head at once.

"Really?" Mouth said. "The Invention? I mean, it was our most sacred book, I thought. It was the story of us. I was ready to kill for it."

"It's been a while, and I was pretty burned out by the time I left," Barney said. "You were at an impressionable age when you lost them, so maybe it was the opposite."

"But you're a sage. Or at least that's what you claimed. You said you achieved the goal," Mouth said.

"Don't take my word for it. I wouldn't, in your situation. You have no way of knowing if I'm telling the truth, or what that even means."

Mouth tried to remember a single line of the Invention, a single beautiful passage or moving sentiment. Everything came as a jumble, and now that Barney had called it doggerel, that's what the words sounded like in her head.

SOPHIE

I lie half awake in the storeroom, remembering the sensation of standing inside a fortress of ice and stone, of feeling welcomed by a whole community, and then how it ended. The Gelet's blood, dark and thick, was still on my hand when I got back to Ahmad and Katrina's place. I can still smell it now. The bracelet hasn't stopped urging me to come back to the night, but I don't know how to make it there. Shouts and discordant music blare from someplace nearby.

Bianca opens the slatted door and stands over me. She looks as if she hasn't slept since the Founding of January: there are puffy blotches under her eyes, which seem red and unable to focus. Her arms keep making tiny gestures, too fast to make sense of. I hope she's come here to sleep next to me, but instead she nudges my shoulder, harder than she probably means to, and says, "Sophie. Do you trust me?"

I almost say yes right away, but something makes me stop and look up at her.

"I need to know," she says. "Because I have a plan, but it won't work unless you trust me with your life. I did it, I found a way for us to go home. We can go back and fix everything we left behind in Xiosphant. We can take down the corrupt machine that decided you were disposable. If Mouth taught me one thing, it's always cut them when they're not looking. But I need to know. Right now. Do you trust me?"

For some reason, I still haven't woken up all the way, even though her voice and her stiff posture alarm me. I ought to be wide awake, alert, but I feel half present.

"What plan?" I whisper. "What are you talking about? There's no way back—"

Bianca rolls her head and shushes me. "You can't ask me that. This is why I said you need to trust me. I'm risking everything, even having this conversation with you. People in this city are so paranoid, they'll lose their minds if they find out what I'm doing."

Everything shrinks in on me, as if the shadows deform and I'm about to be crushed.

She leans closer and I feel her breath on my face. "Remember when I said I have unfinished business in Xiosphant? We both do. You were just telling me you still feel haunted by what they did to you, and maybe the only way for you to get past it is to face those monsters, and to see them brought down. Take it from me, you don't just walk away from the place that made you."

I can tell she expected a different reaction from me—like, she thought I would be excited. But everything about her tone is scaring me.

And meanwhile, I can't stop remembering when the Gelet came and invited me to their city, and then blood, and then blood. Those people thought they were rescuing me.

"I have my own way of dealing with my past," I say. "And we have a chance, we can start over here. We can get jobs. I can work in a coffee shop again. I thought you were having fun here, dancing, going to parties. You keep saying we're famous, and everything is fantastic."

"Sure, yeah, good times. But it's all been a means to an end, and it's finally paying off." Bianca puts her hands on my shoulders, and I feel an immediate flush of comfort, even in the middle of a terrible conversation. "And Argelo isn't going to be fun much longer, from the whispers I'm hearing."

She looks over her shoulder. "I have to go. You need to tell me now: do you trust me or not? Did you mean it on the Sea of Murder when you said you'd always support me?"

I hesitate just a few heartbeats more, and then toss my head, in the Argelan style. "Yes. Of course. You know I do. But you should tell me—"

Bianca's gone. I hear her dress rustle in the room outside, and then the front door clacking shut.

No way I can sleep after that conversation. I get dressed in silver threads and wander down to the place where I'm most likely to find Bianca. On the way down, I keep thinking about the three food dollars. Back at the Gymnasium, I had fallen in love with the idea of newness, and I'd let myself believe that none of our small rebellions would ever have any consequences. Bianca had convinced me the world could start all over again, untethered to the weight of everything that had happened before we were born. But now we're older, and she still can't accept that some burdens are unshakable, fused to the skin, no matter how you try to turn them into unfinished business. And I'm scared she's going to destroy us both.

The Knife is even more packed than ever with people in rainbow clothing, and they're all out of their minds on booze or something else. Two shirtless men embrace each other, one kissing the other's neck, and I look away, blushing, and when I look back, they're gone. As soon as the crowd swallows me up, I feel trapped, stiff, chafed in my armpits by the memory of police gloves. But I breathe, and let the feelings claim me for as long as they need to. I touch my bracelet, and it reminds me of running across ice, on powerful legs. I imagine the community of Gelet, the closeness that comes from navigating around sinkholes and predators together, across vast distances, without any secrets. I try not to think about the dark blood on my hand.

Bianca's sitting at a VIP table on the second floor of the Emergency Session, a nightclub that's tricked out to look like the audience chambers of the old Argelan People's Congress. Austere wood paneling, crimson carpets and wall hangings, framed pictures of men and women with wild hair, wearing stiff collars and thick-rimmed glasses. I've heard bits and pieces about the People's Congress, which was some kind of anarchist regime that governed after the collapse of the Great Argelan Prosperity Company. Bianca sees me and waves me upstairs, past the bouncer.

"Sophie! There you are. I was hoping you'd turn up. You remember Dash, don't you?" Bianca gestures at the only other person sitting in the soundproofed VIP booth: the beautiful man from that fancy ball who told me that was his house. "He was just telling me about this revival of a classic Zagreb opera that he went to recently. It sounds fascinating."

"So charming to see you again."

I stare, until I realize what makes Dash unique, besides the stunning features that I can't identify as being from any one heritage. He's not wearing any insignia to let me know which of the Nine Families he belongs to, the way everyone else in this nightclub is. He sees me looking at all the places his crest could be, and laughs.

"Nope, I'm not wearing one. I don't need to. Anybody who sees me and doesn't know which family I belong to is already in trouble." I still don't get it, so he adds: "I'm the head of the Alva Family. I'm probably the most famous person in Argelo, in all modesty."

"I'll get us drinks," Bianca says, touching my arm and giving me a wink. "Talk amongst yourselves." She hustles down the stairs, leaving me alone with Dash. I lower myself onto the couch opposite him.

"It's good to meet someone who doesn't already know who I am. I can make a first impression for once. Except that I always say the wrong thing, and I'm terrible at meeting new people, so I'm terribly afraid your first impression of me will be a dreadful one." I'm trying to read him, the way I used to read the clients at the Parlour, but Dash's posture gives me nothing. He's so handsome that it hurts to look at him.

"I'm obsessed with Xiosphanti history," Dash adds. "The founders of that city had a valid theory of human nature, but they took it too far. That's the problem with grand social ideas in general, they break if you put too much weight on them."

I realize with a jolt that he's been speaking formal Xiosphanti, even including the time (just after shutters-up), and identifying his social status (foreigner) and mine (student).

"Bianca's the most unusual person I've ever met." Dash doesn't seem to mind that he's the only one talking. "Everybody can't stop gossiping about her. But I think you might be even more unusual, in your own way. Bianca mentioned that the police tried to send you into the night, and you escaped. But you didn't, did you? Escape, I mean. You made it all the way past evening, and survived. I find that just too fascinating. You have no idea how important you are."

I back away from him, burrowing into the crack between the sofa cushions as if I could disappear.

Just then, Bianca comes back with a tray of cocktails. "What did I miss?" she says.

"I was just making an ass of myself," Dash says. "This is just what I was just saying, about being terrible with new people. Everything I say, I sound like a smarmy git."

Bianca sits next to Dash and holds hands with him. "I'm sure you were perfect, just like always." He puts his free arm around her shoulders.

"I miss Xiosphanti food," Dash says, as if that was the conversation we had been having. "There used to be a Xiosphanti restaurant here in Argelo that made that spicy oatmeal, and those odd little cakes that fall apart if you don't eat them right. It was staggeringly expensive, but so worth it."

They both raise their glasses, and after a moment's hesitation, I take mine too. This cocktail is sour, with a cloying aftertaste.

"Maybe I could cook for you," Bianca says, her face just a few centimeters away from Dash's. They look perfect together, the two most ideal faces in the world, with the most immaculate bone structures, and their children would be angels, and the cloying flavor lodges in my throat. I look away, at all the people dancing under a candelabra made of spent bullet casings, before Bianca and Dash start kissing.

Some time later, Dash has to leave to attend some meeting of the leadership of the Nine Families, to address shortages, hyperinflation, the recent interfamily tensions, and other issues. Once Bianca and I are alone, she scoots next to me and gives me her gentlest frown. "I can tell you don't like Dash, but he's a really good guy. He's the only Argelan I've met who understands all the Xiosphanti bullshit I grew up with, all the pressure they used to put on me to live up to some ideal. And he's self-aware enough to poke fun at himself."

"He does that as a tactic," I say. "I don't think we've met the real Dash."

Bianca shakes her head and pulls away from me. "You never really know anybody, in my experience. But Dash and I share the same goals, which is the most important thing for a good relationship. And he's crazy about you. I hope you'll become friends soon."

The vibrations from the floor seep up through my feet, and the stale-cocktail scent overpowers me. "I'll give him a chance. Maybe I'll understand what you see in him." She's already gathering her things. "Is he something to do with the plan you mentioned before? Is he part of whatever you're working on?"

Bianca ignores my questions and smiles, as if all I said was the part about giving Dash a chance. "I have to go. The Unifiers are having a cocktail party. Can you find your own way home? I'm so glad we had this moment together, because you and Dash are both so important to me and I want you to like each other. You'll see. He's going to make our dreams come true."

She hustles down the stairs from the VIP room, into a tangle of sweaty bodies and socialist kitsch. She waves at me from the bottom of the staircase, when I'm still standing at the top.

Ahmad is talking to me about old Khartoum at the kitchen table, while Ali sits nearby, bored because he's heard all of this before. "Everyone in Khartoum was a cyborg, and they all wore bioneural interfaces around their heads, making them smarter than a hundred regular people, and they built on a legacy of Islamic science and math that went back a thousand years. But then we came to this planet, and we were taught that our heritage was meaningless."

"Until I came to Argelo, I didn't think of ancient cultures as having meaning," I say. "Or that anybody tried to suppress them. I just thought, we're on January now, and we decided to leave the old world behind. But I should have known better."

Katrina told me her father was pretty sure he had ancestors in the Zagreb compartment, but her mother's grandparents traced five lineages between them. It's not like anybody kept careful records in the generations after landfall, so you belong to whatever your parents belonged to. Ali has grown up thinking of himself as a descendant of Khartoum, because of his father.

Ahmad asks if I know anything about my mother's Nagpuri roots. I found one single grayscale picture in one of the old books that Bianca rescued from the back of the library, and I used to stare at the image of people in CoolSuits in front of this gorgeous fusion of ancient and modern architecture: grand pointed arches and soaring crystalline vaults. I always wished I could ask my mother what her own parents had told her about our old home.

"Nagpur designed all of the interiors of the Mothership, all the living areas and all the work areas," Ahmad says. "They had the task of engineering an enclosed space that people could stand to live inside for generations, and they used a million tricks of light and shadow to defeat claustrophobia. And then the Mothership had all of the radiation leaks and the explosive decompressions, and all the tiny wars, and then there wasn't enough space for everyone after all. What happened to the Nagpur compartment was the most shameful thing."

Ahmad lowers his head, hands behind his simple linen collar, and just adds, "Everything that's wrong with us now started on the Mothership."

As he speaks, I remember the one brief mention of the Hydroponic Garden Massacre in one of Bianca's old books. The phrase almost sounded funny at the time. But now I feel the same way as when I flew off the edge of the Old Mother. Like there's no bottom to anything, and I could just fall forever. Maybe all this time, I've been lonely for people who were never even born, or a culture I never got to know.

I want to ask Ahmad for more details, but he's already waving his hands as if to say that's all he knows. Or he doesn't want to talk about unpleasant topics in front of Ali.

And then he changes the subject, abruptly. "So. Bianca's not sleeping here, and I kind of feel like she's not really sleeping much anywhere. I can only imagine. You grow up with these strict rules, and then as soon as you taste freedom, you don't know how to handle it." He glances at Ali. "That's why it's better to let the little bastards run wild, and make their mistakes young." Ali scowls, then sticks his tongue out.

I stare at the wall-hanging across from me, with a million shapes all on top of each other. Every time I look, I see a different pattern, circles or diamonds or stars, depending on my angle and how long I gaze.

"Bianca and I have been through frozen hell, and we're still together," I say. "But I keep saving her from herself. I think . . . I think she's my Anchor-Banter."

Ahmad just rolls his eyes. "Don't use words if you don't know what they mean."

At another elaborate party, Bianca kept asking what Anchor-Banter was, and everyone insisted that the only way to understand Anchor-Banter was to read these epic romances, full of duels and battles on the plains, disasters and narrow escapes, and then yell at your friends about them. And then after you got drunk and had terrifying dreams, you'd wake up understanding Anchor-Banter. But I wasn't sure how much of that was a joke.

"What's with that bracelet?" Ahmad asks, startling me out of a reverie. "You keep touching it with an odd expression on your face."

I look at the bracelet, which has an inky stain in the groove between two spikes, which I keep imagining is the blood of that Gelet. "It's a reminder that I owe a debt, and the longer I go without repaying it, the bigger it gets." The rotted metal of the harpoon scrapes my hand again, sticking out of hot vulnerable flesh, as though I'm touching it here and now. I need to get into the night, without any more desperate people shooting at me.

Something occurs to me. "Mouth told me that there are scavengers. They go into the night looking for old technology that our ancestors lost out there. Do you know how I could get in touch with some of them?"

Ahmad laughs. "Well, you do like to live dangerously. But you're in luck. Not only do I know some scavengers, one of them is an old friend of yours."

Reynold traps me in a hug and lifts me off the ground, laughing and shouting for his new friends to come and meet me. "I haven't bothered to look up the other Resourceful Couriers since I got back on my feet, but I was so happy when Ahmad said you wanted to see me." Not the reaction I expected from the man I knocked to the ground with my fist. Is he drunk or something? Yes, he's very drunk. But also sincere. "Everybody, this is Sophie," he shouts. "She helped bring me home after ten enormous pirate boats attacked us."

Reynold's friends come out of the gameroom in a three-story redbrick building, onto the front stoop that bakes under an excess of morning sun.

"I thought you were making that whole story up," says one

of the friends, who sports ferocious whiskers, wild shaggy hair, and overcrowded teeth. "Did they really have ten boats?" Everyone at this gameroom has the same excess hair, including the two women. Reynold looks different with his face enveloped.

I'm wearing my new disguise, a copy of a CoolSuit that I bought from a vendor in the Pit whose racks were half empty. The blouse hangs loose around my midriff, covered with blue fish shapes over a crimson background, and the trousers hang straight down. I put my hair up in a clasp, so I look more like the few other Nagpuri girls I've seen—and less like the best friend of Argelo's latest celebrity. Nobody even glanced at me during my walk here, except another girl in Nagpuri dress, who gave me a quick sideways smile.

Reynold leads me inside a large windowless game lounge with big metal pillars in between the couches and little tables. They don't have any food to share, because the shelves at the local grocery were pretty empty.

Reynold's boss is named Pedro, and he's missing a finger. One other guy sitting in the back is down four, plus his nose appears damaged. Frostbite. I force myself to meet Pedro's gaze as he sizes me up. I hate staring contests.

"Being a scavenger is way better than being a smuggler." Reynold hands me an assortment of angular game pieces. "Even with the cold, and the wildlife attacks. It's short-haul versus long-haul. Plus, instead of semiperishable goods that we have to keep fresh, it's ancient stuff that's been out there forever. I wish I'd been doing this all along."

I choose four pieces, and they spread out a board: Reynold, Pedro, a curvy woman named Susana, and me. They shake a tray full of colored foam, until one foam piece flutters to the ground, and Susana laughs. "Red! I'm on a streak." She rubs her hands together, then puts a piece on the board. Katrina told me that Argelans love games with complicated rules, along with intricate dances and poetry with a strict rhyme scheme and meter: they love structure in anything, except for their actual lives.

"Course, the farther into the night you go, the worse it gets. Harder to move, harder to navigate, even with sensors." Reynold puts his own piece on the board. "The wind, the darkness, the cold. If you go too far out, even the atmosphere gets denser. Plus, something about being in the night makes you go delirious, like it triggers some primitive fear from before our ancestors discovered fire back on Earth."

Susana takes Reynold's piece, and throws all the foam in the air. My move.

"But the profit," Susana says. "The profit margin, it just blows everything else away. Our ancestors had drones! They had shuttles, scoutships, survival suits. They had computers! And most of it is just sitting out there, where it got crashed by the weather, or the wildlife."

"The Gelet," I mutter, too low to hear. "The Gelet broke that stuff on purpose, to keep people away."

"One day we'll find a whole all-terrain cruiser, and I'll die fat and rich," Susana says.

"Our equipment is crap," Pedro says. "I'm just going to come out and say that right away. We have garbage protective gear that we scraped together from a dozen sources, and we only survive if we remember that we're relying on shit."

Something in Pedro's tone tells me this is a recruitment pitch, and they already want me to join.

I can't pronounce this group's name no matter how I try, but it means "Glacier Fools." Whenever Pedro takes the game pieces and fluff, I notice he's careful with his damaged hand.

Reynold's lived in every neighborhood in Argelo, including the Narrows, Khartoumtown, the Snake District, and even the bottom of the Pit. But he likes it here, in Little Merida, where the scents of *sopa de lima* and *poc-chuk* rise up from every stairwell, and embroidered wall hangings depict the shining launch bays of the Merida Space Center, where they crafted the engines and avionics of the Mothership. All the scavengers live upstairs from this gameroom.

After I lose a few more games without ever understanding all the rules, Pedro formally invites me to join their next expedition. I toss my head. Everyone warns me again: this is deadly work, with a high death rate, and I'll probably die. I give another head-toss. Then Pedro hands me a little metal rectangle that'll display an odd shape when they need me.

Reynold walks me outside. Back on the stoop, under the merciless glare, I touch his arm. "Uh. How much do you remember about what happened, after the pirates attacked?"

He rolls his head. "I was pissing blood, from all over my body. Next thing I know, I'm in Argelo, where they have this miraculous wound care." He pauses. "I feel like we went into the night for a moment."

This is going to be harder than I thought, but I have to find a way to talk about this, or I'm done. I look him in the eyes. "I can communicate with the, uh . . . the crocodiles.

They're my . . . friends. I call them the Gelet. They're intelligent and technological, and they want to be friends with everyone. I might be able to teach the rest of you how to talk to them, maybe. But either way, they won't bother you as long as I'm there. The most important thing is, if you see one of them, don't start shooting."

"Honestly," he said. "If we run into a crocodile, we usually just run the other way. If we even see it in time. But I'll tell the others. I mean, if we could have the crocodiles on our side, or even if they just leave us alone, that would make our job twice as easy. Uh . . . so how do you talk to them, anyway?"

I explain three times, squeezing my own thumbs inside my fingers. The whole thing sounds weird when I say it aloud.

Reynold's eyes get wider and he sucks in breath. "Whoa. I don't think I'm drunk enough to even contemplate doing that. I have a feeling that's going to be a hard no, for most of us. But I'll tell the others about this. And for sure, we won't attack any crocodiles if they approach." Then he goes back inside to play another confusing game.

I carry on conversations with Bianca in my head all the time: as I cut across town along the tiny lanes that avoid the traffic around the Knife, as I watch pickpockets work their way through the crowds, as I see the slow corrosion in the girders supporting the big covered walkway. I talk to my imaginary Bianca about impermanence, and how the lack of Timefulness here only makes everything appear more temporary. Like, without small units of time, I'm more aware of the big units of time, the city inhaling the sun-spiked air and exhaling decay. The only thing that never disappears is the past.

This is the sort of conversation that Bianca and I never have anymore, except in my mind. Back in school, we used to talk about everything from big ideas to stupid peeves, but we never discussed our relationship. Now, everything's backward: we profess our undying sisterhood, but we never talk. I find myself going to the dark café, with Abraham's donuts, just to eavesdrop in the starchy, smoky air as the students bicker about the meaning of existence. Sometimes one of the girls who seems about my age looks at me and smiles. Sometimes I even smile back, and feel a different shyness from my normal kind.

Dash and Bianca are both waiting for me when I arrive at the vegetarian restaurant, where the walls and ceiling are made of some kind of artificial diamond that refracts into endless swirls of color. Bianca is leaning toward Dash, lips parted and nostrils flared.

Dash and Bianca have seen a lot of each other since the last time I saw either of them. They ran into each other at an art gallery opening, and then Dash took Bianca to a fondue place, and they went shopping, and toured all the most memorable buildings. The architecture isn't as stunning as Xiosphant's, but there was a revival of Zagreb-style vaulted ceilings and wide towers, and some very fine glasswork and wrought iron, during the era of the Great Argelan Prosperity Company.

"You should have seen it." Bianca looks at Dash the way she used to look at Matthew in the Progressive Students. Except that she also has an involuntary twitch in her left eye, and some redness, from lack of sleep.

I realize that I've never seen any of the things Bianca's wearing, and they don't look like they came from a secondhand store or from the seamstress Katrina sent us to for that ball. The sleeve of her white dress hangs in a shimmering line, and her crystal necklace picks up all the colors coming off the walls. She couldn't have afforded these things with the marks we got from the Couriers—and then I understand what she means when she says she and Dash went shopping: he bought her a new wardrobe. She looks more than ever like one of the pictures of Xiosphanti aristocrats in the silly storybooks that everyone here in Argelo loves.

Dash says, "I grew up famous, and I have a million issues. I should probably try that exhaustion therapy that everyone's talking about. But you two, you're in the spotlight for the first time, aren't you? You can so easily get a kind of false self-image."

One of Dash's favorite tactics is to confess how vulnerable or insecure he is, so everyone else lets their guard down.

"Except"—Bianca helps herself to some kind of lentil paste on flatbread—"Sophie doesn't care what anybody thinks of her. That's one reason she's such a hero." I squirm, but only on the inside. On the outside, I try to look bored.

"Is that true?" Dash leans toward me. "Sophie, do you really not care about anybody's opinion of you? I'm so jealous I'm practically dying."

I just stare at him and fashion my lips into a smile. I try to imagine that I'm standing on the tundra, a hundred kilometers from the nearest light source.

Bianca asked if I trusted her, and I said yes, and I meant it. This thing with Dash is just part of whatever she's planning, and she's in control of the whole situation. I look at the taut line of her pale neck and exposed back, as she leans toward Dash, and I choose to see a harpoon gun, aimed and cocked.

I lie in the storage room, knees to face, half dreaming of all the usual terrors, but half thinking about Bianca and Dash. He's still the most beautiful man I've ever seen, but he's also charming, which is something different. And his charm doesn't work on me, which bothers him. Why does he care what I think? I figure none of this out, but I fall into a short dream in which I'm on the Old Mother and the Xiosphanti police are shooting a Gelet, so its blood sprays onto me.

The signal device wakes me up, with a funny little squiggle. Time to go back to the game lounge and put on some inadequate safety gear with the Glacier Fools.

When I reach the front steps of the gameroom, Mouth is standing out front, cradling a helmet in her hands. She keeps looking downward, with wide-open eyes. "Reynold told me what you were doing, and I asked if I could come along. I still owe you my life."

I toss my head and walk inside.

In the gameroom, Reynold hands me my own survival suit. "You saw Mouth, right?" I toss my head again, then concentrate on arranging these straps and buckles the right way. This looks like a child's drawing of a spacesuit, huge and bulky, with a million pieces that don't quite fit together. Strap bricks to every inch of my body, and I'd move more easily.

Once we're suited up except for helmets, Pedro calls the six of us together, including Susana, Reynold, Mouth, and a laughing blue-eyed girl named Laura. "I cannot emphasize this enough for the newcomers," Pedro said. "Visibility is shit out there. Watch the readouts. Keep track of the person to your immediate right, so you don't lose the group." He talks about the cumbersome procedures, once we find some ancient tech, for freeing it from the ice without causing further damage.

"So, you guys remember what I said before," Reynold says, "about Sophie and the crocodiles."

"We were all pretty drunk," Susana says.

Pedro shushes them and turns to me. "I want to hear this from the source. Reynold says you have some technique for communicating with one of the deadliest predators in the night, and even getting them to help you. And you can teach the rest of us?"

"I was there when she did it," Mouth says. "Couldn't believe how amazing."

"What part of 'I want to hear this from Sophie' did you not understand?" Pedro grunts.

I have that buzzing-under-the-skin feeling that hits whenever I have to talk to strangers, or to a whole group of people at once. But I make myself overcome it, because if this works, if these people can learn to understand the Gelet, then maybe this could be the beginning of other people forming relationships with them, even trading and sharing technology. People will understand that they're friendly, and advanced, and stop trying to eat them all the time. So I talk the Glacier Fools through it, taking time to make sure everything sinks in.

"They'll shield you from the cold," I say. "You won't freeze.

Just expose your face and throat to the little tongues. You'll see their memories, except not with your eyes."

The others, even Reynold, are making remarks and nudging each other. But Pedro glares until they shut up. "We'll follow your lead," Pedro says. "If this works, it could be huge for us."

When I step away from the group, Mouth follows, walking heavily in her suit. "The secret that you've shared," she says, "it's the most precious thing in the world. And you're just opening it to us. I thought everyone was selfish. I thought, that's the world we live in. But then you go and offer this to us. I can't tell you what it means."

"If you try to tell me I'm a saint again," I whisper, "I'm going to bite your face."

Mouth backs away a little, gloved hands raised. "I won't. I know you're just a person. That's what makes this so extraordinary. I know you don't want to see me, but I need to thank you anyway. I keep thinking I've lost all my faith, and then I lose some faith that I forgot I still had. So, thank you."

I turn away and go back to Reynold, who's fastening the last of his suit.

"I hope you don't mind that I told Mouth about your plan to join our crew," he says. "I still can't get past that shitty stunt she pulled the last time we were in Xiosphant. And yet, she's one of the best people to have around in a bloody situation."

I realize I don't hate Mouth anymore. I want to keep hating her, but the hatred just won't come, as though I've used it all up. I look at her struggling to tie the boots on her environment suit with her gloves already on, sweat gleaming on the shaved sides of her scarred head.

The Glacier Fools use a very particular route from their game salon to the edge of night, to minimize the chance someone will see this valuable protective gear just walking around and try to rob us. We weave and jag, go down into disused rail tunnels, and squeeze our bulky bodies through narrow spaces between buildings.

At last the city fades out. I put on my helmet, and I might as well be in space.

The helmet has a visor with a tiny strip of reinforced plastic, so I can see the void outside. There's also a "night vision" display, which shows just lumps of topography; every now and then, a fuzzy shape glows orange or yellow at the edge of my range. The third display has a handful of dots, representing the other Glacier Fools' transponders, plus a little blip at the bottom, which shows that daylight is behind us. My bracelet wakes up.

My own body sounds so loud inside this suit, and I think of my mother saying, *You are an orchestra.*

Once we're walking into the night, the scavengers start talking like kids on a sugar high.

"Did you ever try that kebab place over by the Spoon?"

"It was okay. The kebabs were about half swamp turtle. And nobody calls that neighborhood the Spoon. Just because we have the Knife doesn't mean we also need a neighborhood called the Spoon."

"It makes sense, though. It's actually shaped like a spoon."

"You know what I've been missing lately? Those stuffed mushrooms they used to sell halfway down the Pit. Those were nice."

Every step chills and weakens me, until I'm half dead. The

insulation on these suits is worn thin, patched with tape. I can barely move, and I hear nothing over my own deafening breathing, and my fingers go numb. I've never gone this far into the night, and the night vision just swims. The blobs indicating the other scavengers turn blurry and faint. I could walk off a cliff right now. A snowdrift could fall and crush me to death. I feel my heart drumming, and try to slow my breathing, counting the way I did at the Illyrian Parlour.

Pedro says something about promising readings eighty meters ahead, but a scream tears through the intercom. Then stops. No way to tell who screamed, from which direction, or what happened.

"Laura, was that you?" Pedro says.

"I'm here. I think that was Susana."

"Susana? You there?"

One of the dots on the screen showing our crewmates is fading. No, it's gone.

"Shit. I think it was a bison," Reynold says. "Not that I saw anything, of course. But they come out of nowhere like that."

"It could have been a sinkhole," Mouth volunteers.

"No point standing here, arguing about cause of death, unless we want to be next," Pedro says. "Fucking hell. Susana."

We keep going. My bracelet vibrates so hard I feel like it's yanking my wrist. Stumbling and sweeping my legs, I make my frozen body move in that direction.

"Uh, Sophie. Please stay with the group. I see your transponder, you're going the wrong—"

I ignore Pedro and keep kicking forward. Each step costs twice as much as the last.

My flickering night vision fills with a huge shape, straight ahead. I stop and look up at the rounded body in motion. I look for a pincer, or writhing tentacles. Instead, my screen slowly paints a picture of a bison's open maw, sharp threads pulled taut, ready to slice me into chunks. The mouth grows so big I can't see anything else. Everyone calls my name, but I just freeze.

Nothing happens. And then I realize the bison isn't moving. An eyeblink later, it's gone from my night vision, like something just tore it to pieces.

But, wait—my night vision hasn't gone empty. Tentacles move in the darkness. A pincer snaps open right next to me.

"Damn," Reynold growls. "That is an awful lot of giant, tentacled killer monsters. Trying to remember why this was a good idea."

"They're surrounding us." Laura sounds ready to lose her stomach.

The Gelet make us tiny by comparison, raised on their hind legs. They could embrace each other over our heads, and make a tent for us to cower inside. I feel fear radiate off everyone else. They make little squirming, whimpering noises over the intercom.

I breathe slow, stay in the moment.

Then I realize one of these Gelet is holding something in its front legs: one of those mossy blankets. I move inside, and she and I are wrapped in a cocoon together. Still, the moment I loosen the neck strap on my suit, I feel the wind trying to cut my throat. I show my exposed skin, to prove we're here to listen.

"We went over this." Pedro tries to restore calm. "Everybody, follow Sophie's lead. Let them wrap you up. Show them your throats. That's a fucking order."

I hear them breathing and grumbling as they each get right inside a Gelet's kill radius and unsnap their protective gear. They let in the cold, and brace themselves to let in something else. They can't hear my reassurance over their own moaning.

"I can't." Reynold sounds like he's fumbling with his harpoon gun. "I can't, this is—"

"Trust," I say as loud as my weak voice can go. "I've done this a thousand times."

Then I hear all of them breathing heavier as the other Gelet make contact. I sigh, because they've done it, it's happening. Now they'll understand for themselves. I don't have to be the only one to carry this anymore.

The Gelet inside my "cocoon" comes closer, so I feel the warmth of its tendrils. They touch my face, just for a moment, and—

—I'm with all the Gelet in their city, long before humans first arrived. We had technology that shaped the rivers of water and fire, deep beneath the mantle, and ways to reshape living flesh, and we shared these techniques with everyone. We had music, and poetry, and the belief that you could own history but not the future. We had complicated mating dances, a dozen Gelet at a time joining together at the heart of a mountain, carapaces opening to let fleshy appendages come out and mingle together. Some looked like blades, others like fingers, or strange flowers. All the Gelet tremble in ecstasy, and here and now, I shake with them, as the essence pours out of us all, and into all of us—

—I experience all of this in an eyeblink, and then I pull away, because something's wrong. Loud noises blow out my intercom's speaker. Screams, wails, and curses. And then the crack-neck sound of a harpoon gun discharging.

mouth

When the crocodile opened its jagged maw and Mouth went inside, she saw nothing but darkness, more absolute than night, without even gradations of shadow. Mouth fell with no gravity, no direction, no childhood or old age. Like delirium, but emptier. But then the dark opened, and Mouth found the reason behind it. The crocodiles had other ways of "seeing," and Mouth let go enough to see without eyes.

A great city, shaped like a rose or some fungal bloom, stretched under the ice and extended downward, heated by a geyser and powered by lava. Mouth glimpsed walnut-shaped bodies on walkways, in cubby holes and hammocks. And in deep buried chambers, where they studied the movements of the oceans under the ice, the swirl of the atmosphere. Mouth glimpsed celebrations, rescue missions. Ancient crocodiles built some huge structure—or grew a living creature—to stop a glacier. Around the steam jets at the city's edge, the crocodiles danced.

Ancient memories sluiced into Mouth's brain, cutting across all of her own thoughts and pulling down every structure she'd built to sequester the worst parts of herself. Delirium would have been welcome, compared to this. Mouth struggled to pull away, but the claw held her fast. The crocodile thoughts crowded out her own memories, like she could forget being human all at once. Digging through ice with big forelegs, sifting through snow with tentacles. Mouth felt all her defenses shattering.

Just before Mouth got enough leverage to shove the crocodile away, there was a glimpse of something else. She ran with a group of crocodiles, on a hazardous journey into a scalding vent, to place fleshy seeds, horned with sprouts, in the middle of a volcano. Time passed, and the seeds became wildflowers, spreading their thick petals in the lava, with knotted roots that went deep inside the mantle of January, crossing vast distances. The volcanoes went inactive, or erupted, but the mesh of roots held strong. Mouth felt all the hope, the careful treatment of these blooms, for generations . . . until the flowers were gone. The root system withered. After that, Mouth felt nothing but fear, and a sense of corruption and death.

Somehow, amid all this, there was a message: *Something beautiful died. Everyone will suffer.*

Then Mouth felt the night air again, the paralyzing cold, and fumbled to get her protective garments back in place. Noises came from all around her, too many to separate or understand at first.

"What the fuck—" Reynold sounded undone. "What did I just see?"

"Seeds, far under the ground." Laura was retching. "Giant seeds. Hundreds of squirming shapes."

"I saw death," Pedro said. "I saw nothing . . . but death. My god."

Mouth wanted to speak, help get the situation back together, but she couldn't breathe. She couldn't get back to being Mouth. Part of her was still trying to see without sight, to feel the frozen air with tentacles she didn't have.

"What did you do," Reynold's voice rose.

"Walls of death coming down—"

"What did you do to me?"

"Seeds, goddamn ugly seeds, squirming."

"What did you do?"

Mouth had come into this as nobody, and now these alien memories had surged into all her hollow spaces. Her stomach churned. Strange thoughts that weren't thoughts, visions of life in permanent darkness, a rose-shaped ice city. Mouth was weeping and retching, but she realized the others were much worse. She needed to get a handle on herself.

Reynold shouted, "Keep away—" Then, the bark of a harpoon gun firing.

Mouth got her eyes back and pulled herself back together in time to see one crocodile on her back, a harpoon jutting from her side. The crocodile that had just opened its claw to Mouth was prone on the ice but unharmed, until someone (Pedro?) fell on it screaming. A blur of flailing arms and tentacles, and then Mouth heard nothing but alarms. One of them was the Critical Suit Breach klaxon, which meant someone was about to freeze to death. The others Mouth couldn't recognize, except that all the alarms stopped about the same time the other nearby suits stopped registering living occupants.

Mouth ran back toward Argelo. Stumbling and sliding, collecting bruises on both knees. Every footstep was a battle against the deep snowdrifts and thick ice, but terror kept goading her forward. The suit's readouts were useless, except one: the tiny notch that showed where to find light and warmth again.

When Mouth reached the first glimmers on the skyline, and pulled off the thick headgear, Argelo had vanished.

She sank to her knees, holding on to the ground with both hands, and watched her helmet roll away. The city was just gone. Mouth had another moment of trying to use alien senses she didn't have, as if Argelo were somehow hidden from human awareness. She kept hearing the final screams of the Glacier Fools, but also remembering the image of ruined blooms inside a volcano.

Mouth stumbled in circles, staring at cracks in the dry soil and the thin line of bright orange off in the distance. She tried to listen to the road, but she couldn't make sense of anything. At last she stumbled across some broken-down shacks on the outskirts of Argelo, and realized: she'd come out of the night too far south. As she walked toward density and saw people carrying food or building materials, the world came back to her. But she still felt half present.

She wished she could believe the crocodiles were monsters, and that was why their touch had poisoned her mind. She was pretty sure it was the opposite: she was too void of goodness to share their thoughts. The memory of the dead flowers in the volcano confirmed this to be true.

*

Sophie sat, hunched over, on the steps of Mouth's apartment building. She was covered with dirt and frost burns, and looked like she'd finally lost one thing too many. She straightened when Mouth approached, but didn't stand. Mouth braced herself, because if Sophie hated her before, just imagine now. They were both still wearing their suits, without helmets.

"I didn't know where else to go." Sophie's voice was too quiet, after the howling of the night. "I figured if anybody else came home alive, it would be you." She looked down at the cracked stair. "This was my fault. I made another mistake. I thought I could help you and the others through it, and that this would be the beginning of something."

They sat without talking for a while. Like their brains were so overstuffed with horror they had no space left to put words together.

Mouth felt faint. All this light hurt, after going without, and the alien sensations blared in her mind. "You had never even tried sharing this thing with anyone. There was literally no way you could know what would happen until you tried. We were the ones who let fear control us." She had to close her eyes and bend over. "I need to get indoors. You should come up with me. We'll give you crisps, and some meatloaf that this weird old guy gave me. Nothing like the gourmet dishes you've been eating lately, but still good."

When Mouth squinted her eyes open, Sophie was staring, like she couldn't decide if this was another trap.

"Remember how I said Alyssa would like to see you?" Mouth said. "She keeps asking after you. She misses you."

Sophie hesitated a moment longer, then bobbed her head.

Upstairs, Alyssa took one look at the two of them, and barked a string of Argelan curses. She didn't need her cane much anymore, but she leaned on it as she gathered coffee and dark water and greasy fried things. Sophie fell into the big rattan chair, where Martindale had sat. Mouth slouched opposite.

Sophie's face had always shown her feelings, thanks to her wide hazel eyes and the way her cheeks dimpled whenever she smiled. But now she had just shut down. She wasn't even scowling, like when she'd followed Mouth around back in Xiosphant. She just stared ahead, with her mouth slightly open.

Some time passed, maybe a lot of time, before Mouth could get words out again.

"I'm out there in total nothing, feeling the shadows creep over me, and then this creature is showing me a million things at once. Felt like I was falling into that canyon at the end of the world. My mind keeps vomiting up crocodile memories." Mouth let the steam from the coffee burn her sore eyes. "I don't know how you handle it."

"I don't know. Maybe I just let it overwhelm me. The first time it happened, I was desperate to leave my own body."

Mouth didn't know what to say to make this any better. Mouth had been hoping for some kind of Answer, the kind of truth she couldn't get from Barney, or from the Invention. But it was worse for Sophie—she'd strung way too many hopes onto this one thing, and they'd all broken at once.

This was just too much death at once, without a clean way to mourn.

Alyssa was still piecing together what had happened, and her stream of Argelan curses and sayings still hadn't slowed down.

Sophie looked up at her. "What did you say? That last thing. What was that?"

"Oh," Alyssa said. "I was saying, it's like Mouth is your jinx."

"Wow, thanks," Mouth said. "I already feel bad enough."

This distracted Sophie, so she stopped torturing herself for a moment. "I've been trying to understand that phrase ever since I got here. I thought maybe it meant a troubled friendship, or a love that can't ever become real."

Sophie pronounced "jinx" all wrong, like "*an-kur-ban-tir.*"

Alyssa laughed, scaring Sophie and Mouth, who were both still in shock. "No, not exactly." She explained slowly, in Xiosphanti: "This word just means bad luck. I'm oversimplifying. But your jinx is the person who always shows up and ruins everything for you, just by being there. You can't get rid of them, whatever you do. Like your fate is intertwined with theirs, and you can't escape until you figure out why you're connected. Or if you can learn to live with your jinx, then sometimes the two of you can cooperate to wreck things for everyone else."

"It's more sentimental Argelan shit." Mouth barely had enough energy to be insulted. "And that's not really what it means. It can be a good thing, if you make peace with it."

"That's what I just said," Alyssa said. "Everybody has their own explanation. But mine is the right one. Your jinx could be someone you hate, or a friend, or even a stranger. But you can't ignore them, whoever they are."

Even though Alyssa had just accused Mouth of being an indelible curse on Sophie's life, all this chatter somehow restored a feeling of normality. Like, they were alive and life had continuity, and they were at home, with oily food and bad drinks. You don't come back from the night and start dancing and cracking jokes—let alone a trip where you touched an unthinkable consciousness, and everyone else died. Mouth kept almost shaking and gasping, but she tried to control her tremors, because Sophie needed comfort more.

Sophie kept quiet, except that a few times she blurted out that she had no place to go. She couldn't even stand to be with herself. She couldn't face Ahmad, or Bianca. And she was worried about having to make nice with Dash, who was sort of Bianca's boyfriend now.

"You're staying here," Alyssa said, not like an invitation, but an order. "We never even use that bed, because we're so used to sleeping in a confined space. If Mouth bothers you, I'll kick her out."

Mouth felt weird having Sophie crash in their tiny apartment. She was sure Sophie would never forgive her for almost getting Bianca killed back in Xiosphant, and, probably, Mouth didn't deserve forgiveness. Sophie also seemed to hesitate about staying under their roof after, well, everything. But then Alyssa told her, "Trust me. If Mouth is your jinx, you ought to get used to her garbage. Or if she isn't, then no harm done. Right?"

Alyssa wouldn't hear any more argument, and started wrapping the bed for Sophie, Argelan style.

When Alyssa was out of earshot, Sophie leaned over and said to Mouth: "This idea that you're my 'jinx.' I guess Alyssa is really eager to find a reason why nothing is your fault."

Mouth cringed. "I'm sure you're right. At the same time, though, she also truly does believe in this stuff."

"Alyssa still trusts you. You'd better not ever betray her." Sophie's tone was somewhere between a threat and friendly advice.

That feeling Mouth had gotten when that crocodile first touched her, of toppling into formless shadow, came back for a moment, along with the old familiar pain in that tight spot right behind her brow.

But Mouth just said, "I won't." She couldn't help thinking about the worst part of the crocodile's memories. "I have to ask you something. When the crocodiles—I mean the Gelet— spoke to you before . . . I know it's not speaking, not really, but when they put things in your head . . . Did they show you something about flowers inside a volcano?"

Sophie thought for a moment. "Flowers, no. They did show me how they used lava, deep underground, for power. And they had some huge projects where they created living organisms, deep underground, to try and control the climate. But it went wrong. A lot of their children died from toxic rainfall."

They sat for a long time. Alyssa was in the raised washroom, filling a basin with hot water for Sophie. And for Mouth, who felt less and less like a person who deserved kindness.

"I think I'm having a spiritual crisis," Mouth told Barney, who was basting a large sheep carcass with a two-handed brush and something that looked like tree sap.

"Well, damn," Barney said. "You've been trying to have a

spiritual crisis ever since you came to town. I'm glad you finally succeeded."

"That's not fair," Mouth said.

Mouth had stopped asking Barney about the Citizens, because she couldn't think of any new questions or summon the energy to keep asking the old ones. Mouth just wanted to watch Barney at work, to try to see the saint in him. Maybe the way he seemed to remember all his regulars, and asked them solicitous questions. Or the way he hovered nearby while two young mothers sat, half awake, next to three babbling, kicking toddlers. Barney stood, innocuous as furniture, in case these women needed anything or the children broke something. Mouth watched Barney tend to his three small tables and felt a longing so powerful it choked off some of the flow of blood to her head.

"I know you think I ought to have something to tell you," Barney said, in midstroke of his brush. "That I owe you something, because I walked away before the end."

Mouth didn't react, except to unknot her hands a bit. She didn't know what she wanted anymore.

"I don't know why they didn't give you a name." Barney turned the sheep on its axis. "I think maybe you just weren't impulsive enough for them. They wanted people who would act without stopping to think, to follow their hearts instead of their heads. Sometimes on the road you have to react quickly. But they also didn't want you to think when you ought to be feeling. I don't know if that makes sense."

"I remember them saying that," Mouth said. "I've tried to stop overthinking things ever since."

Barney left the sheep dangling from the ceiling in his small kitchen area and came to sit down next to Mouth. He kneaded his dishtowel into the shape of a thorn and placed it on the table between them.

"Part of me was relieved when you told me how the Citizens ended." Barney winced. "All of their teachings were about standing between these two extremes, and then coming out stronger and with more clarity. When the Citizens never came back to Argelo, and I realized something must have happened, I thought maybe they'd finally given in to the delirium. And I was glad they all just died instead. I know that sounds awful."

Mouth nodded. "They didn't betray the teachings." Then she decided to ask the most important thing. "The crocodiles. They showed me a . . . an experience. A vision. I don't know. They had some kind of flower that they were growing in the lava vents, that opened in the heart of the mountain. And I have this vague memory of seeing those flowers when I was little."

"I don't know anything about that," Barney said. "We went to Mount Abacus all the time. It was one of our sacred places. I usually stayed below and cooked for everybody."

"You don't know anything about it at all?"

"I don't know anything about anything," Barney said. "You want to know what I've learned? That I don't know anything. Time passes, even when you can't see it, and people keep grudges too long and die too soon. I'm just an old fart who makes sheep into meatloaf."

After that, Barney wouldn't answer any more questions, and kept insisting that Mouth should take off for a while because she was scaring away customers. "You stay here any longer, I'm going to make you wash dishes." Mouth's legs had gone numb from sitting too long, but she beat some life back into them.

Sophie stayed at Alyssa and Mouth's place long enough to become a fixture on their bed, sprawled out, sometimes awake, sometimes asleep, and not moving except to eat or wash. Then she was gone, all at once. Alyssa and Mouth were still left with the problem of organizing some kind of memorial for Reynold. Nobody could reach Yulya or Kendrick, not even Ahmad. And Reynold didn't seem to have any other family or friends left in Argelo. So in the end, they held a tiny wake with just Ahmad, Katrina, and Sophie, where everyone except Ahmad swigged from the same flask of swamp vodka.

Afterward, Alyssa and Mouth wandered alone, under a weird-looking sky. The perpetual cloud cover had gotten a shade darker, and instead of the usual even sheets of off-white the clouds had started folding in on themselves. In the middle of the vortex, Mouth thought she saw a pair of beetle eyes, fixed on her personally. Mouth shuddered. "Something's wrong."

"Yeah, that's what I love about Argelo," Alyssa said without looking around. "Something's always wrong. That's what gives the city its special pungency." She pulled the collar of her jacket up around her head and hunched over, in the classic stay-away posture of a hardened Argelan.

They kept walking until they ended up in the Snake District. The light bounced off all the stucco walls and packed-mud rooftops and gave Mouth a kernel of pain behind the center of her forehead. The heat made everything smell rotten. But Alyssa was in a mood after the wake, and she had steered them toward the neighborhood where she'd grown up, more or less on purpose.

"You're not the only one who's reconnected with their heritage lately." Alyssa gazed at a lane between two tall buildings, so narrow you couldn't walk with arms outstretched. Weeds had come up through the cracks between flagstones, mostly those claw-leafed stalks that covered the rocks out past the Southern Wastes. Native to this planet, unlike a lot of the other greencry that ran wild around here.

"I never thought about Argelo much, except as a place to drop off stuff and pick up other stuff, and maybe spend some of our pay on swamp vodka and blue-jean dancers," Alyssa said. "It's only now that I've been stuck here that I'm realizing just how much of Argelo is inside me."

They were walking through the places Alyssa played when she was little, the places her mother and uncles all worked. She kept pointing out where the Chancers, her old crew, had stolen something or tricked somebody. "One time Natalie didn't look in the right place for the insignia and she accidentally robbed a guy with the Unifier crest. We had to stay underground for what felt like our whole lives. Oooh, there's my favorite building that we were paid to set on fire. Don't worry, nobody was inside at the time. You can still see the scorchmarks. Beautiful stripe shapes."

Some of the Chancers had gone south and settled in some dirt-pit, making booze to sell in the city. "I guess I wasn't prepared for nostalgia to kick me in the face the way it did. I guess that's why I wanted to go back into the old gangster life."

Alyssa needed to hear something, but Mouth was coming up empty. Mouth used to know how to respond to things, she had a whole catalog, but now even situations that ought to be familiar left her fumbling in her mind.

Mouth kept picturing snow washing over the faces of the corpses in the night, Reynold and the others, covering them but also distorting their features as they turned solid. The cold and sensory deprivation of full night had torn away some of Mouth's armor, and then something about experiencing life in an utterly different physical shape, and feeling all the foreign emotions, had poked decent-sized holes in her sense of self. But most of all, the image of delicate blossoms in the heart of a mountain felt like a message from death itself.

Mouth said, "Sometimes I wish I had died at the same time as the other nomads. I don't know why I deserved to survive."

"Oh, daylight and ashes. Who cares why you survived? It's probably because you're so annoying that even death couldn't stand to put up with you," Alyssa said.

"I think me surviving was the worst thing that could have happened, because I've only kept a cruel mockery of the Citizens alive in my head."

By now they had gotten back toward the nicer part of the town, where you could hear drums and laughter, and smell the scent of fish pies still crisp from the oven. Plus someone frying stale bread, an Argelan custom, meant to commemorate some citywide moment of confession and reconciliation, a long time ago, that nobody could agree on the details of now.

"I really hoped getting you in touch with that professor would help you to figure out your past, and then you would come back to me," Alyssa said. "But I feel like I'm having to watch my own back, with a bullet wound still healing in my side."

The dead flowers in the core of the mountain seemed different each time Mouth remembered, but she always thought of sickness, corruption, in the heart of the Citizens' holiest place. An enemy of life.

"This is not the Mouth I chose as my sleepmate and road buddy. Remember when we met? You stood out from the rest of the Resourceful Couriers like a daisy in a field of shit. Afraid of nothing, foul-mouthed, full of contempt for everyone's rules. You punched more people than you spoke to. You lied to more people than you let touch you. That's the Mouth I want back."

Mouth tried to take Alyssa's words inside her, as if they were blueprints for something Mouth could build from scraps. "I'll see what I can do," she said.

They kept walking down the winding streets, ducking out of the way of hand-carts and a couple of small lorries. They argued about music and games and whether they were better combined, while Mouth tried to avoid looking up. Until a man fell dead at their feet.

The women who had shot him ran away, guns raised. Mouth was going to shrug this off, but Alyssa spotted the four-winged horse on the man's lapel and said, "We have to kill those ladies." But as soon as they had brought down the two shooters, who wore the Brilliant crest on their jackets, gunshots came from a second-story window. The bullets tore into the two Brilliant corpses as Mouth and Alyssa hunched behind a trash cart. At last Alyssa tagged the second-story shooter and he fell next to the first dead man with the Perfectionist badge.

Mouth's pager lit up at the same time as Alyssa's. Mouth fumbled in one of her pockets for the four-winged-horse badge, which she hardly bothered to wear.

They headed for the Perfectionist HQ. When they were a block away, the sky changed again, and Mouth felt something splash on her face. A droplet of liquid fire. Her skin sizzled, with a sensation like a scalpel cut. Another drop fell, then another, and before Mouth and Alyssa could finish remarking on the first rainfall in ages, this caustic liquid was descending in a constant barrage. People ran for shelter, chemical burns on their faces and hands.

Inside the Perfectionist building, with its dark-stained wood walls and nightclub decor, someone was explaining that this toxic rain had happened a couple other times lately. Scientists said a whole ocean of magma flowed across part of the day, bothering nobody—until recently, when the temperature had increased slightly. Some of the magma had evaporated, and seeded the atmosphere with alkali deposits. The beauty of nature.

Sasha was handing out rifles from a crate. "You took your sweet time getting here."

"What are we even fighting about?" Mouth asked.

Sasha looked at Mouth with a mixture of pity and revulsion. Alyssa kicked Mouth's ankle.

"Blame those assholes, the Superbosses. They made us look weak. And then we had to make a deal with the Alva Family to stay afloat. The peace in Argelo was all about people owing each other favors, an ecosystem. But it was always fragile, and everybody got something. The Jamersons are killing the Absolutists, and the Unifiers are slaughtering the Mandrakes."

At first, Mouth didn't recognize the emotion on the faces of all the Perfectionists: relief. Everyone was relieved to be fighting at last. No more making nice, they could finally kill (almost) everyone who ever got on their nerves.

The rain was too dense to see through. The pavement smoked.

"Fuck the Unifiers!" A woman shoved a burly man onto the pavement, not caring that the rain spattered her face. The man pulled a machete and swung it at the woman, with skinless hands. She splashed his face with rainwater using her bare hands, then sucker-punched him.

Across the street, two men ran past. They held a sheet of metal over their own heads, which would fall unless they both held it up. They kept slashing at each other with knives in their free hands.

Alyssa was talking to one woman in the corner of the space, who had fresh rain burns on her cheek and a gun clutched in both hands. Her name was Janice, and she was an economist who had gone to Perfectionist schools and now lived in Perfectionist housing in the nice part of the dusk, where all her neighbors were Perfectionists too. She spent most of her time trying to solve the problem of hyperinflation when she wasn't trying to kill everyone in sight. "I need to get back out there," she snarled, "I don't need rest, I need justice. I'll rest after justice is done."

"Mouth. Got a job for you." Sasha came over, rifle under one arm. "We need to take over the central food depository. People ought to see we're protecting the food supply, so they'll respect our authority. Plus everyone will need to kiss our asses unless they want to starve. Only trouble is, these dickfaces with bolo guns are guarding it. And we can't risk damaging the food."

"Shouldn't we just wait until the rain stops?" Mouth already knew that was the wrong thing to say.

"Who says the rain is going to stop?" Sasha said.

Mouth was about to argue further, but Alyssa grabbed her arm with both hands and pulled her aside. "We promised to fight for these people. We owe them." She stared at Mouth with a quirk in her left eye. "This is what I keep telling you. I need you to be here for me now, not stuck in the past with dead people who never even cared about you."

Mouth took a rifle from Sasha, then turned back to Alyssa. "I'll see you soon," she said. "I ought to honor my promises, or nobody will put up with me, right?" Alyssa smiled and tossed her head, then wished Mouth luck.

Afterward, Mouth didn't like to think about what came next. You wrap yourself in layers of padding and packing tape, like a parcel, and run through the burning rain as if you could dodge the droplets. Each step kicks up sprays that make you gag. Everything looks gray, almost translucent, and it reminds you of the night vision and its smudgy view of a bloodbath. At last you reach the depository, where the guards sit on the floor and lean against the wall, staring out the window, and you throw a rain-soaked axe into the face of the first one to stand up. The next guard shoots and misses, then shreds your protective layers with a knife. You fall outside, where he headbutts you into a hot puddle. And so on.

Then your only orders are to hold the depository, so you sit with your fellow Perfectionists, plus the people you just killed. Nobody is going to relieve you until the rain stops, and the rain goes on so long you witness the dead bodies decomposing in real time, until someone has enough and flings them outside. The rainfall speeds the process of breaking them down, but it still seems to take forever. At least you're in a food warehouse, so there's plenty to eat.

SOPHIE

A flash illuminates the raindrops outside, turning them into slivers of tinted glass strung between statues caught in distorted poses.

I've memorized every tile on the wall of this Khartoum restaurant, and seen every loop of the fancy wall projections that are supposed to simulate a virtual *souq*. We've almost exhausted their stores of *kisra, aseedaa,* and *kajaik,* and Bianca keeps threatening to make a break for it using a drink tray as a rain-shield. Even with the fancy screens that filter the light into gentle waves, I still have a clear view of the street outside, where a group of men and women slash each other with long blunt knives. Their family emblems have tarnished to the point where people no longer have clear targets. At least half their guns are too old to work under this corrosive downpour, from the shouts I've overheard. I wish with all my heart that I'd been at Ahmad and Katrina's place when the rain started, or even Mouth and Alyssa's.

This view reminds me of the Glacier Fools, and I have to shut my eyes. I keep wondering if any of the Gelet died in that disaster, and whether they think I led them into an ambush on purpose.

"I don't know how you can stand to look out that window," Bianca says from the bar, where she's nursing some sweet liquor. She's still wearing her scoop-necked dress covered with the pearly scales of some rare breed of pheasant that lives past the swamps to the south.

We had come to this restaurant to reconnect, just the two of us, before the next party and the next one after that. But we've been trapped in here for ages, and we haven't talked much. The restaurant staff are all hiding in the back.

Bianca comes toward me. Some wild creature that's been trapped inside me for a long time wants to touch her. To spin around and use my momentum to pull her into my orbit, then clasp my arm around her. I remember how I held her on the Sea of Murder, when death seemed so close that I could say anything. The storm battered us, wrecked our sense of balance, until I thought the skiff would shatter under our feet. That's become my happiest memory.

Now we're in the middle of another vicious storm, surrounded by even more death, and I can't find the right thing to say to make her open up.

So instead, I talk to Bianca about the Hydroponic Garden Massacre, when her ancestors killed mine onboard the Mothership. The Nagpur compartment was all but wiped out, thousands of people, and the survivors were "integrated" into the other six populations, their children raised to forget. There are no pictures, no firsthand accounts, but I sneaked inside the library at Betterment University and found one slender sociology monograph written in Noölang, full of bland statistics that made my heart go cold.

"Everybody talks plenty about what happened with the other compartments, both good and bad," I say in Xiosphanti. "But nobody ever wants to talk about Nagpur."

"That's because it's not constructive," Bianca replies in Xiosphanti for once. "We can't focus on building a better future if we spend all our time agonizing about things that happened a long time ago. And you won't get people to help you change the world by telling them they're descended from criminals. We all spend too much time caught up in the past already, and looking backward all the time is killing us."

"But everything is different now because of what happened then," I say. "Everyone is here, and alive, because the people from Nagpur aren't. My people."

"Your 'people' are the Xiosphanti," Bianca says, "and they're still suffering right now. There are plenty of atrocities and selfish decisions to worry about without having to reach so far back in time. So many mistakes, just since the start of the Circadian Restoration." She speaks Xiosphanti as if the red-and-blue smoke just erupted, and addresses me as a fellow student.

"Ahmad says that everything that's wrong with us is because of things that happened on the Mothership," I say. "Maybe the past is all we are. The same people who flushed thousands of bodies into space went on to invent Circadianism."

Even though Bianca is trying to tell me that the mass murder of my ancestors doesn't matter, that wild creature inside me is climbing all over itself with happiness, because at least Bianca and I are debating again, like in our dorm room.

Bianca gropes and finds a hidden control on one wall that

causes some privacy screens to roll down, covering the window and blocking our view of the dead bodies hissing in the rain. Now the two of us perch behind shuttered windows, and this feels even more like old times.

"What would it even look like for Xiosphant to be fair?" I ask.

"I don't know." Bianca snaps a little, like she's not in the mood to talk anymore. "I suppose we would need to redefine how we think about 'work.' Like, some jobs you can't do your whole life. Some jobs are almost twice as hard as others, and maybe those shifts need to be shorter. Some people have a higher capacity than others. Work is more complicated than people realize."

Bianca still has the look of someone who hasn't slept, more than a nod here or there, in forever. Her head darts, like a cat searching for prey, and she stares, as if she needs to see things for a while before the image settles.

"Who makes those decisions, though? How do you create a system that allocates—"

"I don't know. Stop asking me weird questions. I don't know if you noticed, but we're in the middle of a killzone. I tried to warn you that Argelo was about to stop being fun." Bianca gets up and pours herself another drink, grimacing. She tries to make one for me, too, but I push it away.

I can't hear the fighting outside, because this restaurant has next-level soundproofing.

Bianca comes and sits next to me, touching my shoulder with one palm. "I know that you went and did something reckless. I saw the windburn on your neck, and I heard that Reynold is dead. Why didn't you tell me what you were doing?" She's switched back to Argelan, as if to say the schoolgirl conversation is over. "You said you trusted me, but you really don't."

"You're right, I did something dumb," I say in Argelan. I can't keep all of the bitterness out of my voice. I've held a million inquests inside my own head, but this guilt remains as fresh as ever. "People died, and it was my fault. I was trying to do something good."

"I'm sorry," Bianca says, still touching my shoulder. I feel myself relax into her side. "I know what it's like to want to make things better, and to have it turn to shit. That's how we got here, right?"

She goes to get herself some more liquor, and I say, "I do trust you."

Bianca looks at me, drink in hand, and seems to reach a decision. "When this fucking rain stops, if it ever does, I'm going to show you everything. You can see what we've been working on. Fuck the timetable."

I feel like I'm starting to hallucinate from lack of sleep, so I lie down on the one couch next to the bar, across from the window. I don't expect Bianca to join me, but then I feel her grudgingly work herself into the space beside me. I feel safe, as though her decelerating breath on my face is a hopeful sign that we're still sleepmates, and also road buddies. Our breathing synchronizes into slow iambs, and I drift off.

Then I jerk awake, panting as though I've run a hundred kilometers and I'll never be able to force enough air into my lungs. I don't even remember the dream I was in, but I'm drowning, bloody choking, and then I realize that next to me Bianca is screaming.

Bianca's voice comes in a high rattle, much too loud. She pummels the cushion next to her with both fists. I can't hear what she's screaming, but it's in a rhythm with her punches.

Bianca wakes too, and we both just breathe for a moment, looking opposite ways. She gets up to fetch herself another drink, and smoothes out her shimmering dress.

She sits beside me again, but neither of us goes back to sleep.

We sit without talking, long enough for her drink to disappear and our dreams to feel like places we visited long ago. I hear sounds from the kitchen. I think either the fighting or the rain has stopped. Maybe both.

Maybe this is our last chance to have a conversation, just us two, before whatever is going to happen. "I miss you," I say.

"Me too," she says, staring at the reflective panels on the other end of this enormous space. We are two tiny blobs in a swirl of muted color.

"I really hoped that you and I would reinvent ourselves together," I say, "when we came to Argelo. Everyone said you can be whoever you want here. I thought it would be just you and me, and we could make our own lives, without worrying about anyone else."

"I never would have been happy." Bianca shakes her head. "I can't let go of what happened before. I lost everything, and I was forced to leave Xiosphant, and I couldn't let that be the end of it."

"You didn't lose everything. You didn't lose me."

I feel the way I did when the boat flipped almost on its side, on the Sea of Murder: shivering, my insides going sideways.

She acts as if I didn't say anything. "I never would have been satisfied living a small life, after everything I lost. And now I've found a way to make my life count for something. To be the person I was always meant to be."

"I wish I had been enough for you."

"I miss our old friendship just as much as you do, but that was a long time ago." Bianca takes a breath, and her face closes up. "You died, and you made the decision to stay dead to me. And so I spent too long turning you into a perfect human being in my mind. A martyr, you know? The one good person in this shit-eating world. I hated myself for stealing that money and letting them take you, and I hated everyone who had anything to do with sending you into the night. I wanted to make them pay for what they took from us. I still want that. It's all I think about."

"I'm alive. I'm here." I touch her arm. "You don't have to be angry anymore."

"Oh, really? Thanks. I'll just stop being angry. That's a great idea. Why did I never think of that?" Her laugh feels like a slap. She leans past me and looks out the window, through the crack left by the privacy screen. "Rain's stopped. And the bloodbath seems to be over, too. Let's go. I promised to show you something."

Bianca gets up and walks to the door, without looking back, and her stride makes ripples in the pearly shapes on her dress. "Everything I've done since we got to this city has been to help us survive. And to find a way for us to go back." She walks into the street and almost steps in a puddle of the noxious liquid, but she sidesteps at the last moment.

We make our way down some streets that lead toward a part of town I don't know, where big factories and warehouses cluster around junkyards. Every few steps, we have to avoid either a body or more of the corrosive liquid. Even sleep-deprived and wearing a scalloped formal dress, Bianca plants her feet with perfect sureness, while I keep almost tumbling facedown into a deadly slick, or stepping on someone's discarded blade. The sky still looks darker, and I wonder if the rain will start again.

"Do you think you and I would have stayed friends after the Gymnasium?" Bianca leads me into a covered walkway with a rusty handrail. "I mean, if I hadn't stolen that petty cash, and the cops hadn't used it as a pretext. If we had just kept going, the way we had been. Maybe you and I would have just drifted apart after graduation." She's obviously thought about this a lot.

I think back, and remember the distinguished future that Bianca had been preparing for back in Xiosphant, when she dressed up for all those parties and dinners that I was never invited to. And meanwhile, she dabbled in insurrectionary politics as a way of proving something to herself. I nurtured all these childish fantasies about Bianca changing the world, with me by her side, but I never thought too much about what "by her side" meant. What was I going to be doing while she dazzled everybody?

Bianca waits for me to respond as we travel a series of gantries made of distressed metal. I walk heavy, stooped, with a dull pain in my stomach.

"I don't know. I never had a friend like you before. I don't know what trajectory we were on." I feel as if I've just swallowed a few drops of this toxic runoff. Now that she's spoken, I can see it clearly: we would have lost touch after graduation. I picture us older, pushing past each other on the street and not recognizing each other until we've almost gone too far to wave.

"You and I were good for each other, in this one moment in our lives, when we were young and in love with books and ideas. When we wanted to use our minds instead of sleeping when they told us to. That was our time." We've reached the opening of a dark tunnel. Bianca turns to face me. Her eyes look sunken, in the encroaching gloom. "But now neither of us is the person we thought we would turn into, and we've gone through things together that most people would never even imagine. I just hope you'll be on my side when the time comes."

I'm just staring at Bianca, noticing the raised tendon in her neck, the set of her jaw.

Bianca reaches out and bangs on a mesh gate with barbed wire on top. "Open up. It's me," she says in Argelan. "Dash knows we're here." I'm pretty sure that last part is a lie.

"Don't worry," Bianca says in Xiosphanti, "I still want to save everyone back home. All those people trapped in pointless cycles: work and sleep, work and sleep." She leads me into the pipe-lined tunnel, lit only by a single electric bulb swinging at eye level. "I don't have a whole theory of labor allocation worked out, but I know we can find a better way. You can help."

Bianca's brocaded slippers crunch on the filthy cement floor. I almost brain myself on one of the big metal pipes. "We can't go back to Xiosphant. I keep telling you. You saw how hard it was, coming here. We almost died seven different ways."

"You should know me better than that by now."

Bianca leads me into a hangar, with just a sliver of window along the top of the wall. I realize we've circled around, and we're under one of her favorite nightclubs. Not Punch Face or

Emergency Session, but the one we visited the first time, where the walls themselves are speakers. The one with the glitter that sticks to your skin with some kind of chemical adhesive and doesn't wash off. I hear the triple-beat over our heads: people dancing off the serotonin rush from the killing spree in the rain. She reaches until she finds a light switch, and then I'm looking at ten green-gray vehicles.

"Some of these belong to the Perfectionists, some to the Alva Family, and some to another group," Bianca says. "I already had the outlines of the idea before Dash came along, but he helped me put it together. They've been building these since forever, collecting stuff from the night, or from treasure meteors. I think one of the reasons for this latest skirmish between the families was to get the last few pieces."

These vehicles are all different sizes and shapes, but they all have the same armor, thick and jagged, like a bison's overlapping plates only without any fur. They rest on thick treads with gravity-assist devices to help them cross the roughest terrain— crude, hand-machined versions of the all-terrain cruisers the Founding Settlers drove when they tried to explore the world. Someone has attached spikes to the armor, and there are empty spots where you could add weapons.

These rude metal carcasses remind me of the War Monument back in Xiosphant, the rough edges that scraped me as I hid in its shadow.

"We could bring a small army," Bianca says. "We can do everything we used to talk about in school."

The music upstairs stumbles and recovers, like a drunk man kicking his own foot. I put my hand on the side of the nearest vehicle and feel the shell vibrate. I try to imagine going home like this. With a "small army" of the same people I just watched slashing each other to death for no reason.

"There's still no way," I say, though I have a queasy feeling that I'm wrong. "I mean, these are not amphibious vehicles. You remember the Sea of Murder. You almost fell overboard a couple times. Nobody has the facilities to build the kind of vehicle carriers they had during the Second Argelan War, or the barges from the Fourth."

"But we won't need any boats." Bianca touches my hand where I'm still touching the lorry. "You showed me another way. The sea is frozen over, as solid as rock, in the night. You have this incredible paranormal gift, which I don't claim to understand. But you can communicate with them, with the crocodiles, and they'll help us cross through the night safely. You're the key to all of this, Sophie. Everyone in Argelo has been nursing this dream for generations, especially since their resources have been running out. When I told them about you, their heads almost exploded."

My mind fills with soldiers, uniforms, guns, a forced march into the night. All the old deathly feelings come back, just the same as if I'd never worked so hard to cope with them at all. Police helmets, massacres, the dying sounds of the Glacier Fools—I run through the whole catalog in a heartbeat. But even the memory-panic feels as though it's happening a long way off. I turn to stone, rough-hewn, my head laced with shards of obsidian and granite. I can't see or hear, every breath a struggle. The pragmatic part of me, that voice that keeps me steady and alert in a bad situation, is screaming the worst curses I know.

I concentrate on taking in diesel-scented air through my nose, letting out rank gasps through my mouth.

"You don't know what you're asking." I force the words out, after a long time.

Like slow-dancing with a rockfall.

"I know, I know, they're not your pets. I'm sorry I said that before. They're an intelligent species, with their own society, and maybe one day we'll be strong enough to trade with them. Though, remember that lecturer at the Gymnasium? Dr. Dawson? He always said that in a meeting between any two species, one always domesticates the other. Or they don't coexist. Was he wrong? I don't know."

"They won't do what I ask. I can't even speak to them. Their communication is all one-way." I never explained to her about my bracelet, and now I'm glad.

"They showed up when you called for help. They escorted us to safety. I was there."

Feeling returns to my body, and mostly it consists of nausea. I can't even look at Bianca. I remember all the times I told myself that I would do anything to make her happy, and the memories all have a dark red stain.

"I can't." I stutter. "I just can't. There's no way."

Bianca seems to worry we've been in this hangar too long, so she hustles me back into the tunnel and locks the door behind us. Instead of going back the way we came, she leads me down another junction, and we emerge close to the Knife, right by that row of fish-bread shops. She finds a place that sells crystalized plum syrup on a stick and buys one for each of us.

"I love Argelo, and hate it at the same time." She hands me

my stick, and I bite into it. "But our hometown could use a little dose of Argelo. Progress isn't always decorous. Sophie. I know what I'm doing. And I really want to go home. I want to finish what we started. I thought that's what you wanted too."

The sugar rush, on top of the dead feeling inside me, is making my head throb. I cling to a memory of Bianca saying *both cities, the world*, but I still have a scream caught in my throat that I can't let out.

"Dash and the others, they don't want to hurt anybody," Bianca says. "Their main interest is in reopening trade with Xiosphant, on favorable terms. They need your help with the crocodiles, but also they need my understanding of Xiosphanti governance, or what passes for it. We'll bring hand-picked soldiers who know how to behave themselves. We'll do it with minimal casualties. We'll just force those tools to liberalize, to loosen their chokehold on all the people back home."

My eyes are closed. I don't remember closing them. My mouth is glued with syrup.

"All we want is safe passage," Bianca says. "Nothing else. I know you can do that. The crocodiles are the main reason why every vehicle that ever went into the night is a pile of wreckage."

I don't even know if any Gelet ever want to meet me again, after what happened with the Glacier Fools. I summoned them to a meeting, and then they were ambushed. I've been trying not to lose my mind over it. The Gelet had invited me to come live in their city, before all of that violence. Is that invitation even still open? If I do what Bianca wants, the Gelet would probably despise me once and for all, and they'd be right to.

"Sophie, please." She grabs my arm. My eyes stay shut. "I

know this is scary and strange. I know you wish we could just have a perfect little life together, you and me, but that's not the world we live in." My eyes reopen, but I still can't look at her.

We've finished the gritty sweets. Our sticks are just sticks. I don't know what to say to Bianca. Just a little while ago, I was saying I trusted her.

"Sophie, you've always needed me to push you or whatever, to give you an excuse to do the things you were too scared to do on your own." Still speaking Xiosphanti, Bianca pulls me out into the wet street, where a masked dance party has started. Bianca joins the dancers, pulling me in with her. Her arms fly around my neck, and she speaks in my ear over the drums. "So I'm going to make this easy for you. We're doing this, and it's too late to stop it. Those vehicles are almost ready to go, and you and I are going to do this together. It's already decided. There's no need for you to torture yourself about this."

Her hands rest on my neck, light as moth wings. I try to think of something to say, to change her mind. That feeling I had before—that this is our last chance to talk—is back, stronger than ever, but I still have no voice. Around me, people jostle in masks of velvet and feathers, shrieking with delight. I lean into Bianca's ear, but no words come. I'm lost.

She spies some friends and releases her hold on me, then floats away. I let the crowd separate us. My last glimpse of Bianca is her head bobbing up and down in a churn of upflung arms, as someone ties a pointed mask around her eyes.

mouth

Barney had gotten a musical act at the diner, and it crushed all the customer tables into the other half of the tiny space. A mandolin, a xylophone, a trumpet, and a tin piano argued at cross-purposes. The usual roster of students and shift laborers crowded inside and ignored the spiky metal fence of rhythms and dark chords, even when the old man playing the xylophone started muttering to himself, in a repetitive melody, *had a friend who needed a hand, had a hand that needed a glove, had a glove that needed a mate,* and so on. Mouth wasn't a music lover, but this left her colder than most kinds, and she never saw any evidence that this band brought in any customers. These musicians weren't even playing a board game that you could place side bets on. But with all this racket, Mouth couldn't ask Barney any more questions.

At last the honky-tonk group wore itself out, and the place went empty, and Barney was wiping down tables and moving them back into their old positions. Mouth tried to think of something to say before the diner filled up again.

Barney spoke first. "I know what you want. And it's not going to happen."

"What do I want?"

"You want me to go out on the road with you, the two of us, the last two Citizens. So I can walk you through it. So you can finish your education. There's just no way. I'm too old."

That possibility hadn't even occurred to Mouth. Although now that Barney had brought it up, she could imagine how great it could be. Or they might just kill each other after the first few kilometers.

She laughed. "You think I want the two of us on the road, without anybody else watching our backs? When was the last time you left the city?"

Barney rolled his neck. "Not since you were a kid. Not since I dropped out."

"I told you before. The road isn't the same as back then. Two people out there would be eaten before you could get halfway to the Sea of Murder or the Southern Wastes. You need a whole crew, and a vehicle with a sleeping nook in it, and weapons, and all sorts of other shit. And even then, you'd die."

"Oh." Barney had been in the middle of checking the rack full of spoons, hooks, and knives, but he sat down, as if he'd lost his balance. He turned, all at once, into a person who had a stomach ulcer and heart trouble. "Yeah, you did say."

"The crew I traveled with was ready for anything. We didn't make it."

"So you don't want to go out on the road?"

"I do. I just can't. I've been trying to make my peace with being a city-dweller. I still hate it. But I can't change reality."

"Well, then, I suggest you forget about the Citizens. There's no point in thinking about them, or trying to make sense of anything. Their lessons were only useful on the road, and you can't understand their ways while sitting here, inside walls within walls, between other walls. You can't be on your own and have the mind-set of the Citizens. There's no point. And even if I could teach you any of the old secrets, you couldn't use them here. You can't even see the day and the night at the same time when you're in a city."

"I can't just pretend I grew up in a house," Mouth said.

"Who cares where you grew up? You're here now. The point is, the Citizens' teachings are like one of those wispy pale flowers that used to grow out in the Drylands. Remember those? Imagine ripping it out at the root and trying to plant it in the Noisy Fen."

"I just want to keep our culture alive."

"You can't." Barney had revived and was wiping tables and checking napkins again. "You can't keep something alive that's already dead. You can only preserve the remains, the way that Martindale bullfrog is trying to do. If you want to do something to save our old culture, you should try to help the professor as much as you can. Maybe volunteer as his assistant. He's absolutely the only hope for the thing you say you want."

"That's a horrible thought."

"I don't know why you're so down on him. He's a pompous oaf, but he wants to do the right thing. He cares about this, bless his heart."

Now Mouth was the one sitting and clutching a sudden ulcer.

"I barely thought about the Citizens, all that time bouncing between two cities. It was just a funny story to tell people. But after I learned there was something left, the Invention, I couldn't let go. And I can't just forget again. Especially not now that I've found you."

Barney sighed. "Let's say I could bring all of the Citizens back from the dead. All of their shining ghosts, walking through town, singing one of those dirges that you were so determined to rescue from a vault in Xiosphant. The whole crew, including Cynthia and Yolanda. What then? What could they do that would make you happy? What do you actually want?"

Mouth thought about this for a moment. Bottomless swamp. "Well, they could give me a damn name."

"Bring a book of baby names. We'll flip to a random page, I'll put my finger down. Picking a name is not hard."

"It's not the name. You know that. It's the whole story that goes with it. The personal myth. The identity. They had a whole process."

"Sure, sure. I went through that. I helped others through. It was a nice ceremony. I'm sure they would have gotten to you soon enough, if they hadn't all died. Look, I'm sorry. I don't know how to deal with a thing that you hid from yourself forever and just recently decided was a mortal wound."

Mouth had her forearms in front of her face and her knees in her chest, against some huge projectile. She decided to throw it back in Barney's face.

"What about you? How are you honoring our people? What are you doing? What do you want?"

Barney sighed. "Unlike you, I chose to leave the group. If I'd known I was leaving them to die . . . I don't know. But I didn't know that. So I opened this place as a way to create community. To bring people together. Maybe I aimed too low. I felt like my role in the Citizens was to cook for everyone, but also to help make a space for people to talk. And I told myself I could keep doing that. I welcome people who have no place else to go, and I promise a limited amount of safety to student radicals and people who are on the Nine Families' hit list."

"I've sat in here I don't know how many times," Mouth said, "and I haven't seen you giving sanctuary to anyone." She leaned her chair backward so it rested on two legs and put her feet against the table.

"It doesn't happen all the time." Barney seemed bored with this conversation, yawning and leaning on one hand. "Anyway, I don't owe you any progress reports. I'm retired and an independent business owner. You are the one who has a problem, and I would like to help you solve it if I can. You can't go back on the road, and I wouldn't go back out there even if you paid me in extra life expectancy. You can't get back the Citizens' teachings by talking about them inside a building. How are you going to honor the dead?"

"I don't know." Mouth wanted to say that the dead had never honored her, that if anything, it was they who had left a debt unpaid. But maybe that would sound dumb.

"What have you ever done to help anybody?" Barney leapt to his feet and jabbed a finger at Mouth, who nearly fell flat on her back because she was leaning backward on two chair legs.

"I watched the other Couriers' backs, while they still had backs to watch. I helped these scavengers. I kept Alyssa alive, in spite of all her best efforts."

"A big thing in the Citizens was, we were all responsible for each other," Barney said, sitting back down on his high stool behind the counter. "Sometimes that meant that anybody who wasn't us could eat shit. But we tried to be generous, and interdependence was a big part of the teachings."

"Ugh. So I should go and find some people who are bigger losers than I am, to try and lift them up."

"Yes. I don't know. Maybe. Your own community. Everybody in this town is basically out of their mind. They might be safe under their roofs, but they're more lost in the wilderness than we ever were. You could be doing some good around here."

"I get it." Mouth unkinked herself from her chair. "You want me out of your diner. I'll go bother someone else."

"Sure. I don't care. Do whatever you want."

Afterward, Mouth couldn't stop wondering who she could be a Citizen to, as she looped around the up-and-down streets under a flat gray sky. She had a feeling it was never going to be that simple, that she couldn't just serve meatloaf and tell herself she was honoring the dead. The dead were just like the living: they all wanted something they could never have.

When Mouth got home, Alyssa offered her a hunting knife, holding it by the blade. Mouth took the hilt by instinct, but her fingers lost their strength. The knife stabbed the floor between them.

"Still?" Alyssa said, and cursed.

Lately, whenever Mouth tried to hold a weapon, her fingers turned into cotton strips. She could hold tools, pieces of food, shoes, or whatever, but she couldn't grip a gun or machete to save her life. Her hands wouldn't even assume the shape of fists. This had started right after the rain fight, when she had finished occupying the food depository, and Alyssa still wasn't convinced Mouth wasn't pulling some weird joke.

"You know I wouldn't joke about weapons," Mouth said. "I don't know what's going on with me, but it's probably temporary."

Alyssa sighed and sank into a rattan chair, which was already flaking apart. "This is all my fault. I should have stuck to my original idea and opened a shop. You would have come around after a while. I feel like I threw away a one-time opportunity to start over, try something different."

"What kind of shop, though? You never said." Mouth sat down next to her.

"We could have opened a restaurant, like Ahmad, or that Barney guy." Alyssa laughed. "Or a brewery. Or an antique store, after how much experience we had moving rare goods. Whatever. Something we could grow old doing. Instead, I decided we needed some excitement, and I wanted to help you reconnect with your long-lost nomads."

Mouth shrugged. "Everybody made choices. You already know my regrets."

"I just got blindsided by all my nostalgia for the old times, with the Chancers, once I was actually living here again. I wanted to recapture my glory days as a happy arsonist. And now we're supposed to keep fighting for the Perfectionists, and you can't even defend yourself with a toothpick."

Right on cue, both their pagers went off, with a brand-new symbol that Mouth had never seen before: gnarled in on itself, like a sea-snake. Alyssa had to look this glyph up in the list they'd been given, and then she gasped. "Oh shit. We're being summoned to the White Mansion."

She jumped to her feet, and Mouth followed. While Mouth was pulling the door open, Alyssa handed her a small dark shape, so casually that Mouth couldn't even tell what Alyssa was offering at first. The gun slipped out of Mouth's hand and thudded to the floor. Alyssa cursed. At least the gun's safety was on, so nobody got another new bullet wound.

Mouth had never been to the White Mansion, or even walked near it, because they didn't appreciate loitering in this part of town. But the barbed spikes of the iron fence, the huge marble courtyard, and the ten garrets, each with a window large enough to drive the Couriers' sled through, stirred Mouth even more than she'd expected, with a mixture of awe and disgust.

They'd torn down a dozen tenement buildings, with over a thousand people living in them, to make room for just this one pile, which they'd painted bright enough to throw reflected sunlight in your face.

"I just hope there are snacks," Alyssa said, punching Mouth's arm. "I was a kid when this place was still under construction, and I can't wait to see the inside. But there better be fried oysters, or I'm burning the whole thing down."

"You probably shouldn't talk about arson here," Mouth muttered.

They were met at the front door by a huge bruiser named Jimmy, who worked for the Perfectionists. He had a spiral scar on his hairless scalp, all the way from his eyes to the nape of his neck, and he always boasted that someone had stuck his head into one of those kitchen machines that hollows out a melon from the inside, during a fight that he'd won. Jimmy took all of Alyssa's weapons, and then insisted on searching Mouth five times, because he couldn't believe Mouth was unarmed.

"I know, I know," Alyssa said. "I've been saying." But she didn't tell Jimmy about Mouth's new condition.

Everything in the White Mansion had a scent that reminded Mouth of the first sweet thing she'd ever tasted as a child, when just the concept of sweetness had seemed revelatory.

Jimmy led them down a long hallway, past a huge ballroom with velvet drapes, to a side room that could still fit a hundred people comfortably. There, Bianca was sitting on a huge sofa made of some red leather that Mouth could tell at a glance would be softer than moss.

"There you are!" Bianca waved and gestured to a couple of chairs facing her couch. "Come join me."

Mouth and Alyssa sat, and Jimmy withdrew to the far end of the room, out of earshot. Bianca fixed both of them with her easiest smile, as if they'd all gone to university together. They hadn't talked since Bianca had called Mouth horrifying and almost consigned her to death. Somehow, Mouth found herself thinking about Barney's parting words, about helping people find their way. Any wilderness where Bianca might be lost, Mouth had helped lead her into.

They made chitchat for a few moments, about Argelan food, and poor Reynold, and some rugby game that had been delayed due to rain. Then Bianca got to the point.

"Mouth, I have some excellent news for you. That book you wanted? From the Palace? The one with all the poems and things? We can get it for you. I will hand it to you myself."

At first, Mouth couldn't even process the words Bianca was speaking. A snatch of some other conversation, from a different time and place. Then Alyssa kicked Mouth, and the meaning sank in.

"Oh," Mouth said.

"That's all you're going to say? After everything you put me through just to steal that one book? And now I'm telling you, it's yours."

Mouth tried to bring back the vision she had nurtured in her mind that whole time in Xiosphant, of lifting the crystal volume and paging through it. Seeing all of the old wisdom about how to see both horizons with a clear mind. That vision had quickened her soul back in Xiosphant, but now she just felt sad, and a little lightsick. She couldn't think of the Invention without hearing Barney say "doggerel," or remembering that vision of precious fragile blooms dying inside an ancient mountain, which some old book wasn't going to help her understand.

The Invention might as well be a heap of blank pages now.

"Oh," Mouth said again.

"We're going on a mission soon," Bianca said. "It's a huge secret, but I'm letting you two in on it, because we'll need some stealth experts. We're going back to Xiosphant." She kept talking: armored vehicles, heavy weaponry, a hand-picked force.

Alyssa kept nodding. "You've got it all figured out. This is a solid plan."

Mouth was remembering when Bianca used to ask her,

How many people have you killed? And Mouth had answered with a boastful vagueness, as if the fact that she hadn't kept track made her a better role model. She remembered the first person she'd killed, a tubercular, silt-voiced Argelan man who'd seized her throat from behind when the Citizens' funeral ashes were still fresh on her hands, and the last, one of the men guarding the food depository. But in between?

"You know whose house this is." Bianca gestured at the mahogany walls and the view out the window, of a tiny walled grove of what looked like apple trees. "He runs the Alva Family, which now controls the Perfectionists, who you both swore allegiance to, according to the badges you're wearing. So we could just order you to do this, but I'm choosing to be nice."

"I'm kind of retired from traveling," Alyssa said. "But, well, this sounds like a whole other trip, and I'm dying to see how it turns out. And truth be told, I've been missing all those Xiosphanti grains. Need more fiber in my diet." She elbowed Mouth in the side.

"I thought you would be on your knees thanking me for this opportunity," Bianca said to Mouth. "I honestly don't understand you at all. I used to think you were so wise. I hung on every word you spoke to me. Now you just look like some kind of tragic vagrant."

"A lot's happened," Mouth said. Then she tossed her head. "I promised to help you before, in Xiosphant, but I had my own agenda, and I was selfish, even though I thought it was for a higher cause. So I owe you my help now. You don't need to bribe me."

Bianca's eyes misted up, as sudden as a weather shift on the road. "If you had only said that to me a long time ago, a lot of things might be different now." Then she glanced up at Jimmy, signaling the interview was over. "We'll be in touch about logistics. Keep your pagers with you at all times." She got up and walked out of the room without looking back at them.

SOPHIE

The most famous story of Anchor-Banter, which I still don't completely understand, is about a prince and a tailor, in the fairy-tale version of Xiosphant that everyone loves here: twinkling castles, rowdy banquets, valiant knights. The prince has a perfect life, except he's in love with a beautiful young apprentice in the royal gardens whose touch restores every rare bloom to health. The prince keeps trying to woo her, with tiny flying machines and musicians, but every plan goes awry. And this ugly old royal tailor is always nearby, giving a crooked leer, whenever another disaster ruins the prince's courtship. At last the prince decides to have the tailor imprisoned, on some pretext—but then the prince loses everything and becomes a beggar, outside the walls of his own palace. The beautiful apprentice gardener throws a flower into the former prince's cap every now and then, without knowing him. The prince stays out there for uncounted ages, in the dirt, but his royal garments never tear or sully, and they become a pillow and quilt when the city sleeps. These clothes are a miracle, and at last the prince realizes: that tailor never received proper payment for his work, or credit from the throne. With that, the curse is broken, and the prince is able to return and kill everyone who betrayed him.

The first time I tried to understand this story, I had thought "Anchor-Banter" referred to the apprentice gardener, and the prince's destructive love for her. I didn't even get the thing about the tailor. Alyssa's explanation helped a lot, though the whole thing still seemed incongruously mystical.

Still, Alyssa says when you identify your Anchor-Banter, you have two choices: You can figure out why this person is connected to you. Or you can join forces with them, and cause trouble for everyone else.

According to Mouth, every pile in this scrapyard tells a different story about Argelo. She points out a wire-mesh bundle of filthy, corroded old Founders' Celebration rattles, from a brief period when Argelo tried to mass-produce cheap junk to send to Xiosphant in exchange for food or technology. On the other side, a heap of busted shell casings and shattered bayonets, from the last great war with Xiosphant (either the fifth or the sixth, depending on how you reckoned). She gestures at a wall of garbage that includes: melted plastic farm implements from when the Argelan People's Congress launched an "Everyone Farms" campaign; tarnished badges from political parties and families that nobody even remembers; rust-eaten prospector gear from the heyday of treasure meteorites; packages for various fad cures for lightsickness, fungal infections, and delirium; and rotted placards depicting the great exodus from Xiosphant to Argelo.

I wrap a cloth around my mouth and nose to protect against the fumes from some combination of rotting plastic and battery acid.

"Well, you said you wanted to talk someplace where nobody could hear us," Mouth says, gesturing around at the brightly colored piles.

"Yeah, I did. I need your help, and I don't trust anybody in this blighted city anymore."

Ever since Bianca showed me her invasion fleet, I've been dizzy, as if the sheer weight of my rage has sprung my inner ear. I feel like wrecking this whole city with my bare hands. Every time my anger runs out of fuel, I fall into mourning, as if my feelings for Bianca have gone sour forever. Part of me still can't believe that Bianca has changed, but another buried part has seen this happening for a long time. I keep thinking back to everything that's happened since we left home. The look on Bianca's face after we survived the Sea of Murder, the way she insisted on seeing the Gelet as my servants, the frenzy with which she threw herself into high society. Even the things she said in the storeroom, when we first slept here. She's been planning to use me, almost since we left home.

Mouth is looking at me, and I realize I haven't spoken for a while. "I need you to help me disappear for a while," I say. I start to tell Mouth what Bianca's planning, and it turns out she already knows most of it, except for my part.

"I'll do what I can, but you should know that I can't fight." Mouth looks down. "My hands won't cooperate, no matter what I try, ever since the rainstorm. Wasn't like I chose to become a pacifist or anything, just that my body decided on its own."

Mouth somehow looks even worse than she did after the Glacier Fools. She has fresh burn scars on her neck from that scorching rain, and a cut on her cheek that looks infected. She hasn't been able to keep shaving the sides of her head, and the hair came back uneven.

"I don't need you to fight anybody. Just help me get out of town, find a place to lie low until everyone gives up on this invasion foolishness. Preferably, someplace where I can go into the night without passing through slums full of people with harpoon guns."

Mouth perks up, because here is a challenge that she's comfortable with. She starts spinning out extraction plans, disguises, camouflages, and places I could hide, including a hidden distillery that some of Alyssa's old friends are running, forty kilometers south of here.

"I already promised to help Bianca," Mouth says. "But I guess I can help both of you."

"The Gelet, when I went into the night, they trusted me with something precious," I say. "Not just their shared past, like what they tried to share with you, but even more than that, a . . . a kinship. They chose me to be their friend here in the twilight, and I've failed them over and over, in so many ways. But no matter how I try to make Bianca understand, she still just thinks I have some kind of power that she can use to get what she wants."

I squint at all the bright colors, eaten away by rust or mold. We're surrounded by the detritus of other people's bold visions for the future. I keep gagging on the stench of outgassing polymers.

"You learned to overcome the worst fear and communicate across the great divide, and you've overturned everything we thought we understood about this world," Mouth says, chewing her knuckles. "So of course someone was bound to try and weaponize you. I'm just sorry it was Bianca."

When my mother died, I was just on the cusp of thinking of myself as a separate person, with independent opinions, and I had a hard time separating her death from my own life. I kept thinking I must have done something wrong, or she must have rejected me, and I imagined her final moments over and over: her skin seared away, her final thoughts worrying about the well-being of strangers. Bianca was the first person who ever soothed my derelict heart after that, so of course I threw all of my love at her.

Hernan said my mother would be proud of me. I wonder if it's true, and what she would say if she saw me now. I've taken to wearing the CoolSuit, or even a light cotton sari over a blouse and pants, whenever I go outside without Bianca. At some point, I stopped thinking of this as a disguise, and started just taking comfort in anything that makes me easier in my skin.

Mouth comes back and says, "It's all arranged. Alyssa's on her way to help us. She just had to make a pit stop on her own, to take care of something first."

I start to thank her for the risk she's taking, but just then Alyssa shows up—with Bianca.

"*That* was your pit stop?" Mouth throws her hands over her head. "You went to fetch her?"

"We pledged our loyalty to the Perfectionists, and I take that seriously, not to mention all the promises we just made to Bianca. I wasn't about to sneak around behind her back." Alyssa shrugs. "Plus, I actually think Bianca would make an amazing leader. She kept the Resourceful Couriers from melting down after Omar died, and she's been playing the Argelan game better than most people who were born here."

"Thanks." Bianca nods at Alyssa. "I'd be lucky to have someone like you on my team."

Mouth looks at the two of them with her arms still raised, a comical statue.

"Don't worry: Dash and the others don't know about your little betrayal, and I hope we can keep it that way," Bianca says to Mouth. "I can't believe that right after you promised to help me, you went behind my back and tried to sabotage the mission. Actually, I can believe it, because it's bloody typical. Everything I know about lies and manipulation, I learned from you."

"Both you and Sophie asked for my help, and I couldn't choose between you. But my promise to you still stands."

"Don't blame Mouth," I whisper. "This was my idea."

"Were you even going to say goodbye to me this time?" Bianca comes over to me, shivering in her crimson party dress. "Or were you just going to disappear again, and leave me wondering if you were alive or dead?"

I'd made up my mind that I would never see Bianca again, so she appears like a sliver of lost time. I feel the old yearning to comfort her, to sustain her with my near silence, but then I remember how she laughed as she told me that it was too late to stop her plans, and then the sight of a thorn mask halfway on her face. The cavities in the rough metal vehicles with their fresh uneven coats of paint, large enough to hold the most destructive weapons humanity still has. The casual way she said, *Do you think we would have stayed friends?*

This feeling is the opposite of what a Gelet's touch does to me: I feel crushed by the reality of my own body, my own surroundings, my own mistakes.

"I would have died to avenge you, and you're still at the center of my world, but you won't fucking believe in me," Bianca says.

"You and Sophie are like a single soul in two bodies," Mouth is saying to Bianca. "I've seen how much you care about each other. Don't let it go like this. Just work it out. We can find another way."

I still can't look at Bianca. I close my eyes, and instead I see an assault vehicle with empty weapon ports.

"There is no other way," Bianca says. "We're doomed if these two cities don't start working together. The sky only just pissed alkali a short while ago, remember, and the southern root gardens and orchards are ruined. Argelo is running out of food and clean water, and meanwhile Xiosphant is a collection of ancient machines that can't go much longer. This is a harsh, ugly planet, and we need to pool our resources or we all starve in our own filth."

Alyssa shrugs and says to Mouth, "Can't really argue with any of her logic. Those fucking complacent Xiosphanti need something to wake them up, make them care about the rest of us. Remember when we thought we were going to be stuck there for the rest of our lives? Ugh."

I feel Bianca's hands on my arms, smell the warm yeasty liquor on her breath. "Sophie, I need you. I can't face any of this without you. Everything we used to talk about after curfew, all of the dreams we had, we can make all of it real. When the two of us are united, nothing can stop us. Please look at me. Sophie, please."

I look, just in time to see tears streaking the metallic paint around Bianca's eyes, illuminating the lines on her face. I want to put my arms around her, but I'm still deadlocked.

"Sophie has an amazing gift," Mouth says. "Something that nearly killed me when I tried to do it. She can touch something that maybe nobody else has ever touched. And you're forcing her to use it for destruction."

"For liberation," Bianca says through a wet curtain. "I want to save everyone in Xiosphant from the prison of endless repetition."

"But Sophie doesn't want—" Mouth starts to say.

"Everybody shut up, just shut up, shut up and let me talk. I'm sick of all your stupid voices. Just stop talking, stop talking, shut your faces." The words come out of me in one breath, in a low, guttural rush.

Alyssa, Mouth, and Bianca all stare at me. The night wind rustles through the twine-wrapped bundles of rubbish.

"I never wanted to give up on you," I say to Bianca in Xiosphanti. "All I ever wanted was to keep following you around and seeing each new thing through your eyes. But I can't stand to watch you chasing power, or revenge, or whatever it is that you think you crave. You cannot force me to be your tool of conquest, as if I'm the last section of ablative shielding for one of those war machines. And if you insist on trying, then maybe you were right before, and our friendship belongs in the past."

I pause to draw a toxic breath, the gears of my anger still scraping. And then, I realize. When I spoke Xiosphanti just now, I identified myself as a student, same as always—but I labeled Bianca an aristocrat, my social better. And I used the formal syntax, as if addressing a stranger.

Bianca realizes this the same time as I do, and her face collapses under its coating of reflective paint.

"I've screwed everything up," Bianca says when she can talk again. "But I can still get it right."

Mouth touches my arm. I almost forgot she and Alyssa were here. "If Bianca was telling the truth and nobody else knows what we're doing, then we have a narrow window to get you out of town before everything explodes. She'll be missed long before we will."

I pull away from Bianca. "I'm ready. Let's go."

Mouth looks at Alyssa.

"Well, of course I'm going to help you, you fuckhead," Alyssa groans. "It's not like I was getting used to my life not being a giant nest of fetid swamp dogs or anything."

I'm turning to leave and searching for a way to thank Alyssa and Mouth for the risk they're taking on my behalf, when Bianca speaks.

"Please don't leave me. Please, I can't lose you again." Bianca's voice sounds almost the same as when the police were dragging me away from the Zone House. "Please. I know that I'm selfish, but you make me better, and after everything we've been through we share a bond, you and me, and it goes way beyond any simple college friendship. Sophie, please. I get it, you're scared to go home, but it'll be okay, I won't let anything hurt you ever again. You'll be a hero. Sophie! Don't walk away from me."

I almost walk into a wall of placards, but Alyssa steers me.

Mouth is already muttering to Alyssa about the best routes out of town, the easiest way to vanish. I concentrate on trudging.

And then, from somewhere behind me, Bianca says, "I love you."

All of the strength leaves me and I fall, and Alyssa barely catches my limp body as my eyes wash out. My face feels hot and Alyssa's shoulder smells like soaked-in sweat. Alyssa lays a hand beneath my nape, gingerly, and lets me rest on her as I tremble and spasm. The hurt I've crammed inside every joint and sinew for too long rushes to the surface, and my anger falls away, and I can't hold any of this inside anymore. Nobody speaks, as my jag goes on and on, and I can't think past the words I just heard Bianca speak, I can't stand this hope.

Alyssa's stiff denim shirt is soaked and she supports me, both arms now, without offering any false reassurance.

At last I pull myself upright. "I can't leave her. I just can't."

"Oh." Mouth bites her lip, then shrugs with her head slung forward.

Paint runs down Bianca's cheeks in uneven lines, but she's giving me the smile that used to make me want to dance on my bunk at the Gymnasium. "Thank you," she says. "I'll be by your side the whole time, I promise." She pulls me close, and soon I'm crying in her arms instead of Alyssa's.

My tears mingle with Bianca's, and I realize the two of us

have never cried at the same time before. I'm convulsing and clutching at Bianca, trying to pull her closer and also push her away, and my heart is a dented bell, and the junkyard shrinks in on us, and I hold on tight to her declaration of love, as if it could save me from all of the horrors that lie ahead.

PART

FIVE

SOPHIE

The viewports inside the Command Vehicle darken, then grow opaque as a dense layer of ice covers them. Even with warm air streaming into the passenger section through tiny vents, the walls turn frigid to the touch, and my fingers get numb. All around me, seasoned killers in dark padded uniforms whimper, *Let me out I'm so cold I want to go home we're all going to die out here we're going to die.* Every time our gravity-assist treads stumble over another sharp downgrade, we lurch, and the entire capsule screams. "Everybody shut up," snaps Nai, an elegant older woman who's the leader of the Perfectionists. "You all sound like children." I can't see anyone's face behind their protective faceplate, which makes their wailing seem disembodied—as though delirium has settled upon us like a mist. My armpits chafe and my chest constricts, and I'm caught in my worst terror: strapped down in a tiny enclosed space, surrounded by a whole platoon wearing dark combat gear and helmets, being dragged into the night. Except that this time, I could have escaped. I had a choice, I could have said no. The moans grow louder as the Command Vehicle struggles to stay upright and move forward.

I'm the only one in the passenger section who's not making a sound, and that's only because I'm screaming inside my own head.

"We're fine," says Sasha, a large fussy man who's the second-in-command among the Perfectionists. "Everything's fine. Nothing to worry about. Everything's totally fine. Why should we worry? We're doing great." He keeps saying these things until Nai hisses at him to shut up. A sour odor hangs in the stale air around me. I think of Reynold saying, *Some primitive fear from before our ancestors discovered fire.*

Bianca keeps smiling at me from the front of the Command Vehicle, where she sits with Nai, Dash, Sasha, and an older Alva loyalist named Marcus, all of them still dressed in normal clothes. She kisses Dash, holding his face in one hand, across an instrument panel full of muddy topographic readings and warnings about the dangerous thickness of ice coating our outer shell. Our conversation in the junkyard repeats in my mind, and I can't believe how stupid I was.

Bianca went with me when I said goodbye to Ahmad and Katrina, and she kept nudging me so I wouldn't say anything about where we were going, but also to hurry me along. She said, *It's exciting, we're going on an adventure,* oblivious to how I flinched.

The people around me are still crying, thrashing against their harnesses, making invocations to various gods and devices. Dash is joking about Xiosphanti food again. The indicator lights on the front panel make rainbow trails along the scuffed aluminum walls.

Bianca said she loved me, long after I'd have sacrificed anything to hear her say those words. I would have worn a tower of ribbons and gone to a hundred terrible parties, just so I could pile every shining toy in the world at Bianca's feet. I would have braved every gun and every gloved hand in Xiosphant to bring Bianca jewels from the Palace vault. But now I see her in the cockpit, whispering to Dash and twirling one slender hand for emphasis, and I feel empty.

The vehicle lurches, and someone's gloved fingers grab at my arm for support, and I freeze. I can't breathe. But just as I'm spiraling into panic, I feel a nudge on my right wrist. My bracelet has woken up, and it's urging me deeper into midnight. I take a deep breath and I concentrate on the hum that I feel through my skin. The Gelet haven't given up on me, even after all the times I failed them. They still want me to join them.

All that matters is that bracelet, and the knowledge that my friends are near, and everything else is nothing. Except I don't know what the Gelet will think when they see a fleet of armored vehicles, spiked with weapons, and they realize I've led a whole army to their territory. Bianca's friends designed these vehicles to look just like the ones the Gelet tore to pieces before.

I never loved anybody the way I have loved Bianca. But I know in my shattered core that I would have been a better friend to her if I had walked away in that scrapyard. I need to learn to belong to other people the way everyone else seems to, with one hand in the wind.

*

Something strikes our vehicle, and we rock sideways so hard we're perched on one set of treads for a moment. Then we fall flat again with an impact that crushes me into my safety harness. "What was that?" Nai says, and nobody answers, except to groan. A second impact pushes us off one of our treads, and the vehicle sways harder.

The cockpit's night-vision screen shows a glimpse of fuzzy segmented armor.

"Fucking bison!"

"It's a lot bigger than I thought it would be."

"It's a lot bigger than we are."

"Get it off us!"

"There's more than one of them."

At least three shapes move around us on the screen. We rock onto our side again.

"We can't move forward," Marcus says.

"Shoot them! Shoot them!" Sasha has sweat pooling on his forehead. "Where's the bloody flamethrower?" A woman named Lucy puts on protective gloves and fumbles for a port in the side, letting in a stabbing draft for a moment until the port seals around her wrists. Sasha picks up a short-range radio and shouts, "We're under attack. Roger, you're in the rumbler. Can you get a clear shot?"

Nai starts to say, "No, wait—" Dash tries to slap the radio out of Sasha's hand.

A heartbeat later, I feel an impact that makes my teeth snap together. My neck hurts, and my ears ring.

"You missed the bison, but you hit us," Sasha says into the radio. "Try aiming."

A second mortar blast rattles our vehicle.

"Sasha, you idiot," Nai says. "Tell them to stop shooting at us."

Lucy's flamethrower goes off, turning the night vision a shimmering green, and Lucy shouts, "Got one of them!" The viewport shows an impression of a shrieking round mouth and stringy white fur on fire, then goes dark again.

We're back on our treads, moving forward in fits and starts.

"Bad news," says Marcus. "Those mortars cracked one of our engine casings. We'll have to keep stopping every few kilometers, or the chamber will overheat and flood with toxic fumes."

"We can't stop," Nai says. "We'll get stuck in the ice."

"You should have thought of that before your goon ordered the other vehicle to shoot at us," Dash says. Nai starts to respond, but thinks better of it. Most of the people in this vehicle answer to Dash.

Sasha sees me sitting nearby, and looms over me. "You," he spits. "You're supposed to be the magic talisman that gets us through the night in one piece. That's what we were promised."

I just look up at him. Whatever Sasha sees in my face, it makes him back away, hands raised in a defensive cower.

"Stop bothering Sophie," Bianca says. "She's not an all-purpose protector. She's good if we run into crocodiles."

"Oh god, spare me. Bianca! Everybody swoons whenever you open your mouth, like you're some Xiosphanti princess out of an old storybook." Sasha grunts. "This whole mission was your idea, and we're depending on your friend's so-called magical powers, and I can tell you're just a cheap grifter."

Bianca smiles up at Sasha, as if he just said something innocuous about Zagreb opera, and I can't help feeling a sugary rush of pride in her.

Everybody else in the Command Vehicle goes quiet, not even moaning anymore. We've stopped driving already, because our engines need to cool down. Dash breaks the silence. "Sasha, put on some protective gear and go outside to look at the damage you caused. Take a few engineers with you."

Sasha starts to say, "I don't answer to you," but Nai just gives him a look, and he trails off. His face falls, and he slumps forward. After a moment, he says, "Fine, great. See you soon."

"We've lost number-five troop transport," Marcus says as Sasha puts on the gear, accompanied by two men and a woman from the engine section.

"What does that mean, 'lost'?" Nai says.

"It's just not there anymore. Maybe it fell down a crevasse. The ice is full of fissures."

I can smell the smoke from the cracked engine, and my head swims.

"We . . . lost a vehicle," Nai says.

These are the people that Bianca decided to trust with everything. She tries to give me a conspiratorial smile, cocking one eyebrow. But I just stare past her, at the instrument panel that's gone bright pink with warning lights.

Sasha has his survival gear on, helmet in hand, and he hesitates at the inner hatch. "Okay," he says. "I'm going outside now. If . . . if you still think I should."

"Great," Dash says. "We'll keep it warm for you."

Even though I hate Sasha, this loud stupid bully, I still feel nauseous watching Dash ordering him outside, likely to his death, on a mission that doesn't require his supervision. I kept thinking I had never seen the real Dash, but maybe I just caught a glimpse. Bianca smiles at Dash, and they hold hands.

"I'll be back soon," Sasha says, still hesitating.

But everyone just looks at Sasha until he opens the hatch, bows his head, and goes into the outer chamber with his team, then seals the inner hatch behind them.

"Everybody keep your eyes open for more wildlife," Dash says.

While we're stopped and our engines silenced, the sounds of the night come through. This close to midnight, the wind makes a keening sound, but our exterior visibility is a series of illusions.

Bianca kept saying she had lost everything, right before she showed me this machine for the first time, and maybe this is her way of getting it all back. The social status, the brilliant future, the luxury of idealism in a comfortable chair among friends, all the things she had when I first knew her. I miss that life too, maybe even more than she does and in a deeper cavity of my psyche, but the increasingly thick air of this icebound assault vehicle (sweat and farts and gun residue and engine coolant and terror) is leaving me surer and surer that this whole enterprise says something indelible about her.

My bracelet thrums harder, and I adjust it under my sleeve, trying to send a response, like, *I'm here. I'm sorry about before. I'm here now. I'm sorry for bringing these intruders to you.*

The voices of Sasha and the engineers come over the radio.

"Why is this taking so long?"

"Give us a moment, Sasha. Inspecting the damage."

"I saw something move."

"There are snowdrifts. Motion is pretty much constant out here."

"No, really. I saw—"

"Just keep working. I want to see their faces when I come back in one piece."

"Did you hear that?"

"It's so cold my ears are frozen shut."

"Just keep working."

"Watch out, there's a—"

And then a high shriek, and no sound but the wind again for a while.

"Nikki. Shit. Nikki. Did you even see what got—"

"Stop asking if I see things."

"Nikki's just gone."

"We're seriously all going to die here."

"Stop saying that."

"Okay, I think I sealed the damage. Let's get back inside before—"

And then more screams, which grow louder and more indistinct, a chorus. Then they cease, and we're left with just the wind again.

"Let's go," Dash says to Marcus. "Start the engines."

Everybody looks at Dash for a moment. The radio stays silent. So Marcus takes a deep breath through his upper teeth, eyes stretched open, and then we roll forward. As soon as we're moving again, I feel someone pulling my wrist once more.

The engine seems to hold up, and we tear through the night as if the ghosts of Sasha and the dead engineers are chasing us. The scream of our hastily repaired drive chamber sounds higher and more ravenous than the wind. We catch up to the other vehicles in our fleet, and even pass them, racing forward until our engines protest.

"Gotta slow down," Marcus says. Dash tosses his head.

My bracelet thrums, as if in warning, but before I can make sense of it, I feel a sickening twist, as if the world has come apart underneath us. For one stomach-dropping moment, I think we've fallen into a sinkhole. But no—a splintering, shattering sound comes from two kilometers behind us, and the rear topographic scans show the ice shelf breaking apart. The layers of permafrost unfold like wings, spreading open to reveal the naked ocean below, and all the other vehicles are caught in the middle of it.

mouth

At first, they thought some seismic event had torn through the ice. Or maybe some submerged mine left over from one of those ancient wars, a final revenge from some dead sailor. They bickered and debated, even as the road rose up vertical in front of them. Sweated, spat, pleaded, prayed, boasted, grandstanded. The grav-assist treads pawed at the unsteady fragments of tundra, groping in vain for some purchase. But the mist cleared, and Alyssa spotted the cause of the eruption: one tentacle, covered with iridescent feathers and tipped with a leaf-shaped barb the size of a tenement, had burst upward from the frozen ocean, filling the space like a new monument. One of the giant squids that lurked at the bottom of the Sea of Murder had detected food on the surface, and decided to go hunting.

Alyssa unsnapped her harness, while all the Perfectionists in the number-seven transport wasted time bemoaning their fate, and pushed through the passenger compartment until she reached the cockpit. She leaned over an older Perfectionist loyalist named Winston, who sat in the pilot's seat, and unfastened his safety harness for him. "You better let me drive," she said. Winston hesitated, and she added: "Do you want to live, or do you want to feel good about yourself in your final moments? One of us here knows the Sea of Murder, and it's not you."

Winston slid out of his chair, and Alyssa climbed in, securing herself inside. Mouth came and stood next to her, mostly to watch what promised to be an excellent show.

The fleshy protrusion rose thirty meters over their heads, its tip swaying as if searching for prey. Then it curled, whip-fast, and ensnared two vehicles in a single fluid motion, dragging them back through its hole in the ice.

"Bloody hell," Winston breathed. "Those poor people."

"Pretty quick death. Better than most." Alyssa kept her eyes fixed on the topographic scans, looking for any tiny fluctuations or perturbations in the ice, while easing the ATV forward at a tantalizing speed. They crawled ahead until they reached one of the darkest blue spots, and then Alyssa spun them almost 90 degrees and sped up, so the terrain streaked past for a moment. Then she pulled back on the throttle again, and they were back to baby steps.

"Shouldn't we be just making a break for it, while that monster is distracted?" Jimmy, another senior Perfectionist, muscled his way forward. He was the enormous man with the spiral scar across his hairless scalp, who had searched Mouth and Bianca at the White Mansion. "Why are we playing games instead of just getting the fuck out of here?"

The other five vehicles were following Jimmy's idea, barreling at top speed away from the jagged patch of exposed ocean, toward the waiting Command Vehicle. But the ice ripped open in the space between the rumbler and two of the troop transports, propelling massive chunks at their armored sides. The tip of the squid's tentacle pulled one of the transports down into the ocean, twirling with the measured elegance of a coffee server at the Illyrian Parlour. Then another.

"That's why," Alyssa said. "Any other questions?"

Jimmy's brow furrowed, so that the sharp end of his scar pointed at one glowering eye, while Alyssa executed a three-point turn, and then coasted the vehicle across a thin sheet of permafrost that seemed to tremble as they passed over it.

"I don't trust either of you smugglers," Jimmy was saying to Mouth in a chatty tone, like he was discussing an unsatisfying meal. Jimmy was so tall and wide he had to hunch over inside the troop transport, and his arms kept bumping against the sides. "We should have left you behind in Argelo."

"I wish you had," Mouth said.

Some of the leaders of this expedition, like Nai and Sasha, had wanted to ditch Mouth and Alyssa, or even put them to death for the stunt they tried to pull with Sophie. But Bianca was still convinced that their smuggling experience would be invaluable when (if) this expedition reached the walls of Xiosphant. Mouth still felt bound by the promise she'd made to Bianca at the White Mansion, even though this invasion seemed like a worse and worse idea. At least Mouth had managed to spend some time answering Professor Martindale's countless annoying questions before they left, so whatever happened to her, the memory of the Citizens could be preserved.

The giant squid extended its reach farther over the ice, feathers curving outward as they searched for the other caches of protein. The other three lorries had stopped moving, probably hoping the squid would ignore them if they made no vibrations, but they rested on undulating promontories of ice.

The whole back of Mouth's troop transport was full of people chanting, *Oh fuck fuck shit fuck,* or spilling bodily fluids on the floor. The stench gave Mouth a crushing headache. Alyssa was humming something that Mouth couldn't make out at first, then she twigged: it was that song about the Decapitating Sisters, the two women who could snick a man's head off before his thoughts even reached his gun hand, the pair of them a coordinated neck-severing machine of such beauty that people risked death to watch them work. Alyssa spun the lorry on its axis and scooted away from the tentacle as she broke into the chorus: "And oh, the heads, the heads, the heads, the rolling heads as they danced."

Alyssa had already gotten them past the two fast-expanding holes that the squid had made, and they were gliding forward, with their engines stilled. "Shit," Winston breathed. "We're gonna make it after all."

The fleshy tip of the squid's long arm landed right in front of the ATV, blocking their path. Blotting out the rest of the world, even. The frond-shaped growth wriggled, almost playfully, and its huge feathers undulated in the wind.

"You had to say that," Alyssa grunted at Winston as she squeezed their brake lever, as gentle as soothing a baby.

*

Jimmy fumbled for the thick gloves that would allow him to operate the flamethrower, which was housed in a small alcove next to Mouth's seat. "Gonna teach that thing a lesson, send it back where it belongs." His nostrils flared and his mouth stretched out.

The ground underneath the ATV heaved and buckled, and the spire-sized tentacle turned in a lazy half circle, as if groping for its prey.

"Don't use the fucking flamethrower when we're already on broken ice," Alyssa shouted.

"Don't tell me what to do. I'm going to finish this."

"Mouth, don't let him use the fucking flamethrower."

Mouth was already placing her body between Jimmy and the flamethrower controls. Jimmy balled his fists, and Mouth tried to shape her body into some imitation of a fighting stance. "Step back," Mouth said, "I don't want to hurt you"—as if that was even a possibility. Jimmy took a swing at her head, and she ducked just in time, and then his knee connected with her thigh. Mouth had no room to dodge, and her hands wouldn't even organize into fists.

A clanging filled the compartment, like one of those endless bells in Xiosphant, and Jimmy landed in a heap at Mouth's feet. Alyssa had whacked him in the back of the head, right at the center of his swirl of scar tissue, with a metal spanner.

"Gravestones all over the world have 'Should've Listened to Alyssa the First Time' written on them." Alyssa made sure Jimmy was still breathing, then glanced at Mouth on her way to get the environment suits. By the time Mouth had her helmet and gloves on, Winston had joined them and was getting suited up.

"Any other volunteers?" Alyssa called out, and all of the men and women strapped into seats just looked at the soupy floor. "You know, I'm starting to understand why you complain about city people," she whispered to Mouth.

"So what's the plan?" Winston asked as he clicked his helmet into place.

Alyssa stuffed meal rations and a few explosives into a big duffel bag, which she handed to Mouth. "We're going to use the flamethrower. Just a different way than Jimmy had in mind."

Soon they were trudging through the sightless wind, away from the number-seven troop transport and any hint of warmth. Mouth had the flamethrower perched on her shoulder, and she'd handed the bag full of supplies off to Winston. This suit had much higher-grade night vision than the ancient gear the Glacier Fools had used, but her visibility was only a bit better.

The Citizens used to send young people into the night, with a rope tied around their waists to let them find their way out again, and leave them long enough to experience this unbearable disorientation, so they understood the importance of family, the significance of the people who see and understand you. "Absolution," the Citizens had called that moment of returning to the group after stumbling alone—meaning that the group was accepting you back into its embrace, but also that you understood how absolutely terrible life was without that warmth.

You could mistake the resting tentacle for a natural formation, like a ridge in the snow, from the murky view in this night vision. The transport resembled a misshapen hillock, as a thickening coat of ice covered it, and Mouth wondered if the engine would even run after sitting still too long. Even with the suit, Mouth felt the chill air draining the life from her body. But Alyssa had gotten a jostle back in her walk, even with the effort every step cost.

"You're in a good mood," Mouth said between shivers. "All this time you kept saying you never wanted to travel again, but you're having the time of your life."

"Eh," Alyssa said. "This is a lot different than our usual slog, and the goal is something more than just moving some junk from one city to another. Bianca was right when she said these cities are both screwed unless they work together, and y'know, this feels like an excellent cause."

Alyssa turned her helmet to face Mouth's. Maybe she was smiling, hard to tell.

Mouth kept seeing Alyssa's swagger out here on death's icy threshold, and having two reactions at once. She was happy for Alyssa, and grateful that she'd taken charge and figured out a save. But also, Mouth sensed that something had changed between the two of them, the culmination of all of Alyssa's attempts to fix Mouth back in Argelo. Alyssa had wanted her own crew, people she could count on who shared her goals, and now she'd found that by joining this slapdash invasion. Maybe Alyssa just didn't need Mouth anymore.

They had gotten far enough away from the transport, and Alyssa set about building a pyramid of rations, and setting tiny charges at key points, with fussy artistry. "It has to smell like food, and smolder for a while without melting through the ice," she muttered. From the flamethrower, she removed the fuel tank, which she splashed around her pile. One of the explosives had a crude timer, which they turned to its furthest setting: a picture of a zebra.

"Beautiful." Alyssa seemed to want to stand and admire her own sculpture, but Mouth tugged at her sleeve. By now, the cold had seeped into their joints, hindering their range of motion.

Nobody talked as they trudged back to the ATV, and Mouth could think only about taking off this unwieldy gear and being warm again. She didn't want to think any further than that. They had almost made it back when the puffed end of the squid's tentacle lashed out and poked at the lorry, the edges of its feathers tearing a huge gash in the side.

The squid seemed to be trying to decide if the whole number-seven transport was worth hauling down into the ocean when Alyssa's beautiful pyramid caught fire, a green flash far outshining everything else on the night vision. Like some sacred offering in the wilderness, the pyramid of food and accelerants blazed, sending smoke upward to join the low-lying cloud cover. Alyssa, Mouth, and Winston held their breath inside their helmets until the tentacle slid away from them to go investigate this new source of warmth and nourishing smells.

Mouth had an attack of lightsickness, climbing inside the well-lit transport, until she turned her night vision off. The gash in the side had let in the night air too fast for anyone to react, and their icy bodies were contorted into outlandish shapes, some of them with their mouths still opened to shout a warning or scream for mercy. Jimmy still lay where Alyssa had left him, like he'd never woken up. You would need heavy tools to dislodge these people from where they'd died.

Alyssa ran to the cockpit without bothering to glance at the dead, and gunned the engine, which miraculously still ran. She scooted them forward, as quiet as she could, fumbling at the controls with her thick gloves.

"We're not seriously going to drive across the night in a lorry full of icy corpses." Winston looked over his shoulder and shuddered at the unspeakable tableau.

"Pretty much, yeah," Alyssa said. "You guys should strap in."

"Good thing they're frozen solid." Winston gazed at the faces suspended in terror and agony. "When those defrost, it's going to be revolting."

Once they had gone a kilometer away from the undulating tentacle, Alyssa sped up, and soon they had gotten far enough away that it probably wouldn't find them again. Then they drove past one of the remaining vehicles: the rumbler, upside down, with a busted axle and a hole big enough to do jumping jacks inside.

"So much," Mouth said, "for the invasion."

"We were always going to be outnumbered," Alyssa said. "All the more reason to hit them before they see us coming. Just as long as the Command Vehicle survived."

"There they are." Winston pointed at the screen. "Damn, I didn't think we'd make it."

The Command Vehicle sat alone and motionless, but its lights still blazed, and the external shell appeared intact.

"Damn," Alyssa said. "Damn. What are they—damn damn damn."

As they approached, they could see a dozen huge, prayerful shapes in the darkness, clustered around the Command Vehicle: a congregation of Gelet. The scene looked utterly still, as if everyone had paused to reflect on their situation. Mouth let out a deep breath and tried to pull herself deeper into the frozen crevice of her passenger seat.

SOPHIE

gnore the buzzing from my right wrist, and I take Bianca's chin in my other hand, gentle as picking a pocket. I look down at her, bathed in the cockpit lights: wide perfect face suffused with bitterness and anger and, yes, love, but mostly just weariness. I stare, as if I had the power to preserve this sight in my memory forever. There are so many things I want to ask, in this final moment, but I don't know if I would believe any of her answers.

"I have to go," I whisper, and Bianca's eyes widen. "I have to leave right now. They're waiting for me. The Gelet. I think they want to take me to their city."

"Sophie, listen to yourself. This is delirium. We've all got it, after so long in this nothing wasteland." She grabs my arm, but I shake her off. "There's no crocodile city. There's nothing out there but frostbite and monsters. I get that you have a . . . a bond with these creatures, but don't delude yourself. You can't leave me now, in my literal darkest moment."

"You can come with me." I'm still close enough to murmur in Xiosphanti. I allow myself to believe for a moment that it's not too late, that Bianca and I could still leave everyone else behind. "There is a city. I've seen it."

I try to explain, so she'll at least understand after I'm gone: "I can't do this thing anymore, where we live in a tiny space and pretend it's the whole world. People always have brand-new reasons for doing the same thing over and over. I need to see something new."

The bracelet tugs my wrist again.

All through this conversation, I pretend Bianca and I are alone together—when we're in a severely damaged all-terrain cruiser, soaked with the funk of despair, crammed with every last surviving member of our invasion force. Maybe twenty-five of us, including Mouth and Alyssa, who somehow found us after we gave them up for dead. Their friend, Winston, has removed his environment suit, and I start putting it on.

"We're not going to let you just leave," Dash says, and I ignore him, because this vehicle won't go anywhere unless the Gelet allow it. They appear on the night vision: a dozen, on all sides, with their front legs bent and their pincers bowed in greeting.

"We're almost home," Bianca says. "Don't do something stupid."

I finish putting on everything but the helmet, which I hold in one glove, and I look into Bianca's eyes one last time. All my rage has petered out, and instead I just feel a sadness so violent it's like wings beating inside me, harder and harder, until they snap. I already told Bianca that our friendship belonged to the past, but now it's really true. That's the only way to explain why I'm leaving her like this.

Lucy keeps trying to use the flamethrower on the Gelet, until Dash has to pull her away and push her into the seat I've vacated.

"If you stay, you'll die," I whisper.

"I guess we'll see." Bianca actually smiles, as if she welcomes the challenge.

Just as I put my helmet on, Mouth says, "Can I come?"

I hesitate, and Mouth's expression turns bleak. At some point, she lost any ability to hide what she's feeling. She starts to say something else, about her senselessly dead nomads, and all the other deaths that make less and less sense. I wave for her to shut up and come with me, now or never.

Mouth turns to Alyssa, who says, "Fuck no. Not going to the giant frozen insect hive. I'm sticking with these assholes, because at least I understand them. And I still think we could win this. We were always going to be outnumbered."

"Alyssa," Mouth says. "I know I've let you down before, and you think these people are your crew now. But please, just trust me one last time. Don't throw your life away. Please."

"Just fucking go. Don't give me a whole dance routine."

I tug at Mouth's arm. She aims one last gaze at Alyssa, like a lost child.

Alyssa scoots closer to Bianca, and the two of them exchange little nods—like, they're in this together now. Mouth puts her helmet back on and turns to pull the tiny lever that opens the interior hatch, squaring her shoulders as if she's going to lift something enormous instead of two centimeters of metal.

Dash makes one last lunge to hold me back, and I brush him aside. Mouth and I pass into the outer chamber, and then step out into the sleet-freighted wind.

The Gelet see us coming, and wrap our environment suits with sheets of moss, and a mesh of tentacles. We move away, and the transport growls to life with the hiss of a damaged motor. I shut my eyes for a moment, and then Bianca is gone, vanished into the white wind. The Gelet cradle Mouth and me, leading us into an underground tunnel.

PART

SIX

SOPHIE

I can't stop crying for Bianca, the whole way down. Even with the environment suits, the blankets, and the shelter of the Gelet's tunnels, thick gusts chill my bones, and I picture Bianca surrounded by murderers and thieves, in a failing vehicle. The tunnels lead deeper and deeper under the ice, until we emerge into a cavern where steam rises from hot springs, and I remember promising to hold on to Bianca as long as I have arms. A faint light, pale green in my night vision, comes out of the hot pools, from bacteria or algae, and reveals the sawtooth shape of the walls. Bianca probably hates me now. In her mind, this is just the latest betrayal in a chain that started with me hiding from her after my execution. The Gelet urge us to move faster, into the depths, and I hear the growl of some ancient mechanism.

One of the Gelet seems to feel my agitation, and brushes my arm with one tentacle as we return to a darkness that even my visor can do almost nothing with. I stumble and reel, even with the Gelet guiding me.

My feet throb. Mouth keeps grunting, too. Steam bursts out of the ground and startles me, followed by more intense chills. My legs want to give out, but we keep moving. My disorientation is the size of a million cities, and if the Gelet let go of me for an instant, I'll be lost forever. I can't even tell the size of the space we're moving in, and have to close my eyes and breathe to fight off claustrophobia.

My breath is a piston that drowns out the Gelet's buried engines, and then I let out a wail, which gets louder until it scathes my throat.

I can't stop screaming, after holding it in so long. I scream into my helmet, so deep inside darkness that I have no sense of direction or escape route. I scream myself hoarse, remembering how I put my heart and sinews and guts into saving Bianca from herself, and only became her fool. Mouth says something that I can't hear. My knees fail.

On my knees, a ragged sound tearing from deep inside me, I can't bear this cold.

One of the Gelet pulls me upright, and gently peels the neckpiece off my survival suit. I feel the warm, wet feelers on my skin, and I get a series of impressions—

—a harpoon pierces my side, my own blood slick against my tentacles, fleeing for my life. I limp back home, with the last of my strength, and then I hang in a healing cocoon for an endless, itchy spell. My muscles cramp, and I think about the dream we all crafted among us, here in the city: bringing home our friend from the dusk, leading her down here with us. Finally living together, sharing all our stories with her, maybe even learning her stories, too. We shaped that vision together, and when I leave the husk of my convalescence, all my other friends keep reminding me of the dream we all had. Do I still believe, or did the spear poison my faith as it went into me? I'm not sure. The moment when I laid out that idea before our friend from the dusk, like a whole root system of possibility, is clouded by pain now. I struggle to hold on to that dream, but my memory itself feels wounded, deep in my core between my stomachs, maybe past healing. And then our friend from the dusk is back, and she brings other humans who want to communicate, and I can sense her hope, her courage, like a hot geyser from the deepest permafrost . . . and it's okay. Even when another harpoon cuts through the snowy wind, even when I lose more blood, lose my balance, chip away part of my carapace as a tiny boot comes down, I remember the pure hope that I sensed, bursting out of her. Our friend from the dusk, she carried the other humans to us on the back of that hope. One Gelet falls dead, alongside the three dead humans, but I know her now, our human friend. When I get back to the city, I tell the others that I believe once more—

—Still on my knees, my throat still hot, I gaze up at this Gelet. I notice the hole in her carapace, and I gaze up at her round, sharp-toothed mouth, and the forest of tendrils undulating inside her pincer. Maybe I haven't ruined every-thing after all. Her story settles into me, and I know I'm in the right place. I just hope Bianca is too.

I take a breath, replace my neck strap, and walk forward.

More and more Gelet cluster around us, and the air gets warmer, and that's how I know we've reached the city. Even with the night vision, I only glimpse pieces of the architecture here and there. In the glow from a furnace, I see a chamber stretching over my head, dotted with openings that Gelet climb through, and filled with alien machinery: sharp teeth, curved fulcrums, and blobs of living matter. I feel my way along the curved walls, with Gelet guiding me.

At last we reach a room, shaped like the inside of a bottle, where the light blinds me. I risk taking off my helmet, and I see some writing, in Noölang. Next to me, Mouth hesitates, then removes her helmet too. We're looking at a computer, Khartoum-built like all the computers on the Mothership, and it still works. The Gelet have reverse-engineered its solar cells to use power from the hot springs. The holographic display shivers, but stays readable.

"The Gelet are talking to the Mothership," Mouth says. "But that's . . . I mean, nobody talks to the Mothership, not for twenty generations. We don't even have the protocols anymore."

"Poor Pedro and Susana," I say. "And Reynold. They would have died of happiness if they could see this."

I try to get the computer to give me a real-time view of Xiosphant, so I can zoom in enough to see if Bianca somehow arrived safely. I could at least try to locate the Command Vehicle. The interface is pretty easy to understand. But whatever I do, I only see Xiosphant at some point in the past. Maybe the Mothership is flying over somewhere else now.

Instead, I find a schematic that says something in ancient script like, "Climate Projections: Original and Revised." The original climate projection, from when we arrived here, looks like a steady line, with some increase in temperature due to human industry but a corresponding increase in stabilizing factors. The revised version looks like a tantrum: the lines start out straight, then jerk up and down.

"Well, shit," Mouth said. "Even I can tell that's not good."

"There's going to be more storms, and more disruptions in the water table for both cities. And there's a seventeen percent chance of . . . I can't read this." I squint and try to remember my Noölang class. "Seventeen percent chance of catastrophic atmosphere loss."

"As in, what? Like, we can't breathe anymore?"

I toss my head.

The Gelet have reorganized the file systems, as if they want us to see certain things. The bottom of the display has a row of numbers: "07/20/3207 17:49." I poke at random, and a holographic video appears in the middle of the jumble. A woman wearing some kind of uniform, with features somewhat like Bianca's, looks right at us, and speaks in Noölang.

"My name is Olivia. I don't know if anybody will ever see this. I've been inside this alien city for twenty-nine Earth rotations, according to this computer. When we detected this place with our orbital scans, we couldn't have known how deep it goes, and most of the teams concluded it was either a natural ice formation or some sort of burrow system. I remember Richardson and Mbatha suggested it could be a built structure, but everyone else regarded this as a fringe theory at best, based on flimsy data. If only the rest of the science teams could see the interior structures and the complexity of these systems. These creatures are so much more advanced than we could have guessed, and they make me want to redefine all my ideas of technological and societal development."

She looks in all directions, as if she's scared that she'll be caught. "These natives seem to regard geoengineering and bioengineering as two branches of the same discipline. They've rebuilt both themselves and their environment to cope with this planet's unique challenges. Back on Earth, people theorized that a tidally locked planet would need some kind of 'air-conditioning' system, circulating hot air from the near side to the far side, to avoid weather instability and atmospheric disruption. And these creatures seem to have created something even better, using networked chains of flora to sequester and redistribute heat energy. They cultivate them inside dormant volcanoes and lava vents. It's incredible."

I'm not sure how much Mouth understands, but the word "flora," combined with "volcanoes," makes her stare.

"They use a form of touch telepathy, via this bodily secretion that's somewhere between a neurotransmitter and a pheromone," Olivia says. "They touch you, and you can share their memories, and the memories they've taken from others. There appears to be an olfactory component. Except that I can't always tell if they're showing me the past or their ideas for the future."

She shudders without any warning, weeping into her sleeve. "They want to . . . they want to make me the same as them. They have a surgery, or some kind of procedure, that will change me, so I can communicate the way they do. They've shown me what they're planning, and I won't let them. I still have the medi-kit, and I can take all my palliatives at once. I won't let go of my humanity. If anybody ever finds this video, please know, these creatures are not our friends.

They want to remake us, the same way they've changed their environment and themselves. If you see this, fight them, fight them with your last—"

The video cuts out. I'm left staring at an empty space, feeling sorrow for a woman who died a long time ago, one way or another.

Then the meaning of her words starts to sink in, and I feel so light my whole body might be made out of billowing silk. *Oh, of course.* I want to laugh, and then I do laugh, and I keep laughing, harder and more raucous, until I realize Mouth is staring.

I start to explain what Olivia said, but Mouth understood most of it. Her nomads used Noölang for everything sacred.

"Why would they let us watch that?" Mouth says.

"Because they wanted to make sure we understood what they plan to do with us: give us their gift of communication."

"Okay, so how do we defend ourselves . . . I mean, I told you, I can't fight anymore. And even if I could—"

"I want this." I take Mouth's shoulders and look into her wide-open eyes. "I'm going to say yes. I need to talk to the Gelet as an equal. And I am so tired of using this clumsy human voice. I never even liked talking. People lie every time they speak. I can finally understand, and be understood, and oh, of course I am going to do this! I have never wanted anything half as much."

"But your humanity!" Mouth grips the side of the computer table with both hands. "I mean, you can't let go of—"

"Did you actually read any of Mayhew's writing? Back when you were pretending to be a young radical?" I ignore Mouth's squirming, because we're past that now. "He talked a lot about human nature. We can't stay the same forever. New world, new people."

Mouth startles me by quoting from Mayhew's *Treatise on Inhumanity,* almost verbatim: "'We measure the freedom of human beings by their ability to change with their environment. The only truly alien influence is the dead grasping fingers of our own past.' But still, stop and think. You'll be throwing away everything . . ." She pauses and looks down at her boots. "You know what? I'm the worst person to give anybody advice. Do what you want."

"Thank you."

All this hope catches me off-balance. I'm scared, too— what if they kill me by accident? What if I look hideous to other humans? But this is worth any risk. Everything I've lost and suffered, all of it will be a cheap price if this works.

"But there's no way I'm letting them do that to me," Mouth says.

"I don't think you should. The one time you tried to communicate with them, you couldn't handle it. Any more than the others." I flinch at the memory of the scavengers, arguing about whether there should be a Spoon to go with the Knife. I'll never stop blaming myself for that bloodbath, even if the Gelet have forgiven me. I need to do better. And now, maybe I can.

I sit in three-quarter darkness, holding conversations with Bianca in my head. "Don't go," I tell her. "You don't want to go home. You want to go back to being the person you used to be. Even if you succeed in conquering Xiosphant with a handful of foreigners, you'll only be killing what's left of your old self. Come with me to the Gelet city. We'll sit in the dark and ask each other stupid questions, and keep each other warm." But even an imaginary Bianca won't listen to me. She's probably dead by now.

I'm not ready for how much I miss people, after always wishing I could escape from them. I hear Mouth grumbling in the opposite corner, but I've never been this far from a crowd before. Their loud voices, the inadvertent touches, and the scraps of personal information that people always give in passing. All the tiny ways that people help each other to exist.

Food appears from time to time, dropped in my lap from someplace: weird pastes that feel clammy in my mouth but warm in my stomach; roots; and, once or twice, some freeze-dried rations from the Mothership, still edible after so long. I sleep a lot, on a makeshift bed of old survival gear.

At last some Gelet come and herd me into a cavernous space, whose dimensions I only discern because of the echoes of my own stumbles. Every time I move, I almost topple. One of these Gelet puts her pincer around my face, the first time they've done this since I came inside the city, and shows me what they plan to do: an array of dark spikes going into soft flesh, and a cradle of bone being pried apart with great care. I see things that look like worms and blobs of fat being stuffed inside a cavity that wasn't meant to hold them. Skin being reshaped.

I understand: This will be painful. This will be impossible to undo. They'll need to take me apart and reassemble me, and they cannot guarantee mastery.

"Yes," I say. "Yes. Do it. I want that. Please. Yes."

They can't tell that I'm agreeing, so I spread my arms as wide as I can, indicating openness.

"I'm ready. I want to be able to speak to you. I want to be part of your society. Let's do this."

I keep broadcasting eagerness, as loud as I can. I can't contemplate that kind of pain, let alone the disfigurement, without going stiff with fear. But I know for sure, this is what I came here for.

Even when they take me into the chamber and remove all my clothing, exposing me to a chill, leavened by heat from deep-running springs, I don't flinch. When they offer some sedatives from some old human medi-kit, I take them eagerly. In a half doze, I have inklings that they're opening me up and taking away pieces, somewhere below my floating head. The drugs help me not to mind, but I don't mind in any case. They can take anything, as long as they give me what they promised.

When they finish remaking me, they seal up my insides, while one of them envelopes my forehead in her pincer, tenderly, showing me a comforting memory (dream?) of a snowdrift being rearranged, slowly, by a languid wind that moves tons of loose powder in ornate whorls. Kilometers of bright lace, in constant motion.

mouth

Mouth sat in one of the Gelet's weird sticky hammocks and heard their limbs scuttling in the trails going up and down outside the room where she was resting up. They had left a stack of old human books in here, and she'd read a couple of them in the meager illumination. Mouth didn't think she was a prisoner, exactly, but if she wandered out into the Gelet city, she'd just get lost, or wind up in total darkness. And the thought of exploring this hive filled Mouth with dread. The Citizens had been fond of dread, which they'd viewed as a profound spiritual rapture that suffused your whole body, even to the hairs on your skin and the arches of your feet. Dread lasted longer, and went deeper, than awe or joy.

Mouth couldn't force her mind to accept that she was in this alien place, with its hissing turbines and its swarming creatures. Instead, she tried to picture Alyssa sitting down here with her, and to guess what Alyssa would say about all this.

Maybe Mouth and Alyssa had never seen each other clearly. Mouth had always thought of Alyssa as a fully formed person who had already made all her big choices. But really, Alyssa had been a kid when they'd first met, and Mouth had only lately known Alyssa as an adult. She'd been trying to step up and become a boss for ages, but her relationship with Mouth had remained stuck in their old dynamic. And maybe she'd always cling to the impression of Mouth that she had formed as a wild-eyed girl with messy hair, leaving home for the first time.

Two pairs of snapping pincers appeared next to Mouth's hammock, and a tentacle brushed her skin. She flinched but didn't try to pull away. Up close, without the deafening wind, she could hear the teeth clicking in the wide mouth, and see the oily secretion glistening on the grubs in between the pincers. The Gelet smelled like damp cloth and fresh-baked bread, and they didn't have "heads" at all. Instead, these protrusions rose over their front legs, like your thumb climbs out of your wrist, and culminated in those two big indentations that seemed to change shape, looking sad or wistful or mirthful as the light shifted.

The Gelet guided Mouth out of the hammock and gave her something to wear: a kind of dry moss or algae that hugged her body wherever she wrapped it around herself, and kept her warm and comfortable. Then they led her into a maze of shadows.

Mouth had lost her night-vision helmet along with the rest of her gear, and she saw nothing but depthless chasms and knife edges everywhere. The tentacles steadied her but also wore away at her calm, with their soft cilia and thick flesh. In the occasional flickering from distant foundries and bioluminescent growths, Mouth glimpsed segmented bodies moving in the dark, and she jumped each time. She had no reserves of bloody-mindedness left. She lost track of how many turns they took, or how many paces, and she started to believe she'd never see again.

They arrived at a large space, one of those high vaults with a number of galleries or balconies coming off at regular intervals, all the way up to the black pinprick of sky. Light came from far ahead, pale yellow and red. Four or five Gelet stood together, with all of their pincers turned sideways and open wide, to allow all of their tendrils to connect in some group conversation. Their gaping pincers, all interlocking, looked like those thistles that were overrunning the shore of the Sea of Murder. Their hind legs flexed. Mouth turned away by instinct, then forced herself to look, and saw that one of these Gelet was not a Gelet at all.

Sophie disengaged herself from the group and walked toward Mouth, who almost didn't recognize her. She walked taller, with her head raised, and she had a blissful smile on her face, even amid all the gloom. Mouth was so distracted by her new posture and attitude she almost didn't notice the tentacles rising up from Sophie's back, or the wormy flesh wriggling on her chest, below the collarbone.

Then, once Mouth saw those things, she couldn't see anything else. She felt sick to her stomach.

"There you are," Sophie said, then shook her head. "It feels strange to speak aloud now." She guided Mouth until they were sitting on a kind of bench that was lit by a greenish glow from some living flesh hanging over their heads.

"So you . . . wow. So you did it. You went ahead and became . . . this," Mouth said. "They never even thought of making a law against what you've done, but you're still the greatest outlaw in history."

"Coming from you, that's a compliment. Right?"

Mouth didn't know what to say. She sat on her hands and stammered, without making any syllables. She knew what would happen now: Sophie would want to slime her so she could communicate without words. Maybe she'd force Mouth to experience her memories of witnessing all of Mouth's selfish behavior, when they'd first met and Mouth had been tricking Bianca, and this would be the final strike to Mouth's heart.

But Sophie didn't come any closer. "You'll get used to it," she said in a near-inaudible voice that sounded like the old Sophie again.

"I'm sure I will," Mouth said.

Mouth could hear the husky sound of Sophie's new appendages rubbing together in distress.

"You know, you don't have to be alone," Sophie said after they had sat for a while. "This pain you're holding inside yourself, all the memories of your dead nomads. You could share it with everyone here, if you became like me. You just form the memory in your head, and anyone you touched could remember it too, and share it. You don't know how light it feels."

"I can't do what you've done," Mouth said. "I really can't. I used to be brave, but . . ." Even thinking about the deaths of the Citizens, too, brought a desolation, like the whole of the road was wound around the inside of her frame. Mouth didn't want to share that anguish, to make it common property. She didn't want consolation, or a sponge to soak up her grief.

But then, on some weird light-starved impulse, Mouth

said: "But I can tell you about it, and you can share the memory of me telling you with your friends, if you want."

Sophie nodded.

Mouth talked until she tasted salt and bile. She told Sophie how she'd heard the voices in the distance, and then seen these blue creatures filling all the spaces around and between the Citizens. The chopping and whirring of a million pairs of wings, the whole encampment turned to a blue haze. The Priors, the helpers, the old people, the children, all singing with pain, until they went silent. Mouth running on her awkward child legs, fresh from a growth spurt, toward an orchard of skeletons with blue petals clinging. And then the shiny wings were gone, leaving just bones in the dirt. Mouth had painstakingly collected every one of those bones, even the smallest, even the ones that crumbled in her hand, and piled them in one spot. Then she'd fumbled with a tinderbox, trying to turn all the tiny wheels and open the valves, but only succeeded in burning her own fingers. At last she got a spark but the bones wouldn't catch until she'd baled dead grass from a kilometer away and spread it, and then the flame near took her face off.

Mouth had almost lost the power of speech by the time she got to the part where she'd walked away from the still-burning pyre and gotten lost, going in circles, even though the night was right there and the day on the other side, and you could see the plume of smoke. Her eyes stung, her heart beat louder and louder.

She had no strength left when she finished telling the story, and this was the most she had ever told anyone about what had happened, even Barney.

"I am going to be walking away from that fire for the rest of my life," she said, and this was something she had never admitted to herself before. "My hair could turn to white silk, my skin could turn to dry leaves, and I would still be walking with my back to the flames that consumed what was left of my people. I'm not ever going to be Argelan, or Xiosphanti, or Gelet, or any other nationality."

Mouth risked looking at Sophie. The girl's human eyes had a layer of moisture in them and around them, and her face was trembling. The thicket of fingers coming out of her upper rib cage wriggled, but the human face showed sadness, kindness, helplessness. Sophie rose, and without saying a word she went to share Mouth's testimonial with the Gelet.

Mouth sat alone, in a split-wall chamber that seemed dimmer than ever. She stared past the opening in the wall, into a superstructure of swaying material that looked like coral or limestone. The city's motors sounded like submerged avalanches.

Gelet came to fetch Mouth, three of them with their tentacles spread in a gesture that looked like sheltering, or guarding. Mouth had almost gotten used to not seeing, except for when a shape appeared nearby and startled her. They seemed to handle her with more care this time, after getting her story from Sophie, and the gentle nudges and enveloping tentacles only made Mouth angrier, because she was not some injured child. She pushed the Gelet off her, and made her own way.

She was so intent on brushing off her escort she marched right into a Gelet's waiting tendrils.

As soon as the slippery digits made contact, Mouth was somewhere else. She had known this was coming, had tried to prepare so she wouldn't lose her mind again. No fear, just stillness. But this Gelet vision was even more vivid than before—but also easier to understand, instead of the jumble of images they had dumped on her last time.

Mouth stood on the edge of the night, observing the road with inhuman senses. A mob of people walked from place to place, carrying everything on their backs or in a few carriages, straying into places that humans had never invaded before.

The Citizens became bolder as their numbers grew, and they even started going into Mount Abacus, the great rocky fist on the other side of the world from Xiosphant and Argelo. From the Gelet's vantage point, Mouth watched the Citizens climbing into the mountain that straddled the road, exploring every crack until they found this miraculous substance: a dry, chalky bloom that glowed in the dark and crumbled as they pulled it out of the caves. Mouth remembered the acrid smell of that stuff, the way the Citizens would smear it on their faces for some of their rituals, how they would gather every last bit, because it had a million uses. The Citizens had called that substance nightfire, because of the way it glowed in the dark.

Gelet had spent lifetimes cultivating this bloom. Mouth felt their terror and shock as it was stripped away, as the root system deep inside the vents began to wither and collapse. These plants laced throughout the world, collecting heat energy on the day side and redirecting it to the night, exhaling gases that calmed the skies. Over several visits, the Citizens ripped out every piece of nightfire they could find, until the sky changed. The clouds whirled until they ripped at the ice sheets and created brand-new mountains, as big as Mount Abacus, that moved through the night with the force of a million harpoon guns firing over and over.

A walking mountain of ice, with caustic liquid falling inside it—just like the downpour that had left burn scars on Mouth's scalp and hands—came upon a Gelet nest full of untold thousands of newborns. The protective layers of rock and coral collapsed, turning to sharp fragments, and then the rain burned everything that had been exposed to the air. These fresh infants screamed as they suffocated and starved, no way to save them.

As they struggled to save their young, the Gelet saw the Citizens going back to harvest another batch of the nightfire.

Mouth knew what was coming next, and she tried to pull away from these tendrils. But the Gelet held her fast. The blue swarm, a last resort, something the Gelet had created long ago to deal with a species of pests coming in from the road. She felt their remorse as the blue knives took wing from a hatchery deep under the ice and flew to the nearest food source in the warm twilight.

Mouth was screaming and pushing the Gelet with her hands and feet. She begged for release. She bit her own tongue and kept barking. She wailed and thrashed. The emptiness inside her was worse than ten thousand bones burnt to ash. When they let go, she fell on her hands and face, watering the dirt and clawing at her own scars.

She threw up on the floor and her own knees, the remains of some meal supplements the Gelet had rescued from a human transport coming in ugly pieces. The puke in her mouth only reminded her of the noxious rainfall that had flooded the Gelet's nest and destroyed their children.

"Please," Mouth said over and over, as if she could petition some authority to take away the ugliness.

The Gelet waited until she had stopped writhing and making sounds, and then they reached out, lightly, as if she could still lash out or fall to pieces. They helped her to her feet and led her back to the chamber with the hammock, the old books, and the bags of freeze-dried survival rations from some doomed ancient expedition into the night.

SOPHIE

You can go to the fifth central hub, downtown, and get these boiled chestnuts from a chef who gets them direct from the source, a chestnut patch buried under the thickest part of the night. Jean told me about it. The chestnuts melt against the roof of my mouth—so rich, after a diet of ancient human field rations. And once you've had enough chestnuts, you can go down the side chute and find yourself in a party where the "music" is made by an orchestra of countless tiny trumpets, which pressurize and depressurize the air around me in subtle fluctuations that human ears couldn't even register. Here in the midnight city, there's always a gathering, a celebration, someplace. I explore until my feet hurt, and I keep coming across another marvel. Like a school, where children, whose pincers look more like beaks, learn science and math from a teacher whose pincer encompasses all five of their tiny foreheads at once. (Their math begins with geometric shapes, and builds to patterns that remind me of the hangings on Ahmad's walls.) And just up the street, there's a theater where a dozen Gelet hang from stone ledges, and lean in to wrap all their pincers around a great tangle of flesh descending from the ceiling, which imparts a story to all of them at the same time. At another spot, a wide chamber with a low ceiling, the Gelet play a sport involving ice crystals and pressure-sensitive pads.

I navigate the city and almost don't care when I walk in total darkness, except when I suddenly notice, and I heave with terror for a moment. I still get too scared to move from time to time, thinking of cops forcing me up a mountain, or a bloodbath under toxic rain, or being trapped in the Command Vehicle. But I've shared all of those memories with the Gelet, in as much detail as I could stand—and in the process I've learned to look at each terror, to peel it apart into tiny moments, and to place it alongside the countless generations of their memories that I've been absorbing. I've joined a family whose firsthand experience traces back to before humans even had a concept of history.

I haven't seen what my new shape looks like, not with my eyes anyway, but my whole sense of my boundaries and my personal space has changed. I can "see" things happening far away, and "hear" the shape of the walls, thanks to my tentacles, which are smaller than a normal Gelet's. I don't always know exactly what I'm sensing, but it gets easier over time.

Nobody tries to stop me from roaming, now that I'm healed enough to move without feeling a million hacksaws tearing into me with every step. Everywhere I go, they're curious, but polite. When someone does stop me to ask a question, it's more along the lines of "How are you enjoying your stay?" or "Is there anything you need?" I'm the first foreigner among them in countless generations, maybe since the woman in that video, but they know me already.

When someone asks how I'm enjoying my stay, it comes not as words, but as a set of images and memory fragments that somehow evoke the concept of a solicitous host. When I reply, I babble. I share a memory of when I first arrived in Argelo, and I was scared to be in this crazy stormy city, and Ahmad taught me to make this fish bread that they all eat there. And I share another memory of Argelo, the first time I went to the Pit on my own, not to look for Bianca but because I craved those vapors. And how I felt, seeing people who celebrated having ancestors from Nagpur, for the first time. Then a flash of all the kindness I've received thus far, here in the midnight city.

This is way too much information, but they just send back an image of a perfect ice crystal: a kind of smile.

I keep trying to understand what the Gelet believe in. What religion, what politics? They give vague answers, like images of rock faces being worn away by the wind, or huge power generators turning somewhere underground. I wonder if one of these Gelet is Rose, my friend from the Old Mother, but they've all shared those memories among themselves, so everyone seems to feel as though they personally were up there with me. Gelet don't have names, like humans, but each newborn Gelet is given a kind of blessing, or hope for their future. So Jean's personal blessing was something like "good learner, future genius," and the part of my brain that still uses language decided to shorten that to "Jean." I'm not even sure how I tell each individual Gelet apart, but it's some combination of scent, variations in size and shape, and some kind of "hum" that my new senses can perceive.

Exhaustion has a sudden reach for toppling me off my heels and bringing back the pain from my surgeries. I'll explore, sticking my head into every archway—there are no doors here—and thrill at the discovery of a shop floor where Gelet are toiling in a circle over a set of gears that they shape according to a design they are sharing via touch. Or, in the next opening, a great bath where hot springs rise up and the Gelet cleanse their bodies. And then, just as I'm feeling the hunger to discover more, I'll teeter and fall. The cold seeps back into my bones, and I remember I'm trapped underground, in total darkness, and my head spins.

The first few times I grow weak and sleep-deprived, some Gelet lift me and take me back to the room with the bed, where I recovered from surgery. But after that, they find it easier to bring me to the place where they themselves rest.

In a great plaza, lined with brick and slabs of polished granite, Gelet throng, hundreds at a time, and pile themselves into slings and specially grown hammocks, which suspend their carapaces in a mist that feels warm and sweet. I bathe in the spray, which grows thicker and clings to my skin. The liquid fills the air until I float in a sensation of reassurance and acceptance, surrounded by all my friends.

Just as I slip into a dream, I remember the words that suicidal woman said in the hologram: *they seem to regard geoengineering and bioengineering as the same thing.* Of course, I think drowsily, of course they built a whole cave system where the vapors cause changes to their minds and soothe their bodies.

In my dream, I enter another level of the midnight city: a

river of solid ice that encases but does not feel cold, rushing into a frozen reservoir under a sky full of stars. I've never seen stars, except once at the Sea of Murder, and these keep growing and shrinking, changing their position, flaring and subsiding. Time rolls backward, and tall cities emerge from the tundra, great gleaming fortresses that withstand storms and quakes for countless generations. These cities climb into the night, drawing energy from the relentless wind and the flows of water and lava under the surface, and then I see them being built piece by piece. A whole earlier Gelet civilization rises up in front of me, after I already saw it fall.

I witness the slow progress of history, the changing shape of Gelet society, long before humans arrived.

A huge presence comes among us sleepers, and I cannot tell if it's inside the dream with us, or out in the plaza where our physical bodies are suspended in the solidified mist, which has formed sticky trails attached to my skin. One way or the other, this new arrival looms over all of us, much taller than a normal Gelet, with a pincer that looks large enough to encompass my entire body.

Somehow I can tell this is the leader, or more like the magistrate, of the Gelet, from the way all the other dreamers lower their pincers and focus their minds. This magistrate turns to each of us in turn, searching our hearts and examining our stories, with tendrils that slip past our skins and bones, and all of the walls we might have tried to build around our souls. When the magistrate comes to me, a powerful mind reaches all the way inside me and takes stock, and there's a long, terrible pause. I start to worry—maybe I've failed, been found wanting, or made a mistake. I panic, even in my sleep, twitching and contorting. But the magistrate just reaches all the way inside me and pulls out a childish memory I half forgot, from grammar school. Back when Mark tried to snatch my hand and I ran away from him, and then I was startled by the freedom, the safety, of not being courted. I feel that memory rise to the surface, coming to define me, but also becoming known to the other Gelet through our shared sleep.

I still obsess about whether this magistrate approves of me, but then I realize: this leader, whoever she is, has been dead since long before my grandparents' grandparents were born. This visitor is a shared memory, kept alive in all of us. I start to wonder if the entire government of the Gelet is made up of ghosts and dreams.

Most of my sleep is not so dramatic. I feel the motion of hot liquids underground, the cycles of water and lava and tectonics, and I sense the life of the planet, from deep underground to the high atmosphere, from beginning to end. At one point, I lie in the mesh, on an undulating hammock, and sense the motion of a glacier across the night: steady, unreasonable, pure.

I start to crave that experience of dozing on the hammock surrounded by Gelet, linked by sticky webs of shared memory, or secondhand fantasies.

For some reason, I keep thinking of all the Gelet as "she," but I don't know if they have any concept of male or female, or anything else. I've glimpsed how they reproduce, and they have many types of protrusions and openings, so everyone shares something and also takes something inside themselves. And then their babies start out as an unformed mass, inside a fungal mesh, although I've only glimpsed all this in their memories.

The spires of the midnight city soar hundreds of meters over the main plaza, made of some kind of crystal agate that sings, actually sings to my human ears, as the hot vapors come up from far below. Every time I go out into the city, I find something else that amazes me. A fountain channels water from some deep aquifer and makes it soar in two intersecting arcs that end in funnels that vanish inside the walls. A huge turbine spins in the depths, and powers a hundred ravenous machines. A ribbon of lava never stops streaming, close enough to singe me as I sidle past on the boulevard downtown.

When I'm not in the plaza, asleep among the Gelet, I visit the laboratory where they brew strains of amino acids that are designed to help them survive the latest unstable weather events, like these caustic rains. They've built a structure inside solid rock that I realize is a kind of centrifuge, in which specially grown shells whirl around too fast for even my new senses to encompass. When the circle stops spinning, a Gelet lifts one of these "vials" out delicately, aided by the fine motor control of her thousands of cilia.

I even find the hidden cul-de-sacs where the city's vices happen—the deep pit where Gelet meet to consume the powder from drying and grinding up certain roots, which makes them dream of running away from their friends and just getting lost in the night alone. Or the tiny nooks where the Gelet disappear, when they think nobody can see them, to connect to memories and fantasies that are forbidden for one reason or another: things everyone agrees were better left behind. No matter how often I ask, I can never quite understand what they forbid, and how.

Soon, I know the streets of this city better than I ever knew Argelo. I know just where to turn to find the back passage that leads to a tiny workshop, and sometimes they've gotten some old computers working, so they can play a skein of sad music from my homeworld, the sounds of strings and drums teased by long-dead fingers, echoing through the ice and stone of the midnight city. I also know where to go to find an ice slide that carries me down forty or fifty meters, in a hair-raising glide path, straight into the middle of a festival where puppets reenact a famous scene: the arrival of humans on the bright edge of the day.

The humans emerged from their shuttles and landers, intent on striding onto the surface of this new planet. And then they all fell on the ground, in pain. The higher gravity, the stinky air, the white light, all made them go fetal. They stayed down, moaning, for ages. Some of them never got up again. Many of the colonists who had survived the wars and accidents and atrocities onboard the Mothership died soon after arrival.

Far away, in the night, the Gelet set about trying to understand these people: how they lived, how they communicated, what they worked for. After some of the humans had tried to go into the night, and the Gelet had been forced to bring down their flying machines and wreck their lorries, the Gelet understood about speech. But even once they reproduced the vibrations, the Gelet couldn't replicate them.

They couldn't ask the magistrate for advice, because she

had been dead for generations, and as far as she was concerned the dusk remained quiet, a clean buffer before the turbulence of the day.

People in Xiosphant never knew how close the city came to destruction. The Young Father is a dormant volcano, and the Gelet had a lot of experience controlling those. They couldn't understand us, but they took our machines apart, and our technology told a story about people who never quit building and killing. They swapped ideas back and forth, of what could happen: humans invading the night in force, launching some extreme terraforming project, ordering the Mothership to drop meteorites on the midnight city. Plus if they waited, Xiosphant could become too well protected for them to destroy.

The city survived because the Gelet made a better assessment of humanity's technical abilities. They saw we were losing touch with the Mothership, and we didn't have the meta-materials we needed to keep building onboard control systems, weather shielding, and various other things. We showed lots of ingenuity in inventing new ways to produce food and handle our waste, and keep people alive in this environment, but most of our technology was sliding backward. But also, they saw us digging up metals from our mountains and the meteors we'd brought down—copper, bauxite, cobalt—and saw how we could be useful.

After many visits to the hammocks in the plaza, sharing the collective memory/dream, I realize that human civilization is based on forgetting. If I own a pair of shoes that used to belong to you, then my ownership relies on your forgetfulness. Humans are experts at storing knowledge and forgetting facts, which is why we saw this city from orbit and then pushed all the evidence into a hole. And I can't help thinking of what Bianca said when I asked her about the Hydroponic Garden Massacre: that progress requires us to curate the past, to remove from history things that aren't "constructive." I don't know if our power to forget makes humans stronger, more self-destructive, or maybe both.

The Mothership still has a store of ancient media from Earth, and when I find my way back to the bottle-shaped room with the computer I call up images and films of Nagpur. They called it the Winter Capital, but the holographic recordings show a red sky and people wearing light summer clothes in bright colors. They move along walkways and tramlines that look like filaments, strung high above the gleaming domes and stupas on the ground. There are films of people dancing in unison; doing a coming-of-age ritual that involves wrapping a thread around a boy about Ali's age; building vast swarms of tiny robots that soar outside the weather-shield; sharing a meal of thick bread and vegetables that look like nothing I've seen before; sending probes deep inside the Earth to harvest geological energy. These clips have numbers at the bottom that start with things like "2439," and I'm realizing this is some archaic calendar. Then I find a hologram stamped with "2527," showing a family from Nagpur: mother, father, squirming giggling son, all wearing modified CoolSuits with an emblem on them. Someone I can't see asks in Noölang, "Are you excited to be leaving home? What are your hopes for this long voyage?" The father jokes, "I just hope those Calgary idiots don't make a mess of the sewers, or it's going to be a long flight." The mother slaps his arm, lightly, and looks straight ahead. "I hope Partha makes plenty of friends on the ship, and doesn't end up mixing with the wrong kids. Peer pressure in an enclosed environment is always the worst." Her husband rolls his eyes, but she ignores him. "Partha's children, or maybe his grandchildren, will live to see this new planet. I hope they remember where they came from." The image fades. I'll never know what happened to Partha, though I can guess. But now that I've seen these things, I can share them with everyone, and they'll never disappear, even after the Mothership's systems fail.

Jean has a broken left tentacle that the Gelet could not fix, even with all their advanced biohacking. She can still lift small objects with her other tentacle, and can make adjustments to the great machines underground with her cilia. She worked some stints in the farms, the foundries, and the water-treatment canals, but the physical labor wore her out, and meanwhile she has a good personality for teaching and counseling. That's why they encourage Jean to spend time with me. She shows me the memory of traveling across an ice floe in the middle of a violent snowfall, when a nearby outcropping broke just as she passed, sending sharp rocks cascading down. From her viewpoint, the snow grew teeth. She was trapped under the rock for a painful age until her friends could get her out, and her whole left side is still racked with chronic pain. She also shows me the rockfall from the viewpoint of a few others who witnessed it from a distance: the mountain crag coming apart, the boulders in free fall. By now, she remembers the disaster as much from far away as up close, because she and others have shared the distant vantage point so many times. Maybe that's good for her recovery.

The Gelet work hard, without getting rewarded with food dollars or marks, or threatened with conscription. Instead, they just talk about work all the time. Everyone shares their memories of all the work they've done, and thus everybody knows just how hard everybody else has worked since the last time they've gotten together. Nobody ever lies, and I don't know if they're exactly capable of lying.

Jean still moves different from the others, and everybody knows her story. After her accident, Jean fell into a deep depression that nobody could shake her out of, according to another Gelet, whom I've started calling River. River and I are sitting in a sort of canteen, eating stewed roots that look odd but taste like roast pheasant, and her pincer is wide open so I can extend my tendrils and entangle them with hers. I'm still getting used to doing that.

According to River, Jean wasn't depressed just because of the chronic pain, but because everybody treated her different. Every time they shared memories, even of unrelated things, the Gelet couldn't help letting their worry about Jean, even their pity, leak through, and this made her flesh crawl underneath her carapace. Everyone talked among themselves about how to make Jean feel better, and then they couldn't hide this from her. Their concern for Jean became an infestation that left sticky strands of poison through every thought and desire they shared, however benign.

This had happened before. Long before humans arrived on January, another Gelet was caught in a tectonic experiment that went awry. This scientist was unhurt physically, but she kept reliving the fear and pain, the feeling as the plate shifted and everything came unstuck. The moment when she realized everything was not under control after all, and then the rest of her team died. All the others revisited her memory of that instant when power gave way to powerlessness, but it was not their memory, it was hers. They all observed her sullenness since the accident, and they talked endlessly about how to cheer her up. So they showed her comforting memories of when someone else had survived a bison attack, or they shared with her their recollections of happy occasions. But the more they tried to help her, the more they reminded her of how bad she was feeling, and the worse she felt. This turned into a self-reinforcing spiral, and eventually she killed herself.

So everybody tried to handle Jean differently. They knew Jean was a gentle soul, with more patience than most, so they gave her a job working with the newborn children, just split off from the mass. They all had noticed those moments when Jean showed her gentleness, and everyone shared them more and more. *You're the only one who can do this.* Jean knew perfectly well that she was being handled, that they were all going out of their way to support her, but she decided to put up with it, and anyway she liked her new job.

But everybody still notices Jean's injury, even when they try not to, and she hates the moments when they pause in her presence. The way their tentacles quiver as they try not to sense what's right in front of them. That's one thing Jean likes about spending time with me: her difference is nothing compared to mine. When the two of us walk around together, nobody even notices her.

I have no idea how long I've been in the midnight city, but my old life feels like a surreal dream. I've healed enough to start thinking about finding a job here. Like, I could help harvest roots or grubs from the deep crevices that a regular Gelet can't get inside. Or I could help in one of the laboratories, because I've always loved science. Bianca used to say that Xiosphant's only goal was to keep things the same and maintain our current level of technology, and that this forced Xiosphanti scientists into a contradiction—because the true goal of science is to make progress and discover new things. But Gelet science seems to be different, with experiments that have been in progress for generations, involving processes that move too slowly to observe in one lifetime. Plus, since the climate destabilized, their main goal has been to protect future generations. They can remember every disaster, the same way they remember every failed experiment from the past.

When I picture myself, I no longer imagine a shy girl with high cheekbones, a round face, and swept-back black hair. Instead, I'm a collection of tendrils and limbs: smaller than a regular Gelet and less mobile, but still the same in the ways that matter. I no longer notice when I'm in the dark for long periods, because my senses are all about the vibrations underground, the nonvisible wavelengths of radiation that swim around me, the movement of other people nearby.

I'm with River in one of those smaller salons, where the natural warmth from the springs comes up through a big spout in the middle of the room, and I'm cozy in a blanket of bioengineered fuzz. I'm drowsing, my tendrils braided with River's without sharing any particular thought, and River sends me a memory that I must have shared sometime in the past.

I'm a human, in Argelo, and Bianca is saying, "—this amazing drink that you are about to try for the very first—" and then the taste of an Amanuensis, the sweet kick, still delicious after all this time.

I don't know what makes me sicker: seeing Bianca, smelling the sugary sweat that fogged the air in Punch Face, or just being exposed to human speech again. Whatever it is, I have a panic reaction that feels like an old forgotten friend, along with the agony of reawakening parts of myself that I put to sleep, long ages ago. I excuse myself and pull away from River. I need to take care of myself, by myself.

I haven't even wanted to think too much about the memories of my old life since I got used to living here. The few times lately that someone brought up a memory that I had shared about my family, or Bianca, or the Parlour, or going to the White Mansion in Argelo, I would just freeze up. People learned not to talk to me about that weird, messy human stuff.

Some time later, Jean and I are leaning against the wall after we've just watched one of those puppet shows, and I don't even notice that my tendrils are fully extended and linked to Jean's—until she shares a memory of the time I followed Bianca around Xiosphant and I saw her meeting with Mouth, in a roomful of guns. The memory is there, as fresh as a moment ago: Bianca's neck poking out of her fashionable coat, her hair pinned back, the sneaky way she looked around, as if she didn't realize how easy she was to follow, the weight of my longing as I hid from her. All at once, I'm young and foolish and unaltered, and pining for someone who thinks I'm dead.

I turn firm and brittle, choke on my own breath. I haven't shared any memories of being human in a long time, but I must have shared a lot of them, early on, when I was learning to communicate.

I almost pull away from Jean, break the connection. But I don't want her to go around sharing a memory of me being an oversensitive fool with everybody else. So I just try to relax and take it in. I chose to make this moment available, so I can't blame Jean if she decides to give it back to me.

But then more human memories flood back, one by one. The first time I almost died on the Sea of Murder. My failed attempt to avoid joining Bianca's invasion plan. The Curfew Patrol chasing Bianca and me, while alarms blare all around us. The Glacier Fools shouting in their delirium.

Now, I lose control of my breathing altogether. I pant faster, without drawing any oxygen. I feel light-headed, my limbs gone dead, and all my old memory-panic is back. I can't stand to think of myself as having a human body, or a voice that could expel sounds that human ears could catch and ingest. I thought I'd made peace with these memories.

I'm not handling this as well as Jean hoped—and that's when I realize: this is something the Gelet have decided to do. They're going to keep reminding me of what it felt like to be among humans, until I can take it without breathing too fast, going numb, or throwing angry, misshapen thoughts back at them. Jean shows me a happy memory of a glacier until I stop twitching and fighting. Still, all of these memories, one after the other, crush me with so much anger, love, and fear, I still feel my skin crawl, my heart pound, a pain like lightsickness, only worse.

For the first time since they put these tendrils and all these other new organs inside me, I want to tear it all out with my bare hands.

Jean wants to understand why I can't handle the memories that I chose to share in the first place. How can I explain, in a way that a Gelet will understand?

I share a memory with Jean of my lowest moment ever— not the part when the cops pulled me out of the Zone House and forced me up a mountainside and I knew my life was over, but later, afterward, when I soaked in a hot bath at the Illyrian Parlour. When I was safe but knew I'd never be safe again, warm but chilled inside, scrubbed but forever dirty. And the one thing that consoled me in that moment was tucking myself back inside the memory that Rose had shared, of running in the night with all the other Gelet, on our way to build something with our powerful limbs.

I keep showing Jean, over and over, how that borrowed memory saved me at my lowest point. I capture the exact moment when my despair gave way to wonder.

Jean still doesn't get why even my happiest experiences of living with humans bring me nothing but pain. Even after everything Jean went through, she still thinks happy memories ought to cheer you up.

A while later, I'm not even surprised when another Gelet, whom I call Felice, wants to give me back another memory I shared long ago.

I'm back in the dorm, and Bianca and I are sitting and studying after she's returned from some party or formal ball, and this one kept her away from me forever. I'm staring at my book, trying to concentrate, but then I look up at Bianca, who's already looking at me with this tiny smile. I make some face at her, and she breaks into cackles, and then we're both laughing.

That's it, the whole memory. Felice teases out all of the little details, like the way Bianca's smile starts sad and then the indentations around her mouth and eyes change shape. The surprise in Bianca's face when I make whatever face I'm making, and then the giggle.

I tense up, but Felice is already showing me a comforting memory of snow washing across an ice field, kilometers away from anything.

I don't know why the Gelet are trying to hurt me like this. Except, of *course* I know.

I find myself going to all my favorite places in the midnight city, greedy to stockpile memories for what I already realize is coming. The area where they put new organs inside me, removing part of a lung, feels sore and fatigued. Some strain, deep under the skin and bone.

I clamber down, out of my favorite hammock in the plaza, and Jean and River are both standing nearby, come to visit me. They both open their pincers, extending their tendrils to touch my chest. I brace myself for another old memory of when I was human.

Instead, though, Jean and River show me a plan. Me, as I am now—with sensitive, vulnerable tendrils on my sternum, two tentacles climbing out of my back, and indistinct shapes on my abdomen—walking the streets of Xiosphant. Using the gifts the Gelet have given me to help other humans understand. In time, recruiting other humans who can become like me, so we can create whole families of hybrids, who can also recruit.

They're going to send me away. Send me *home*. Looking like this, hideous to human eyes, with no protection. I saw this coming, but I wasn't prepared, and trying to see myself through the eyes of Xiosphanti makes me feel sick to my core. I let out a tiny gasp, which sounds monstrously loud to me after so long keeping silent.

mouth

Mouth almost went into a coma after the Gelet showed her how they had destroyed the Citizens. She wanted to. She even tried to. She made every effort to let the darkness around her suffuse her. She could not recall the walking mountain of ice, weeping its astringent blood, without hand tremors. She could never accept the Gelet visions, or whatever they were, in any case, but her mind could do almost nothing with that toxic ice, destroying a crèche full of infants, except rebel against itself.

The Citizens never even knew what they had done. They invented myths about the Gelet—servants of the Elementals, or teeth in the jaws of eternal darkness—but all of those fables were about what the Gelet could do for people, or to people. The Citizens had stayed blameless in their own cosmology, until the very end.

Her mind kept offering up more and more details of what they had shown her, as if Mouth couldn't process it all at once. No way to shut off the thoughts, even when she slept.

Sophie had not been present when Mouth had received the story of the nightfire. She had stayed away on purpose. But she came to Mouth's bedchamber much later, crouched under the hammock so she was just a voice drifting from the bottom of the room. Mouth sometimes lunged, to pull her closer or to push her away, but she was never within reach. Sophie spoke haltingly, because she had never loved talking even when she'd had no other way.

"The nature of the Gelet's consciousness is such that, I mean, you have to understand, the past is all one." Sophie stammered far below Mouth's bed. "To the Gelet, the decision to spare Xiosphant from destruction is as fresh as when they chose to wipe out the Citizens, even though they took place so many generations apart. For the Gelet, they both happened at the same time. I think they evolved this way because they live in never-ending darkness, with frozen winds that obliterate all sound and erase all writing. They worked for hundreds of generations to stabilize their climate by engineering special flora, and, to them, that work also just happened."

Mouth never responded to anything Sophie said, other than with her arms and legs.

"Humans couldn't have survived on this planet without all the work the Gelet had done before we got here," Sophie said. "We wouldn't have lasted more than a generation or two before the storms would have wiped us out. The farmwheels in Xiosphant, the fisheries and orchards of Argelo, they wouldn't even have existed. Everything we keep fighting over."

Sophie grew tired of speaking, as Mouth had known she would. If she climbed up and tried to use her new body parts to send ideas or memories straight to Mouth's hind brain, Mouth was scared she might hurt Sophie involuntarily, even with her pacifist hands. But Sophie never came near. Mouth just heard Sophie breathing, over the scrape of the stone engines.

Mouth had her own personal memory of the blue swarm, the bones that broke apart when she tried to gather them up, the flames too close to her face. This was her own experience, and now that she'd worked so hard to reconstruct it for Barney and then Sophie, she couldn't push it back into the hole where she'd kept it for so long. But she also couldn't get rid of the memory of the great spout of ice, drizzling deadly slush as it traveled. Both things made her want to shut down.

"I eavesdropped when you met with Bianca, back when you wanted to trick her into helping you steal your poetry book," Sophie said from the darkness below. "I remember you said, 'The truth should hurt. Truth should knock you on your butt. Lies make it easy to stand.'"

Mouth broke her silence at last. "You paid more attention to me than I paid to myself."

"The Gelet have been giving me back my own memories, which is the first cruel thing they've ever done to me. But you sounded impressive. I actually wanted to believe you."

"I was just repeating things I heard somewhere," Mouth said. "Things the Citizens used to say, things I overheard in political meetings. I combined them, changed them around."

"That's all anyone ever does," Sophie said. "People never say anything new."

Sophie fell silent again, but she wouldn't leave Mouth alone. Like Mouth had taken some bad pills, and Sophie had to hold vigil while she rode them out. Mouth tried a couple times to say that Sophie owed her nothing, but Sophie just stayed, on the floor, breathing quietly.

"I want to show you something," Sophie said after a long time. "I think it'll be easier coming from me than from one of the Gelet."

Mouth understood what Sophie meant by "show," and she began to protest, to protect her face and neck with upthrust elbows.

But Sophie shushed Mouth and made soothing noises, and touched her rain-scarred neck with one palm. Sophie's face caught the one shaft of light coming into the chamber from some distant furnace, and her round features looked more composed than Mouth had ever seen. Maybe they'd changed places at some point: Mouth was the scared kid now. Sophie kissed between Mouth's eyes, which gave out more of their seemingly endless supply of tears.

"Don't worry," Sophie said. "I can take you down gently."

Mouth nodded at last. "Okay. Do it." Sophie's face jostled, and Mouth realized that this was her own body shaking. She made herself go slack.

Sophie leaned closer, until her chest was touching Mouth's, and then her wriggling little tongues snaked out. Mouth stiffened again at the last moment, but she felt the light touch of a few dozen surfaces, almost like moistened fingers, making contact with less pressure than the Gelet had used. Sophie shushed Mouth again. Her face was so close that she had three eyes, and you could feel her breathing almost like it was your own.

When Mouth closed her eyes, she could see something taking shape, an image or something, but it felt like an afterimage, a half impression. The picture kept pulsing in and out, and Mouth found herself concentrating, straining to see it more clearly.

"There you go," Sophie said. "Just let it take you."

Mouth leaned back in the hammock to let Sophie put more weight onto her. She felt Sophie's knees around her waist, Sophie's body resting against hers, and Sophie's face on her face. Then she went into Sophie's vision, and all these sensations vanished.

Sophie wasn't showing Mouth a memory, the way Mouth had expected. She had braced herself for another glimpse into the terrible features of history or, worse, some slice of their shared past from Sophie's perspective. Instead, they were flying, Sophie and Mouth, floating above the clouds that had been the upper limit of the world for Mouth's entire life. Mouth looked at Sophie, who was gliding with a placid focus in her eyes, like she did this every day. Sophie gazed upward, and Mouth followed her line of sight to see the blackness of the sky overhead, dotted with tiny lights. A rounded mirror splashed them with reflected light, and Mouth realized this was the moon.

How are we doing this? Mouth tried to ask Sophie, but there was no air up here.

Sophie's voice came, from somewhere far away. "This isn't a memory, not really. Some of it is. The Gelet have memories of being in flying machines that they've shared with me. But this is also just my imagination, mixing with the real sensations. Think of it as a fantasy."

Mouth could see the sweep of the ground, passing under-neath, in between the thick ropes of clouds. The ground was pitch dark, because they were over the night, and the clouds wouldn't let even a drop of moonlight through. Mouth wasn't sure how they could see down there, but this made dream sense rather than regular sense. They passed over the curve of the world, and Mouth saw a burning light on the horizon. She tried to turn and fly in the opposite direction, because the sunlight would shrivel her to cinders, but Sophie kept driving forward. "Nothing can hurt us," she whispered.

In the dream, Sophie gave Mouth a tiny smile, like they were two fliers moving independent of each other, and then they came into more light than Mouth had ever seen. Even through the clouds, she could see the arid ground sizzling, the very dirt being scoured by hot winds. How Sophie had gotten this image, Mouth couldn't guess, since Gelet would never be able to withstand full daylight, in a flying machine or otherwise. Then Mouth looked down and saw crystal formations, gleaming and pulsing: another city.

Sophie pointed upward, and at last Mouth knew where she had gotten these images of the day, seen from above. A spaceship passed right over their heads: a silver shape, like a man crouching on his elbows and knees, with the sun painting its ancient skin a million shades of red and blue, rippling into each other. The Mothership had never stopped waiting, never lost faith in the people crawling in the dirt below.

They flew through clouds, ducked around tiny windstorms, and wove in and out of the day. Sophie beckoned Mouth with one finger, and they flew higher and higher, up into the blackness, past the edge of the atmosphere. They hovered far above even the Mothership, near the great yellow-orange crags of the moon. And they looked at January, the bright half and the dark half, not motionless at all but always turning. The day wasn't just red fire, but had veins of blue and green, like jewels against a bright cloak. The night had a texture like velvet, with a dark purple sheen to it. Mouth stood in space, looking down at the world, and she was flooded with an emotion she couldn't even identify. She almost couldn't stand how beautiful January was from up here, and how wonderfully wrong it felt, to see so much daylight with what seemed to be her own eyes.

They drifted down, not even seeming to get any closer to the clouds at first, then picked up speed. Mouth almost screamed as she fell into the cloud layer, but it became a laugh instead. The clouds yawned and swallowed them, and then they descended in the night, racing over frozen peaks and canyons wider than anything on the road. At last they found the city in the middle of the night, and descended through an airshaft. Mouth saw her own body, inside a tiny chamber, with Sophie sprawled on top of her, and then she fell inside her own head and her eyes opened.

Mouth realized her clothes were soaked with sweat, and she and Sophie were stuck to each other. She didn't want to peel away, because she felt her heart drumming, her blood so rich it dazzled her eyes, her skin wide awake. Sophie had given her an incredible gift, and she didn't know what to do with it. She pulled her arms out from between Sophie's knees, and hugged Sophie as tight as she could.

"I thought you hated me," Mouth whispered in Sophie's ear.

"I did, for a long time." Sophie was breathing in sharp bursts. "But you're my jinx. I guess I have to find a way to live with you."

"I'm . . ." Mouth felt overcome for a moment, with stammering tears. "I'm sorry about Bianca. I'm sorry for all of it. I keep wishing I had died with the rest of the Citizens. I wish we hadn't destroyed this delicate miracle that the Gelet had created. We should have paid attention."

"Bianca made her own choices." Sophie raised herself up, so she was kneeling across Mouth's waist and lap. "The rest of it, I don't know. But Bianca, she deserves to take the blame for her mistakes. I wanted to put all of it on you so I could keep her pure in my mind, but that's not fair to her, either. I still blame you for the parts that were yours, but . . ."

Mouth sat, her hands just touching Sophie's. "I thought if I could make up for what I did with Bianca and the others . . . I thought I could be a good person. But now, I feel like . . . I don't know. I feel like I should do something to make sure what happened to the Citizens never happens again."

Sophie twitched with fear, like Mouth could be about to suggest doing something drastic: revenge or something. And maybe Mouth should hate these creatures for killing her people, who had never intended any harm. But she couldn't get the image of the marching icecap, full of burning rain, out of her head.

Mouth shook her head. "I mean, people need to understand. Maybe more people need to become like you."

"They already told me that they want me to go back, to find other humans who could become hybrids," Sophie said. "I don't want to. I want to live here forever. You don't even know how great it is, being able to share everything."

Mouth would never forgive the Gelet for what they had

done, but she could understand it. You might mistake understanding for forgiveness, but if you did, then the unforgiven wrong would catch you off guard, like a cramp, just as you reached for generosity.

Sophie led Mouth on tours of the city, which had innumerable wonders when you perceived it through Sophie's senses. Mouth learned not to cringe, at least not too much, when Gelet came near. Some of their food tasted decent when you got used to the slurry texture and rough, chewy edges.

Sophie still wanted to convince Mouth to give in, to let go of humanity and learn to perceive all the beauty, the dream geography, of this city. To become like her. But Mouth would never have simple feelings about the Gelet, and there would always be some hate in the mix. Plus, her mind couldn't open itself up the way Sophie's did. If Mouth tried to live with those new senses, plus all of the vivid access to other people's memories and ideas, her head would explode. "Even if I didn't have all this toxic emotion, I wouldn't have the right kind of brain," Mouth kept trying to explain.

"This is the way to make sure history doesn't repeat itself, you said so yourself."

Mouth shook her head. Memories still pressed on the upper part of her spine. "You'll find other people who can handle it, you're good at reading people. You can find the ones who have nothing to lose, who have learned to listen with both ears so they can know when the powerful will come down on them next. The people Bianca was willing to die for. You'll spot them, and offer them a different chance."

"I can't," Sophie said. "This is going to destroy me. However sick you feel inside, when you imagine letting the Gelet reach you ever again, imagine that times a hundred. That's how I feel about going back among humans. Even if I were normal. But looking like this . . . everyone who sees me will be disgusted."

Mouth had gotten used to how Sophie looked. Her face was the same as ever, her eyes still clear and searching, her mouth wide and expressive. She had a protective hide around her shoulders and torso, which could appear like a suit if you weren't looking carefully. But the tentacles, which seemed to help her see in the dark, and the moist grubs, which grew under her collarbone and waved like kelp in the water, would be harder to disguise.

"I think you're beautiful," Mouth said.

Sophie just scowled. "I'll be dead the moment I set foot in Xiosphant."

Mouth knew the next few words she spoke would change her life, maybe ruin what was left of it. But she had no choice: "I'll protect you." Sophie was staring at her, and maybe didn't know how to trust someone whose head was a sealed vault. Mouth added, "I still can't fight, or use a weapon. And I know I haven't always kept my promises. But I mean it. I'll guard you with my life."

Sophie seemed like she was about to say something back, then thought better of it. She didn't speak the whole rest of the time they walked around the city, even though Mouth couldn't make much sense of the "tour" without Sophie's narration.

They walked through giant chambers and around the edges of deep pits, but though Mouth could take in just enough detail to recognize tremendous engineering, she mostly saw just tentacles and huge legs moving in the gloom.

No matter what Mouth said now, Sophie had stopped talking, as if they'd stepped back in time to when they had been strangers. Mouth tried to break through her wall, by making awkward jokes about the noxious gin-and-milk that everyone insisted on drinking in Xiosphant, but Sophie just shrugged and kept walking. Mouth lost Sophie a few times, but then Sophie would tug at Mouth's wrist from out of the darkness. Mouth ended up back in her hammock, alone, with a few boxes of freeze-dried survival rations for company. One of them contained actual chocolate, which was more tart than she had expected.

Mouth had nothing to do but lie there, with a riot of ghosts. She read more books, and also decided that the sides of her head had healed enough to shave them once more, using some supplies from an old medi-kit. She had no clue how long she stayed there alone, but when Sophie reappeared, she still wasn't speaking. This went on so long Mouth almost forgot what Sophie's voice even sounded like.

SOPHIE

I can't go back to Xiosphant. I'll die. I'd rather go into the night and freeze to death than return to the city that tried so hard to break me. Especially looking like this.

I try to explain to Jean: I imagine running out into the night, exposing myself to the elements, and I make the image as real as I can. This terrifies Jean, who was considered a suicide risk for such a long time, but she still responds with the same old idea of me walking among my own kind again, happy and useful. The decision has been made.

But who made this decision? I've been understanding their society for so long, and I know the city backward and forward—I even met the magistrate—but I still don't know who's in charge, or how I can change their mind. I have no clue what they believe in, what principles guide their decisions. Nobody even understands when I try to ask. I show them the prince and the Privy Council, or the Nine Families, and they grasp that some humans are treated better than others. They respond with a memory of a time, right after Jean was hurt in that snowy rockslide, when the others tried to bring Jean her favorite foods, or play complicated music involving countless pressure variations.

I slip away from Jean and sneak down to the deepest, hottest levels of the city, where nobody's ever brought me. If there's a leader, or a ruling council, or something, it must be down here somewhere. I search every tunnel, but never find any seat of power.

Then I stumble into a wide, rocky chamber that's so hot I have to shield my eyes. Sweat pours down my face. In the middle of this vault, a fleshy mass writhes inside a sticky web. These are the half-born children, just like Rose showed me so long ago, still hungry and sick. Still stunted from the toxins leaching through the ice and soil, with nubs where their pincers ought to be and thin wriggling limbs coming off their clay-soft skin. Their distress comes through my cilia, as if my new senses pick up some chemical they're giving off, and the sudden weight of despair crushes me. They're trapped, with no way to see a future, and everything hurts, and nobody can bring them any comfort. Rose already shared an impression of these suffering children, but this feels different. I want to step forward and cradle the entire brood in my arms. I can't stand in front of all this misery and do nothing, and these might as well be my own children. I feel hotter and hotter, until I have to flee, back the way I came, back to the cool silence.

Afterward, those fear chemicals soak into me, and I keep remembering. It's worse each time.

Nothing will change, unless more humans learn to be like me. I remember the climate projections, and the rising trend line. We can't fix this problem in my lifetime, or even several lifetimes, but we need to start now. There are places Gelet can't go and things they can't do, but humans can.

I treat this decision the way I learned to treat my memory-panic. I stop, and I give myself space to feel all the worst emotions. Then I move forward.

One by one, each of the Gelet shares their favorite impression of me. River remembers me volunteering to be changed, how my determination never wavered, even though I had seen that ancient hologram. Jean volunteers some moment of kindness that I didn't even remember, when I reached out to make sure she was okay. Felice recalls how I laughed, watching the puppet show about humans. The Gelet who suffered a harpoon wound and still showed up again when I brought the Glacier Fools, whom I haven't seen since I was changed, shares a random memory of me helping some children cross a narrow walkway. Another Gelet was there on the Sea of Murder, when I was trapped on the ice with the Resourceful Couriers, and shows me how brave I was.

At last a Gelet I've never seen here in the city approaches, shy and hesitant, and opens her pincer to share her own memory: me climbing to the plateau of the Old Mother, to thank her for saving me. Rose holds up my father's timepiece, carefully, at the end of one tentacle.

Mouth won't stop chattering, even as I'm trying to say goodbye to my whole family. We ride some kind of seed-shaped carriage, part volcanic rock and part living creature, through steep ice tunnels. Mouth's head is freshly shaved, and she's wearing her environment suit again. But mine doesn't fit anymore, so I'm just covered with layers of protective moss. I shiver, though not from the cold, and share again my worst memories of Xiosphant: cops dragging me into the street and shooting protestors, the Curfew Patrol aiming guns at Bianca and me. But Rose and the others already know how vicious Xiosphant can be, since their friends have been sliced up and roasted there.

Rose keeps reminding me of when I used to visit her. She shows me how I looked that first time, out on the ice wearing my secondhand trendy clothes, dying and terrified. She showed me that memory before, but this time I can identify more easily with Rose's perspective.

I'm Rose, and I see this human, shivering from cold and terrified rage, and she does that animal thing of tensing to fight or run. But then, instead, she does something no human has ever willingly done before: tilt her head back, let my tendrils touch her bare flesh. I feel Rose's surprise, her euphoria, the sense that something perverted and maybe wonderful is happening.

When I came to the city, Rose stayed away, because she needed this to work so much she was worried that she would overwhelm me. But she shared everyone else's impressions of me, and helped to shape the consensus that the time had come for me to go home.

I try to ask Rose the question that's been bothering me since I came here: What do the Gelet believe in? I have to ask several times, and then she seems to get it, because she unfolds an ancient memory, the oldest that anyone has ever shared with me. Or maybe not a memory, a legend—or a little of both. I can tell its age by the smooth edges, the lack of sensory detail, and the easy flow of the events, the same way humans can spot that a story has been told and retold by a long chain of people, because it makes too much sense.

Long ago, before the first civilization that I saw rise and fall in those shared visions, everyone lived in scattered burrows all over the night, with no more than a hundred people per burrow. They wove their tendrils together when anyone wanted to share information about what she had seen, or done. Or somebody might come up with a simple idea that she shared with everyone else, like a way to harvest more roots and grubs to feed into the web where their children were developing. Or how to strengthen their barriers against iceslides and avalanches.

And that's when their greatest love story took place. These two people, who had grown up in different burrows, came together after some brutal ice storms drove them away from their homes. The two refugees became inseparable, and their tendrils were intertwined whenever they weren't working or eating. They slept with their pincers wrapped around each other, in their own mossy nook where the cool air ran over their carapaces. Their dreams flowed back and forth between them, and their memories of fleeing their homes blended together until they almost shared the same past. Everyone else recoiled, because this couldn't be healthy for them, plus they were excluding the rest of the community, which was hurtful. People tried to pry the two of them apart, physically, or sent one or the other of them on long errands outside the burrow. At last one of the oldest and most patient of the burrow's residents decided to talk to both of them together, and find out exactly what perversion they had been drawn into—and then there were three of them. Entangled, inextricable. People began talking about evicting all three of them.

What had seduced them into this unnatural closeness? A set of designs for a water wheel, using the nearby underground river to operate a crude mill that would help them separate out the poisonous part of some mushrooms that grew in the caves. This was such a complex idea that one person couldn't invent it alone and then share it with everyone else—the concept needed to be shaped among two or more people, working together. They couldn't even share it with the others until they had the concept. And these lovers had discovered a powerful thrill, a joy that went all the way down to their stomachs, in weaving a big idea together. Like some wild rapture, the sensation of helping others to imagine something bigger than yourselves.

Somehow, this weird love story is the foundation of this community's politics, or religion. Rose lingers on the oddest parts, like when they finally reveal their invention to the rest of the community, or the tenderness when the couple becomes a trio. I sense the echoes from all the countless other times that people have passed this legend around, and the lesson that comes with it: to join with others to shape a future is the holiest act. This is hard work, and it never stops being hard, but this collective dreaming/designing is the only way we get to keep surviving, and this practice defines us as a community. Even the other communities that live apart from the midnight city, scattered all over the night in smaller cities or towns, share this origin story.

Just as she finishes explaining, we roll to a stop. I look out and see the unmistakable crags of the Old Mother rising over the permafrost, with just a tiny wedge of light behind it. I squint as hard as I can, but the light still burns.

PART

SEVEN

mouth

Xiosphant's decorative carvings leered down as its brick walls closed in on them. Gables overhung the acute angles at the intersection of two streets, as if daring you to say these corners weren't square. Mouth had always loathed this city, but now every step took her deeper into the past. First the shady side of town, the Warrens, with all the factories and warehouses where she'd attended all those meetings, then the fancy coffee salon where Sophie had worked— boarded up, long since closed— and the Low Road, where the Resourceful Couriers had toasted with swamp vodka. Grungy metal slats covered the windows, and the Curfew Patrols stomped the cobblestones, while people slept in their shrouded bedrooms. But the patrols never came close, because Sophie could sense them from a kilometer away, with the same alien organs she had used to find a half-repaired fissure in the wall facing the Old Mother.

Sophie kept gazing up at the shutters as if they would open and swallow her. The Gelet had given her a big musty cloak that disguised the new shape of her body, except for when she became agitated and her tentacles moved around under the cape, which happened all the time. Mouth still wore the remains of her environment suit, just in case she didn't already look enough like a foreigner. The sky grew lighter as they walked deeper into town, and Mouth's head pounded more and more after so long underground.

"They're going to dissect me." Sophie's voice barely carried over the final bell before shutters-down. "They'll catch us, and then they'll dissect me."

"Not gonna happen," Mouth said. "This town tried to kill you once, and you laughed it off. You lived for ages as a condemned criminal here, and you never got caught. You know this town better than anybody, and you are too smart for these tight-asses. If it comes down to you versus the whole damn city of Xiosphant, my money's on you."

Sophie didn't respond.

Neither of them discussed the implications of the old familiar shutters, or the Curfew Patrols, or all the other little indications that Xiosphant was still a conformist hole. Alyssa and Bianca had been left with only one vehicle and a tiny force, with kilometers of tundra yet to cross, and both Sophie and Mouth had already come to terms with their probable deaths. As much as they ever could.

Another bell, and all the slumbering houses yawned. Mouth would never get used to the spooky way this town went from empty to frantic in an eyeblink. People poured through doors, stuffing breakfast into their mouths, rushing to their jobs in half-fastened coveralls and safety gear, already scheming to get ten kinds of money. Mouth and Sophie hustled off the street into the tiniest alleyway, in the shadows, to stay hidden—but also because all these arms and legs, all these voices, all at once, felt like an assault. You forget just how noisy and smelly people are.

Sophie was already fretting out about how she would accomplish her mission. How she could find anyone who could look at her without screaming for help or alerting the cops— let alone someone who could share her gift without suffering full-on delirium, the way the Glacier Fools and Mouth had. She studied everyone who passed on the street, looking this way and that.

"This whole town is engineered to make you feel like you're always running out of time," Mouth said. "But we can take this slow. The one thing we do have to accomplish soon is getting me a better disguise, and also scoring some food dollars." They had a satchel with some of those freeze-dried rations, plus some roots that tasted like pheasant according to Sophie. But those things wouldn't last forever, plus Mouth had aspirations of getting very, very drunk and holding a private wake for Alyssa. Mouth had been sober for too long. "Also, we need whatever money you use to pay for crashspace."

"Infrastructure chits," Sophie said. "The Illyrian Parlour is boarded up. No idea what happened to Hernan, and Jeremy. My father and my brother Thom wouldn't accept me even before all this. So I don't know where we can go." She touched the star-shaped bracelet on her wrist.

Mouth pondered. "I know someone. One of my least favorite people in the world."

*

The streets were too crowded for ghosts, even when they stuck to all the side lanes. They passed near the Gymnasium, where Sophie had been a student. The place where they'd probably bring a freak of nature to their laboratories for dissection. She pulled her rough wool cloak tighter, hunched over, and cast sharp glances in every direction.

They passed a pile of rubble on the light side of town where Mouth was pretty sure she'd seen a large brick building last time, with some of those fancy high-tech decorations. Didn't look like a controlled demolition, and they built these things to last. Mouth stopped and stared, but Sophie didn't seem interested. Until they passed another pile, this time of whitestone and iron girders, and another. "What kind of weapon—" Mouth said.

Sophie shook her head. "Not a weapon. Weather." She kept walking.

Mouth kept getting lost in this fake grid, and felt immobilized by lightsickness. But at last they came to the roofing plant, and the wire cage around George the Bank's office.

"Mouth! Never thought I'd see your ugly face again." George got out of his chair and opened some dark water. "How did you make it back here? And who's that hiding behind you?"

"This is Sophie," Mouth gestured. "A lot has happened. So, uh, I was hoping for some scratch. We left a lot of valuable gear with you when we had to leave town last time. Now I'm back for a while, and I want to get set up." Speaking Xiosphanti again felt like the return of an old toothache. She had to bite her tongue to get the right verb constructions for George (manager) and herself (barbarian).

"Well, I almost feel like you owe me money, rather than the other way around," George said. "You left me in a raw bitch of a situation when you skipped town. They were arresting anyone who might have shaken hands with you vagrants. But also, you're trying to call in a favor that someone already used up. Your friend Alyssa made the exact same argument, and I gave her all that I could spare."

"Alyssa came here? How long ago?"

You might as well have stuffed Mouth into a cannon and shot her over the city.

"I think it was four shutter-cycles ago." George shrugged. "Eight Honesty after Pink."

"I thought she was dead. I can't believe she survived that fiasco."

"She said the same thing about you. Like you'd gone into the night to die."

"We all went into the night to die. Some of us were better at it than others."

"Can't tell you where she is now. Don't know if you saw the rubble, but we had a cyclone. It swooped down, wrecked a couple city blocks, and then dispersed." George sighed, even though this devastation was probably good for the roofing business. "And meanwhile, things in Xiosphant have gotten somewhat complicated, politically."

"Have we ever had a conversation where you didn't say that?"

George took another sip of dark water, and seemed to be debating whether it was worth throwing away some money just to get Mouth out of his office.

"Here." He handed Mouth a wad of food dollars,

infrastructure chits, and a few other types of cash. Mouth also found a big hat and a Xiosphanti poncho that would cover her scarred head and strange clothes—maybe the exact same items that Mouth had worn before. And Sophie picked up a lacy fringe to pin around her ankles.

"Consider this a retainer," George said. "I might have a job for you pretty soon, so check back."

Mouth started to thank him, but then saw the face at the center of one of the food dollars. Not the best likeness, but they'd captured the eyes pretty well. Hold the dollar one way, she seemed to gaze at Mouth like she believed that they would transform this town together. Look at the money from a higher angle, and she looked furious at Mouth's betrayal. You could follow the entire course of their relationship, just by moving a dollar around.

Bianca.

"Our new vice regent," George said. "I told you: complicated. Whole new government."

Mouth showed the money to Sophie, who swayed like she might faint, or drop to her knees. Cloak moving up in the back, just a little. She stared into those eyes, and seemed to have a whole different dialogue with them than Mouth. Then Sophie looked up and saw George studying her too, trying to guess what this was about. She straightened up and cleansed all emotion from her face.

"I have to go see her," Sophie said.

"I don't think that's a good idea just yet." Mouth gestured at George. "Like the man said, it's complicated."

"It's Bianca."

"Let's just take this one step at a time. If I can find Alyssa, she can give us the——"

George looked out his window and cursed. "Hide. Hide now!" He gestured for Mouth and Sophie to get behind the row of filing cabinets, with the info crystals where Mouth had first learned about the Palace vault, with the Invention.

"So good to see you and your friends," George was saying to a visitor. "Want some dark water?"

"George, this is not a social call, and I don't appreciate seeing you drink during business time. The work is behind schedule." It was a man's voice, with a slight Argelan accent. Mouth took a moment to identify the speaker, whom she hadn't heard speaking Xiosphanti before. "We don't want to have to play rough."

"Dash, don't be like that. Your new Palace roof is going to be beautiful, made of wrought iron. People will wonder if you had it fabbed somehow." Mouth had never heard George sound so upset, not even when she'd quoted a political slogan by accident. No, not upset. Terrified. George was terror-stricken. Mouth didn't much care what happened to George, but this still made her nauseous. "I mean. We're also overbooked, thanks to all the cyclone damage. And we're doing this job for you guys for free."

"You're not doing it for free, George. You're doing your patriotic duty. When you say things like that, I feel as though you don't appreciate the honor we're giving you."

Sophie moved forward, to do something. Confront Dash? Punch him, the way she did Reynold that one time? Strangle him with her tentacles? Mouth got in her way and whispered,

"Not now. Not here." Sophie hunched down again.

"Of course, we're honored," George said. "Such an honor."

The next thing Mouth heard was a loud crack, followed by George making a sound like a starving baby.

"So," Dash said over George's wailing. "The way I understand, your facility is just qualified to receive infrastructure chits. Am I right? Great. So the only way you can get other types of money is through private arrangements." George let out a high gasp. Dash continued: "Y'know, I wonder if somebody should look into that. Make sure it's all on the level."

"If you were going to threaten me with a currency fraud investigation . . ." George panted. "Why did you have to break my leg?"

You could hear in Dash's voice that he was flipping his hands. "I don't know. Nostalgia, mostly. Or maybe homesickness. Plus, pain drives the message home." His footsteps moved away, then stopped. "Oh, one more thing. I heard you had a visit from a mutual friend."

"She—ahhh. Wanted my help. I didn't."

"Next time you meet an enemy of the state, tell me. Of course, Alyssa's been handled. We built her a special dungeon under the Palace. So romantic, just like those storybooks I used to love. Okay, see you, George."

Alyssa had never seemed so free as the last time Mouth had seen her, and now she was in some ironically "romantic" dungeon. Mouth found herself desperately wishing she was still able to inflict harm.

Mouth and Sophie waited until they were sure Dash was gone, then rushed out and tried to help set George's broken leg. "Just go," he hissed. "I'll be fine. Clean break. Go. Never come back."

So they took their money, including the food dollars with the haunting eyes, and left. Now, with Mouth's big hat and Sophie's hood, they both looked fully ridiculous.

"We have to rescue Bianca," Sophie said when they got out on the street. "It's obvious they're holding her prisoner in the Palace. Using her as a figurehead while Dash and his goons run everything."

"Keep your voice down." Words that Mouth never expected to say to Sophie. "I don't know what's going on, and neither do you. But now we know where Alyssa is. I learned the hard way, breaking into that Palace is impossible, but I bet anything this new dungeon is a different matter. They probably built it adjacent to the sewers."

Sophie stared at Mouth, maybe thinking that Mouth would rescue Alyssa and let Bianca rot, for selfish reasons. There was a nugget of truth to this.

"Just let me talk to Alyssa first," Mouth said. "We need more information. Please just hang tight for now."

Sophie started to argue, then just shrugged and said, "Okay. Go see your friend. I'll be fine."

"You're not going to try and see Bianca?"

"No, of course not. Go do what you have to do."

So Mouth left Sophie hiding in an air vent on a redbrick tower, and hoped for the best.

SOPHIE

Bianca has learned this way of flexing her wrist joint when she listens, and her eyes draw closer as her nose wrinkles. She perches on a wooden chaise with gold leaf, with a crimson gown hanging off one shoulder, and a tiny glass of some fluky green spirit sitting on a side table next to her. Dash is here, talking to her about the delays in finishing the new Palace roof, and she's giving him an exasperated look.

"This is important. We need a stronger roof, before the next cyclone comes over the Young Father and just rips everything apart," she says.

Seeing Bianca again, my heart gets pulled off-kilter. All of my old feelings rise up out of the past, as though her smile and her voice have the power to bend light, restructure time, make everything new.

"This is not what I thought I'd be spending my time doing here, in the Clockwork City," Dash says in Argelan.

"What did you think you'd be doing, Dash?" Bianca laughs. "Just eating fancy cakes all the time? Doing elaborate dances, and scattering petals everywhere? I'm dying to know."

He shakes his head. "I used to find your sarcasm so intoxicating. I actually thought about marrying you, did you know that? I pictured you and me marching through Founders' Square, wearing the most resplendent silks and lace, and getting the High Magistrate to officiate the biggest wedding this town ever saw."

"We executed the High Magistrate, remember? It was a whole occasion."

This Palace probably is impossible to sneak into, just as Mouth said—unless you have your own tentacles, with cilia that grip harder than any mechanical clamps. I managed to keep them hidden under my cloak, even as they helped me scale the wall overlooking the quiet rear plaza, adjacent to the market stalls. I could sense the Palace guards moving underneath me, hear their chatter. Any moment, they were going to look up and see me, and I would die. I had to stop and melt into the wall a few times until I felt calm again. But I had no choice. I needed to see her. Now I'm clinging to the ledge outside her window.

"I'm not the marrying type," Bianca is saying to Dash. "But we did have fun, didn't we? We make a good team, and we're just getting started."

Dash comes over to the window to look out over the city, and I scoot out of the way just in time. "This town always sounded so adorable when that fussy old tutor was teaching me Xiosphanti. All the elaborate phrasings, and the way every moment in time seemed to have its own special name. But the real Xiosphant turned out to be just a sad gray husk."

I don't need to see Bianca's face to know she bristles at that. "You'll learn to love this town the way I do. And maybe then you'll understand how to get what you want without shouting and hitting people."

"Sure. Maybe." Dash turns away and heads for the door to Bianca's gilt-edged chamber. "But for now, I have to go browbeat more tradespeople. I wish we could just throw another party."

"We'll party when we have a reason to celebrate."

"That's a barbaric notion. Parties are only fun if they're unreasonable. See you later."

They kiss for several endless heartbeats, and then Dash walks out, shutting the door behind him.

I only came here to learn more information, as Mouth suggested, and now I've learned quite a bit. So I should leave, quietly as I came, slip away and plan my next move. But she's so close to me, and I never thought I'd get another chance to speak to her again, and her flowery scent reaches me from all the way across the room. Maybe now that I can communicate in a whole new way, everything can be different between us.

I'm next to Bianca before she even knows I'm there.

Bianca looks up and lets out a gasp. Her face turns to clay and she coughs, spits, and starts to cry. The liqueur glass falls and lands intact. She gasps for breath, with a hyperactive twist to her mouth and red borders around her eyes. Bianca and I are both stiff, made of brittle wire, until she reaches out and pulls me into a hug. I pull her head onto my shoulder, careful to keep my tendrils away, and she weeps on my neck.

Neither of us talks for a long time, and I'm flooded with an emotion that I can't even name. I told myself I was finished with Bianca, but this feeling clamps onto me with sharp teeth, sunk deep.

Then I break the silence, for once. "I thought you were dead. I thought you died out there in the night, or else when you tried to invade here. But you won. You won. I can't even imagine."

"We were so lucky," she says between sobs. "I can't believe you're alive too. I didn't want that to be our last conversation. Here you are, back from the dead one more time, but this time I have even more things that I never got to say. I couldn't believe you just walked away and left us there, lost in the middle of the ice fields."

"I asked you to come with me."

Bianca doesn't seem to hear me. "You promised to trust me and stick with me, forever. And then you left me to die in the wilderness. But I didn't die. We made it home. We won."

I mourned Bianca so hard in the midnight city, I forgot how alive she really was. Now I step back and look at her. The multilayered hairstyle, jewelry, and shimmering turquoise powder around her eyelids can't distract from the radiance of her eyes. She could conquer anything.

"We came over the side of the Old Mountain, and here was Xiosphant, just wide open." She pours herself another green drink. "We only had one transport left, remember, and just two dozen soldiers. But this city never saw us coming. I knew they would never expect anyone to invade from the night, and those blockheads assumed that people would only attack the city when their shutters were open, because they'd gotten so used to thinking of their sleep cycle as natural. The Curfew

Patrols were pathetic. By the time everyone opened their shutters, we were inside the Palace, and we had captured the prince. We killed the vice regent, and all the Privy Council, everybody, and then we were in charge."

She uses the most informal syntax, as if we were cousins by marriage, not vice regent and outlaw. And something inside me, underneath my spread of tendrils, opens up at the sound of Bianca's voice: like clear water flowing down the side of one of those marble fountains, in just the right amount of partial sunlight, back in Argelo. I almost don't care that she's telling me about murdering so many people.

This is the tallest room I've ever been in, with walls a good four or five meters high, and a vibrant painting of the Xiosphanti crest, Gelet and tigers embracing, on the ceiling.

Her drink scathes her throat, and she coughs, and then smiles at me, so I feel myself flush. "Back at the Gymnasium, I always wished I could be more like you. You used to talk about how you had clawed your way out of the dark side of town, and meanwhile I was just swept along by other people's expectations. You were just so real, Sophie, as if you couldn't help being yourself. Maybe this whole time, I've been trying to find the person that I can't help being."

The burnt-orange aroma of her liqueur overcomes my new senses, and I'm overaware of a hum in the room, something grinding against itself. I can't get rid of the dumb fantasy that I've somehow scored one more chance with Bianca, that I can still fix things between us.

"But so, you won," I say. "And you were in charge. Right? And you had all these reforms, I remember you talked about them so often, all these reforms you wanted to make."

She sighs and covers her face with one hand. "We tried. We really did. But you can't just change one part of the system without upsetting the rest of it. The farmwheels turn on a strict schedule that synchronizes perfectly with the shutters going up and down, and the water pumps are optimized for the farmwheels, but also for everybody washing at certain times. The sewage is optimized for peak times as well. And so on. You start tinkering, and the whole city falls apart, and then everybody starves."

I don't know what to say. Everything she's saying about the system, we were taught in school, until we all knew it by heart. But she's acting as if she just discovered it for the first time.

"Oh, it's one thing to read about it." She laughs and rolls her eyes at my expression. "But I didn't really get it until I tried to make adjustments. Plus meanwhile, I have just a small number of Argelan fighters left who are loyal to Dash and me. Mostly, I have to rely on the Palace guards, and they're only behind me so long as I have the prince in a safe place. I've been hand-picking my own people, smart Xiosphanti, to take key jobs. But I still have to rely on the old bureaucrats and administrators to implement my decisions, and they fight me every step of the way."

When we first became friends, and Bianca used to pull the forgotten history books out of the back of the library at the Gymnasium, this act of revealing a different past seemed to me a magical power. But now I keep wondering if there were books she chose to leave on the shelf, which talked about all the crimes of saviors, like the Hydroponic Garden Massacre.

Maybe if she had read deeper, things would be different now.

Bianca sighs. "Then after that freak cyclone, everyone was scared, and frightened people always crave stability. Sophie, I really need someone I can count on here, and I still wish that could be you."

I look out from her balcony, at a view of Xiosphant I've never seen. The town looks so clean, all of the beige and crimson rooftops catching the dusk rays. You can't even see the tiny patch of cyclone damage, let alone any other blemishes. A glow comes from the top of the Young Father and casts a curtain of illumination over the warm side of town, and then as I turn my head to the left the light dissipates, until darkness lands at the feet of the Old Mother.

"I can't believe you didn't actually change anything." I can see the market and the big shops on the Boulevard, and the housing towers dotting the skyline. "You were going to make everything better. All of these people trapped in cycles, the same thing over and over, everyone yearning for freedom. You were going to fix it."

"Give me time. A generation from now, you'll see the change. We're going to reopen trade with Argelo, and people will be exposed to new ideas, new ways of living."

I look away from the balcony and check Bianca out again: the rigid posture, the fidgeting ankles, the tight jaw. She's trapped herself here in this Palace, and underneath her brash surface she's terrified, more than when we almost drowned on the Sea of Murder. She got everything she thought she wanted, and now she's barely holding on.

All I want to do is rescue Bianca one last time, save her

from herself, as if all her mistakes—her crimes—are just another handful of food dollars that I can take on myself. The ache grows inside me until it feels too big to contain, and I want to carry her away from here.

But we're past that now. There's only one thing I have left to offer her.

"I need someone to count on, and I wish that could be you," she says again. "I don't know how you survived, and I want to hear all about it. But you came back to me, and now you can help me make all of this right. I've always imagined doing all of this with you by my side."

"I've been living in the midnight city." I choose my words carefully. "Everything I told you before was true. I came back here because I have something incredible to show to all the people, and you're the one I always wanted to share everything with. What you said just now, about how you couldn't change the system even once you were in charge, I can help you fix that. I have a way to change everything. And you and I could finally understand each other, and stop hurting each other all the time. We could be real."

As I say those things, I feel as though I'm shaping a possible future in my mind, and inviting Bianca to shape it with me. The holiest act. I can almost see it becoming real, and maybe coming here was worth the risk after all.

"So that hive of ice monsters gave you a new political theory? Or some kind of organizational tool? I'm intrigued."

Bianca keeps looking over her shoulder at the door, as if expecting Dash to come back. Or Nai, if Nai is somehow still alive. I stay close to the balcony, because if either of those people show up, I'll swing out the window and up onto the roof in an instant.

I can't help drawing my cloak tighter, to disguise the shape of my body from her. "I need to know. What scares you so much about the idea that the Gelet could be people? You wanted to use them in your invasion, so why couldn't you accept them as equals?"

She ticks on her fingers. "Because if they're people, then what does that make us? Invaders? Is our struggle here even meaningful, if we're just squabbling on the margins of their history? Because I've eaten crocodile meat, at some of those feasts I used to go to. Because I didn't want to lose the Sophie I knew—you know, the sweet, passionate girl who always lit up my world—and it scared me to think of you becoming something I couldn't even understand."

I should leave now. The calculating part of me, the part that somehow kept me alive in the midst of so much death, is yelling for me to get out of here. But I stay.

"I've never heard you admit to being scared before." I move back toward her, and she actually smiles at me. Her smile still has the same power as always. I feel my center of gravity rise.

"I never had to say. You've always known," she says, "and you've always helped me get through it. So okay. I'm here. What did you want to show me?"

I hesitate just a moment longer, then I let my cloak fall open. Bianca sees my tendrils, up above the neckline of my simple shift, and the motion of tentacles behind my head, and lets out a high gasp.

Bianca heaves, and speaks in a guttural rush. "Your

body . . . oh shit . . . What did they do to you? What did they turn you into? Fuck, are you even human anymore? How can you stand to be— I think I'm going to throw up—" She makes clicking sounds in the back of her throat.

I have a sudden flash of Mouth saying, "I think you're beautiful," as though my subconscious is trying to protect me.

"I'm still me," I plead. "I haven't changed. I'm still Sophie."

She spits and thrashes, looking past me. "No. Oh no, no, no, this is worse than I could have imagined. They turned you into . . . This is so much worse. We're going to have to study you. Are they planning on doing this to other people? Is this what you wanted to show me, this . . . this contamination? Is it contagious? Are you going to try and infect me?"

"No, wait," I babble, because she's reaching for some velvet cord that will summon guards or servants. "Just wait and listen to me for once, Bianca, I haven't even shown you what I was going to show you. Please stop. I promise it'll be okay. I could never hurt you."

As I lean toward her, I reach for a comforting memory: the pot of tea that we always took from the common room and kept on the squat little table in our dorm room at the Gymnasium. Before all of this, back when life was simple. I remember one quiet moment when she poured tea for me, and I keep it in my head, the fragile stillness of it, so I can give it to her.

But Bianca squirms and lashes out with one fist as my tendrils make contact, and I can't find the memory of pouring tea anymore. Instead, all I can think of is staring at her from behind the War Monument, with a barrier of misshapen waves between us. My mind skips to the time I followed her and spied on her in a political meeting full of guns, and then standing in the corner of some party in Argelo, observing her. Then I'm watching someone tie a mask around her face as she recedes into a crowd. Studying her and Dash across a crowded nightclub.

"How many times did you spy on me? Were you just stalking me all the time—" Bianca makes another gagging sound.

I can't come up with a memory that's not of me watching Bianca from a distance. My heart is shaking itself to pieces and my tendrils tear at my skin with the effort of maintaining contact. I fumble for a happy memory and—

—Bianca is lying next to me on her bed, in our dorm room, whispering in my ear, and her breath makes my skin so sensitive that I would evaporate if she even touched me and then her body touches mine just for a moment and I feel a shiver and I've never even let myself want anything with the part of me that rejoices in desiring—

—Now, here, in the Palace, Bianca pulls away from me, just as I've realized how dangerous that last memory was, the feelings I've never even confessed to myself.

Bianca makes a noise between a roar and a howl, and throws me so hard I land halfway across the room.

"You forced yourself into my mind and you . . . Standing here with those grubby oily worms coming out of your body, thinking those disgusting thoughts about me. I can't even stand to look at you. They didn't turn you into a monster, you were always a monster. How did I not know this?"

Bianca's words have a thicket of sharp edges, and I'm still paralyzed, thinking about that desire that I never even let into myself. Bianca spits at me that I'm perverted, revolting, a creep.

All the blood is rushing to my head and I'm drowning, but there must be something I can say right now. I didn't stalk her—and my love isn't selfish—and I'm scared I overwhelmed her with too many memories at once. I try to blurt an explanation. "I just wanted to save—"

My shoulder is on fire. The pain spreads to my left arm and my left side. A man in a bright green breastplate has come in the door and fired an antique pulse maser at me. The wound mostly cauterized on contact, but blood still dribbles out of my shoulder. I scream.

Bianca yells at her man not to kill me, they need me alive. I pull away as she shouts at the guards pouring into the room not to shoot, for fuck's sake. I reach the balcony, where I'd plotted an easy parabola—flipping onto the railing and then up to the roof. But I've lost flesh, and I'm losing blood. I try to climb, but I slip on my own mess, and I fall instead. My tentacles only just save me, catching on the Palace wall, as I drop to the balcony one floor down.

mouth

Mouth climbed down into the sewer and made her foul way under the Founders' Square and the market stalls, to the pristine clay pipe that she was pretty sure led into the dungeon's latrine. The pipe itself was too narrow, so she set about weakening the mortar around one of the big new stones at the base of the dungeon wall. Whoever built this new dungeon had done a poor job with the masonry, probably because Dash had broken their arms for not working fast enough. The big granite block wobbled as the mortar crumbled under pressure from the scraper in Mouth's belt, but she still needed several lifetimes to loosen the block and pull it out of the way. Then she could climb up through the commode itself, which stunk just as much as she'd expected. She pushed aside the rotting wooden boards over the commode.

The single-room dungeon had one prisoner: Alyssa wore a chain attached to a shackle around her ankle, with the other end bolted to the wall. She looked so much older Mouth didn't recognize her at first. Her skin clung to an emaciated face, and she bent almost double. Her eyes focused on Mouth with effort.

"You look like hot puke," Mouth whispered. "Hold still."

She found a file inside her tool belt and started sawing through the chain on Alyssa's ankle.

"Make up your mind," Alyssa hissed. "You ditch me, then you come back."

"Shut up and let me work."

"Can't wait to hear your latest rationalization." Alyssa sounded like mossy rock being dragged over rotten wood. "Not that I don't bear some of the blame for this shitfest. I believed in Bianca—like, really believed. I spent a lot of time encouraging her to step up, after you vanished on us. Become the brilliant leader that she was meant to be. I think I may have miscalculated. Pretty much as soon as we finished murdering the entire government, I was suddenly 'not reliable.' I mean, fuck. I'm the most reliable person there is."

"Shhh," Mouth said. "You'll have plenty of time to explain how this is really my fault after we get out of here."

Alyssa shook her head. "You're just going to ditch me again."

"No, I'm not." Mouth was about halfway through the chain, and she'd only had to switch hands three times. Both hands were raw and throbbing.

That was when the alarms started ringing. Not from the dungeon, from the Palace above. Mouth cursed. *Sophie.*

"I have to go," Mouth said. "I'll leave you the file. The commode leads to a stone I removed, then the sewers."

"You literally said a moment ago that you wouldn't abandon me."

Mouth paused with one foot in the toilet, and sighed.

"I have a duty. I'm Sophie's bodyguard, and she's an idiot.

She's also the future of humanity, sort of. Keep working on your chain."

Mouth had wasted too much time already. The alarms blared, and boots crashed on the pavement above. She swung back down into the sewer, trying to guess which pipe led to the fancy toilets. She picked one that looked likely, and took a hammer to the fixtures until she had made an opening. At least the alarms and shouts drowned out the racket of her clumsy swings.

"She's not even human anymore," Bianca said. "She got into my chamber and attacked me with some kind of psychic powers. It was horrible. We need to capture her alive if we can."

Mouth couldn't get over how good the inside of the Palace smelled: like fresh-cut pine, even over the sewage she tracked onto the floor (which was made of a stone so soft and warm Mouth wanted to lie down on it for a while). The Inner Council Chamber had gleaming walls of something that looked like glass but wasn't, and the furniture was a mixture of handcrafted high-end wood and machine-fabbed steel and plastic. Beautiful ancient devices, some of them dating back to the Mothership, covered every surface.

Most of the clamor rang out from upstairs, but shouts came from the outer hallway surrounding this level. "She's down here!" Mouth ran toward the voices.

Sophie cowered under her big cloak, hiding between two pillars, with guards closing in on her. She held her shoulder in one hand, like they'd winged her already. Just as Mouth made eye contact with Sophie, all the guards spotted Mouth.

Mouth gestured for Sophie to stay put, then ran for the nearest window, making as much commotion as she could, sliding across the polished floor. The first two rifle shots missed, but the third went through her shoulder, turning her right arm into a useless decoration. The fourth hit her left leg. She hoped this distraction had helped Sophie to escape, however unlikely that might be.

As Mouth started to bleed out on the fancy carpet, she remembered when the Resourceful Couriers had tried to get into the rug import business, working with this one community of weavers who had a workshop in the Pit back in Argelo, using techniques they claimed to have brought all the way from Earth. The Couriers had hauled a pile of their wares all the way to Xiosphant, only to find they were cheap rugs that someone had dyed just well enough to fool a group of rubes. At least now Mouth's blood was soaking into what appeared to be a genuine antique, which meant she would have some revenge, even in death. Nothing would ever get blood out of this carpet.

"Oh, for—" Bianca was standing over her, wearing an off-the-shoulder crimson gown. "Mouth. I should have known." She turned to the nearest guard. "Get her cleaned and patched up. Then put her in the dungeon. I want to know everything she can tell us about this monstrosity."

Bianca leaned in close enough that Mouth could see the redness in her eyes, and the insomnia lines. Bianca looked almost as prematurely aged as Alyssa. "I should have expected you'd be here, after that creature showed up in my house. I want you to know that I destroyed your stupid poetry book the first chance I got."

Mouth didn't even know what book Bianca was talking about at first, and then she remembered about the Invention. She tried to shrug, but that was not happening with this bullet wound. She also couldn't scrounge enough air to say anything about that "creature" being the only one who ever really loved Bianca. Or the fact that Bianca had been happy to use Sophie's unique connection to January's natives to play her geopolitical games. Mouth had summoned endless quantities of air back when she'd been saying whatever Bianca wanted to hear, but now every breath came with a sharp pain in her chest, like her lung had gotten wrapped in barbed wire.

Alyssa rolled her eyes when Mouth fell on her hands and knees in the dungeon, and the guards shackled her to another chain. "Well, you did say you would be back." The guards locked the door behind them.

Mouth still couldn't breathe. They had cleaned her bullet wounds and applied some sealant, but one of them felt like it still had shrapnel. She made an asthmatic rattle instead of words.

Alyssa looked around to make sure the guards had left, and then pulled the file out of her sleeve and sawed through her chain, which was close to breaking. "This file is worthless," she said. "What happened to the good one we used to have? The one with the specially hardened iron surface? I know you had it last."

Mouth couldn't get enough breath to answer, but also honestly wasn't sure. The good file had been in that cloth bag, back in Argelo, maybe.

"You lose everything." Alyssa rubbed the file faster. "I can't leave a single thing with you. Literally anything I put in your hands, it's just . . . gone." One last frenzy of tugging, and her chain snapped.

Halfway to the commode, Alyssa paused and looked at Mouth, who was on the floor, hugging her knees and trying to breathe. "You only just let me down, *again*."

Mouth tried to gasp that she was sorry. She had broken in here to rescue Alyssa in the first place. She had never wanted to leave Alyssa behind in the night.

"Give me one reason I shouldn't just let you stay here. Even half a reason. I'm so tired of your garbage."

Mouth managed to squeeze out, "You have no . . . other friends. Everyone else . . . is dead."

"Good point. Hold still, asshole." Mouth passed out while Alyssa was filing.

A rhythmic series of slaps across her cheek made her upper bullet wound throb, and she realized her ankle was no longer chained. Mouth lurched to her feet, swaying.

"We don't have long," Alyssa said. "When they realize we're gone, they're going to notice the mess you made of that toilet. Nice subtle work, by the way."

Alyssa hoisted Mouth over her shoulder and helped her stumble through the slippery tunnel that smelled like generations of diarrhea. Mouth breathed into Alyssa's ear, barely managing to croak, "Can we," and some time later, "start over?"

No response to that, except that much later, when Mouth had collapsed on a bed in a tiny flop that Alyssa had rented over a tannery in the Warrens, and Alyssa was poking a tiny syringe into Mouth's lung, she heard Alyssa say, in Argelan: "There's no starting over. There's only starting again."

Mouth tossed her head.

"So, you're Sophie's bodyguard now?"

Mouth tossed her head again. "Need to find her." She could breathe a little better now.

"Ugh. That girl. Beginning to think you're each other's jinxes. Well, okay." She sighed. "I haven't thrown my life away for a lost cause in a little while. Tell me about it when you can talk."

"Okay." Mouth passed out again.

When Mouth regained consciousness in a filthy room darkened by shutters, she half expected Alyssa to be gone. But Alyssa sat at the tiny cork table, dismantling the shackle on her own ankle, and that was the most beautiful surprise of all. Mouth attempted to smile up at Alyssa, who smiled back and reached to take her hand. Mouth squeezed Alyssa's palm, like some talisman promising safety, redemption, or maybe just not dying alone.

Mouth took a deep, miraculous breath. "When I thought you were dead, I was planning one hell of a wake. I was going to get so drunk I'd never see straight again."

Alyssa snorted. "I never got a chance to drink to you being dead either. Your wake was going to be incredible: those gross cakes you always liked, fancy high-end liquor, plus maybe some little kids who could sing and pretend to be sad."

"Your wake would have been way better than that," Mouth

said. "I was going to set a few dozen firebombs all over town, in honor of your career as a child arsonist. Heaps of food. Including those disgusting cactus-pork crisps. Liters of swamp vodka. The whole town would have passed out."

"Fuck off. Your wake would have been the best wake in the history of wakes." Alyssa poked Mouth's leg. "Flowers and parades and flamethrowers, and I would have given a whole speech about how you were too dumb to live, but too fuck-faced to die of stab wounds or gunshots, like everyone else."

As she spoke, Alyssa leaned forward and put one arm around Mouth's uninjured shoulder and leaned on her chest, with care. Mouth heard a sigh of almost unbearable tenderness.

"Your wake would have ended with a thousand more people dead," Mouth said.

"Pffft. Your wake would have been an extinction-level event." Alyssa moved closer, until all of Mouth's uninjured parts were swathed in arms and legs. "But now I guess we'll just have to drink to being alive, like boring people."

They fell asleep tangled in each other, like old times.

SOPHIE

I see my face everywhere: a terrible likeness printed with streaky ink on the Palace's ancient printing press, but still me. Bianca gives a speech in the Founders' Square, standing in the same spot where her predecessor as vice regent announced a reduction in med-creds and triggered a riot. "We've been invaded by something evil that followed us out of the night," Bianca says. Behind her, the prince looks pale and lightsick. "Some creature that we've never seen before has learned to imitate human form. It may look like a beautiful woman, but don't let it get close, because its slightest touch will end your life." Around me, the crowd shrills. I pull my hood tighter, hiding my face. I can't help remembering when I was swept up by this same mob, and imagining what they'll do if they find me this time.

Then I close my eyes, and let the feelings take hold of me, before I remind myself that I'm not trapped now. I'm strong, and I can climb any surface, and I can sense danger approaching before it even sees me.

I keep thinking that if I could have just showed Bianca that one memory of drinking tea, when we were too young to understand anything, things would have turned out differently. The teapot was like a harmless sun, radiating heat without the assault of light, and we clustered around it, gossiping and making up stories about what we were going to do when we got free.

As I leave the Square, my cloak snags on the rusted metal of an old stairway rail, revealing the shape of my body for one eyeblink. I'm not sure if anyone saw, but I duck into an alley piled with old linens and climb one wall, gripping with the ends of my tentacles. Around the next corner, I scale an eave and hide on a crumbling sill covered with laser-carved angels while people walk underneath me.

I don't know what happened to that teapot. My old memories haven't gotten any clearer thanks to my gift, and I only remember what I remember. So the teapot only lives in that one moment, and a few others. Maybe we broke it, maybe it got lost, maybe it's still in a cupboard at the Gymnasium somewhere. In my recollection, it had green cornflowers painted on it, and a thin crack where the lid connected.

I take refuge in the very hottest part of town. Corroded corrugated aluminum, hot to the touch, right next to my face. I huddle there, sweating and suffocating, during the twelfth bell, the recessional chimes, and, at last, the shutters-up warning. My shoulder still burns, and I worry it's infected. I've been so stupid. The Gelet are counting on my help, but I can't stop throwing away my life for Bianca. It's all I ever do.

Mouth probably died at the Palace. Even now that Bianca is lost to me, the idea of Mouth being dead cuts deeper than I could have expected. I remember her story of the blue wings, and the way the Gelet recoiled when I conveyed it to them. I should have helped Mouth find another name, one that didn't remind her constantly of bones and lost chances.

My love for Bianca feels like a feature of the landscape that recedes farther into the distance the longer I stare. I wonder how much she's sleeping now that she's home, and whether she dreams of me.

I need to leave my hiding place to find some food, and that's when I spot the symbol. Painted in yellow on the peeling stucco wall of an empty shoe factory, the glyph twists in on itself, with the shape of wings and one long tooth. I stare awhile before I remember where I saw it before: on some of the books in Hernan's study, at the Illyrian Parlour. I hesitate one moment longer, and then push open the tiny door.

Jeremy crouches in a wide-armed chair next to a coffee urn in the style of Old Zagreb, with a cloudy ancient copy of a Mayhew tract in both hands. Cyrus the marmot stretches out on one arm of the chair, grumbling. Jeremy looks up and smiles at me. "You made it. I saw your picture all over town, so I tried to leave a message that only you would understand. I'm so glad you're here."

He gives me food, and clean water, and a place to sit, and then he sets about tending my shoulder.

Jeremy talks twice as fast as before, now that we're a long way from the Parlour. And meanwhile, Cyrus seems even more languid than ever, though he cozies up to Jeremy the same way he used to with Hernan. Jeremy says Hernan kept the

Parlour open for a while, and things seemed to quiet down after I left. But some time later, there was another crackdown on anti-Circadianist elements, and Hernan had to close shop after all. This all happened ages ago. I keep being shocked by how much time passed while I was away. It's already 4 Silence after Crimson, according to the calendar on the wall. Hernan ended up on the run, and eventually died of an infection that spread to his blood.

Besides Cyrus and the samovar, Jeremy has saved a few other things from the Parlour. He digs in a wooden crate until he pulls out a scrap of wax paper: my mother's painting of me standing near some barley stalks. "Hernan told me to give you this, if I ever saw you again." I stare at the tiny figure, whose face is turned away, and the light, from somewhere out of the frame, that limns her cheek and the tips of the newly harvested crops. I count every brushstroke, as if I could see my mother's hand if I concentrate hard enough. And then I roll it, tenderly, and tuck it inside a pouch in my cloak.

Then I sit with Jeremy, and he tells me about the new Uprising: he and his friends are working to unseat our new vice regent and her foreign allies. This dusty storage room, scorching even with the shutters closed, is one of his hideouts.

"All of that training Hernan gave us." Jeremy shakes his head. "Turns out it's quite helpful for politics. I know how to fire people up, by doing more or less the opposite of what you and I used to do."

I start to try to explain about Bianca, how I still believe she never wanted to hurt anyone, even now, and Jeremy hushes me.

"I don't need you to tell me anything," he says. "I want you to show me."

I just stare. His face, lit by a single beam from an old handheld light, looks like a landscape of arid gullies. Cyrus is peering up at me too; maybe he recognizes me, or wonders what's going on.

"You want me to . . ." I whisper.

"That's why I made all this effort to find you. I've been hearing rumors, from someone who works at the Palace and heard her talking to Dash after you got away. They say that you can show people the things you've seen, and that's why the vice regent is scared of you. You know all her secrets, you know the whole truth about her, and anyone who touches you can experience it, as if they had been there in person."

I hesitate, fingering the sides of my cloak.

"Please, show me," he says again.

I open my cloak. When I bring the tendrils closer to his face, he lets out a slow breath, like steam escaping the coffee urn. I show him Bianca speaking to the Progressive Students, then try to take him through the glimmering parties in Argelo, Bianca flirting with these oligarchs, and the fleet of armored vehicles. Forcing myself to revisit these things feels like a whole new kind of memory-panic, except with crushing sadness instead of anxiety.

Jeremy untangles his face from my tendrils, and I realize after a moment that he's shaking with happiness.

"This . . . this is amazing. You could be the single most effective recruitment tool in the history of political organizing. People will want to try this for themselves, and once they do, they'll be on our side forever. I can see why the vice regent is scared out of her mind."

I step away from him, all my senses heightened as if danger could arrive from anywhere. This storage room feels both too claustrophobic and too exposed.

"I didn't come back home to be some living piece of propaganda," I say.

"She's trying to destroy you," Jeremy says. "You have to destroy her first. That's how it works."

"Thanks for the food." I move away from him, climbing the half stairway toward the blinding glare coming through the doorframe. "And for tending my shoulder. I feel much better. Please take good care of Cyrus."

Hearing his name, Cyrus growls and stretches his pseudopods.

"Please stay here. I have an extra bedroll. We can talk more later. You don't have to rush into anything. But this is a way for both of us to get our lives back. Now that I've experienced your power, I . . ." Jeremy rushes behind me, hands raised, but makes no move to stop me. "You can control the thing that most of us are controlled by. We could do so much together."

I pause at the door. "If you want to become like me," I say, "climb the Old Mother and just wait at the top. Go alone, no weapons. They'll come and find you." Then I walk outside, shielding my face against the sunbaked heat, and hurry back to my hiding place before the shutters open.

My shoulder still burns, and I don't know whether to curse myself or Bianca against the pain. I needed to run away from Jeremy, because I was afraid I would end up agreeing to let myself be used again. Maybe I'd have tried to share the story of

Bianca in a way that made people want to forgive her, even as they rise up against her. And that might be the only way I'll ever get to share my abilities with anyone, without them reacting the way the Glacier Fools did, or Bianca. People can stand things for the sake of politics that they would never endure for love or profit. But even if I could do that to Bianca without loathing myself, I know I couldn't stand to deliver that story to people, over and over. I would turn to ice if I even tried.

The shutters open, and close again, and open again, while I hold myself still and keep my back to the brazier of the Young Father. My shoulder still hurts when I move, but I think it's getting better.

I sleep inside my crawlspace without any regard to the state of the shutters, and maybe I've just been away too long to sink back into the old rhythm. If anything, now I prefer going out when everyone else sleeps. I don't fear the Curfew Patrols, not with all my new senses, and Xiosphant looks lovelier when you can see every stone and adornment without people in the way, the interplay of ancient technology and the more recent handcrafted imitations. I can't believe how much odd little things delight me, like a fluttering wrapper from the cakes we used to get at grammar school, or a sign for the Grand Cinema, the tiny space where they screen old hard-light dramas. Sometimes I catch the acrid scent of tannery smoke, or notice the shimmer of the air in the Cold Front, and I can't help feeling this tawdry nostalgia.

But actual people are more complicated. After so much exposure to Argelan culture, I can't look at random strangers here in Xiosphant without trying to guess which compartment their families traveled in, and how that lines up with their social class here.

A Curfew Patrol marches away from me, nowhere nearby, but I hear another set of footsteps that sound more furtive, stopping and starting as if someone keeps hiding. I creep over the lintels and around the smokestacks of bleached-brick buildings, getting closer to the temperate zone, until I lower myself into the street in front of Alyssa.

"You nearly gave me a heart attack," she says in Argelan. "We'd better get off the street. I know a place we can lie low." I follow her down more alleys until I realize we're circling closer to the Palace and I'm sure that I've trusted the wrong person again. But at the edge of the fanciest street market, Alyssa opens a trapdoor and helps me into a small space under one of the market stalls. This is the closest to the night I've been in a while, and my bracelet gives a faint buzz.

Alyssa shines a small torch around the tiny wooden space. "We waited out the curfew in here on my first visit to Xiosphant. Mouth was bleeding all over the place. Look, you can still see the stains."

Her curly brown hair is longer, and she has a couple of new scars on the left side of her face, right next to her wide, protruding ear. She winces when she moves, and even her smile has thicker lines, but her laugh still sounds the same as ever. I hug her and she leans on my shoulder for a moment.

"Mouth sent me to find you. I'm not letting her out of bed until her lung sounds like a lung again. But she's been climbing out of her skin with worry. She made me promise to keep looking for you."

"I can't believe Mouth is alive. I saw her take at least two bullets at the Palace."

"Must be tough to be a masochist when your entire body is scar tissue, without a single nerve ending left." Alyssa seems to laugh, but then she stares at me with her mouth pursed. "She was willing to die for you. She didn't even hesitate."

"You should have seen her face when she heard that you were alive, and then when she found out you were in a dungeon. I've never seen joy go dark so fast."

"Huh." She raises her eyes for a moment, thinking about Mouth, then looks back at me. "I suppose you're going to just show me what her face looked like. That's your new thing, right?"

I wince, thinking about Jeremy. All his big plans for me.

"I'm not anybody's recording device," I say.

"Good. The only thing that makes life tolerable is that people forget all the stupid things I say as soon as I've finished saying them."

We sit in the tiny hutch under the market square for a while, and I can tell this place brings back conflicted old memories for Alyssa. She mentioned Mouth's blood, long since dried.

I think something and say it at the same time: "You've always been the strongest, out of all of us."

Alyssa half laughs, half just shakes her head. "Doesn't feel like it, most of the time. But then I think about my ancestors, and everything they went through for me to be here, and I just find a way. That's what this town tried to keep you from having, I guess, because they wanted you to be weak. And now look at you."

The scent of old blood has been thickening since we closed the lid, along with a musty loam funk. Something about this earthiness reminds me of the Resourceful Couriers' sleep nook.

"Mouth searched for ages for something to believe in, and I couldn't give it to her," Alyssa says. "Even this Barney guy, who used to be one of the Citizens, couldn't. But you did. And now she wants me to join your cult, or your security detail, whichever. But . . . I can't be disappointed again. I just can't. The next disappointment is going to snap me in half."

I want to say that I don't need Mouth's protection, or Alyssa's either. But Mouth just took two bullets for me. So I say, "What will you do, if Mouth wants to stay with me, and you decide not to?"

"Don't know. I can't go home. I guess I could turn mercenary, see if the new Uprising wants a fighter. But I think I need a break from overthrowing governments for a while. I could work at a dive bar. The Low Road, maybe." She makes a peevish noise with her mouth. "I really thought Bianca was going to be great. She had me convinced. How do I know it's going to be any different if I decide to follow you?"

I watch her face close enough to see a flicker of hope, in among all the twinges. I don't want anybody to follow me, or to believe in me. I want to sleep for another five or six turns of the shutters.

But I was sent back here to teach. So I feel the calm settle into me.

"There won't be any safe place soon," I say. "Good weather's gone forever. Imagine if the next cyclone hits one of the farmwheels."

"All the more reason to lie low," Alyssa says. "Why should I put my faith in you now?"

I breathe deep, as if I could take time itself into my lungs and hold it there until I'm ready for the next moment to arrive.

"Don't believe in me," I say. "Believe in them."

I spread my arms and unwrap my cloak to let her see, if she wants to see. Alyssa hesitates a moment, then comes forward.

I bring her down easy, remembering all my mistakes, and show her nothing but the play of snow on the wind, until I feel her relax into it. Then I bring her inside the city in the middle of the night, down through walls of ice and living matter, which resonate with all the music from below. I show her the galleries, the huge girders, strengthened by fire from the center of the world, and supported by a shared history that goes all the way back to the taming of the sky. The Gelet approach, not as some inhuman shapes that swarm out of a hostile landscape, but as friends whose tentacles extend in welcome and whose pincers open to let you see inside their hearts. I close in on one memory in particular, of when Rose held up my father's timepiece, and how this looked to my human eyes as well as to my new senses, all the ways I knew she was keeping faith with me. I don't try to tell a story, or share a chain of events, I just open up the feeling of being home, in a place where everybody knows your damage, and I let it seep out of me. The memories I have to share are clean and true.

When I disengage, Alyssa holds me tighter, as though she doesn't want me to ever let go. Her eyes are so wet they look like silver.

ACKNOWLEDGMENTS

Writing this book felt like stumbling around in total darkness, a lot of the time. I'm supremely grateful to everyone who helped me find my way. Any screwups and faults are all my responsibility, but most of what's good about this book is due to the generosity and kindness of many others.

First and foremost, I am hugely and eternally indebted to Miriam Weinberg, my editor, whose brilliant sense of story and razor-sharp sensibility made a huge difference. Large sections of this book only work because Miriam spent hours on the phone with me helping me to see where I had swept important stuff under the rug, and to figure out what this book was actually about. Miriam is the most patient genius around.

Also, Patrick Nielsen Hayden didn't run screaming when I told him I wanted to follow *All the Birds in the Sky* with a dark, serious story about a tidally locked planet. I'm also super grateful to everyone else at Tor, including the fantastic Kirsten Brink, magical punk rock icon Patty Garcia, super art director Irene Gallo, the eagle-eyed copy editor Liana Krissoff, and tons of others. And at Titan Books, I'm super grateful to Ella

Chappell, Lydia Gittins, and everyone else who has supported this book.

Also my astute and fearless agent, Russ Galen, supported me every step of the way, no matter how weird and indescribable the book started to sound.

I also have to thank my sensitivity reader, K. Tempest Bradford, who put up with a million questions and offered keen insights on my elaborate future history of Earth and beyond. Thanks also to all my beta readers: Claire Light, Liz Henry, Elizabeth McKenzie, Isabel Yap, Baruch Porras-Hernandez, Wonder Dave, Jessy Randall, Nicole Gluckstern, Kate Erickson, Shobha Rao, and anyone else I've forgotten. Claire, in particular, spent ages generously helping me with the emotional beats and the world-building in this story.

Josh Friedman took a chance and hired me to work on the *Snowpiercer* TV show when I was struggling to finish this book. Getting to listen to some of the smartest people around geek out about story structure (including the aforementioned Kate Erickson, plus Alexandra McNally, Erica Saleh, Halley Gross, Heather Regnier, and Lucas O'Connor) made all the difference when I left behind their oppressive society on the edge of a frozen wasteland, and returned to my own.

Thanks also to my manager, Nate Miller, for getting me that gig and for everything he's done to support my writing.

So many other people have helped me with my writing and helped me to learn from my storytelling mistakes; I could be here all day listing them. I've learned from the best.

Thanks to everyone on Twitter who answered my tidally locked–planet questions back in 2013, and to everyone who's helped me with the science since then. Lindy Elkins-Tanton at Arizona State University patiently answered my geophysics questions, and I also got some useful feedback from Aomawa Shields and Dorian Abbot. Berkeley's Terry Johnson had a lot of thoughts about the Gelet's weather manipulation.

I'm aware that the science in this book is fudged in some cases, and in others the scientific consensus changed while I was in the middle of writing. Which happens. But these generous scientists, as well as all the papers I read about tidally locked planets, were invaluable in shaping this book.

Superstar economist Noah Smith kindly read my book and patiently argued with me about the admittedly gonzo economy I had created for Xiosphant. I don't think I convinced him to go work for the Xiosphanti Central Bank, alas.

And most of all, as always, I have to thank my partner and hero, Annalee Newitz, who inspires me in a million ways, and with whom I always want to share all the science, all the stories, and all the mapo tofu.

ABOUT THE AUTHOR

Charlie Jane Anders is the author of *All the Birds in the Sky*, which won the Nebula, Crawford, and Locus awards, and *Choir Boy*, which won a Lambda Literary Award. Her novel has also appeared on *Time Magazine*'s list of the 10 best novels of 2016. She is the author of a novella called *Rock Manning Goes For Broke* and a short story collection called "Six Months, Three Days, Five Others". Her short fiction has appeared in *Tor.com, Boston Review, Tin House, Conjunctions, The Magazine of Fantasy and Science Fiction, Wired Magazine, Slate, Asimov's Science Fiction, Lightspeed, ZYZZYVA, Catamaran Literary Review, McSweeney's Internet Tendency* and tons of anthologies. Her story "Six Months, Three Days" won a Hugo Award, and her story "Don't Press Charges And I Won't Sue" won a Theodore Sturgeon Award. Charlie Jane also organizes the monthly Writers With Drinks reading series, and co-hosts the podcast Our Opinions Are Correct with Annalee Newitz.

ALL THE BIRDS IN THE SKY
CHARLIE JANE ANDERS

From the former editor-in-chief of io9.com comes a stunning novel about the end of our world—and the beginning of our future.

Patricia is a witch who can communicate with birds. Laurence is a mad scientist and inventor of the two-second time machine. As teenagers they gravitate towards one another, sharing in the horrors of growing up weird.

When they later reconnect as adults, Laurence is an engineering genius living in near-future San Francisco, trying to stop the planet falling apart through technological intervention. Meanwhile, Patricia is a graduate of Eltisley Maze, the hidden academy for the magically gifted, and works with her fellow magicians to secretly repair the earth's ever-growing ailments.

As they each take sides in a cataclysmic war between science and magic, *All the Birds in the Sky* sees Laurence and Patricia try to make sense of life, sex and adulthood on the brink of the apocalypse.

"A brave, genre-bending debut"
Independent

"Heartfelt, ambitious and dynamic"
Financial Times

"Clever and wonderfully weird"
Publishers Weekly

TITANBOOKS.COM

For more fantastic fiction, author events, exclusive
excerpts, competitions, limited editions and more

VISIT OUR WEBSITE
titanbooks.com

LIKE US ON FACEBOOK
facebook.com/titanbooks

FOLLOW US ON TWITTER
@TitanBooks

EMAIL US
readerfeedback@titanemail.com